Flickering

Flame

Clifton LaBree

Published by
Fading Shadows Imprint
New Boston, New Hampshire

Paperback ISBN: 978-0-9746450-3-2

Cover by Vivian LaBree

Colonial Series Books

Flickering Flame *(Book One)*

A historical novel, about the Cullen family who settled in Portsmouth, New Hampshire, and their participation in events prior to the French and Indian War. Freedom and opportunity were on the march, but it extracted a heavy price. Frontier settlers were ruthlessly killed and butchered by rampaging Indians lead by French officers and Jesuit priests who frequently incited them to greater levels of inhumanity...

Raising the Torch *(Book Two)*

A continuation of the saga from *Flickering Flame*, Colonial Series book one, of the Cullen family in Colonial Portsmouth. This is a moving story of love and sacrifice when a small colony had the audacity to fight for independence from their motherland...

Dedicated to my wife Pauline, and my family, with thanks for all their support and encouragement

Chapter One

Twelve-year-old Daniel Cullen braced himself against the rail. The violent rolling and pitching of the heavily laden merchant sailing vessel not only frightened him, it also made him sick. He did not know what to expect on the long voyage to the colonies called America. The seaworthiness of the ship in heavy seas filled him with anxiety. Suddenly, the ship rolled even further to the port, throwing him on top of the rail. Frantically he tried to regain his balance. He felt weak and dizzy and began to vomit. As he teetered precariously on the rail, Daniel felt two strong arms pull him back to safety.

"Be careful, Laddie. The north Atlantic can act up a bit," exclaimed the sailor, noting a greenish hue around Daniel's eyes. "Go down below and you'll feel better. Ask the cook for some hardtack and chew small bites slowly. It'll settle your stomach."

Nodding his head, Daniel groped for the rail on the stairway leading to the galley. He turned to the sailor with large glistening eyes, "Thanks for helping me. My mother warned me not to be a bother."

"You've been a quiet passenger on the trip so far, my boy. You've been no bother to me. I have a son about your age back in Liverpool," the sailor replied. "The storm has about blown itself out now. Find a quiet spot near the middle of the ship where you can lie down. Within a couple of hours you'll be back to normal."

"I'll try that," Daniel answered, carefully clutching the rail. The aromas from the kitchen almost made him retch again.

The elderly cook, a short hunchback man who walked with a limp, took one look at Daniel and pointed to the set of stairs to the storage hold. Daniel passed him without a word. The hold was filled to capacity with paper, sugar, molasses, and several boxes of glass. He located a flat spot on top of the molasses barrels and lay down.

Movements of the ship were much less noticeable than when he had been on deck.

"You look a mite piqued, my boy," the cook said, entering the storage room. "Don't worry, it'll soon pass. Every sailor gets the sickness once in a while. Here, try some soda crackers and hardtack. They'll stop the dry heaves that accompany an empty stomach."

"Thank you," responded Daniel, accepting the crackers with shaky fingers. He broke off small bite-size pieces and began to chew them.

"That's the way, lad. Where are you heading all by yourself?" the cook asked.

"I'm supposed to meet my uncles. One lives in Portsmouth and the other lives in York. My mother made me promise to continue school, so I'm going to live with the uncle that lives in York, because he is near a school in the village. My father died several months ago."

"You'll love the new land. As soon as you set foot on the shore, you'll feel the excitement and energy that's in the air. Miles upon miles of land are available for those who can set roots in it. There's nothing like it in Scotland or England where all the land is taken by the Crown or rich land barons. If I were a younger man without this lump on my back and the bum ankle, I would've jumped ship long ago and found me a place to live in peace and quiet on my own piece of God's earth." There was a wistful look in the cook's sensitive eyes.

"I think the hardtack is already working, sir," Daniel said, sighing with relief. Tired, he laid his head back down on the molasses barrel.

"Well, rest a while, lad. It's the best thing for you. In a day or two, we'll be within sight of the Isle of Shoal off the Portsmouth coast."

"Thank you for everything, sir."

"Everyone calls me Ben."

"Thank you, Ben," said Daniel, closing his eyes.

Feeling better after eating the hardtack and crackers, Daniel lay in the dark storage compartment and thought of his home in Aberdeen. He had been homesick ever since the ship pulled up anchor and put out to sea.

Daniel's mother was a frail, petite lady who, day after day, worked hard cleaning and scrubbing the floors in a wealthy landowner's mansion. As long as he could remember, she would return, exhausted, to their small apartment above the stables. As soon as she came through the door, she laid down to rest. Daniel could especially remember the cough that seemed to come from the depths of her lungs and left her gasping for breath. The sound always frightened him. Even at his young age, he knew that she was seriously ill, or she would have accompanied him on the journey to America. His two uncles had sent enough money for both of them to make the passage.

Slowly, tears began to roll down his angular cheek bones into his ears. He knew when he hugged his mother and kissed her good-bye before boarding the ship, that it was probably the last time he would see her. He wanted to stay, but she insisted that he take the trip when space became available.

She had told him just before he boarded the ship: "Sailing for the new land was a cherished dream your father and I shared for the three of us. Now that your father has gone, it is with a heavy heart that I send you alone on the long, perilous journey. You go with my blessings, Son. I'll follow you when the time is right, and I'm a little stronger."

"Why can't you come now, Mother?" he had cried in protest.

"I'm indentured to the master of the house where I work, Danny. Soon my debt will be paid. I want you to go where you can own the land you work, and the fruits of your labor will be yours. That had been a dream of your father's since I married him. To own land is to be free." Tears had filled her eyes and she continued to pour out her heart. "You go, Danny. My love will always be with you. Listen to your uncles. They loved your father very much and will be proud to have you come to their new homes. I have enclosed in your pack the papers you will need to claim the land your father was granted by the Crown for his service in the Army. Now that your father is unable to fulfill his dreams of land, you will have to do it for him, my Son. Be strong and make us both proud. Love of my life, blood of my blood, now go and don't look back. May God guide your footsteps, Son."

She had kissed him one last time and gently pushed him out the door, closing it behind him. He had heard her crying on the other side of the door and was reluctant to leave, but he dutifully picked up his heavy pack and began walking down the hill overlooking the Aberdeen docks where the merchant ship was waiting.

Sailors had been busy unfurling the sails to catch the winds when he crossed the gangplank. As the heavy ship slowly pulled away from the shore, he watched the large mansion on the hill for some sign of his mother. If she was watching the ship, he never saw her. The shore became a tiny speck in the wake of the vessel. Sobs had wrenched his slender body while the ship sliced a path through the dark waters towards a new life and a new land far from home.

For a long time Daniel remained in that dream-like state between deep sleep and drowsiness. When he opened his eyes, it was so dark he could not see his hand inches from his face. The steady groan and squeal of the wooden timbers frightened him, and for a moment he did not know where he was. The aroma of boiled tea began to filter into the storage hold, and then he remembered. He sat up on the barrel.

Suddenly, a ray of light shined down the ladder-like steps. "Daniel, me boy. Can you hear me?" Daniel recognized Ben's voice.

"I hear you, Ben," he replied, carefully feeling his way toward the lantern Ben held.

"I've got some fresh tea that might help to settle your stomach," Ben announced.

"I must have fallen asleep."

"That yea did, lad. I heard your snores way into the galley," Ben chuckled, setting his lantern on a large table. "I've got a spot of tea for yea."

"I thought I'd never want to eat or drink again after being so seasick, but a cup of tea will go good, Ben. Thanks."

"That's the way it is. Here, sit at the table and let's enjoy a quiet tea before the morning watch ends, and the hungry galoots start charging down here like starved cattle." Ben placed a steaming hot cup in front of Daniel. Ben had a way of softly snorting when he was pleased about something.

"You mean I slept all through the night down there?" exclaimed Daniel, looking out one of the hatchways onto the deck.

"You sure did, lad, and it's what worked the sickness out of yea. Don't eat too much for the rest of the trip and drink plenty of tea. I've found that works best."

"Mmm, it sure tastes good. Thanks, Ben. It's been a long passage. I'll be glad to be back on land again."

"The ship has become a home to me," Ben said, taking a seat at the table, and a long sip of tea. "Would you believe that when we tie up at the dock, I find it awkward trying to walk on a surface that's not moving under my feet? If you would be of a mind to help me, we could gig for codfish today."

"I've never done that before, but have seen the fishermen at home come in with boats filled with cod."

"Well, it doesn't take much skill, lad. When we hit a school of cod, we simply throw in a gig line and pull it up, hoping that some fish get hooked on the barbed gigs attached to the line. Sometimes you can fill every gig. The cod is not much of a fighter compared to many fish. Everyone on board looks forward to fresh fish in this section of the Atlantic."

"It sounds like fun, Ben," Daniel eagerly answered. The trip had been long, and he was bored walking around the ship trying to keep out of the way of the sailors. "It'll be good to do something useful for a change."

"I thought you might say that," Ben replied. "Would you like a bowl of rice before you start?"

"I'm a little hungry," Daniel admitted.

Later that morning, the ship came upon a large school of codfish, and the Captain ordered two small rowboats into the water secured to each side of the ship. Two men were placed in each boat, one in the rear and the other at the bow to gig for codfish. Daniel climbed down into the boat on the starboard side and watched the seasoned sailor in the bow cast out a line of about twenty feet to the side of the boat, then pulled the line in with both hands. He had hooked three large codfish on the first throw. Cod were so numerous that he could have scooped one out with his hand. The school extended a hundred feet or more from the ship. Daniel was amazed at the ease of the catch and did the same to the line Ben had given to him. His first throw hooked four fish, and it was all he could do to pull the line over the gunwale of the boat.

"That's the way it's done, lad," said the sailor in the boat with Daniel. "We feast tonight on sweet codfish!"

Daniel continued to throw his line in the water until it was played out, and wound it in. Each throw hooked at least two fish. Several times a fish was hooked but managed to wiggle its way free of the barbed hooks before Daniel could get them into the boat. The fish catch began to fill the boat. Ben's helper, nicknamed "Cookie" by the crew, climbed down into the boat to collect the fish in large buckets.

The fishermen remained in the boats for two hours. The school of cod had disappeared as quickly as it had been sighted. They had collected enough to feed the crew for several days. It was a delicacy, for near the end of their journey, food supplies were scant, and they had been subsisting on hardtack, rice, and tea. Daniel was glad to have a chance to rest. His arms ached, and his hands were raw and bleeding from pulling on the gig line, but he felt good being able to do something useful. He was of the opinion that he had caught almost as many of the fish as his experienced companion in the boat.

Captain Tanner helped the men pull the small boats back on the main deck. Then, he turned to Daniel with a broad grin on his face. "You did well, son. How's the stomach feel today?"

"Much better, sir," Daniel answered, still excited about his performance. "I've never seen so many fish."

"At this time of year we often come across them. Would you mind coming to my cabin?" Captain Tanner requested. "I want to discuss some things with you." Captain Tanner was a short, portly man with a ruddy complexion. He handled the responsibility of his rank with grace and a good sense of humor. The crew liked him because he was fair and understanding, but he was harsh on shirkers.

"Yes, sir," Daniel answered, following the Captain to his spacious quarters on the stern deck of the ship.

"I have something that belongs to you," explained the Captain, noting the puzzled look on Daniel's face. Opening the door to his quarters, Captain Tanner held the door for Daniel and closed it behind them.

The large room was light and cheerful with windows looking to the stern and on both sides of the ship. Charts and nautical equipment were visible on a large table, and a small bunk took up one wall. A large bookshelf filled with many volumes that occupied the opposite side of the room caught Daniel's eye. He was drawn to the books.

"Come, Daniel, you can sit up here at the table," suggested the Captain, pointing to a chair. "I have here on the table some maps showing the grant of land that you will one day own. Don't be surprised, son. Before we left Aberdeen I had a long conversation with your mother. She made me promise to look after you and to see you safely delivered to your uncles."

"It's something my mother would do," Daniel's heart warmed, thinking of his mother and how much she loved him.

"Your mother is a fine lady, and I knew your father, too."

"You did?" Daniel was surprised.

"We soldiered together for a few years in India and in the colonies. Your two uncles were also in the same regiment. The four of us grew up in Aberdeen and were good friends. Your father planned to return to the colonies in America after we returned to England." Captain Tanner left the table and opened a large trunk next to his bunk. "I have here a pouch that your mother entrusted to me so that I could pass it on to you when we reached America. Tomorrow morning we should be tied up at the dock in Portsmouth."

"So soon?"

"If all goes well, Daniel. This pouch includes a few things from your father." Captain Tanner emptied the pouch on the table and opened a wooden case. It contained two pistols with walnut handles, exquisitely crafted as a matched pair. They came from India. The case also contained a bullet mold, a flask of gunpowder, and a supply of flints.

Daniel's eyes opened wide. He had never seen these pistols at their house in Aberdeen. He knew that his father had been a soldier, yet he rarely talked about his experiences. Daniel had remembered his father's absence from home and how sad his mother had been. She had worried all the time he was gone. Once he had left the army, his parents used to spend hours looking at the map Captain Tanner had on the table. They had dreamed of a time when they could come to America and become landowners, but the years dragged by with his father working sunup to sundown in the livery stable of the mansion on the hill. Their dreams of a better life sustained them for a while, but, alas, the dreams remained out of reach, and Daniel had now inherited them.

"Go ahead, lad," said Captain Tanner noting the mist in Daniel's eyes, understanding the sad memories that filled his heart. "Don't hold it back. My, you look so much like your father when he was your age. I was always proud to call Dan Cullen my friend. Hold your head up high, son, yea come from good stock."

Daniel shook his head at the Captain. "I remember seeing maps like this at home."

"Well, these maps are yours, Daniel. They describe your tract of land on the east shore of the Connecticut River. Your two uncles own land adjoining yours. Your mother told me that you have the deed to the land in your pack."

"Yes, sir," Daniel replied, wiping his eyes with his arm.

"Tomorrow we'll tie up to Market Street dock in Portsmouth," Captain Tanner announced, closing the pistol case. "I'll hold these things for you here in my quarters until we dock. You should get a good night's rest. I'm sure that tomorrow will be a very busy day for you, Daniel."

Chapter Two

That night Daniel tossed and turned restlessly in his bunk. Most of the crew had been to the colonies several times over the past few years. Some were from America and planned to take advantage of land available to those willing to build a home and live on their tracts. Daniel had heard them talk a lot about their desire to move to the new frontier. The prospects of being attacked by Indians sounded exciting to him, but he had mixed feelings about being a part of the migration to the new lands.

Most of the land was being given away by the English Crown authority in large charters to people who had served the Crown well. Daniel's father was an example. The gift of "free" land was not without some risk and danger. When the white men first landed on the shores, some Native Americans were willing to share the land where they hunted, fished, and grew crops. Initially, the Indians had greeted the new settlers with generosity. That changed, when the concept of land ownership complicated the situation. The Indians could never reconcile themselves to think of land as being "owned" the way the British understood the purchase and sale of land. According to the native population, land did not belong to any person or group of people. They could negotiate hunting and fishing "rights," but that was a far cry from outright possession of the land itself. Land was sacred to the Indian like the sun, moon, and stars. They were unable to grasp the concept of ownership as understood by the white settlers. This grievance was at the heart of the conflict between the white men and the native Indian tribes, and there was little prospect of it being resolved.

Daniel had heard the sailors talk about the conflict and its dangers. He was impressed with their descriptions of rampaging Indians attacking helpless homesteaders who had pressed the frontier to the west and north. The idea of being scalped by the redskins, as the sailors

9

called the Indians, was frightening and sent shivers up and down his spine.

Someone on deck shouted: "Land ahoy!"

The announcement brought Daniel out of his bunk scrambling to get dressed. Racing for the ladder leading to the deck, he joined the crowd and pushed through to the rail for his first glimpse of America.

Captain Tanner approached Daniel. "Yonder to the starboard is Mount Agamenticus on the coastal plain. It is a helpful navigation guide to Portsmouth on the Piscataqua River. Off to our port you'll notice a small group of islands known as the Isle of Shoals. They've been a fishing center for a hundred years. The catches of codfish have exceeded those from any other place in the Atlantic."

"I can understand that after the way we caught them yesterday," Daniel answered. The new land was beginning to take shape to him. It was no longer a land of imagination or dreams. Here, before him, was physical evidence of its existence, and it gave him a strange feeling that this was where he belonged. "How long before we land in Portsmouth, Captain Tanner?"

"About an hour, lad."

Daniel passed from starboard to port as the ship made its way toward the Piscataqua River. The wind was out of the northwest, so they dropped anchor at the mouth of the river and waited a half hour for the tide to change. An incoming tide would carry the ship up the river with very little sail necessary. A few seconds after Captain Tanner gave the order to lift anchor, the heavy craft began to move into the narrow channel of the river. He ordered an extra sailor to stand by at the wheel, because the currents in the river were some of the most treacherous waters on the coast of the new land. If the navigator was not alert or strong enough to counteract the current, the ship could be dashed against the rocky shores in seconds.

Captain Tanner pointed out the British Fort William and Mary at New Castle on the port side of the ship to Daniel. Its perimeter and revetments for the heavy guns visible from the river were made of brick and granite. On the starboard shore another fortification could be seen, Fort Fisher. It was built on a prominent hill overlooking the river. The large caliber guns that protruded from their revetments impressed the 12-year old. If both forts opened fire upon a ship in the river, there would be little chance of hiding or maneuvering. He hoped that the men tending the guns knew that Captain Tanner's ship was friendly.

Several small islands with landing docks dotted the riverbed. Fishermen waved from the islands as they passed, and Daniel waved back. The docking of a merchant ship from England was a happy occasion for the inhabitants of the city. The Captain skillfully guided his helmsmen, and the ship gently came to a stop against the massive pilings at the Market Street Wharf in Portsmouth. Gangplanks were quickly placed so that sailors could run ashore with lines to secure the ship to the sturdy mooring shafts.

Portsmouth was a larger city than Daniel had imagined. The waterfront was filled with wooden houses and red brick buildings. Anxious to go ashore, Daniel ran to his berthing area below for a single canvas bag that had belonged to his father. Ben intercepted him at the base of the ladder.

"You look excited, Daniel," Ben noted. "I have something for yea, lad. I've kept them for a long time with the hope that maybe, just maybe, I would be able to drop anchor on a small farm of me own." He caught his breath and handed Daniel a beautifully decorated knife in a leather sheath. "A young lad like you in a new land will find many uses for a knife. Take it, Daniel, and remember me whenever ye use it."

Daniel was touched by the simple man's generosity and sensitivity. "Thank you, Ben. It's a beautiful tool. Take good care of yourself, Ben. I'll always remember your kindness. Thank you, again." Daniel held out his hand to the faithful cook.

"I have a feeling that you'll do well in this new land, me lad," Ben replied, brushing his hand away, giving Daniel a heartfelt hug. "Now go, laddie, and make your mark so that all of us who know you will be proud."

"Good-bye, Ben," Daniel sadly replied, shouldering his bag. Part way up the ladder he turned to wave at Ben, then climbed onto the deck and headed for the gangplank.

Captain Tanner intercepted Daniel. "This is where we part, lad. I've got your pouch here. Put it in your pack if you have room."

Daniel accepted the pouch from the Captain and placed it away in his pack, which was already heavy, but he was determined to handle it by himself. Captain Tanner scanned the crowd congregated at the wharf to greet the ship from the vantage point of the elevated deck.

"Ah," exclaimed Captain Tanner, spotting the Cullen brothers. "I see your uncles. Their red hair is spiked with gray, but I'd recognize them anywhere. You're about to step into Portsmouth, New Hampshire, a part of the Massachusetts Bay Colony."

He led Daniel down the slender gangplank to the dock, where both of them experienced the strange sensation of walking on solid ground instead of on a pitching and rolling deck. At first it seemed difficult, but after a few steps they became accustomed to the sure-footed feel of dry land. Captain Tanner led the way to two men conversing with others on the wharf.

"It's been a long time since we were together, Lee and Earl Cullen," cried Captain Tanner enthusiastically.

Daniel was all eyes. The two men Captain Tanner addressed were his uncles, but they were strangers to him. They resembled his father with their broad shoulders and dark red hair liberally splashed with gray and white especially around the ears and temples.

"Well, if it isn't Sergeant Tanner. You haven't changed much," replied one of the uncles in good humor.

"A little more weight around the midriff," laughed the Captain. "I have here your nephew Daniel Cullen – one fine boy in my estimation. Dan, this is your Uncle Earl and your Uncle Lee."

Daniel was uncertain if he should shake hands or bow or what. He dropped his pack on the wooden wharf, after which his Uncle Earl effortlessly picked him up and embraced him in a crushing bear hug. "You look just like your father except for your dark brown hair, lad. Welcome to America. I hope you'll like it here with Lee and me. We've been looking forward to your arrival ever since your dear mother wrote to us this past winter. How is she?"

"She's not doing very well. I'm worried for her," Daniel answered soberly.

"I'm your Uncle Lee, Daniel," said his second uncle, also warmly embracing him. "It's been a long time since I saw you as a mere baby in your mother's arms. It's sad that your father cannot be here to celebrate this happy occasion."

"Who's to say that he isn't with us, Lee," said Captain Tanner. "I'm sure that the fine man I called my best friend will look after his son and guide his footsteps."

"You speak the truth, Sergeant Tanner," Lee acknowledged with a calm demeanor. "It's really nice to see an old friend. I had heard that you have often carried cargo to Boston."

"Yes, and I've been here at Portsmouth a few times. It seems good not to have to march the miles we used to do in the Army," laughed the jovial Captain.

"I don't mean to change the subject," Earl Cullen mentioned, noticing the flag flapping on the merchant ship. "We've got a good wind out of the northwest which will counteract the incoming tide in the river. I'd like to take advantage of it and clear the harbor as soon as possible. Did you have just this one pack, Daniel?"

"Yes, sir," Daniel replied.

Earl Cullen shook hands with Captain Tanner and his brother Lee. "We'll be back shortly to give you and your family a chance to visit and get better acquainted with Daniel. You can help us shove off if you like."

"I wish you luck, Daniel," said Captain Tanner. "I hope to see you Cullen brothers again. If you'll pardon me, I've got a cargo hold filled with goods for your fair city."

Lee and Earl walked to Earl's small skiff tied up at the dock north of the merchant ship. Daniel picked up his pack and followed their long easy strides. The boat was tiny compared to the ship Daniel had just left. It had a single sail with a tiller instead of a wheel, and it had a small enclosed cabin in the center of the boat. Earl jumped down into the boat and took Daniel's pack and placed it in the cabin.

"Say good-bye to your Uncle Lee and jump aboard, Daniel. The wind is perfect for us to make good time. We're going to head back down the river and go up the coast a short ways to York Village."

Daniel turned to his Uncle Lee and received a warm hug from the large man, then jumped into the boat. Lee untied the two mooring lines and gave the trim craft a powerful push out from the wharf. The tide pulled the front of the boat upriver until Earl pulled the sail out full to the top of the lanyard, then, the bow of the boat gently turned down stream as the wind filled the sail. Earl remained at the tiller and motioned Daniel to take a seat beside him. They waved to Lee on the wharf as they passed behind the merchant ship and headed back out to sea.

A melancholic feeling came over Daniel as they passed the sturdy ship which had safely carried him across the North Atlantic, a stretch of water that Captain Tanner had told him could be the most dangerous in the world. Off to the port side he noticed a large ship being constructed with freshly peeled trees being used as masts.

"That's Rising Castle Island, Daniel," Uncle Earl said, pointing to the unfinished ship. "When the ship is completed, it will be launched into the water by removing the heavy blocks under the keel and bow. Then, it'll slide down the greased poles into the water. This skiff was built there a couple of years ago."

Daniel studied his Uncle Earl. Like his father, Daniel, Sr., Earl and Lee were tall with a muscular large-boned frame. Daniel had been with his Uncle for a few short minutes, and felt at ease in his presence.

The short journey to Maine gave Daniel a chance to assess his reaction to the new land his mother and father had dreamed of for as long as he could remember. As exciting as the occasion was for him, an element of sadness limited his joy. Tall pine trees and sturdy oaks and ash lined the rivers and coast. They were much larger than in his native Scotland. He didn't see much open field or pasture land near the coastal region.

The small craft sailed rapidly past the two forts at the end of the river and into the estuary, where Uncle Earl turned north along the Atlantic coast, staying as close to the shore as prudent seamanship dictated. He asked Daniel to loosen the sails about one fourth. Mount Agamenticus loomed larger and larger out of the flat coastal plain. A few minutes after leaving the estuary, they entered a harbor with calm waters. Uncle Earl told Daniel that it was the York River, and they were going to travel inland a mile or so to his house on their right.

Uncle Earl held the boat in midstream for several minutes. Eventually, he turned the boat to a landing dock on the shore. Daniel quickly collapsed the sail as instructed and looked at the large two-story house sitting prominently on a bluff overlooking the river. As soon as the boat touched the dock, he jumped out to secure it to the mooring posts.

"Well, Daniel. This is where you can call home. Let's grab your pack and meet your Aunt Ursula and Cousin Ellen," said Uncle Earl.

Chapter Three

The long set of stairs from the dock up the bank to the house exhausted Daniel, who had insisted on carrying his own pack, and his Uncle Earl let him. The home would have been considered a grand mansion back in Scotland. His Uncle had been successful in business affairs, and it was evident by the size and eloquence of the main house and its surroundings. The house had an attached barn which housed their two horses and their soap and candle manufacturing equipment. A small portion of the barn, located on the road that passed close by the house, was used as a display and sales area.

Aunt Ursula was a heavy-set lady with long gray hair that fell lose about her shoulders. She welcomed Daniel with an enthusiastic hug. She looked tired and was wearing a white close-fitting bonnet. She insisted that both he and his uncle remove their shoes at the door, clothing was to be hung on the clothes pegs. Daniel would soon learn that holding a position of prestige within the community was very important to the Cullen family.

His cousin Ellen was tall and slender and a bundle of energy. She had dark brown eyes and auburn hair, and was two years younger than Daniel. He thought she was beautiful. She seemed to be a happy child and was pleased to welcome Daniel into their family fold. Ellen was born in York shortly after her father had left the British Army and settled in the colonies.

That first night at the supper table, Daniel enjoyed a popular food called kedgeree. It contained wild rice, beans, lentils, smoked codfish and hard-boiled eggs, and was served piping-hot. He learned that it was a staple in the colonies. He had been all day without anything to eat, and it tasted good. They talked about the school which was about a half mile from the house in the village of York. Ellen attended regularly and was able to read and write. Uncle Earl told him that he could attend school with Ellen. However, Daniel had to understand that his chores around the house came before school, and occasionally, when there was a large supply of hot tallow or beeswax in the heavy cast-iron kettle, he would be expected, along with all the rest of the family, to help dip candles.

Daniel had been tutored to read and write at home by his mother and occasionally by his father, who had stressed the importance of an education. Daniel's skills were as advanced as Ellen's who had been in school for five years. He was anxious to go to school, for he had a curious mind and derived pleasure and a sense of achievement learning new things about the world around him. His father had told him that he was a good student, and he should take advantage of every opportunity to advance his education.

Uncertain about his acceptability, Daniel asked, "Will the teacher object to my being a foreigner?"

"Not at all, Daniel," Uncle Earl replied with a smile. "I'm sure that your mother, who is very intelligent, has done well by you in that respect. The new school in the village has only one requirement, and that is the desire to learn and the ability to do so."

"What do they teach?" Daniel asked.

"Several subjects are touched upon, lad," Aunt Ursula told him. "The teacher will cover some of the basics in mathematics and the principles of religious doctrine – remember that we Scotch are strong Presbyterians. The laws of the land will be covered, and you'll have a chance to read and understand stories and poems that will be fun and exciting. Every emotion that man is capable of experiencing has been described at some time and place by the great writers of the world. The ability to read and understand the written word is a wonderful gift that has the potential of opening many doors for us as we travel on the path of life."

Daniel nodded that he understood what his Aunt was saying. His mother had also told him the same thing. She had encouraged discipline and warned him about complacency. "One is never too old to learn," was one of her favorite expressions.

Days went by quickly for Daniel. He adapted to the routines established by his aunt and uncle in their home. He worked a little bit every day on the firewood supply. His primary chore was to maintain an adequate supply of wood for the six fireplaces in the house. Whenever he entered the house he carried an armful of wood. The kitchen fireplace, which was used for heat and cooking, burned four times more fuel wood. The three foot pieces for the kitchen were heavy and awkward to carry, and he was thankful that it was closest to the firewood lean-to. Occasionally, he and Ellen would have fun throwing dried kernels of corn into the red coals of the large fireplace, where they popped and were thrown back at them. Sometimes they could catch them if they were quick enough.

The new land was full of surprises, and Daniel was learning more and more about it every day. The Cullens worked hard and were considered successful by the standards of other families in the village, yet they ate simple, hearty foods like most working families. Two of the most popular foods in the colonies became Daniel's favorites, hasty pudding and apple pies. Hasty pudding was made by heating cornmeal in a small amount of water until it thickened. It was usually eaten hot with dried apples and maple syrup added as desired. It could also be eaten cold when it was thinly sliced and used like bread. He found it very filling and nourishing.

Apple pies were a daily staple food in the colonies. Composed of sliced or whole apples wrapped in a heavy crust of dough made from wheat, barley, or oat flour, it was eaten hot or cold all year round. When fresh apples were no longer available, dried apple slices were soaked in hot water and used. Apple harvest time was a busy period when bushels of apples were sliced and strung on flax strings in the attic or any other room where they could dry before they spoiled.

Some foods like oranges, lemons, raisins, and sugar were scarce and a real treat when they were shipped to the colonies. Daniel had eaten them in Scotland, but that was much closer to those places in the world that grew them.

One day in June, Ellen and Daniel were carding flax fibers in the barn. Ellen held the long stringy stocks of flax while Daniel used the carding brush to comb the fibers like combing snarls from their hair. The fibers were separated and used to make the wick for candles. Several fibers were attached to a board a few inches apart and hung down the length of the candles to be made. Twenty to thirty wicks hung down from the board and were dipped in the hot liquid tallow. The flower and seeds from the flax plant were distilled to produce linseed oil.

The first dip was the hardest because the string could become tangled. Daniel held the board level and dipped the strings into the hot tallow. Then he slowly pulled them out and held them over the large kettle while Ellen used sharp scissors to trim any excess tallow from the bottom of the candle. It was then placed on a rack allowing the tallow to harden before it was dipped several more times until the candle was the correct size. Ellen and Daniel liked to do candles when the tallow was mixed with concentrated bayberry. It filled the barn with a fresh, clean scent.

One day during the last week in June, Ellen and Daniel were walking home from school when they noticed a wagon being loaded with candles and soap. It was their Uncle Lee packing up a supply of stuff for himself and friends in Portsmouth.

"Well, look who we have here," exclaimed Uncle Lee, jumping off the wagon to embrace each of them. He held Daniel at arms length and examined him from head to toe. "I swear, you've grown since we last saw you, lad. Yea are a picture of your father. How have yea been doing? Has my brother Earl worked your fingers to a bone?"

"No, sir," replied Daniel, sharing Ellen's enthusiasm about Uncle Lee's visit.

"He's a good lad, Lee," remarked Uncle Earl. "He takes responsibility seriously like big Dan used to do, and he's proven to be a student his teacher is proud of. Erin has done well by him, God rest her soul!"

Daniel detected a solemn note in Uncle Earl's voice, and looked into Uncle Lee's eyes. They were sad! Instantly, without being told, he knew what was wrong. "Is it my mother?" he cried.

"Yes, Daniel, it is true," Uncle Lee answered in a wavering voice. "I received word last night. One of our cousins in Aberdeen sent a letter to us on a ship that tied up in Portsmouth late yesterday. I'm so sorry, lad..." Lee took his young nephew in his strong arms again. Tears formed in Lee's eyes. Everyone in the family had loved the gentle soft-spoken Erin. She was one of the world's givers who asked very little for herself.

"I had a premonition that she would never be able to make the crossing, but I prayed that God would grant her the strength so that I could see her again... She deserved a chance for a new life. She would have loved it here in America," Daniel cried, still clinging to his Uncle Lee.

"Aye, there is truth in your words, lad. Sometimes life isn't fair, but we have to go on and not judge why things happen the way they do," Uncle Lee continued in a steady voice. "I know it's little comfort now, son, but be thankful for all the years yea had with her. I'm sorry to be the bearer of such painful news. I came as quickly as I could."

Daniel held on to the reassuring Uncle Lee and recalled the last time he saw his mother. Her color was bad, and she was breathing hard. He could hear the rattle of phlegm in her lungs... He now realized why she had been so insistent on his leaving for America on the next available ship out of Aberdeen. She knew that she was dying and did not want him to witness her last days. The thought of her unselfish devotion to him enveloped him in sadness. What he wouldn't give to be able to tell her how much he loved her. Tears gushed from his dark eyes and ran down his cheeks. He began to sob convulsively and gasped for breath. Ellen and his two uncles stood silently around him and shared his sorrow.

"No words can make the pain go away, lad," Uncle Earl solemnly said. "But you're not alone in this world. Your new family in this young land loves you for who you are. You'll never be alone."

"I'm sorry, Dan," Ellen cried with him. She could never know what her cousin was feeling, but seeing him react to the death of his mother touched her deeply and she felt helpless in her inability to console him. Daniel was in emotional shock. He heard the voices of those around him, yet was impervious to the words they were saying.

Lee turned to Earl and told him that he should be leaving now. He wanted to pass over the Piscataqua River ferry before night closed in. They had agreed that it might be better for Daniel to return with Lee to Portsmouth. The change might help him overcome the grief that he now carried. Aunt Ursula packed Daniel's things in his faithful canvas pack and placed it on the wagon. Ellen and her parents reluctantly said good-bye to Daniel. Uncle Lee helped him into the wagon. Ellen and her mother and father watched them slowly travel up the road toward the village, waving one last time as it disappeared around the corner.

Uncle Lee respected Daniel's desire to remain silent. Small talk was awkward at times like this. The sturdy Belgian mare pulled the loaded wagon with ease. The sun was beginning to dip towards the western horizon. A couple of miles out of York village they came to the first ferry, the one over the York River. Uncle Lee mentioned to Daniel that it was the same river that flowed by his Uncle Earl's house. Daniel nodded in acknowledgment. Lee paid the ferry owner with a dozen candles as they drove the wagon off the small barge to the Kittery side of the river.

Daniel watched the passing landscape with an indifferent eye. Corn and flax were growing in several fields that had been cleared for farming. The distinctive blue flower of the flax plant could be seen in most of the cultivated plots of open land. The terrain was undulating and the amount of wooded land continued to surprise him. Trees lined the fields and pastures in Scotland. Here they continued as far as the eye could see - sturdy oaks and maples and tall majestic evergreens that had a sweet clean smell. They arrived at the Kittery side of the Piscataqua River while the sun was still visible. The ferry was a much larger and more elaborate operation than the one they had used on the York River.

The ferry was located several hundred feet north of the Market Street Wharf where Daniel first stepped foot in the New World. The tide was coming in, so a line was attached to the ferry and ran across the river south two hundred feet north of the landing dock. When the ferry was released from the eastern shore, the incoming tide pulled it across the river at the end of the rope, guided by a taut line from landing to landing, like a giant pendulum, with no effort required. Once it was on the western shore at Portsmouth, the ferry could be slung back to the Kittery side by using lines positioned in similar fashion north of the ferry route, while the lines on the opposite shore were left slack. All the attendants had to do was loosen or tighten the appropriate lines, and the ferry was propelled across the river with ease. When the tide was at ebb there was always movement of fresh inland water flowing to the sea.

Uncle Lee's house and print shop were located at the northern outskirts of Portsmouth, close to the Piscataqua River on a street that led to Market Square, the center of the city. The print shop was located in two rooms of the house with access to the street. At the rear of the house was a large barn where they housed their two horses. A large pasture ran down to the river with a rail fence all around the perimeter. They owned fifteen acres.

Uncle Lee pulled the wagon under the shelter of the barn and stopped. He turned to Daniel. "We're home. I hope you like it here with your Aunt Maureen and me. I've owned the land for twenty years. Your Dad once visited here when I was single and living in the barn. He liked the setting, and I'm hoping that you'll like it, too."

Daniel felt as welcome as he had with Uncle Earl and Aunt Ursula. "My mother told me that as long as there are Cullens in the new world, I will have a place to stay. I now know what she meant by that."

"Don't ever forget those things your mother and father told yea, lad," advised Uncle Lee, climbing out of the wagon. "I'll unhook the horse and put him in the stall; then we can go inside and have supper with your Aunt Maureen."

"I can help rub him down," Daniel offered. "I often helped my father with the horses at the livery stable of the big house."

"I'd appreciate that, Dan. Many hands make work lighter. We'll put old Andy in the stall here beside the wagon. He's gentle as a lamb and should walk right into the stall as soon as we unhitch him."

Andy did as Uncle Lee predicted and started to eat the oats Daniel had placed in the manger. It brought a smile to Daniel's face. Lee saw the reaction and placed an arm around his shoulders directing him towards the door leading through a storage shed into the modest house.

Maureen Cullen met them at the door. She was a short slender lady with gray hair tied in a bun at the base of her head. Her flashing green eyes made Daniel feel that she was looking through him instead of at him. It made some people feel uncomfortable, but he disregarded the intensity of her observation, and noted her warm caring smile that lit up her face. She was a complete contrast to his Aunt Ursula.

"I've been sitting here by the fire wondering what Erin Cullen's son would look like, and I'm not disappointed, Daniel. Welcome to our home." She spread her arms out to him. He found comfort and peace in her strong embrace. She reminded him of his mother and, once again, tears welled in his eyes.

Lee looked upon the two with a smile. He was still very much in love with his wife and showed it in many ways. He knew that Maureen had that uniquely wonderful touch of bringing serenity and harmony to the sorrowful situation that Daniel was now experiencing. Therefore, Lee had gently insisted that Daniel accompany him back to

Portsmouth. Dan was already experiencing the relaxed, unpretentious atmosphere that emanated from the gentle lady. It was a gift she dispensed with grace and charm.

"I'm glad to be here, Aunt Maureen. My mother told me that you and she were good friends," Daniel said, wiping his eyes with his shirt sleeve.

"I loved your mother like a sister," confided Aunt Maureen in her reassuring melodious voice. "I also knew your father well. I'm so sorry that dear Erin is no longer with us. She had more dreams and plans for this new land than any of us, and I'm going to remember her with a smile on my lips and be thankful that memories of her are so very special. I can promise you that she's with us now in this room and will always be your guiding angel, so wipe those tears from your eyes and accept the legacy she and your father have given you." Aunt Maureen kissed him on the top of his head and held him for a long time.

Daniel withdrew from her embrace feeling better and smiled at his good fortune.

Chapter Four

The bedroom Aunt Maureen assigned to Daniel was the same room their son, Ronald, had used. Five years ago, he was killed by renegade Indians while helping to build a cabin northwest of Portsmouth. His uncle and aunt rarely mentioned their son's name. Daniel thought about the loss of a child and wondered if it was as painful to Aunt Maureen and Uncle Lee as the death of his father had been to his mother and himself.

The light of his single candle barely illuminated the bedroom. The smooth pine panels still smelled fresh and clean. The single dormer window looked out over the northern roof of the house. He could see some lights still burning near the Piscataqua River to the right. He sat at the small desk near the window and examined the books neatly lined up at the front of the desk. The books were on elementary mathematics and geometry, and there were several volumes of plays by Shakespeare. Several goose quill pens and a half-filled inkwell were also neatly lined up on the desk.

Hanging on the wall above the desk was a British Army uniform, probably belonging to his Uncle Lee, for his father had a similar one hanging on a clothes post in their apartment at Aberdeen. The jacket was the traditional scarlet red; however, the blue cuffs, lapels, and collar identified it as the uniform of the Royal Scotch Regiment that Daniel's father and two brothers had served so faithfully.

A British Brown Bess musket hung on two pegs above the uniform. The musket still smelled of gunpowder. The firearm sent a shiver through his youthful body, wondering what stories the weapon could tell if it could talk. The Cullen brothers had served with the Royal Scotch Regiment in India trying to pacify radical religious fanatics, and they had served in the southern portions of the colonies fighting Indians, French, and Spanish troops who claimed the same portions of the continent. Daniel touched the triangular bayonet on the musket and was surprised at how sharp it was.

Daniel collected his sack and unpacked his two pistols examining them carefully. They were a trifle large for his small hand, but he was confident that he would grow enough to use them. His father had been a fine marksman, and he wanted to be like his father.

Later that first night, loud noises at the neighbor's farm awoke Daniel from a sound sleep. Men were shouting in threatening tones. Daniel leaped to the window and saw a haystack on fire. It was close to Uncle Lee's pasture fence and lit up the night sky. Angry men hollered and Daniel could see movement in the background of the fire. He heard footsteps downstairs and Uncle Lee called to him.

"Daniel, do you hear me?"

"Yes, sir," he replied sharply.

"There's a nasty disturbance at our neighbor's place. I'm on my way over there. Would you please come down to stay with your aunt while I'm gone? You should barricade the door after I leave and open it for no one except me. Is that understood?"

"Yes, I'm on my way down." Daniel replied, hurrying downstairs to find Aunt Maureen sitting at the foot of the stairs with a candle in her hand staring at the barricaded door.

"Come, sit beside me, Daniel. Don't be alarmed by this," Aunt Maureen requested in a strained voice.

"What's going on, Aunt Maureen?" he asked in an excited voice, thinking about what he would do if somebody tried to force his way into the house during his Uncle's absence.

"It's a long story, child, and I'm afraid it's not very complimentary," she answered, grasping his hand and squeezing it reassuringly.

They listened in silence as the angry voices began to calm down. Lee's authoritative voice demanded that the men be quiet, "And make certain that the fire does not extend beyond the haystack."

"Is Uncle Lee in any danger?" Daniel asked.

"Your Uncle is one of the most respected men in the village. Whoever the men are, they'll listen to him," she answered confidently.

"What's wrong?" Daniel urgently asked again.

"Our neighbor, Thom Cameron, is a hard working man who minds his own business. Your Uncle Lee and I have found him to be a very kind and helpful neighbor. His wife, Melinda Cameron, is an Ojibwa Indian squaw. They were married and Thom brought her here to his farm." Aunt Maureen's voice wavered for a moment and continued. "As you know, our son Ronald was killed by a wandering band of Saint Francis Indians. I have a hatred for them that will never leave me, yet I've tried to differentiate between the vicious savages responsible for his death, and the rest of the native peoples. After all, some white people are just as vicious and cruel, and that doesn't mean that all white people are that way. That same logic should be applied to the Indians who inhabited this same land we now own."

"I can understand that, Aunt Maureen," Daniel told her with a nod of his head.

"I like Melinda Cameron regardless of her race. She's a good mother, a faithful wife, and a very hard working person. Her world is her family, and that's as it should be. She does domestic work at some of the wealthy homes in the village. Many people resent her presence and look down on her. I'm not sure what this incident is about this morning, but it may concern the Cameron's daughter, Lavina, who recently returned from a missionary school in Vermont near the Canadian border. Lavina is about your age. I've known the child since she was born. She's an intelligent girl with good manners, and I like her. Come, let's start a fire and enjoy a cup of hot tea."

The fireplace had been banked by Uncle Lee just before he retired for the night. Daniel removed the gray ashes covering the live coals and sprinkled a handful of dried pine shavings over them. He built up a square platform of dry firewood beneath the heavy cast iron teakettle Aunt Maureen filled with water. The teakettle hung from a heavy pivot arm inches from the leaping flames.

Daniel went to the window and stared into the darkness while the water was heating. The fire had been doused and the loud voices had disappeared. Suddenly, there was an urgent pounding on the door. Lee Cullen demanded that they let him in. Daniel nervously yanked the heavy timber away from the door jamb and opened the door for his uncle. Lee Cullen stepped across the threshold holding a young girl in his arms.

"Oh my," Maureen cried, coming to her husband's side.

"It's all right, Maureen. Lavina has been frightened by the drunken trio that attacked her and her mother as they were walking home from

25

a late party at the Wentworth home." Lee placed the girl in the rocking chair beside the fireplace as if she was a toy doll.

Daniel was all eyes. His Uncle Lee's gentleness reminded him of his own father. The girl was crying uncontrollably holding her face in her two hands.

Maureen went to the girl and placed her arms around her. "You're safe here with us, Lavina. Please, can you hear me?" There was no response. The girl continued to cry hysterically. Maureen looked up at her husband with questioning eyes, shaking her head.

Lee looked on helplessly and said, "She was not hurt physically, but the trauma and fear of what might have happened is unthinkable."

Maureen took a deep breath and slapped Lavina across the face hard enough to shock her. Lavina stopped screaming. Maureen collected Lavina in her protective arms and apologized. "Please forgive me, dear child, forgive me for striking you, Lavina. Would you like some hot tea?"

The girl nodded, "Yes," and began wiping the tears from her face with a handkerchief Maureen had given her.

Daniel continued to stare at the girl. She was shorter than him by three or four inches. Her long black hair was done up in two braids that hung down in front of her shoulders. He had never seen an Indian up close. The color of her skin was more copper or bronze than black like some Negroes he had seen working on the docks in Portsmouth.

The water began to boil in the teakettle. Daniel swiveled it away from the fire and lifted it from the hook with a heavy cloth. Uncle Lee threw a handful of tea into a porcelain teapot and held it so that Daniel could pour the boiling water into the pot.

"A warm cup of strong tea will calm all of us," Lee said, stirring the pot and setting it on the small table beside the fireplace. "This has been quite an introduction to Portsmouth for you, Daniel. This young lady is our neighbor's daughter, Lavina Cameron. She has just returned from a missionary school in Vermont, known as the New Hampshire Grants. Lavina, this is my nephew, Daniel Cullen. He recently came to us from Scotland across the ocean."

Lavina raised her dark swollen eyes to look at Daniel. "I'm glad to meet you, Daniel Cullen." Her voice was soft and melodious, unlike what Daniel had expected, and she spoke perfect English!

"Daniel stayed for a while with my brother in York. Do you remember the place? I brought you with me once when I went to get a supply of soap and candles. You were just a little girl then," Lee said in a calm, comforting voice. "You must remember, young lady, you were not the cause of what happened tonight."

"What did happen?" Maureen asked, placing a cup of hot tea in Lavina's hands, turning toward her husband.

"As I understand it," Lee explained, choosing his words carefully, "Lavina and her mother had worked into the early hours of the morning at the Wentworth home, cleaning up after a long celebration. On their way home, they were confronted by several men who had been drinking at the local brewery. Melinda and Lavina tried to avoid them by walking on the other side of the roadway, but the men caught up with them and began shouting obscene threats. Melinda was badly bruised when one of the men tripped her and began to paw at her clothing. Young Lavina attacked the attacker, scratching, and clawing at his face. The fury of her defense startled the men momentarily, so that Lavina had time to help her mother off the ground. Then they ran as fast as they could toward home. Thom had heard the loud voices and came outside just as Melinda and Lavina ran into the yard. He attacked the men following them with his bare fists, but was overpowered. He was on the ground when I got there. Like all cowards, they backed down and disappeared into the night when confronted squarely. Thom has a nasty bang on his head, and Melinda is very shaken up."

"I should go to them," cried Maureen, placing her tea cup on the table.

"They're all right, Maureen," Lee interrupted her. "I offered to take Lavina for the night so that they can care for each other. In the morning, we'll check on them, and then I'm going to the constable. I recognized two of the men, and I intend to press charges against them. Our streets must be safe for our citizens."

Lavina had been sipping the tea listening to every word Lee said. She had always liked the Cullens, and felt secure knowing that they lived nearby. "Will the men be punished?" she asked in a wavering voice. "Is there justice for Indians, too?"

Lee looked at the frightened girl staring into the red coals of the fireplace. "I understand why you ask the question, Lavina, and you have good reason for doing so, but laws should protect all citizens equally. The way man interprets and administers those laws may reflect the bigotry in our culture, but the law must always stand steadfast."

Daniel was moved by the eloquence of his uncle's defense of the helpless Indian girl, even though he did not completely understand everything he was saying. Lavina lifted her eyes to look at Lee. Daniel saw pride and dignity beyond anything he had ever experienced. It was a defining moment he would often recall, and that night he was proud to call himself a Cullen.

The next morning, the sound of a door closing on the barn woke Daniel. It was a clear sunny day outside, and he could smell smoke. Springing out of bed, Daniel looked out the window and saw his Uncle Lee tending a small fire in a metal container on the floor of a smokehouse in the middle of the pasture. It was a common practice to smoke and dry ham, bacon, codfish, and any other meat or fish to extend their storage life. The sweet smell of bacon and ham being smoked made Daniel hungry. He washed up in the wash basin on a small bureau in the room, and rushed downstairs to the kitchen. Aunt Maureen was busy at the fireplace.

She turned to him and smiled. "Good morning, Daniel. I'm glad you could sleep. It was a busy evening. I have some oatmeal for you, and Lee just brought some fresh cool milk from the springhouse. Are you hungry?"

"Yes I am, Aunt Maureen. I apologize for sleeping so late. My mother made me promise to be helpful and do my share of the chores wherever I stay. I intend to do that."

Aunt Maureen motioned for him to sit down at the table. "I'm sure you do, Daniel. You don't need to apologize for sleeping late. I could have done that too, but Lee was up at his usual time. Perhaps, I'll take a short nap this afternoon," she chuckled impishly.

"Has Lavina already gone home?"

"By the time we got up, she had gotten the fire going and was finishing a cup of tea. I suspect that she did not sleep a wink. She returned home after thanking us. I like that child, and admire her dignity in the face of cruel prejudices expressed by some people. Lee accompanied her home. I guess everything is all right with her mother and father."

"Did Uncle Lee complain to the constable?"

"Yes," Aunt Maureen stated emphatically. "I would not be surprised that he might write an editorial about the incident in his paper."

"What is his paper?" Daniel questioned with interest.

"Lee makes several copies of his newspaper every other week. He calls it the COASTAL BEACON. A few merchants advertise their wares in the paper and Lee collects tidbits and announcements of special events of current interest in the area. He makes enough money from the advertisements to pay for printing and distribution of the paper, and offers it free to the general public. It is quite popular and has a loyal following. Your Uncle Lee is a writer and has a reputation of being a crusader. He's an eloquent spokesperson for the common man and a respected foe of the privileged and wealthy families of the area. Even his adversaries like Lee, because he's honest and is endowed with an extraordinary sense of decency and fair play."

Daniel listened with intense interest to his aunt's words. "Will I be able to help him in the print shop?" Daniel asked.

"You certainly will. There's always something that needs to be done."

"Our nephew has recovered from a long night," Lee announced, entering the house. Daniel smelled smoke. "How are you this morning, lad?"

"I'm fine, sir. I smelled the smokehouse, and it made me hungry," Daniel smiled.

"I'm using a combination of dry corn cobs and green sugar maple wood to finish off our last batch of bacon and ham," Lee told him, taking a seat at the table. "If you have any more oatmeal, Maureen, I could eat another serving. It's going to be a busy day."

"I was just telling Daniel about the COASTAL BEACON," said Maureen, setting another bowl for her husband.

They engaged in small talk about the paper and events of the morning. Maureen was busy around the fireplace while they talked. Daniel watched her carefully place two dozen or more eggs in a heavy kettle of water and swing it out over the flames to boil. He knew what she was doing for his mother did it often. As soon as the eggs were cooked, they were peeled and immersed in a brine of sugar, vinegar, and mustard seeds. A few days later they were tasty pickled eggs, of which he was most fond.

After eating, Daniel volunteered to feed and water the horses in the barn and clean out the stalls. His Uncle Lee announced that he was going to town for a while and winked at Daniel as he left. Daniel energetically attacked the chores, pleased to be able to do something to help out. When he had the barn well-organized, he filled the wood box in the kitchen with dry firewood and resupplied the fireplace in his aunt's and uncle's bedroom.

Lee returned midday with a satisfied look on his face. He approached Daniel who was splitting wood behind the barn. Daniel found his smile contagious, for his Uncle was a contented human being!

"Dan, me lad," he called. "I have some good news. Several merchants from the area are forming a supply train destined for the town of Charlestown on the Connecticut River. A fort is being built there to defend the town and settlers nearby from Indian raids. It'll be almost a hundred miles through rugged country and take about five days to get there and four days to return. Would you like to accompany me on the trip?"

Chapter Five

There was a sense of excitement in the air since Uncle Lee announced that Daniel could go along on a trip through the sparsely settled portions of the state. The possibility of being attacked by roaming bands of Indians and/or French troops was very real. Later that afternoon, Uncle Lee told Daniel that he could take one of his pistols with him, and asked permission to take the second pistol of the collection for his own use on the trip. It was an easier weapon to carry on a freight wagon than a firelock musket. Daniel enthusiastically agreed. The request made Daniel's heart beat a little faster and increased his desire to accompany his uncle.

Lee showed Daniel how to shoot the flintlock firearm. They walked through the barn to the pasture where Uncle Lee patiently demonstrated the proper steps to safely fire the pistols.

The first step was to load the barrel with the correct amount of powder. Uncle Lee showed Daniel his bullet pouch from the British Army which contained several prepackaged measures of gunpowder for the British Brown Bess musket. The Brown Bess barrel had a bore size of three quarters of an inch in diameter. Daniel's pistols had less than a half inch diameter bore, so slightly less than half of the powder in the paper packet would be required for each discharge. To load the pistol, the gunpowder was poured down the barrel, then a lead bullet inserted, followed by a wad of paper or cloth about twice the diameter of the bore. The wad was placed after the bullet to hold the charge in the pistol. Finally, the charge was rammed firmly to the bottom of the barrel with the wooden ram attached under the pistol's barrel. The firearm could be safely carried in this charged condition.

Uncle Lee continued with his instructions, talking slowly and precisely about each step. To fire the pistol, after the barrel had been charged, a small amount of gunpowder was placed in the priming pan and the cover (frizzen) closed over the pan. He cautioned Daniel that if he was in a desperate situation for rapid fire, the priming pan could be filled before the barrel was charged; however, for a pistol, which was carried in a vertical position, it was safer to prime the pan last. Then, he pulled the hammer back with his thumb, took aim, and gently squeezed the trigger. A piece of flint was held in place by a spring-loaded gooseneck-shaped hammer. When the trigger was pulled, it released the spring, allowing the hammer to strike the L-shaped piece of steel covering the pan. Sparks from the flint would ignite the powder in the pan which then ignited the main charge through a small hole in the barrel.

Lee noted Daniel's intense focus on his instructions and liked that serious side of the young man. "Now, all we have to do is see how the pistol shoots." Uncle Lee raised the pistol in his right arm, fully extended it and pulled the trigger. A sharp "ka-boom" filled the air and a puff of smoke rose from the pistol.

"Wow!" exclaimed Daniel. "That's loud."

"Well, half of a powder packet is a maximum load, but it should handle the charge safely for a few years. I hit the piece of wood I was aiming at. These are fine weapons, Daniel, and are a wonderful heritage from your father. Now, watch carefully. I'll repeat the steps and fire one more time."

Lee fired again and hit the same block of wood on the pile at the end of the pasture, then he passed the pistol off to Daniel. Repeating the steps as instructed, Daniel flinched when he first pulled the trigger. His uncle grinned and told him that it was a natural reaction the first few times. They stayed in the pasture until Daniel was able to fire and hit the piece of wood. The shooting lesson was a rite of passage in Daniel's life, representing a step towards manhood.

After the shooting demonstration, Daniel and Uncle Lee loaded the wagon with boxes of candles, soap, blankets, kegs of nails, and several barrels of dried, smoked codfish for the inhabitants of the fort at Charlestown. They left space for hay and oats for the two horses, and for the bedding, tent, food, and cooking utensils necessary for the trip.

The loaded wagon was too heavy for "Andy" to pull for long periods of time, so Thom Cameron offered the use of his Belgian draft horse, "Gabriel." The two horses had frequently worked as a team and had the capacity to pull the wagon day after day without straining either animal. That evening Thom and his daughter Lavina brought his mare to Lee's barn. Lee and Daniel met them at the barn door with a lantern.

"I appreciate the loan of Gabriel for the trip, Thom. That way Andy can be a little lazier," Lee chuckled. He sometimes saw things that amused him that others failed to appreciate.

"I'm glad to help, Lee. I'd be going with you if things were different, but I don't think it's a good time for me to leave." answered Thom Cameron in a deep sonorous voice. He was a tall thin man with white hair and deep-set eyes. He moved with easy fluid motions.

"I understand, Thom. I think it's a wise decision. I just wish it could be different for you and your family," Lee told him, placing a comforting hand on his shoulder. "In time, things will get better, but the way the French have been increasing their raids and debaucheries on isolated settlements, I would not plan on much improvement for a while."

Lavina took the reins from her father and led Gabriel toward the stall Andy occupied. Daniel held the lantern for her and opened the stall gate. Lavina was shy as she tied Gabriel to the stall stanchion. She turned to Daniel and asked: "Are you going with your uncle?"

"Yes, we're leaving at the break of dawn," he answered. He could still picture her crying in the kitchen. "I hope you were not hurt last night. Uncle Lee spoke to the constable so that the men will be punished."

"I feel bad that it happened right after I returned home. My mother is still very upset about the incident." She stepped out from the stall and closed the gate. "Old Gabe is about the same age as Andy. He loves carrots. While you're gone my mother and father will look after your Aunt Maureen. I'll probably stay with her evenings."

"I like the way people help their neighbors in this new land. It's not that way in Scotland where everyone seems to be too busy with their own affairs. I think I'm going to like it here," Daniel confided in her.

She giggled at him. "You talk different than the local boys."

He smiled at her frankness. "I guess I do."

"Come along, Lavina. These men have lots to do for the coming trip. Don't worry about Maureen, Lee. We'll look out for her," Thom said, waving good-bye.

"I have no doubts, Thom, thanks. Good night to you, and you, too, Lavina."

"Good night, Mr. Cullen, and you too, Daniel," she replied, skipping after her father.

The next morning Daniel and his Uncle Lee left the farm just as the sun was breaking above the eastern horizon. Seven wagons joined the train at different points along the road heading west. Lee led the way with his wagon on the first day. It had been agreed that, at the end of each day, the point position was taken by the next wagon in line and the lead wagon would rotate to the rear of the train. That way everybody shared equally the dusty conditions behind the supply column.

Daniel sat on the seat beside his Uncle Lee watching the surrounding landscape with interest. Their first point of destination was the Merrimack River, about two days travel from Portsmouth. Uncle Lee had traveled the route a couple of times. Daniel heard him mention to the other teamsters that the Merrimack was the largest river they would cross and a well-traveled track led to Thornton Ferry. By mid-day they had made good progress over tracks that connected small settlements to Portsmouth. The horses needed to be fed, watered, and rested, so the train pulled off the trail on the east side of the Oyster River, which could be forded without any difficulty.

While the horses and men were eating and relaxing, a long column of oxen teams pulling full-length white pine trees passed by. Two oxen pulled a single tree over one hundred feet long, mounted on two axles with large wheels, one at each end of the tree. They were destined for Portsmouth where they would be shipped to England and used for masts on newly constructed ships. The mast trees were a valuable natural resource and the Crown had scouted the area and marked suitable trees with a brand. This was resented by the local settlers and land owners. Daniel counted twenty mast trees pass by.

According to his Uncle Lee, the prospect of sighting Indians between Portsmouth and the Merrimack River was slight. Daniel was constantly scanning the passing terrain for a chance encounter. England and France had declared war with each other again, and the news of the clashes between them were becoming more frequent and bloody. Protection of the nearby settlers was the main reason for constructing the fort called Number Four at Charlestown, New

Hampshire. It was the fourth and most northerly settlement on the Connecticut River.

Daniel had heard tales about the border situation from various sources over the last two years, but it was only after Uncle Lee described the big picture involving two powerful nations, that Daniel understood the gravity of the situation. Uncle Lee was convinced that full-scale war was inevitable before the dispute of land west of the Hudson River in New York, including the Ohio River Valley, could be determined, and settlers could farm their lands in peace. Officially, war had been declared between France and England, but in reality, raids and conflicts had always been a part of the region regardless of peace treaties.

The French had legitimately claimed portions of the continent from the Saint Lawrence River south to the Atlantic coast. French explorers were some of the first to view the vast stretches of land, and had built forts throughout the Great Lakes and Ohio Valley to support their claims. The English had also laid claim to the same lands and viewed the French influence in the Ohio Valley as a way of limiting English expansion westward. The French had developed a lucrative fur trade in the region and in northern Canada, including Hudson Bay. The French had fewer military resources on the continent, and to increase their strength, they enlisted the assistance of many Indian tribes, notably those belonging to the Iroquois confederation. They were mortal enemies of the less aggressive Algonquin tribes from the New England region. Uncle Lee told Daniel that Lavina and her mother were Ojibwa, who were some of the first native people to greet and welcome the white men to their shores as friends. As time passed, that relationship changed and became confrontational, primarily because the two races viewed the ownership of land differently.

To the Indian, the concept of ownership of the land was in conflict with their basic beliefs that animals, trees, rocks, the land, and the sky all have souls and spirits. How can a person own what has been given to all the inhabitants of the earth? The white settlers came to the shores in search of land, free land, to raise their crops and families in peace and without the yoke of tyranny. They were accustomed to English law that gave them the right to measure, sell, and purchase the land as ultimate owners and possessors of the land and everything that grew on it. The Indian recognized hunting privileges on portions of the land they shared with selected tribes. That distinction was vigorously defended, and was the closest thing to ownership that they were capable of understanding.

When the white men purchased land from the Indians, the native peoples viewed the transaction the same as sharing hunting privileges, not as outright possession that could deny others access to the land. Given the situation, contests for the land became vicious and bloody. The Indians were in a constant state of conflict with their neighboring tribes over hunting privileges. Powerful tribes displaced the less powerful. Their concept of hunting privileges was much like the English concept of land ownership, and the tribes settled differences on the battlefield. There was little room for compromise with either party. The Indians that had inhabited the Atlantic coast were defeated and pushed north and west into regions already claimed by the French and their Iroquois allies. An eruption was inevitable. It was only a matter of when and where.

They crossed the Merrimack River late on the second day at a small settlement called Thornton Ferry. The ferrying system was very similar to the one used across the Piscataqua in Portsmouth. By then, Daniel's rear end was hurting from the rough bouncing of the wagon. Even a blanket didn't help that much, so he walked beside the wagon for long stretches at a time. He drove the team every few hours so that Uncle Lee could walk and limber up his legs. Once when his uncle was walking beside the rear wheel he heard grinding noises coming from the hub – the axle needed to be greased. Lee signaled to the rest of the train that he would have to stop.

In just a few minutes, he told Daniel to hold the wagon off the ground with a wagon jack while he removed the wheel and applied liberal amounts of beef tallow around the axle. A minute later, the wheel was replaced and tightened, and the wagon was once again ready to roll. It was a familiar and necessary maintenance routine frequently carried out.

After passing over the Merrimack River, Daniel saw fewer and fewer clearings or log cabins. They drove for hours without seeing any evidence that man had ever been there except for the two wagon tracks, which were becoming narrower, especially in areas of thick forest. There was something ominous about the dark wilderness, and Daniel stayed close to his Uncle Lee and fingered the pistol under his shirt jacket. They were approaching the frontier, that land between the settlements and Indian territory where survival of the fittest was the law.

On the third day, the train encountered two men standing beside the road. They hailed the point wagon and asked if they could hitch a ride. The teamster told them to find a comfortable place to sit, which they did in the cargo area directly behind the front seat. About a mile further, the road took a sharp right hand turn to get around a granite ledge outcrop. The first two wagons had disappeared around the bend and the train came to a halt. Daniel and his uncle were the third wagon from the rear of the train. The minute the wagons stopped, a concerned frown came over Lee's face, and he whispered for Daniel to take over the reins.

Before Daniel could answer, Uncle Lee rolled off the wagon to the ground and crawled into the brush on the right side of the road. Daniel was frightened. What if something was to happen to his uncle? He strained his eyes to see where he was and saw nothing. Lee entered the woods without being seen and rushed cautiously to the point where he thought the lead wagons would be positioned. He silently crawled onto the overlooking ledge. His worst fears were confirmed!

Evidently, two other men had been waiting down the road at the bend so that they could steal up to four wagons. The highwaymen had already pulled two teamsters from the first two wagons and were marching them back along the train on the side opposite from where he was located on the rock. One of the teamsters had already spotted Lee on the rock. Lee moved carefully to his left so that he could see his wagon. To his dismay the seat was empty! Daniel was nowhere in sight. He looked behind him and saw Daniel crawling to him, pistol in hand. Lee put his finger to his lips and whispered in his ears.

"Stay beside me and do as I do, we don't want to shoot unless it's necessary. If I do shoot, you refrain from pulling the trigger, for we'll be defenseless then. Is that understood?"

Daniel nodded his head soberly. Lee saw the determined look and patted him on the shoulder. Lee stood up while the four men held only two of the teamsters on the ground. He cocked the pistol and aimed at the easiest target of the four men, hollering in a loud voice: "Drop any weapons you may have."

Daniel followed his example and pointed his pistol at one of the thieves. The gun wavered under the tension of the moment. The four thieves looked up and were surprised at the two pistols pointing at them. They were armed with a pistol and two muskets. There was fear in their eyes. The two muskets were quickly dropped as the men held up their hands to show that they were empty. The one with the pistol hesitated.

"You can try it, buster, but I'd think hard and long about making any rash moves if I were you. These matched pistols have a hair trigger, so drop it, before they accidentally go off," Lee shouted in a penetrating voice. The man dropped the pistol and resigned himself to his fate. "Now, the four of you move to the front of the train."

They did as they were told. The two teamsters grabbed some rope and tied the four bandits together so that they could walk beside the point wagon. No one in the train wanted them to take up space or weight in any of the wagons.

That night, the bandits were still tied together while the teamsters took two-hour shifts keeping guard. Daniel insisted on taking a turn, so the guard duty time was lowered to an hour and a half. His tour came at midnight while a full moon made the night bright and clear. He stood a few feet from the men, leaning against a tree with his pistol in his hand. It was loaded and primed. All he had to do to fire was cock the weapon and pull the trigger. All during his allotted time at guard duty, he was asking himself if he could really pull the trigger and shoot a man if the situation warranted it.

Daniel noticed that one of the men kept fidgeting with his tied hands, and walked closer to him to see what was wrong, keeping his eyes wide open. Without warning, a clenched fist caught Daniel beside the head knocking him sideways dropping the pistol. The man's hands were free of his ropes! Daniel knew he was in danger, the man outweighed him by a hundred pounds. For a few seconds Daniel was disoriented and screamed for help. The man who had hit him was untying the ropes on his feet. Daniel reached for the knife Ben had given to him and confronted the man just as he leaped against Daniel grasping for his throat. The two fell to the ground. Daniel could not breathe and felt faint. His last instinct was to lift the knife in an arc and drive it into the side of his assailant. He heard a cry of pain and passed out.

Chapter Six

Lee heard Daniel's scream and leaped to his feet, running to the place where the prisoners were being held. He saw Daniel lying on the ground with one of the thieves crawling into the relative safety of the forest. He overtook the prisoner, grabbing him by the collar. The prisoner threw a rock at Lee. It bounced across his chest and infuriated him. With a powerful swing of his arm, Lee landed a blow against the prisoner's head, knocking him off his feet, unconscious. Lee then leaped to Daniel's side and checked for a pulse.

Daniel groggily sat up. By then the other teamsters had gathered around and secured the unconscious prisoner to the wagon. The knife was still in Daniel's hand. It was too dark to see the blood on the blade, but he could feel the thick sticky substance on the handle.

"Are you all right, Daniel?" Uncle Lee demanded, kneeling down to examine him more closely in the limited light.

Daniel was embarrassed that the prisoner had caught him off guard. "He had gotten untied without my knowing it. He thumped me a good one beside the head. Is he badly hurt?"

"I can't tell for sure," Uncle Lee explained calmly. "He had some fight left in him, so he's not too severely wounded. You did well, Daniel. The man was desperate, and he could have killed you. These four scums will bear closer watching until we get to the fort. We'll put them on a small ration of food for good measure."

Lee gave instructions to the teamsters that he would take over as guard and suggested that they all rest for the remainder of the night. He sat beside Daniel with his back against a tree facing the prisoners. In a short time, Daniel succumbed to sleep and rested his head against his Uncle's shoulder. Lee smiled recalling the bravery of his young nephew. There was much about Daniel that reminded Lee of his deceased brother. Even now, after all the years, Lee still mourned the loss. He would have been proud of his son's performance that night.

39

Daniel slept soundly, snoring softly in his uncle's ear. Lee smiled, sitting quietly, watching the dark skies filled with sparkling stars. He liked the night. Somehow it was easier to think and plan things in the hush of the evening. He had often wondered where life would take him. He had traveled all around the world with his brothers in the service of their King. It had been a hard life, yet, it had built a resiliency and determination in him that sustained him in times of adversity. The unknown no longer held him hostage to fear.

Wherever Lee went, he was looked up to as a leader. His brothers had always recognized the traits and had chided him about getting promotions when they received none. The responsibility bothered him at times for he often felt inadequate. If he had a chance to live his life over again, he would choose to become a more educated man than he was. Words came easy to him when he was doing his editorials, for he felt strongly about what he wanted to say. His thirst for knowledge had never been quenched.

The morning came with a brilliance that warmed the men's aching muscles stiffened by the hard ground they had slept on. The wagon train soon picked up the cadence of the methodical advance to the Connecticut River. The cart track was cleared of small trees and brush, while the larger trees and rocks were left for some later period of road building. The path of least resistance was their guide. The track wound in and around these obstacles over rolling hills and deep valleys filled with small fordable streams.

Their first glimpse of the Connecticut River came on their fifth day of travel near a small gathering of cabins at a locale known as Walpole. There the train turned north at a junction on the improved roadway that followed the river. Fort Number Four was ten miles to the north. Clearings and cabins with a soft plume of wood smoke rising from the chimneys were much more numerous along the river. Beautiful garden crops filled the areas opened to the sun around the cabins. The fertile flood plains of the river were easier to till. Further inland, the rockiness of the soil discouraged many settlers, who found it too difficult to eke out a living.

The supply train was met with great relief and much cheering by the men building the fort. Daniel felt like a celebrity. A contingent of British soldiers were helping the construction workers. They provided a defensive force against attack by the French and Indians who frequently used the river as a means of transportation for lightning-quick raids along the Connecticut River valley. One of the soldiers directed the train into the partially completed stockade by way of the south gate, where the roadway ran between two buildings connected by a massive overhead structure called the great chamber. It was a strong two-story fortified framework containing the main gate to the fort. The open room above served as barracks for soldiers, storage area, and meeting place for town and church congregations.

Daniel looked in awe at the fort under construction. Heavy hand-hewn beams of white pine and hemlock served as a framework for the structures. Long beams spanned the roadway under the great room between the two houses at each corner. The stockade walls were constructed from logs thirty feet and longer placed in a trench dug so as to connect the houses that made up the corners and center portions of the perimeter stockade. The poles were firmly secured four inches apart from each other so that no one could pass through the opening, and it would be difficult for the Indians to burn the walls down.

Within a short time after their arrival, the prisoners had been turned over to the soldiers, the wagons had been unloaded, and the supplies placed in storage areas under cover. The food was carried into the great chamber. Daniel helped to carry the barrels of dried codfish up the stairs to the large open space above the roadway. It was the largest room he had ever seen. One of the soldiers pointed out the watch tower which was in the corner next to the stairs to the great room. Daniel and his Uncle Lee climbed the steep winding staircase into the observation tower. They looked out over a large section of land between the fort and the Connecticut River that had been cleared of trees and bushes. It was known as Great Meadows. It was possible to look north and south for miles along the river.

Lee inspected the fortifications with an experienced eye and nodded his head in approval. "Well, Daniel, what do you think of this fort? The settlers nearby can come here and be relatively safe. The homes and belongings they leave behind will probably be burned or destroyed, but at least this structure gives them some measure of security that enhances their chances of survival."

"I imagined that it would be built of stone like the castles in Scotland," Daniel replied, impressed with the view from the tower.

"The presence of abundant forests in this new land make wood a useful source of building material. Productive forests in England or Scotland are scarce," Uncle Lee said, studying the military rational for the structure. "The fort was built to be a safe refuge from raids by the French and Indians attacking across the open land next to the river. An experienced warrior of any nationality would make the simple decision to attack the fort at the rear away from the river. A stockade will hold off an attacking force for a while, but inevitably, all stockades fail. I expect that the commander of the fort realizes that potential threat."

"Do you think it will really be attacked?" Daniel asked.

"It's a sure thing, Daniel. The frontier we're standing on right now will never be safe from French and Indian attacks until England or France withdraw from the claims they have both made for large territories in the continent, especially on this frontier area west to the Mississippi River."

Daniel looked at his Uncle Lee, who continuously surprised him with the depth of his knowledge of current events. They climbed down from the narrow staircase to the watch tower and entered the great chamber, the main defense position of the fortification. Several British soldiers with their colorful red tunics were looking through the small openings built into the thick walls. It was dark inside, even though several candles placed on tables distributed around the outer walls were burning. Daniel and his uncle paused a moment to adjust to the darkness of the interior. Lee instantly recognized a man sitting at a table holding one of the candles.

Lee approached the table with long powerful strides. "I may be wrong, but I do believe that I recognize an old friend. Come along, Daniel, he'll want to meet you." Uncle Lee grasped Daniel by the arm and walked with him to the table, and excitedly announced: "It's been a few years, but I'm certain that it's John Akins."

The man turned around and looked at Lee, removing his small set of glasses. He blinked for a moment and a sad shadow of despair crossed his face. It was immediately replaced with a forced smile. "Lee Cullen, it has been a while, hasn't it?" cried John Akins, embracing his old friend. "It's great to see you again, Lee. . ." He sat back down and began weeping, holding his head in his two hands.

"My God, John, what's wrong?" He had never seen his soldiering friend so despondent and laid a comforting hand on John's trembling shoulder. "Take your time, old friend."

A passing soldier motioned for Lee to come a little closer and spoke in a whisper, "Your friend's wife was killed by Indians two nights ago."

"No, no," Lee shook his head in disbelief. "Thanks for letting me know, sergeant. John and I both served with the Royal Scotch several years ago."

"Aye, and it looks like he'll be needing a friend," replied the sergeant, returning to his station at the openings in the walls.

A tall gray-haired British Captain approached the table and sat down beside John Akins. "Mr. Akins, do you hear me? This is Captain Stevens, commandant of the fort. Dr. Hastings has asked me to find you and report that your daughter has come out of her coma and is resting in my quarters. Do you understand, Sir?"

"Yes, yes, I understand, Captain Stevens. Thank you," answered John Akins, lifting his head to look for Lee. "Lee Cullen is here somewhere. Ah, there you are, old friend."

Lee announced himself to the well-built Captain Stevens. "Is there anything I can do to help, John? I'm so sorry to hear the bad news. It seems as if it was only yesterday that you and Molly were married. Talk to me, John. I heard the Captain here mention a daughter," Lee pleaded.

"Yes, my daughter, Mary," John Akins struggled to talk coherently. The grief was beyond his power to control. He was a small, white-haired man with a wiry frame and dark penetrating eyes. He looked as if he was still reliving the savage scene all over again.

Captain Stevens looked on sympathetically and said, "Your wagon train has arrived at an opportune time, Mr. Cullen. Thank you for the supplies. A special thanks is in order for the supply of newspapers that you have published in Portsmouth. News from the outside world is scarce."

"It's a very small paper," Lee told him modestly. "Our readership is limited to the coastal community of Portsmouth. The editorials produce quite a lot of interest from dissenting views," Lee chuckled to himself.

"Well, I've got matters that need my attention. It's been a pleasure meeting you, Mr. Cullen. Good luck, and have a safe return trip." Captain Stevens rose from the table and turned to John Akins. "My quarters are available for your use, Mr. Akins. Doctor Hastings is there with your daughter now."

"Thank you, Captain Stevens. I appreciate the offer."

Lee shook the Captain's hand as he left the great chamber. Lee noticed that John Akins had been reading a copy of his newspaper lying on the table.

"I was looking at your paper, Lee. You always were a bit of a thinker. You accurately describe our situation here," John Akins said, carefully studying Daniel. "This lad is Daniel's boy, isn't he?"

"That he is, John. Looks like him, doesn't he? His name is also Daniel. Dan this is an old friend of mine and your dad, John Akins," Lee introduced them.

"The spitting image," replied John. "I'm glad to know you, lad."

"I'm pleased to meet you, too, Mr. Akins," answered Daniel, grasping the bereaved man's trembling hand. A copy of the COASTAL BEACON, was lying on the table. "This is the first time I've seen the paper. May I read it, Uncle Lee?"

"Of course, Daniel. Why don't you and I step outside for some fresh air, John. It's dark and stuffy in here. We'll be outside, Daniel."

"Okay, sir," he answered, turning his attention to the editorial written in the paper:

The struggle for the North American continent has involved the major powers of Europe – France, England, Spain, and Holland.

While the English were colonizing the Atlantic seaboard, France was firmly establishing a foothold along the Saint Lawrence River to our north, and Nova Scotia to our east. The Spanish claimed lands west of the Mississippi and in Florida. The Dutch were caught in the area of the Hudson River valley area between the designs of Spain and France.

Armed conflict was guaranteed the moment more than one nation professed claims for lands in the new world. Spain, England, and Holland have resolved their differences, sometimes on the field of battle in a war that began seventeen years ago and ended in the Treaty of Vienna in 1731.

Brutal and savage Indian raids have been made upon New Hampshire settlers for fifty years. Their brutality and savagery were condoned and even encouraged by the French military and the much hated black robes, the Jesuit priests, who frequently accompany them on their raids. Isolated hamlets have been burned and their inhabitants tortured, scalped, and butchered.

The Peace treaty of Utrecht (1714) was only a temporary cease fire between the French and British. The day it was signed, both sides willfully violated the agreements.

In April, 1725, Captain John Lovewell commanded forty-six men and marched against the Indian town of Pequawket. They were ambushed by a large force of Indians. Captain Lovewell was killed in the first volley. The survivors fought off the attack with a very heavy loss to the Indians. Threats to settlers in the area were diminished. There have been no attacks against the settlers in the eastern portion of the state since Captain Lovewell's courageous raid to eliminate the danger. Similar operations will have to be duplicated along the western New Hampshire frontier east of the Connecticut River before any level of peace or security can be had by the beleaguered homesteaders.

Daniel read the article again and came away from the table with a better understanding of the tempestuous relationship that existed between France and England and a fear of the dangers that surrounded the small fortification in the wilderness. He left the great chamber and walked downstairs into the stockade looking for his uncle.

Captain Stevens noticed the boy. "Your Uncle Lee is in the house to your right beneath the great chamber, lad." The Captain pointed to the door.

Lee and John Akins had made their way to the quarters of Captain Stevens beneath the watch tower. Doctor Hastings was standing over a young girl lying on a small lounge in the main room. He was an elderly man with friendly eyes and a smiling demeanor. John Akins introduced Lee to the doctor and asked about his daughter.

"Your daughter, Mary, is still traumatized by the events that took place, Mister Akins. She's going to need a lot of rest and a lot of loving care. She's a fragile girl, and we have no way of knowing what kind of effect the sights she has seen will have on her. I expect that in time, she'll recover completely, but I would caution you against returning to the cabin where her ordeal began."

"I just can't leave my Molly right now, Doctor... I just can't," John Akins cried with tears streaming down his face. He kneeled down to Mary and brushed her blond hair away from her ears. She opened her eyes and stared at him. "It's all right, Mary. You're safe now... You're safe now."

Daniel quietly walked into the room and saw the slight figure lying on the small bed. He didn't say anything. He just stared at the look on the girl's face, wondering what horrors it had taken to produce such a forlorn lifeless stare.

Doctor Hastings took Lee to one side and spoke in a whisper: "Your friend has just lost his wife, Molly. She was beaten, tortured, and raped before she was killed. John had left the cabin to get a pail of water at the spring house when the savages struck with a Jesuit leading them on to greater outrages. John heard their cries for help and surprised the savages, killing one with his bare hands. The others fled in a hurry, scalping his wife before they left. His swift actions saved Mary, here, from a similar death, but he was too late to save his wife."

"What can be done to help her, Doctor?" Lee asked, concerned for the child's welfare.

"Our knowledge is woefully limited, Mr. Cullen. The best thing for the girl right now is an atmosphere of peace and serenity. Just possibly, she may be able to work through the nightmares on her own, or there's the possibility that she may withdraw further. At that point, maybe we will have lost her for good. I just don't know."

Daniel and Uncle Lee left John Akins alone with the doctor and his daughter, and checked the status of the wagons. They planned to stay within the unfinished walls of the fort for the night. The teamsters had pulled the wagons outside of the fort, parking them along the road they would be taking in the morning. The horses were unhitched and turned into a corral beside the eastern wall of the stockade.

A large fire was being built in the center of the stockade. Heavy cast iron kettles filled with water were placed on grills to heat. Tea was a staple drink on the frontier. Venison steaks were cut into thin strips and hung from a battery of spits hanging over the dancing flames. The fire generated a feeling of camaraderie and contentment to those who sat around it. The relatively large number of men in the compound was assurance against an Indian attack, and the Native Americans rarely attacked at night.

Daniel and his uncle ate heartily. Three of the wagons had been filled with furs to be auctioned off at Portsmouth. As the men were prepared to turn in for the night, a dispatch rider from Boston arrived, creating a flourish of speculation. The rider announced in a dry, dusty voice that the French had attacked and now occupied Port Royal (Annapolis), Nova Scotia.

To many of the men, the news was dismissed as irrelevant to what was taking place in the wilds of New England. Lee had a different take on the situation and was uncomfortable with his conclusions. The fact that the French were emboldened enough to make such an attack against British-held Nova Scotia was evidence that they were determined to insure their claims of conquest with military force. He saw a possibility that in the not-too-distant future, the New World could erupt in violent combat. The victor would then be able to, once and for all, legitimately lay claim to the land stretching through the Ohio River valley and beyond the mighty Mississippi River. The prediction Lee had made could now be unfolding. He feared the frontier was about to explode.

Daniel shuddered as he closed his eyes and pulled the blanket over him. Dark and ominous shadows were about to descend on the frontier

Chapter Seven

The next morning, Daniel awoke to a cool, damp day. It had rained during the night, and his bedroll was drenched. He looked for Uncle Lee, but he was nowhere in sight, and his bedroll was missing, too. A large fire in the center of the compound was being rekindled in preparation for breakfast, which one of the cooks told him would be venison jerky, hot tea, and oatmeal with maple syrup. Wondering what had happened to his uncle, Daniel went through the main gate to the parked wagons and saw no one. Then he checked the corral and was relieved. Uncle Lee had already fed Andy and Gabe and thrown blankets over them.

"I was worried," admitted Daniel, helping his uncle harness the horses.

"The rain was just enough last night to chill the horses. They may be big, powerful brutes, but they can get sick over the slightest thing like this sudden shower and a drop in temperature. Musty hay will make them terribly sick, too. A cow will sort the good hay out and not eat it, but a horse will eat and make himself sick every time. They rarely learn from old mistakes. I guess that makes them dumber than cows," Uncle Lee chuckled with a shake of his head.

Daniel liked to hear him do that. He seemed to quietly amuse himself. This trip into the wilderness had taught Daniel much about himself and his Uncle Lee. It came natural for him to take charge of events such as he displayed with the thieves on the trail. He had the mark of a leader who was able to inspire maximum effort by just being himself. Daniel's mother had told him that his Uncle Lee and his father were cut from the same cloth, and that he should not be afraid to trust him. Uncle Lee would not let him down.

"We'll leave the horses here for now. I'm hungry as a bear after hibernating all winter," Uncle Lee smiled at Daniel. "You've done well on this trip, lad. I'm proud of you. Let's get something to eat! We have a slight change of plan for the return trip."

"A change of plan?" Daniel questioned with a frown.

"Aye. We're going to take Mary Akins back home with us. She can't stay here, and she is not able to return to their cabin in her condition. If the situation were reversed, John Akins would do the same thing for me. I owe the man my life. Someday I'll tell you about it. Anyway, it's already decided, and Mary seems to be in agreement. What do you think, lad?"

"I think it's the right thing to do," he replied firmly, still touched by the depth of the horrors she experienced. "She's so helpless... what do I want to say? Vulnerable?"

"That she is, Daniel. When we return to Portsmouth, would you like to help me in the print shop, or would you prefer to return to York with your Uncle Earl?"

"I'd rather be with you and Aunt Maureen in Portsmouth," Daniel hastened to reply. "I was going to ask you about helping out with the paper. I would like to be able to write the way you do and explain complicated things with everyday words."

Lee smiled at his nephew. The boy seemed genuinely happy about the prospect. Daniel had all the attributes of being a partner. Uncle Lee fondly placed an arm around his shoulder as they waited in line to be served.

Later, the seven wagons started their return trip to Portsmouth. Three of them carried the fur pelts, and the remainder were empty. When they were closer to home, the teamsters loaded the wagons with firewood where there was a greater supply than along the coast.

Lee had accepted the gift of a feather mattress from Captain Stevens for Mary Akins' use on the bumpy journey to the coast. The mattress was placed on the bed of the wagon, and they had built a framework over the bed on which they placed a heavy blanket to shade the sun in the day and the rain at night. When she saw the arrangement, she seemed pleased that an effort had been made for her comfort.

Mary sat on the bench beside Lee for several miles. The day was damp and dark without a trace of sunshine. Daniel noticed that she wore Indian style moccasins made from deerskin, and her long dress was woven from flax fibers. She wore a visored bonnet much like his

Aunt Ursula, and he wondered if she removed it when she went to bed at night.

The two men accompanying Mary made it clear to her that the body of the wagon and the bed were her private domain, and they would honor her privacy at all times. She thanked both of them. She silently rode beside Lee for hours, staring straight in front of her.

Occasionally, soft cries pierced her moist lips. Daniel and Uncle Lee tried to console her when she was overcome. Daniel felt sorry for her and looked for ways to take her mind off the tragedy she had witnessed by pointing out interesting scenes along the way. She initially resented his efforts, but he persisted, and soon he was able to elicit a begrudged smile. His empathy was sincere, for he still mourned the loss of his father and mother. That was not the same thing as seeing them savaged by Indians, but he understood the loss.

At the end of that first day, they pulled off the roadway into a wooded area near Walpole, veering away from the Connecticut River and headed east. Collecting dry firewood was impossible, so Uncle Lee directed Daniel to collect some white birch bark with his knife. He found a clump nearby and sliced off several pieces about a foot in length and returned to the campsite where Lee and Mary had collected sticks for the fire. They were wet, but Lee was confident that he could have a roaring fire going soon. The fire would smoke, but it would create enough heat to boil water for tea and warm up a supply of dried venison.

Lee broke the white birch bark into smaller pieces and placed them in a single pile. Then he sprinkled a small amount of gunpowder from his pistol's priming pan and plugged the fire hole into the pistol's main charge. After layering several rows of small-sized firewood on top of the bark, he held his pistol on the side and pulled the trigger. Instantly a spark ignited the powder, which in turn started the birch bark on fire. Lee chuckled to himself and enjoyed the approving glances of the two young people. Before Lee did anything else, he removed the fire hole plug and recharged the pan. After, he placed the pistol under his shirt so that it would not get wet.

Two days later, Uncle Lee and Daniel filled the empty portion of the wagon with seasoned firewood at a crossroads settlement in Londonderry on the eastern side of the Merrimack River. Many of the settlers supplemented their income by cutting and splitting firewood they sold to travelers on the busy route between the coast and the vast interior of the Grants. They made sure that Mary still had plenty of room in the wagon. During the course of the journey back home, they had established systematic routines whereby everybody did their share. Daniel and Mary collected firewood whenever they stopped for the evening or for a rest. Lee took over the chore of meal preparation and the feeding of the horses. After they had eaten the evening meal, Daniel and Uncle Lee rubbed down the horses while Mary cleaned up the dishes and campsite before getting ready for the night. The two men usually slept under the wagon.

On the last day of the trip, Mary confided to Daniel that he and his uncle snored a lot at night. For some reason he could not understand, Daniel was a little angry that she told him. She seemed to be pleased telling him that she knew. Her condition noticeably improved with every mile they traveled away from the Connecticut Valley.

Daniel was glad to be back in familiar territory. People waved and said "hello" to Uncle Lee as they drove through the streets of Portsmouth. He good-naturedly waved back and continued on his way, arriving home early in the afternoon. Uncle Lee drove the team and wagon into the barn, coming to a stop opposite the horse stalls.

"Mary Akins, here we are at our home. I'll take you into the house to introduce you to my wife, Maureen, but before we do that, I want you to know that while you are with us, you are an honored guest in our home. No harm will ever reach you, and you have only to mention it to Maureen or me if there's something not to your liking. Do you understand what I'm trying to say, lass?"

"I do," she replied hesitantly. "Thank you for telling me that. Father called you his best friend."

"Why don't you and Mary go in, Uncle Lee. I'll take care of the horses," Daniel suggested.

"Thanks, Daniel. Come, Mary, let's meet Maureen. I hope that you'll feel comfortable with us."

Daniel brushed Gabe and Andy before hitching them into the stalls. He gave each of them an extra ration of oats as a reward for their faithful service on the trip. The blankets they had used on the trip were musty, so he spread them on the fence rails to air.

As he was piling the firewood against the barn wall, Lavina entered the barn.

"We saw you pass by," she said shyly. "How was the trip?"

"It was long and dusty, Lavina. Old Gabe and Andy did a good job. I just brushed and fed them," Daniel replied. "It's good to be back."

"Your Aunt Maureen missed the two of you while you were gone. We kept busy. She showed me how the printing press works and the two of us made up thirty copies of anniversaries, birthdays and notices of local events," Lavina smiled, proud of the achievement.

"Well, that beats all," exclaimed Daniel. "Here I was looking forward to helping Uncle Lee on the press, and you beat me to it." They both laughed. "We have a visitor that will be staying with us. She's in the house now with Uncle Lee and Aunt Maureen. Go ahead in and introduce yourself, Lavina. I'll finish unloading the wagon and be right in."

"All right," Lavina answered and headed for the house.

A minute later, Daniel heard a piercing scream from Mary. A second later, Lavina burst out the door and ran to her house, crying. Daniel called for her, but she refused to answer. He ran into the house, meeting Uncle Lee at the door. "What's wrong?"

"The second Mary saw Lavina, she changed and became hysterical. Lavina most likely triggered the ugly memories she's been trying to deal with. Lavina ran out without saying a word. It was over before anyone could say a thing," Uncle Lee explained, nervously walking back and forth in the kitchen. He was concerned for Mary, of course, but he was also concerned about Lavina who was completely blameless.

Mary was sitting at the large table near the fireplace cradling her head in her hands. Aunt Maureen grabbed Daniel and warmly embraced him. "It's so nice to have my two men back home with me. I believe you've grown since I last saw you, Daniel!"

It pleased Daniel to know that she missed him. "We're glad to be back, too. Mary has had a bad time," he said, looking at Mary's frail and tensed body. He had an urge to comfort her but did not know how. "I'm sorry, Mary. I should have come in with Lavina instead of sending her in alone. Maybe I could have made her presence less threatening for you."

"I'm going to the Cameron's," Lee told his wife. "I owe Lavina an explanation."

"Yes, I think it's in order. She was such a good companion for me while you were gone," said Maureen.

"May I come with you, Uncle Lee?" Daniel asked with a frustrated look on his face. "After all, I sent Lavina in the house without thinking of Mary's delicate condition. I should have prepared her, or at least been with her."

"Of course, come along, lad." The two left for the Cameron home. "This eruption between Mary and Lavina is symptomatic of the future. I have some bad feelings about it. The storm that is brewing across the land is going to make for difficult times. Mary and her father are examples of the kind of hatred and fear that will envelope the land. The Akins are justified in feeling the way they do, but not every Indian is in that category. We must never forget that the first settlers to the shores of this land were met by the native peoples with generous gestures, sharing their knowledge and culture with our descendants."

"I've heard that in school," replied Daniel, absorbing every word his Uncle Lee said.

"The Camerons have lived quietly in this community with a minimum of disturbances such as happened the day you came to stay with us. Most of the people in Portsmouth who know the Camerons accept them without malice. Good people are good people, and it has nothing to do with race."

"Mr. Cameron is over there by the barn," Daniel pointed.

"Hello, Thom. We've come to see about Lavina and apologize for what happened." Uncle Lee explained to Thom Cameron what Mary Akins had recently experienced. "She's going to stay with us for a while. We're concerned for her, of course, and we're also concerned about Lavina. We want to at least explain why she received such a startling reception."

"I understand, Lee," answered Thom Cameron, nervously fidgeting with the handle of his shovel. "Lavina is in the house. She was terribly upset." He gave a resigned shrug of the shoulders. There was a sad air of helplessness about him. He turned to Lee, filled with anguish: "What am I going to do, Lee? There are some hard times ahead. Anyone can see that. Tensions are running high. I'm afraid for my family, and I'm sickened by the thought that I may not be able to protect them if things go wrong. I'm also frightened that I may end up killing someone who threatens my wife and daughter, if the situation becomes that desperate. If I do that, who will look after them when they put me away?"

Daniel was stunned by the intensity of Thom Cameron's feelings. Any man would kill to defend his family if it became necessary. Thom Cameron was correct, though, if he was to kill a white man defending his native family, he would receive different treatment than a man defending a white family.

"I wish I had an answer for that, Thom," Lee answered in a strained voice. "I've been having similar thoughts about the road ahead of us. Let me say this one thing to you, Thom. No one could have more generous or trustworthy neighbors than Maureen and I have in you and Melinda. I pledge to you that I will help you defend your family, anytime, anyplace, without exception. And I'll be proud to stand at your side."

"Thank you for that, Lee. Come, let's see about Lavina." Thom led the way into the log cabin they called home.

The cabin was roomy, clean and orderly, and smelled of fresh bread. The large central room was a combination living room and kitchen. Two rooms were on either side of the large fireplace that took up most of the northern wall. They could hear Lavina crying in the open loft to their left. Mrs. Cameron greeted them as they entered the cabin. Daniel was curious how she would be, for he had never met her. He was shocked, for she was unlike anything he had imagined. She wore a light doeskin dress with frills along the sleeves and a colorful white belt around her waist. Her black hair was done up in two tightly woven braids with red ribbons tied on the ends like Lavina. Mrs. Cameron was a beautiful woman by any standard.

"Welcome to our home, Lee," she said in a soft, melodious voice. "This must be, Daniel, whom I've heard much about. I'm Lavina's mother, and I'm glad to meet you."

Lee spoke first. "It's good to see you, Melinda. Yes, this is my nephew, Daniel."

"I'm glad to meet you, Mrs. Cameron. We came to see about Lavina. I'm probably to blame. I should have warned her about what happened to Mary and should have accompanied her to make the introduction. I feel bad that Lavina is the object of fear, for she does not deserve that."

"You speak well, Daniel Cullen," she looked up at the loft. "Lavina, please come down and speak to our neighbors." Lavina slowly climbed down the ladder on the wall. Her mother collected Lavina in her arms as she touched the floor.

They explained what had happened to Mary, and Daniel apologized for not telling her. "I'm sorry, Lavina. I did not want you to be hurt in any way. Aunt Maureen is explaining the situation to Mary now. Don't take it personally," Daniel pleaded.

"How can I not take it personally, Daniel? Mary was frightened by what I am, not who I am. I understand and feel better now that you and Mr. Cullen have come to explain it to my family. Thank you for being so kind."

Lee acknowledged her thanks. "I also came to say thank you for helping Maureen while we were away. Gabe and Andy did a good job taking us to the Connecticut River and back without a problem. Daniel gave them an extra ration of oats, which I'm sure they're enjoying right now."

"You're a very kind and intelligent man, Mr. Cullen," Lavina said in a tremulous voice. She looked at her father who knew what she was going to say, and his eyes watered. "I love my mother and father and am proud of who they are. How is it possible to be an Indian and a white woman at the same time? Your society and my mother's society will not accept me for what I am, a half breed. Part of both, but neither. . . Can you tell me who I'm supposed to be?"

The cry for help left Lee speechless.

Chapter Eight

Daniel and Lee left the Cameron home brimming with feelings neither of them could easily define. Dan wanted to assure Lavina that he was a friend, and the fact that she was part Indian had nothing to do with it. That evening, he laid awake for hours trying to imagine how he would feel if their positions were reversed.

His first encounter with racial prejudice and its ugly manifestations, that night Lavina and her mother were attacked, had left an impression on him. He did not understand why another person's race or culture could fan such hatred. The Camerons lived in peace and did not bother anyone. They certainly were not a threat to others. In different circumstances, he could even imagine Mrs. Cameron being appreciated for her beauty alone. He knew that true beauty came from within; like the sunshine, it warmed those who stood in its rays. Daniel knew, for he had lived with a most beautiful lady, his mother.

That same night, Uncle Lee was quieter than usual. He was glad to be back in the arms of his beloved, but a nagging apprehension clouded his joy.

Maureen ran her soft fingers across his closed eyes and kissed them. "What's wrong, Lee?"

"I don't rightly know, Maureen. Lavina was hysterical, but she calmed down and spoke from her heart in a way that touched me. The young girl described her anguish in a more compelling way than I could ever attempt. I saw her dilemma and wanted to comfort her. The only consolation that could work would be to change mankind." He told her what Lavina had told him and Dan.

Maureen thought about her remarks. "While you were gone, she stayed with me every night. Each day we followed your journey in our minds. She is quite familiar with that part of the state and worried about both of you. She was a wonderful companion. The mission school certainly was thorough with her education. She's more accomplished in her ability to read and write than me. There is goodness in her heart. This outbreak with Mary Akins will pass. You worry a lot and care for people. I love you for that. Don't ever change, Lee Cullen."

"Lavina's pain seemed to go deeper than a simple person-to-person confrontation. It would be nice to think that tomorrow and beyond will be better days for our circle of friends, but I have a premonition that this unrest that is shaking the world is going to touch our foothold in this new land. I fear that the eruption of violence is close at hand…"

She placed an impatient finger to his lips. "Hush, my darling, and hold me tight."

Mary Akin slept in a small room overlooking the front entrance to the house. Maureen Cullen impressed upon her that it was her private domain, and she should use it as a place of refuge when she felt the need to be alone. The home to which Mr. Cullen and Daniel had brought her was a happy one and she felt comfortable and secure within its walls. Hopefully, the frightful memories that embraced her would slowly fade away.

That summer of 1744 had changed the Cullen family. Daniel came to be an important part of the family, and Mary Akins, a child of the forest, blossomed under the nurturing care of Maureen and Lee. All agreed that Mary should attend a school as soon as possible. She had never attended school on a steady basis, but she was able to read and write on a very elementary level. The Cullen's were strong in the belief that the ability to read opened up a whole new world of opportunity. It was the single most important skill in enriching a person's life. Mary was excited for the opportunity and grasped it with enthusiasm.

Lee also encouraged Daniel to build upon his foundation of knowledge obtained in York and in the neighborhood school he attended in Aberdeen. The Portsmouth school was within walking distance. Daniel and Mary attended classes every morning for five hours and came home midday, when they were anxious to burn off their pent-up energy. Mary helped Maureen in the house with chores, washing, and cleaning. She was quick to adapt to the loom that Maureen used to make cloth. Weaving on the loom was Mary's favorite pastime. She created unique designs with different colored fibers that she and Maureen boiled in berries.

Daniel eagerly searched for all the information he could find about printing. Uncle Lee's printing room was located on the first floor in the shed connecting the house to the barn. He had a small library with a desk in a room adjacent to the press. The first time Daniel walked into the press room, the thick scent of linseed oil greeted him. His uncle mixed lampblack with the linseed oil to produce the ink for the press. It was expensive to purchase it from England the way he did spare parts for his press and all of the paper they printed. He told Daniel that it was a messy job mixing the two ingredients.

According to Lee, every major city in the new land had a printing press. Boston was blessed with several and the first paper in the colonies, *Courant,* was being produced at Hartford, which began operations thirty eight years ago. Presses were not being produced in the colonies yet. Lee's press was made in England by the Vale Company.

The first day Daniel helped in the press room, Uncle Lee told him with a grin, that the first thing necessary was some material worthy of being printed. A writer had to have something he wanted to say that was important for people to know. Once the material was decided on, Uncle Lee would take his composing rule and measure the layout of the message on the sheet of paper being used. A completed sheet was printed one at a time. The layout took some getting used to because the cast metal type of upper and lower fonts required that it be assembled in the reverse of the normal way words and sentences were read. The type was pressed into a wooden board with slotted lines spaced close together. This board was placed on a moveable sliding table beneath the upright portion of the press, the type was freshly inked with leather hand-held ink balls. A sheet of paper or cloth was placed between the clean sheet of paper being imprinted and the platen, the heavy structure that presses the paper to the inked type. The press was lowered by means of a long rod so that it touched the freshly inked surface firmly.

A thin framework hinged to the base of the press (frisket) held the sheet to be printed over the inked type. Once the impression was made, the platen was raised out of the way, the frisket was hinged free of the type, and the printed sheet was removed and placed to dry on lines or rods usually built overhead. The cycle was repeated for every printed sheet.

Uncle Lee told Daniel that the quality of a print was judged by many things. Most of all, it was imperative that the press itself had to be securely bolted to the floor, and that all of its joints should be tight and braced to minimize lateral movement, no matter how slight, which would leave the printed sheet blurred. Care had to be used in removing the printed sheet, and ink must be evenly applied to the surface of the cast type. Excessive ink on the printed sheet in the form of blotches were called "monks." The name was also applied to a printer who was careless about the quality of work he did, and was most uncomplimentary.

Lavina had avoided the Cullens for several weeks that summer. One day she came face to face with Mary and Daniel walking home from school while she was running an errand for her mother. They met at the northern tip of North Mill Pond.

Daniel recognized Lavina. "Hello, Lavina. I was hoping we'd see you soon. You're looking well."

Lavina was dressed in a long Lindsey wool dress with a small white bonnet on her head. Her black braids with red ribbons were hanging over the front of her shoulders. She smiled guardedly, unsure how she would be greeted. "I've been really busy caring for the farm. Father has been ill."

"I'm Mary Akins," Mary told her. "I've wanted to apologize for my behavior the last time we met. I'm sorry if I frightened you, and I did not intend to insult you. I'll be staying at the Cullens for awhile."

"I accept your apology," Lavina replied with a smile. "I'm sorry about your mother. I'd like to be your friend. I have a few in Portsmouth, but one can never have too many friends." The two girls looked into each others' eyes and saw a reflection of sadness.

"It's nice that we met like this. I'm helping Uncle Lee in the print room," Daniel explained proudly. The longer he looked at Lavina, the more he realized that she looked a lot like her mother, and was growing more beautiful every day.

They talked about the school and the latest paper Uncle Lee had published. Daniel boasted that he had printed every one of the fifty copies without a single monk. The three laughed about his modesty! They went their separate ways with a spring to their steps and a warm glow in their hearts. The lazy summer turned to a brisk fall filled with bright colors more brilliant than ever. Mary had confirmation from her father that she would stay with the Cullens for the next year, or until he thought it safe for her to come to the cabin.

The long, cold days and heavy snowfall of winter limited their outside activity. School hours were increased for Mary and Daniel. Mary was a good student. By the year's end, she was reading at an adult level. She was pleased with her accomplishments and shared them with Lavina who encouraged her to greater levels.

The peace that reigned between the Cullen and Cameron household was a contradiction to the border warfare that continued unabated between the French, their Indian allies, and the English settlers threading their way into the disputed areas claimed by the French. Even in northern New Hampshire, an occasional attack against settlers took place, especially in the Connecticut River Valley.

The prophecy that Uncle Lee had editorialized about in the summer of 1744 was steadily becoming a reality. The controversial rival claims of France and Great Britain for the lands west of the Allegheny Mountains and in maritime Canada was approaching a climax, creating fear and anxiety throughout the new world.

Each year the frontier settlements pushed westward toward the setting sun, drawn by the fertile lands of the Ohio River Valley. The land was a lucrative attraction to those frontiersmen who had tried and failed to make a living on the rocky hillside farms of New Hampshire and Vermont. It also became a destination to the newcomers from every part of Europe. Scotch and Irish settlers outnumbered any other nationality. The concept of private ownership of land fueled the ubiquitous march to the setting sun.

The French from Acadia and Cape Breton frequently violated the New England coastline, raiding and looting the relatively helpless commercial traffic between Europe and America. Whenever the colonists and the small remnants of the British fleet attempted to retaliate, the French retreated to the secure port at Louisbourg, Cape Breton.

The colonists from Portsmouth to Boston viewed Louisbourg as an unacceptable threat to their security and ability to conduct free trade. Early in the summer of 1745, Massachusetts took the lead and began assembling seven regiments of militia from New England. New

Hampshire raised one regiment and sent it to Boston, where shipping and supplies were being gathered for the long desired expedition to neutralize Fort Louisbourg. Lee Cullen had offered his services to the effort as a Captain in command of a company from New Hampshire. He served under an old acquaintance from Kittery, Maine, William Pepperell, a militia officer in charge of the expedition. The New England armada en route to Nova Scotia was scattered by a storm and met at Canso, Nova Scotia, where the troops had a chance to do some much-needed training. A British Navy Squadron arrived from England and accompanied the armada that laid siege to the fortress at Louisbourg in May 1745. The siege lasted for seven weeks.

During that seven week period, Captain Lee Cullen's men were riddled with disease and boredom as the fleet bided its time waiting for the spring ice to leave Gabarus Bay, south of the fortress. Once the spring drift ice left, the Americans entered the Bay, which would act as the main anchorage for the fleet during the siege. Lee's company was part of a group who went ashore about three miles from the fortress against slight resistance. Several of the New Englanders were wounded, but they had established a small beachhead ashore forcing the French to retreat. The New Englanders' vanguard scouts determined that the land to the rear of the fortress at its northern extremity was swampy and that the fortress was vulnerable from that vantage point.

That first day ashore, Lee's company landed supplies and more troops. The French countered the New Englanders by evacuating the Fort's Royal Battery to the north. The French were afraid that the Louisbourg garrison could be lost if the colonists pressed a vigorous attack. Consequently, they spiked the cannons so that the colonists could not turn them against the French garrison. Lee's company hastily followed at the heels of the retreating enemy troops and occupied the battery. The easy capture of enemy territory boosted morale considerably. The vantage point became even more desirable when the touch holes were drilled out. One day after the battery was occupied, the cannons were in action against their former owners. It was an accomplishment that stirred the colonists to greater efforts.

The siege continued day after day, week after week. The essence of a siege was to remain committed. Eventually, every fortress would have to yield to a determined and prolonged blockade. Much of the militia troops were sick from the cold and wet climate. Dysentery was rampant among the soldiers. Lee was also a victim of the debilitating sickness, known among the troops as the "bloody flux."

The final assault came on June 26, when the ships entered the harbor intending to mount capitulating attacks from both land and sea. The French surrendered and the New Englanders celebrated the "greatest triumph of conquest." Commander Pepperell reported that the victory had cost about twelve hundred lives. It was a victory that Lee shared with a note to Maureen.

> July 4, 1745
>
> Cape Breton Island

My Dearest wife,

The French commander was given the opportunity to surrender on May 15th, but he refused to do so until the fortress lacked the ability to resist. His answer came from the mouth of a cannon. We obliged him and he did surrender on the twenty-sixth of June.

The surrender terms allowed the French to be repatriated with any moveable property they possessed. Our men have been outraged by the generous gesture of the British higher command. The men were promised the chance to collect "reasonable" booty if they were victorious. Now much of the valuables have been denied them. We'll have to keep a tight reign on discipline.

Colonel Nathaniel Meserve, the shipwright from Badger's Island, has been our New Hampshire Regimental commander. He's done a great job of it, too. He was instrumental in the successful capitulation of the fortress. He had constructed massive sledges capable of hauling cannons across the mud flats. Manpower was used instead of draft horses because the mud was too thick. The batteries were manned at the edge of the mud flats so that they could reach the fortress with their heavy caliber barrels. The French were unable to counter battery fire. It was a superb performance by a fine soldier.

I think often of you. Say hi to Dan and Mary. If Dan had been a little older, I would have brought him along on this triumphant journey. We have made history here at Fort Louisbourg. Many of the troops are staying to restore the fort. My company of volunteers is scheduled to return within a couple of weeks. I'm ready to go home.

I've been bothered by dysentery since I arrived in Canada. It has drained me of strength, and I know I've lost some weight. The hard campaigning that soldiers are expected to do is more difficult than I remembered. Perhaps, I'll refuse a future commission. Younger bodies than my fifty-five years can handle the strain. I know that experience is important, but it must be accompanied by a strong, resilient body. I'm finding myself deficient in that department.

The captain of a supply ship promised to drop off my letter to you. I send my love to you by way of the stars that shine on both of us tonight. Thank you, my dearest Maureen, for being my wife. How lucky I am!!!

Love, Lee

Chapter Nine

When Captain Lee Cullen walked through the door of his home, September, 1745, Maureen burst into tears, horrified to see him in such an emaciated condition. She rushed into his arms and lifted her lips to him. Her heart cried out in silence, "What have they done to you, my darling?" She withheld her questions, knowing that he would explain in his own time. For now he was home safe in her arms. Her prayers had been answered.

"I'm never going to let you go again, Lee," she cried, laying her head on his chest.

He was too weary to answer her and basked in the warmth of her serene presence. His home and Maureen were all that mattered to him. He understood what she was saying, and for the present, was inclined to agree, but he was an old soldier who would answer the call to arms when it was necessary.

By the spring of 1746, Lee was back to his normal self, thanks to Maureen's tender care. One evening, he attended a meeting of the Portsmouth Council where he was told that, according to the latest courier rider from Boston, the French fleet was assembling a strike force to be used against the cocky New Englanders at Boston as a retaliatory measure for their capture of Louisbourg. That event was the source of much celebration throughout the colonies. The daring raid was praised for its courage and initiative.

The euphoria of the fall and winter changed drastically in the spring when the Bostonians learned that the French fleet was preparing a strike. Boston was ill-prepared to repel such a force, and the population was terror-stricken. That summer of 1746, Daniel suggested that he leave school so that he could spend more time in the print shop. He also suggested that his Uncle Lee should spend more time writing about current events. Daniel solemnly promised that he would print every word that his uncle produced. Lavina and Mary also offered to help. Daniel laughed with his uncle when he promised to be "monk"-free on the editorials, too. Uncle Lee was enthused about the proposition, and gave it considerable thought.

Lee realized that the explosive times needed to be discussed with calm, rational intelligence, and he felt that on many issues, he had something to say. Now that he was surrounded by a healthy, energetic bunch of youngsters, he decided to take the challenge and spent some quiet time in his little office. His first article was about the French threat to Boston and other towns on the Atlantic shore. It read:

The French fleet is not a dire threat to Portsmouth. It may do some damage in Boston, but the chances of its destroying or occupying the city is doubtful.

If, by chance, the fleet does decide to come up the Piscataqua River to attack Portsmouth and our neighbors in Kittery, Maine, we are capable of greeting them with coastal gunfire that will cripple them. The first fortress to broadside the fleet would be the batteries at Odiorne Point. If they continued up the channel, Fort William and Mary and Fort Fisher were capable of intersecting lines of fire that could devastate the ships. Or, they may allow the ships to proceed without interruption and then sink the last one or two ships so that the channel is blocked. Few Naval officers would ever let themselves be placed in that situation.

It is my belief that the threat of the French fleet is overblown and is robbing us of vital energy and resources. We should be fortifying more of the area along the Connecticut River, where raids are carried out by the French and Indians with impunity and are rarely punished. Our dedicated New Hampshire Rangers are doing a good job, but they cannot be everywhere at the same time. My recommendation is that we should concentrate efforts by supplying and manning Fort Number Four at Charlestown better than we have in the past. The threat of attack is greater now than it was two years ago. The French have increased their military strength and enrolled more of the native tribes to do their dirty work for them, making our frontier more dangerous.

England has not sent additional troops to our shores for a long time, even though their war against France may potentially be won or lost here in America. We will defend ourselves with resolve if that becomes necessary, but we have a right to expect the motherland to provide adequate means to protect her children, and are requesting that long overdue level of protection. We can only hope that the Crown hears our cry from the wilderness.

The summer solstice celebration in Portsmouth was an annual event that most residents looked forward to. It took place the third week in June, when planting was completed, and crops were beginning to break through the ground. It was a day of picnics, contests for the best baked apple pie, competition for the best rifle and pistol shots in the turkey shoots, and the best archers in the community. Lee had won the turkey shoot several years in a row with his British musket.

Lee had helped his print shop workers put out a list of events for the day. Daniel let it be known that he was going to try his luck at the pistol turkey shoot, and had been practicing regularly behind the barn. His Uncle Lee made a modest wager with him about who gets the turkey. Daniel was somewhat embarrassed to compete with his uncle, but accepted the wager. The loser had to buy the turkey. His uncle winked at him with a smug look on his face as they shook hands.

The day before the celebration, Daniel purchased a new shirt and pair of pants and tried them on in the privacy of his room. He looked at himself in the mirror and was satisfied that the new clothing fit him better than his everyday homespun wear. Daniel had grown three inches taller since arriving in New England. At fourteen years old, he was developing into a handsome young man.

The next day, Daniel was waiting outside the house with a four-seated wagon that Lee kept in the barn for special occasions and a young mare they had recently purchased. Daniel had shined the harness and groomed the mare before hitching them up. Uncle Lee had left early to visit with the Council and planned to meet them at the square. Daniel was dressed in his new clothes, patiently waiting for his Aunt Maureen and Mary to come out of the house.

Aunt Maureen was dressed in a light green dress and a white bonnet. She was lovely as usual and offered Daniel her hand to help her into the wagon. "Mary will be along any minute now. You're going to be surprised."

Just then, Mary opened the door and stood for a second at the edge of the porch. Daniel turned to look at her. He gulped hard and blushed profusely. "Is that you, Mary?" he asked.

"You know it is, Dan," she replied, nervously walking toward the wagon. Her blond hair was done up so that her long curls hung about her shoulders down to the middle of her back. She wore a lace bonnet like Aunt Maureen, and her dark blue dress amplified the lightness of her golden curls. Her flashing blue eyes looked at Dan who could not take his eyes from her. She smiled and accepted his hand to help her step up in the wagon.

Daniel walked around the wagon and climbed beside Aunt Maureen. His Aunt winked at him as if to say, "I told you so." Taking the reins in his strong hands, he drove through the center of town and parked the horse and wagon at a watering tub and hitching post. He had a ration of hay and oats stored in the wagon to feed the mare later in the day. He watched Mary and his aunt excitedly mingle with the crowd.

The first contest to get under way was the turkey pistol shoot. Twelve contestants were entered and Daniel was registered to shoot first. Each contestant was allowed to take three shots; one free-standing position, the second from a kneeling position, and the third sitting with arms resting on a table.

The target was not a live turkey, but a white circle within a black turkey drawn on paper. Uncle Lee and Daniel had printed a hundred sheets of the target. The center of the target was placed over the heart of the turkey with three small rings separated an inch apart in concentric circles. Each ring counted ten points. The total score was determined by measuring the distance from the center of each bullet. A "0" score was perfect.

Dan nervously took his position at the shooter table. The three shots had to be made within two minutes. Sweat beads formed on his forehead as he faced the target fifty feet away. It looked small to him from that distance. When the cowbell rang, he methodically primed and loaded his pistol and shot in all three positions. His shooting time was a minute and a half, a good time. He saw his Uncle Lee standing in the crowd behind him, smiling. The target was collected and the holes measured. Two were an inch from the center and the third was three inches, giving him a total score of five.

"I'm proud of you, Daniel," exclaimed Uncle Lee, helping him collect his loading supplies. "I'm not so sure I can match that with old Bess here," he chuckled.

When all of the pistol shooters were finished, the judge announced the scores. Daniel received the best score and would compete against the winning musket shooter. The best shooter would win the turkey.

About midday, Uncle Lee took his position at the shooting table and efficiently fired his three shots in quick succession in one and a quarter minutes. The target for the rifle competition was spaced one hundred-fifty feet from the shooters. He used to brag to Daniel that his company of Royal Scotch was capable of carrying out a sustained fire of four shots per minute. Lee's score tallied to seven. He turned to Dan and shook his head, "Well, Daniel, it's between you and me. May the best man win." The crowd of onlookers cheered the contestants.

Daniel grinned and shook his hand.

New targets were set, and since Daniel had the better of the two scores, he shot first. He worked well under pressure, and once again, in precise measured movements, he fired and loaded in rapid sequence. He scored seven.

Without any delay, Lee took his place at the table and held ready for the cowbell. He was precision in motion, and instead of ramming the charge to the end of the barrel with the wooden ramrod, he banged the butt of the musket against the ground to set the powder and ball charge in the barrel. When he brought the musket to his shoulder, he did not hold the sights on the target. First, he aligned the target with the top of the sight and slowly lifted the musket. When the barrel was over the target, he gently squeezed the trigger. He waited calmly for the scores to be read. He received a score of seven, the same as Daniel. They had tied!

Daniel ran to his uncle and embraced him. "I was hoping that you would try your best and not let me win. What a day this has been!" They both won two live turkeys.

Lee suggested that the judge auction the two turkeys, with the proceeds going to the town militia's refreshment fund. It was met with cheers of approval.

After securing their firearms in a box in the rear of the wagon, Daniel and Uncle Lee looked around for Mary and Aunt Maureen. They found them in Market Square looking at some new glassware that had recently arrived from London. Dan instantly recognized Aunt Maureen and Mary but could not place the person with them. As they drew closer, he realized that it was Lavina's mother, Melinda. She wore a pale yellow dress with her hair loose over her shoulders.

"Daniel, me boy," exclaimed Uncle Lee. "I do believe we are in the company of the three prettiest ladies in town." The three ladies received his compliments with modest smiles. He turned to Melinda and bowed slightly. "Where's Lavina?"

"Lavina is tuning her father's violin and restringing a new one that her father traded for a horse last week," Melinda told them. There was always a proud confident aura about her. Daniel thought that Melinda Cameron was a lady at peace with herself.

"I didn't know that Lavina played the violin," said Mary, watching Daniel. "I know that you two are bursting to tell us who won the shooting event."

Uncle Lee began with enthusiasm. "I thought that I was going to show this young man how old soldiers can shoot, and I did pretty good with old Brown Bess. Truthfulness requires that I inform all of you that he matched me with a pistol, which is harder to shoot with accuracy. I thought I'd show him how it's done, but he ended up showing me! It must be a sign of old age creeping up on me," he chuckled and placed a proud arm around Daniel's shoulder.

The highlight of the solstice celebration was the collection of musicians that intermittently played throughout the day. At dusk, a large array of lanterns were lit around Market Square in preparation for the evening dance. It was a much-enjoyed finale. In earlier periods, the Puritans had banned dancing, but as the years passed fewer and fewer of the die-hard believers existed, so dancing became the centerpiece of the annual celebration.

Lavina and her father walked across Market Square to the front of the large church where two wagons had been placed back to back to act as a stage for the musicians and speakers. Music was traditionally the highlight of the celebration, and it was rare when the square was not filled to capacity. Daniel watched Mr. Cameron and Lavina as they mounted the stairs to the wagon. She wore a white Lindsey dress with her trade mark braids tied off with red ribbons.

Uncle Lee put Daniel's thoughts to words. "Now there goes one of the loveliest young ladies in the colonies."

Melinda watched her daughter with glowing pride. "She is lovely, isn't she?"

Maureen squeezed her Ojibwa friend's hand and said, "She's the image of her mother."

Melinda smiled at her neighbor. It was a compliment that touched her, for she knew that Maureen was not one to make idle comments.

A few minutes after tuning their instruments, the air was filled with music. There were three violins, two banjos, a cello, and a harpsichord. Lavina sat beside her father who often played at weddings and other events in town. The ensemble played a variety of songs, most of them traditional Scotch-Irish folk songs, waltzes, and a couple of Spanish fandangoes.

The sun was slowly setting in the west, casting shadows across Market Square. Lanterns hung around the square were lit creating an intimate atmosphere the dancers enjoyed. The band stopped playing to take a short intermission to get refreshments. Thom Cameron motioned for the attention of the crowd, beckoning for them to be quiet for a moment.

He had an announcement to make. "Friends and neighbors, it's nice to see so many familiar faces and a lot of new additions to our community. We've enjoyed playing for you. While we take a rest for a few minutes, I'm proud to announce that I've been able to talk my lovely daughter, Lavina, into playing a solo for us. She's selected an old ballad from the Emerald Isles that never ceases to pluck our hearts." Thom turned to his daughter and embraced her, whispering in her ear, "Your beauty matches what is in your heart, my dear. Now, forget the audience out there and embrace the music." He released her and climbed down the stairs.

Lavina stepped closer to the edge of the wagon, curtsied to the crowd, and raised the violin to her shoulder. Heeding her father's experienced advice, she closed her eyes and began her interpretation of the music. With a quick run up and down the scale, she paused a moment and began to play *Londonderry Aire*. Before she had completed the first few bars of the composition, she had captured the ear of the audience. It told the story of a soldier leaving for war and of the sad ending when he returns. From the soft beginning to the finale crescendo, her strong, nimble fingers ran up and down the strings with the skill of a master musician.

Lavina's music was magical. It lifted their hearts and brought tears to many. She held the high notes for a long time, making long sweeps across the strings with the full length of the bow. All the while her eyes were closed, for she, too, was a part of the music. The song always evoked a feeling of sadness and melancholy within her. Lavina ended the selection holding the highest note for a long time as if it was passing them by and eventually fading away. She opened her eyes and removed the violin from her shoulder. There was a long silence, and for a moment she was afraid that the audience did not like the selection. The members of the audience had become a part of the music, experiencing its exquisite message, and it took a few seconds for them to be released from its power. Then, the crowd erupted in spontaneous applause.

Lavina's father ran up the stairs and embraced his daughter again. "You played the best I've ever heard you. Take a bow and do an encore if you like." Thom jumped off the wagon and joined the crowd in clapping for a virtuoso performance. No father could be prouder than he was of Lavina at that magical moment.

Lavina lifted the violin and began a series of traditional Scotch-Irish songs such as *Minstrel Boy, Kilgary Mountain*, and *Down by the Sally Gardens.*

Tears filled Melinda's eyes as she watched her daughter perform. Tonight she had won the crowd with her excellence, for music transcends all languages and cultures. Maureen placed an arm around Melinda and said, "I'm so proud of her, Melinda, she plays beautifully."

Daniel listened to the performance with rapt attention. It was hard for him to imagine that the Lavina he knew so well was making such heart-warming music. It was a rich moment of discovery for him. How much more was there to his friend?

Lavina completed the encore medleys, stepped down from the wagon, and walked to her mother. Melinda saw the moist film in her daughter's eyes and was not surprised. Lavina always cried when she played with such emotion. Everyone congratulated her. Her modesty appreciated their enthusiasm but shunned affectionate hugs and kisses in public. It took a while for Lavina to transition from the emotional high of the performance to the reality of her mother offering her a piece of apple pie. She was hungry and sipped on a cup of hot tea.

The other musicians began to take their positions on the wagons. Thom Cameron came to get Lavina. "We'll be going for another session. Would you give us the honor?" he asked with a wink, smiling at his wife. "Our daughter has touched a few hearts tonight!" And he was gone with Lavina in tow.

The balance of the evening was spent listening to the music and dancing in the Square. Lee and Maureen danced several sets, and then Lee asked Melinda to dance. She accepted, and they glided around the square. She was light and graceful with her movements. They bumped into Daniel and Mary a couple of times, and everyone laughed. About nine o'clock, Lee admitted that he was danced out. Maureen, too, was tired and suggested that they call it a night and go home. They offered to take Melinda home. She accepted and went to the wagon stage to let Thom and Lavina know that she was leaving with the Cullens. She blew each a kiss and left the Square.

Mary and Daniel promised to be home by eleven. They were enjoying the excitement of the evening too much to quit so soon. Mary danced every dance with Daniel. He was inexperienced, but he made an effort and improved as the night progressed. The slower dances, especially the waltzes, were easier for him. Mary liked being in Daniel's arms. She had seen him daily for the past two years, yet she knew very little about his innermost thoughts.

"Are you enjoying yourself, Daniel, or are you just doing this because you think I do and are too much of a gentleman to let me know?"

"What a question to ask," he exclaimed. "I've never been much of a dancer, but it's fun. I like to see the people enjoying themselves. The music is wonderful. I've never heard such beautiful music before. It kind of gives you a lift." Daniel breathed deeply and continued. "You look wonderful tonight, Mary. All the boys have been watching you."

"In case you haven't noticed, Daniel, a lot of the girls have been looking at you all evening, too," she replied, holding him a little tighter. They danced to a dark corner into the shadows across from the church. She laid her cheek against his chest. He had grown considerably taller in the past two years. "Dan," she said in a shaky voice.

"What, Mary?"

"Will you miss me when I return to my father's place?" she asked in a questioning tone.

"Of course, why do you ask?"

She lifted her head to look into his eyes. The light was not very good, but she saw well enough to know that he was being truthful. Then she kissed him. His first kiss. Her warm lips were soft, and he felt a tingle run through his body. "I believe I've fallen in love with you, Daniel. I know we're young, but I'm sure I'll feel the same way in the years to come."

"I know that when you leave, I'll miss you a lot, Mary," Daniel replied. The sudden rush of emotion left him searching for the right words. "I'm not experienced enough to say with conviction that I love you. I'm not sure how one defines love. I see Uncle Lee and Aunt Maureen care and look after each other because they love. My parents were the same way. I can say that I like being responsible for your safety and have ever since you came from Fort Four. What I'm trying to say in a childish way is I probably do love you, too. I like being with you. If all of that adds up to love then, yes, I can say that I love you."

She kissed him again. "I wanted you to know how I felt about you. I'm not sure when I'll be leaving, but it will be before the fall."

"So soon?"

"Yes," she answered.

Daniel kissed her on the forehead. "I'll worry about you. Maybe we can visit once in a while."

"I hope we can at least do that."

A slow waltz was playing, and they danced out of the shadows near the musicians. They waved to Thom Cameron and Lavina, motioning that they were going to leave and walk home.

Lavina watched their every move with a heavy heart. After they had gone, small tears formed in her dark eyes. She understood what was taking place between Daniel and Mary, and it hurt.

Chapter Ten

Seven years later, April 1, 1753

Daniel was no stranger to death or to the savagery of Indians when they taunted and tortured their captives. He had frequently witnessed their talent for brutality and barbarous assaults upon the human body when he had served for a year with a small group of bordermen who roamed the wilderness between the civilized settlements in New Hampshire and Canada. The rangers were hired as scouts and as frontier sentinels, keeping track of the movement of Indians within striking distance of new settlers who had the courage to stake out their piece of land in defiance of the risks to themselves and family alike.

Daniel had witnessed indescribable mutilation and inhuman cruelty on the part of the Abenaki Indians from Saint Francis. Generations of tribesmen had settled in an area where the Saint Francis River joins the mighty Saint Lawrence River in Canada. They freely inhabited the northern New Hampshire wilderness, raiding and terrorizing the area at will. The only force they had to fear were the occasional encounters with groups of rangers who were versed and experienced in woodcraft tactics. They fought the native population on their own terms, bringing some level of security and stability to the frontier. Daniel had found that their methods of torture and retribution were little different from that of the Abenaki, but such severe measures were all that stood between the defenseless homesteader and the fearsome Saint Francis raiders.

Daniel had left the ranger's ranks to marry Mary Akins. He had fallen deeply in love with her. The awakening of his feelings at the summer solstice dance seven years ago, had grown to the point where he asked for her hand in marriage. It had proved to be a good union. They were happy and content with each other as they planned and built their log cabin on the tract of land Daniel received from his father on the Connecticut River.

An inch of light snow had fallen the night before. Daniel woke early, saw the snow, and hoped to pick up a fresh deer track. Fresh venison would add to their austere diet and supplement their food stores. He left Mary and Lee II while they were still sleeping. John Akins had been helping Mary and Daniel complete their log cabin. He was awake and had waved to Daniel, understanding what he was about to do. Daniel quietly left the log cabin, checking on the Jersey cow they had walked all the way from Londonderry.

John Akins was an experienced soldier like Daniel's Uncle Lee. They had discussed the risks of living on the frontier. Mary's mother had been a victim nine years ago, and the potential for an attack was perhaps even greater now. The French had succeeded in using the native population as a weapon against the British settlers. Regardless of the existence of a truce or peace treaty between France and Great Britain, clashes along the border were a constant fact of life. Lately, the intensity had increased, yet Mary had been willing to take the chance with their son. Generally, incidents were taking place further north as the settlers reached closer and closer to Canada.

Once he left sight of the cabin, Daniel paused and leaned against a large white ash tree so that he could carefully survey the scene. The air was brisk and fresh. He liked the promise of spring that gave birth to a new life in the wilderness. He breathed deeply, savoring the freshness. Checking the priming of his rifle often was a habit he had developed in the rangers. The leather wrapping he always kept around the flintlock mechanism was readily removable in a hurry if necessary. He always kept one of his pistols covered under his hunting jacket.

A couple of deer had sampled the salt lick John Akins had brought with him and placed on a deer-run so that it could be observed from a distance. Salt was scarce in the area, and the deer and moose were attracted to it. A mile or so from the cabin, Daniel spotted fresh deer tracks and kneeled against a beech tree to check his weapon. He used a musket with a rifled barrel that fired a half inch bullet. It was more accurate and capable of shooting farther than his Uncle Lee's English musket. The rifle had been custom-manufactured by a Portsmouth gunsmith specifically for Daniel. It was a birthday present from his Uncle Lee and Aunt Maureen.

He was checking the priming of the flintlock when he saw movement off to his left. It was just a blur. Daniel remained motionless and meticulously scanned the area. A doe was heading for the salt lick! Rising slowly behind the tree, Daniel brought the rifle to his shoulder and waited for the deer to cross between two trees straight ahead in his line of sight. The instant the deer appeared, he gently squeezed the trigger. The deer collapsed with a hole through her heart. He reloaded the rifle before leaving his position.

The morning was cool, and Daniel's fingers were numb from handling the rifle. He began dressing the deer, warming his hands beneath the hide. While Daniel was busy doing that, he continued to be alert. The soft layer of snow would not last too long, but it could still silence movement in the forest so that he would not be able to hear it. Daniel quickly dressed the deer and began dragging it towards the cabin, pleased with his morning's work. Mary would be happy to have the extra meat for their larder.

An hour later, Daniel came in view of the cabin, exhausted from dragging the deer. He was instantly alarmed, there was no smoke coming from the chimney! A roaring fire was always the norm by midmorning. Daniel dropped the doe and ran as fast as he could past the shelter for the cow toward the front of the cabin. His prize Jersey cow had been butchered, the ground was covered with blood and a hind quarter was missing. Sick with dread at what he would find, Daniel leaped to the porch and opened the door, almost tripping over John Akins dead body. It was dark inside, but he could see the inert form of his wife lying on the bed with Lee II tucked under her arm.

Mary had been bludgeoned to death. Little Lee II had almost been cut in two by a savage tomahawk blow. A loud howl pierced Daniel's lips as he grasped Mary in his arms. Her blood spilled on his hunting jacket. Her body was still warm, but lifeless! All three of the bodies had been scalped, leaving their facial expressions fixed in horror. He knew that the Abenaki relished the horror of scalping their victims while they were still alive. Upon closer examination, Daniel discovered that Mary had been raped before she died. A deep "x" was carved on her lower abdomen.

John Akins' body was pulverized with knife cuts and tomahawk blows. He must have put up a brave defense, but the butchers had to leave his lifeless body even more mutilated. They had stuffed his mouth with feces. Another cry of rage filled the still air of the New Hampshire wilderness. Too sick to completely believe what had taken place, Daniel slid to the floor of the cabin and wept for a long time. The cabin wreaked with the smell of death.

Filled with a rage and thirst for revenge, Daniel pulled himself upright and fled the cabin circling around to pick up the Indian's retreating tracks. There were three separate tracks leading towards the place they had landed their canoe. Pushing the image of death from his mind, Daniel was determined to extract retribution from the savages that butchered his defenseless family. A fire had not been started in the fireplace, so he concluded that they must have struck shortly after he left. Maybe they were waiting and watched him leave. He noted where they had pushed their canoe from the shore and assumed that they would continue downstream looking for other likely targets.

Daniel ran as fast as his feet could propel him southward along the river, surveying the full breadth of the fast moving Connecticut for signs of movement. If God was on his side, he would have a chance to confront the savages he desperately wanted to kill, slowly if possible.

Five miles south of his cabin, Daniel knew that there was another one visible from the river. It was empty for the winter, but maybe the hostile Indians did not know that, and he could intercept them. The cabin was situated on a prominent rock formation with an excellent view of the river. Daniel dropped to his knees behind a clump of river ash saplings as soon as he came in sight of the cabin. He remained motionless studying the scene. He was in luck. The Indians had landed on the shore close to where he was hiding. He stealthily crawled closer to see their tracks in the fast disappearing snow, and waited for their return.

His patience paid dividends when Daniel saw the three heavily painted warriors leisurely walking back towards their canoe. His mind raced through a plan of attack. If he shot the Indian closest to the canoe with his rifle, and the next in line with his pistol, he could close with the last member of the group with his knife. Carefully and in slow motion he removed his pistol from beneath his shirt and tucked it loosely under his belt, cocking it first. Then he brought the rifle to his shoulder and waited for the first Indian to reach the canoe. They seemed to be unconcerned and were joking with each other. Fresh scalps, dripping with blood, hung from their waists!

With a clear line of fire, Daniel pulled the trigger of the rifle and quickly jumped to his feet with pistol in hand. The second man in line turned in time to see Daniel looking at him over the sights of his pistol. Fear filled his eyes as the handgun fired, catching the savage in the neck. The first two warriors dropped to the ground, leaving the third alone staring at Daniel in disbelief. He looked around; there might have been more than one man attacking them.

With a powerful lunge of his muscular legs, Daniel plowed into the third Indian who had leaped toward the canoe. Daniel caught him in mid-air, driving his knife into his side. The Indian cried out in pain. They landed in the water and continued to struggle. The Indian managed to swing his tomahawk in a glancing blow against Daniel's shoulder. Too intense on the task at hand, Daniel shrugged the blow off and buried his knife into the savage's stomach. The Indian was still alive when Daniel pulled him from the water onto the shore. With a precise circular motion he cut a ring around the Indian's head and grasped his hair removing the scalp in one swift motion. It was accompanied by a cry of anguish from the Abenaki who raised his hands to his bloody head.

Daniel checked to see if the other two were still alive. They appeared to be dead, yet he scalped them anyway. The act would normally have sickened Daniel, but the adrenaline was running too high for him to regret it. There was a sense of euphoria that he had attacked and overcome the three butchers of his family. Remorse might come later, but at that moment, he felt empowered and was emboldened to extract more retribution.

The third Indian was still alive. Daniel took him by the arm and lifted him off the ground balancing him against a red maple tree. Their eyes met. Terror and fear in the eyes of an Indian was a sight that made him feel good. With every ounce of strength in him, Daniel swung the trusty knife Ben had given him many years ago into the groin of the dying Indian. It penetrated the Indian's body and sunk deep into the wood of the tree, holding the savage upright as blood ran down over his grotesque facial features. Weeping moans escaped from the bloodied human figure. Daniel watched for several seconds, hoping that the savage was suffering as his family had.

Daniel retrieved his rifle and pistol, and loaded them before returning to the scene of his carnage. The canoe was filled with some provisions and two French muzzle loaders. The Indian he had staked to the tree was dead when he removed his knife. He cleaned it in the river before returning it to the sheath. Daniel left the three savages where they fell, hoping that others might see that justice had been administered. Then he pushed off from shore in their canoe and headed north against the strong current of the Connecticut River. He had avenged the mutilation and death of his family, but it had not been enough.

Daniel slowly approached his cabin in a state of physical and emotional numbness. He kept asking himself the same questions: "Why, in the big scheme of life, was it necessary for Mary and his son to die so ignobly, and what did it accomplish except pain and misery? And what kind of threat did a gentle old soldier like John Akins constitute? Why...? Why...?" The presence of death again made him physically ill, and he retched until there was nothing left for him to purge.

The sun was beginning to set, and long shadows covered the ground he had selected to bury the three bodies. The first thing Daniel did was to collect red hot coals from the banked fireplace ashes so that he could build fires on top of the frozen ground to melt the frost remaining in the soil. Spring was late in coming. Normally the ground would have been soft and muddy by April, but cold weather and snow continued. All night long, Daniel labored digging two graves. When they were completed, he used the last of his strength to wrap Mary and little Lee with two heavy blankets and placed them in the first grave and John Akins in the second grave. The first shovel of freshly dug soil he placed over Mary and Lee II almost destroyed him. Tears rolled down his face in streams blinding him. No man should ever have to bury a loved one who died so tragically! In his heart he knew that the inert body he was covering with soil was no longer the Mary he had loved and cared for. Her soul had gone home where she would wait for him to come to her.

When the burials were completed, Daniel was amazed that he had been able to carry it out without losing his mind. The pain and loss were so deep that, at one point, he entertained a powerful urge to find release from the depression he was suffering. It would have been easy to use the pistol and end the misery. He dismissed it as an act of cowardice. His desire for revenge and justice soon overcame the momentary thought of self-destruction.

He returned to the cabin for a kettle of water and some tea, bringing them out to the fires roaring next to the new graves. He exited the cabin as quickly as possible. The memories it held were too powerful for him to deal with. Hot tea warmed and settled his churning stomach. For the rest of the night Daniel sat beside the graves, mourning his loss and remembering the life he had shared with his Mary.

A few days after the solstice celebration in Portsmouth seven years ago, Daniel and his Uncle Lee had left with several other supply wagons for Fort Number Four in Charlestown with Mary. Her father was waiting for them at the fort. The trip had been awkward for both of them. Bashful glances took place when they thought Uncle Lee was not looking. Later, they learned that he noticed every subtle nuance, and smiled at the wonderful innocence of first love. Their parting at the fort had been sad for each of them. Daniel had written a letter to Mary and had secretly placed it in her small trunk. When she wrote her first letter to him, she told him it made her cry for happiness when she discovered it.

It was on that same trip that Daniel and Uncle Lee had borrowed a couple of fast horses from the militia garrison still commanded by the competent Captain Stevens. They had ridden rapidly north along the Connecticut River, past Hanover, to the fifty acre tract of land that his father had left for him. It bordered the river for several hundred yards. Walking around on his own land gave him a grand feeling of euphoria and satisfaction. He knew then that he had to return to it as soon as he could. It was a small piece of the universe that he could call his very own.

A year later, 1747, the fort at Charlestown was attacked by a large band of Abenaki led by French officers. Settlers from the area had rushed to the relative safety of the stockade. After three days and nights of fighting, the small contingent of thirty one men garrisoning the fort beat off the attacks. The whipped Indians broke off the engagement, leaving behind many of their dead comrades.

The tempo of violence increased monthly along the frontier. Within a year, the Peace Treaty of Aix-la-Chapelle was signed by

France and Great Britain. The document engendered a seething resentment on the part of the New Englanders against England. It returned Fort Louisbourg at Cape Breton back to the French. New England colonists rightly felt that their sacrifice was squandered and unappreciated by this meaningless pronouncement. Uncle Lee had written a stinging editorial against the treaty, which left a festering discontent that would eventually erupt in years to come.

Daniel had helped his Uncle Lee in the print shop during those years between adolescence and adulthood. He grew in physical stature as an equal to his powerfully built Uncle Lee. Always soft spoken, Daniel retained the good manners his mother had taught him. He grew in wisdom commensurate to his imposing size and had developed a knack for writing.

He became popular in the community, especially among the young ladies. He had been amused by their attention, but he thought only of Mary and knew that someday they would be married.

Mary and her father had come to visit the Cullens that summer of 1751. Daniel had proposed to her during that visit, and she accepted his offer with a thankful heart. The wedding ceremony took place in the Portsmouth Presbyterian Church with a few friends attending the ceremony. Mary was radiant in her white gown and veil. Daniel could still picture her bright eyes and the way she smiled. It was the happiest moment Daniel had ever experienced. They temporarily moved in with John Akins while Daniel built their new cabin on the claim.

Daniel remembered Lavina with a sad shake of his head. They had been good friends for a long time. He knew that she had feelings for him that he did not reciprocate. One day, when they were alone in the print shop, Daniel mentioned that he and Mary planned to marry when they were both twenty. The announcement was like a physical blow to Lavina. She quickly left the room to hide her tears. Daniel knew what was troubling her, and it hurt him to know that he was finding happiness which his best friend did not share. He valued her friendship and respected her for many things, especially for her generous, giving nature. He had always liked her; he simply never loved her the way he did Mary, and he told her so that same day.

"You know, Lavina, I've loved and respected you like a sister that I never had. We've been friends for too long not to be honest with each

81

other. I'm sorry if I hurt you in saying that, but it's the truth," he explained in a calm, deliberate way.

"I, too, have enjoyed your friendship, Daniel. I'm not blaming you or Mary, who is a dear friend, also. I wish both of you much happiness together," replied Lavina with sad eyes.

One day Lavina had confided in Daniel in a wistful, melodious voice. "I am an Ojibwa from my mother and a white person from my father, an Englishman. I have been raised in your world, yet it will not accept me because I am not white. It would also be impossible for me to live and survive in the wilderness as a native Indian. I'm what you would call a misfit, a half-breed who lives in a world of my own."

"Don't punish yourself like this, Lavina."

She paused a moment and continued, avoiding his penetrating appraisal. "My heart was blind to reality. I know now that it was foolish and unwise. Even if you had similar feelings, it could not work. Your circle of friends would avoid you because of me. I'm like those dark-skinned people from Africa, the slaves. I'm part of two worlds and cannot be accepted in either. What am I to do? Must I, too, follow the sun along the path of my ancestors in the hope of finding an answer to my dilemma?"

The questions she posed in parting still troubled him. There were no answers for her. Several days later, Daniel opened the print shop, hoping to see Lavina. She did not show up for three days, so Daniel went to the Cameron's home and asked for her. She was in the great room of the cabin talking with her mother, who graciously excused herself when she saw the troubled look on Daniel's face.

"I was concerned about you, Lavina, and stopped by to see you," Daniel had told her, feeling awkward and responsible for her discontent.

"I've been getting things ready for a return to the missionary school in northern Vermont," she explained without looking at him. "More and more Native Americans are expressing a desire to learn English. The project for a school at Hanover on the Connecticut River has not materialized yet, but several people are working on the project. When the border is free of wilderness warfare, maybe it will come someday."

Daniel was concerned about her safety. "Won't you be in danger?"

"You forget that I'm a Native American, too, and am able to move freely within their territory without harm, Daniel."

"When are you leaving, Lavina?"

"Early in the morning, Daniel. I had planned to say good-bye to you and the Cullens. I love them both very much and have felt safe and comfortable being their neighbor. You've grown into a fine young man any girl would be proud to claim, Daniel. Mary is fortunate, and so are you, for she's a wonderful person. You two deserve each other."

"Thank you, Lavina," Daniel had cried, searching for the right words. "I wish you luck in your new work. I've always been proud to call you my friend."

"Thank you."

Daniel took her into his arms and held her for a long time. "I'll miss you. I wish you a safe journey, and always remember, that if you ever need a friend or a helping hand, please promise to call on me, and I'll be there. I'm going to miss you, Lavina."

"I'll miss you, too, Daniel. Now go before I fall apart." She stretched on tiptoes to kiss him, then firmly pushed him out the door.

Daniel remembered, and wept at the sight of the newly dug graves.

Chapter Eleven

The sun rose the next morning, erasing the long shadows that had hung over the graves. Daniel was an empty shell of a man numbed to the reality that his life had changed forever. He had no more tears to shed. Mary's death had filled him with a profound resolve to extract justice for the unwarranted slaying.

Daniel warmed his tea from the kettle sitting on the dying coals and wondered what had happened to Lavina. He never felt so alone in his life and needed a friend. It was strange that he should think of her sitting beside his wife's grave. It was ironic, Mary was the best friend he ever had, and another was a half-breed Indian maiden.

It would be impossible for him to stay at the cabin. He knew that he had to keep busy or go out of his mind. Returning to Fort Number Four would give him a destination and an opportunity to see what jobs might be available. Maybe he could link up with some of the ranger units on the frontier. Right now, he had no desire to return to Portsmouth. Too many memories waited for him there. He had to let Uncle Lee and Aunt Maureen know what had happened. His cabin would not be safe for a family until the Indian menace had been eliminated.

The melting snow had filled the Connecticut River to capacity. Daniel guided the canoe close to the eastern bank ever watchful of potential dangers behind every bush and tree. His injured shoulder was painful, and he alternated the paddle from hand to hand to no avail. He sprinkled cool water on the shoulder for relief.

Daniel passed the small settlement of Hanover without stopping. Wood smoke curled from chimneys of the cabins clustered near the riverbank. An hour later, Daniel leaped from the canoe and pulled it out of the water onto the grassy shore of great meadow at Fort Number Four. He waved to the vigilant lookout in the watch tower and made his way to the front gate of the fort. His first visit was to the quarters of Doctor Hastings located on the ground floor beneath the watch tower.

The elderly doctor examined the bruise with an experienced eye. "You took a hard blow without breaking the skin, Mr. Cullen. There's not much I can do except rub some cooling salve on it for relief. You'll be sore and stiff for a few days. Moderate exercise will aid healing. May I ask how you received the blow?"

With a calmness that surprised him, Daniel explained what had taken place. "I came to the fort to get a word to Uncle Lee and to see what was available for work. I don't really know where to go from here."

"Don't even think of tomorrow. Work on getting through the day. Time is the only thing that really helps. I'm so sorry to hear about your family. Sadly, it is an ever increasing story on the border, and I fear that we are in for a more turbulent period ahead." He had seen first-hand the cruelties committed on the pioneers who dared to push the limits of civilization. At times, he wondered if the price was worth the struggle for more land. "There was talk of a supply train being organized for a trip to Fort Anne or Fort Edward on the Hudson River," continued the Doctor.

"Thank you, Doctor Hastings," said Daniel, preparing to leave. "May I ask you for one more favor, sir?"

"If it's within my power."

"I need to write a letter to my Uncle Lee Cullen in Portsmouth. May I borrow paper and pen and leave it with you to send with the next party leaving for Portsmouth?"

"Of course you may. Take a seat at my desk and use the pen and paper. If you'll excuse me, I have some sick patients in the great room upstairs. Just leave the letter on the desk, and I'll see that it gets delivered."

"Thank you, sir." Daniel took a seat at the upright desk and composed a letter.

April 4, 1753
Fort Number Four

Dear Uncle Lee and Aunt Maureen,

The news I deliver in this letter is horrendous. Mary, Lee II, and John Akins have been the latest victims of the Abenaki and the French soldiers and priests who direct them. It's hard to imagine that men of God could be capable of encouraging such brutality and depravity, and impossible for me to adequately describe what was done to my family.

I know that I should come home to Portsmouth, but I have too much hatred and rage that needs to be worked off before I return to the civilized world. Only now, after experiencing their loss, can I appreciate how difficult it must have been for Mary to witness the death of her mother.

I plan to stay here on the border for a while. Both of you are often in my thoughts.

Pray for me

Daniel

That evening, Daniel took refuge in an empty lean-to built around the stockade and stretched out on a bed of straw. Within minutes he was sound asleep. Even in his dreams, ugly thoughts invaded his mind. He felt he had abandoned Mary and his son by leaving them alone in their cold graves. Now that he was away from them, he had an urge to return. All night long, he fitfully tossed and turned. He woke to the smell of hot tea brewing in an open fire beside the lean-to.

A heavy-set teamster saw Daniel rise from his straw bed. "There's plenty of tea and venison if you care to join me, stranger."

"It smells delicious. Thanks for the offer," Daniel replied, warming himself at the fire. He was stiff, and his shoulder ached more than ever. "My name is Daniel Cullen. I came in yesterday looking for some work. Do you know if there's any available? Doctor Hastings told me that a supply column was staging for a trip to the Hudson."

"I'm Harry Worth, and you're right, Daniel," said the teamster. "There's an Army supply column going to Fort Anne. It won't leave for another ten days or so. I've got two wagons filled with powder and lead shot. If you want a job, I'm sure there'll be plenty to choose from."

"Sounds good to me," Daniel replied, savoring the warm tea. He thought about returning to the cabin until the wagons were ready to leave. His thirst for revenge was strong. Daniel thanked Harry for the food and drink, purchased some supplies at the fort, and headed north against the current on the river intent on retribution.

A plan had been developing in his head during the night. Perhaps he could trap some Indians. The thought occupied his mind, replacing the visions of his lovely Mary lying on their bed in a pool of her own blood. If he started a fire in the cabin early in the morning, perhaps marauding Indians from the river might think it was an easy target. He could lie patiently undercover away from the cabin in range of his rifle.

When Daniel arrived at his cabin, he searched the riverbank to the north and located an ideal ambush site about five hundred feet upstream. There was a low marshy area between the river and the elevated observation point he had selected. Clumps of white birch saplings gave excellent cover. He could wait there undetected and observe the river for a long distance northward. He could sleep in the cabin with relative safety. They did not fight at night because they believed that their spirits might be lost in the darkness. It would give him a chance to rest and prepare food for the day. Before departing in the morning, he could bank the fire with some green wood. The smoke would be easily noticed by travelers on the river.

For two days Daniel stood a silent vigil at his vantage point without success. Early on the third day he saw two Abenaki warriors paddling a canoe towards him. His heart pounded in anticipation. He double checked his rifle and pistol priming, looking forward to an encounter with the savages. They spotted the heavy discharge of smoke coming from his stone chimney and guided their canoe to shore near a clump of alder bushes that would conceal it.

They landed a short distance from Daniel's observation post. Armed with tomahawks and knives, they scanned the surrounding area with experienced eyes. Daniel was sitting motionless against a white birch tree holding a branch heavy with leaves in front of his face and body. One of the Indians looked directly at his position without detecting him. Daniel breathed easier when they turned to approach the cabin from the rear. They were within easy distance for his rifle. He carefully cocked the weapon and sighted at an opening in the leaves.

The instant the lead warrior entered the space, Daniel squeezed the trigger. Daniel's first shot hit the man between the shoulders below the neck, spinning him around. Before the warrior had hit the ground,

Daniel had pulled his pistol from the belt, cocked it and fired at the second intruder who was looking for the source of the gunfire. Both Indians were killed instantly.

The success of his vigil buoyed his spirits. He wondered how many innocent lives he saved by eliminating those two warriors and felt gratified. He ran to the two corpses, scalped them, and threw them into the river. He claimed the canoe and pulled it farther into the forest to conceal it from prying eyes.

For six days Daniel stood at his lonely post and surveyed every traveler that traversed the river in either direction. Several white settlers used the river for travel to and from their claims, the same as Daniel and Mary had done. On one occasion, he recognized a large Indian raiding party with a priest and a French soldier in three canoes. He was determined to eliminate as many as he could. They showed no sign of being attracted to his cabin, so he steadied himself behind a sturdy red oak tree and took aim at the Abenaki warrior at the helm of the first canoe. His first shot hit the Abenaki, knocking him into the water. A loud cry rang from his lips the instant he was hit. Daniel reloaded with maximum powder charge and fired two more shots before the canoes were out of sight. He knew that he had hit three of the targets, but had no way of verifying if he had killed them or not. The vile priest in the second canoe grabbed a paddle and began paddling furiously. Daniel was tempted to make a snap shot and trust to luck, but the canoe was too far away.

He was enjoying the hide-and-seek game. His craving for revenge was being nourished with each kill. He knew the supply train was scheduled to leave Fort Number Four soon, yet, he still considered staying at his post to continue the deadly game. Daniel dismissed the thought and allowed himself one more day at his river-side post.

On the morning of the last day, he saw a lone canoe being paddled from the rear by one person. He recognized the traditional frilled hunting shirt and the long black hair of an Indian. The canoe was traveling close to the eastern shore where he could get a good shot. Without hesitation, he stood against the large red oak tree which hid him well, cocked the hammer, aimed, and fired. The loud scream from the canoe electrified every nerve in his body. It was the scream of a woman. He saw the figure lean forward, still grasping the paddle which hung in the water acting as a rudder for the canoe. It pulled the canoe to the shore close by the cabin. In a flash, Daniel lost the euphoria and empowerment that his vigil had given him. A woman... He had shot a defenseless woman! Leaving his rifle behind, he desperately ran to catch the canoe before the strong current swept it downstream. He leaped into the water to pull it to shore. The figure slumped over the gunwale, almost touching the water, was a young squaw.

Daniel effortlessly grasped her small body from the canoe and placed her on a grassy location beside the river. He reached for her wrist and breathed easier when he felt a strong steady pulse. At least she was not dead! His bullet had shattered her left arm and grazed her shoulder. Blood was splattered all over her upper body, even her hair. Sick with regret, he took his knife and cut away the deerskin hunting shirt to expose the wound. It was bleeding profusely. Daniel ran into the cabin to get clean clothing for bandages and wound them tightly around the squaw's arm to stop the bleeding and keep the wound from getting infected. He made a simple sling to support the arm. The woman opened her eyes as he was bending over her tying the sling in place. They were filled with fear. She tried to sit up, and he restrained her. Just then, he heard a strange noise coming from the canoe. The cry of a small baby echoed in the wilderness.

"It can't be," he exclaimed, running to the canoe. There lying in the bottom of the fragile birch bark craft, wrapped in a decorated deerskin hide, was a small baby. A flap from the deerskin covered the baby's head. He lifted the flap to expose a five or six month old baby smiling at him! "My God, what have I done...? What have I done...?"

He picked the baby up and brought it to the woman on the ground. He thought the baby was probably a girl. The woman lying on the ground saw Daniel bring the baby to her. Tears, the largest Daniel had ever seen, formed in her eyes and ran down into her ears. She reached out for the baby with her right arm. He placed the baby beside her. He went again to the canoe to see if there was anything there for the baby to eat. A woven ash basket contained a supply of dried sphagnum moss and a container of honey. He carried them to the woman, placing them within her reach. The woman was frightened and began to shake uncontrollably.

"She's going into shock," Daniel thought. He knew that the woman's life was threatened if he did not hurry to wrap blankets around her. She could slip into a coma any minute. He placed the baby on the woman's stomach, picked them both off the ground and ran toward the cabin. Fear filled her eyes. He had seen that same look from animals when they were cornered and had no way to escape. Daniel burst through the cabin door placing the woman and baby on the bed beside the fireplace and wrapped them both in warm blankets.

Beneath a deep layer of wood ashes, Daniel found a few live coals in the fireplace and started the fire using dry pitch pine shavings. Soon, he had a roaring fire going. He replenished the supply of wood next to the fireplace and ran to the river for a pail of clean water to fill a cast iron tea kettle on a grate next to the crackling flames.

Tea would be ready soon. Daniel lifted the blankets to check if the woman had stopped shaking and to his surprise, she had unfastened the hunting shirt and was nursing the baby. She defiantly looked at him. Tormented by the knowledge that he had shot a nursing mother, tears filled his eyes. "I wish I could tell you how sorry I am," he murmured, turning away from her.

"I understand some English," a weak, frightened voice answered. She modestly pulled the cover over her naked breast and looked away from him.

Daniel looked at her. "I really am sorry for what I've done to you. I acted out of hatred for those who killed my son and wife and had no intention of hurting a woman. Your arm is broken. Are you injured anywhere else?"

"I hurt all over," she replied in a low voice. "The bullet hit my arm and bruised my shoulder."

"It will be dark soon. It's too late to get to Fort Number Four by sundown. First thing in the morning, I'll take you to the fort. There's a doctor there."

She nodded and appeared to be relieved to hear his plan for her.

"I'm making some hot tea. Would you like a cup?" he asked.

"Yes, I need liquids to feed the baby," she answered reluctantly. "Why did you shoot me? I was not a threat to you."

Daniel reflected on her question and studied her calmly nursing the baby. He had watched Mary lying in the same bed nursing Lee II just a few hours before he found them dead. How could he tell this woman of the forest how much hatred he carried for those who murdered his family? He did not answer her. Instead, he made tea and placed a hot cup on a stool beside the bed. It was not necessary for him to justify his reasons. He had made a mistake and had apologized for it. He stared for a long time at the flickering flames in the fireplace. The blood stains from John Akins' murder and scalping were noticeable on the floor and on one of the blankets he had hurriedly snatched from the bed. Was it John's or was it Mary's blood on the blanket partially covering the nursing Indian woman? He jumped to his feet, snatched the blanket off her and threw it into the fireplace. Then, he walked into the bedroom for a clean blanket and placed it over her body.

The crackling fire and the reality that Mary was really gone struck him like a heavy blow. For days he had kept busy thinking only of revenge, pushing the ugly images of their mutilated bodies from his mind. The blood-stained blanket had wrenched him from denial. Tears fell across his rugged weather-beaten face, and pain ripped him apart. Daniel sat before the fireplace and wept uncontrollably, holding his head in his two hands.

When Daniel finally stirred, the fire was low. He threw another log on the fire and checked the squaw and baby. The mother was sleeping with the child tucked tightly in her right arm. The baby smiled at him. Guilt and shame filled his heart, his random act of violence made him no better than the men that murdered his child. All night, Daniel kept a brisk fire burning. When daybreak came, he rushed to his lookout for the rifle and loaded and primed it before entering the cabin. He heard the baby cry for a few seconds and was silent. "She must be nursing the infant," he thought.

He entered the cabin and said, "I can heat some rice and corn meal to eat. With dried fruit mixed in, it makes a pretty tasty breakfast. As soon as we finish eating, I'll take you to the fort. Do you want something?"

"I am hungry," she replied.

"When you're finished nursing the baby, you can place her in the cradle here beside the fireplace," Daniel pointed to a small cradle Lee II had used. "If you want, I can change the baby for you. I have some dry moss in the cabin for that purpose."

She studied his face. "My arm hurts more this morning," she hesitantly admitted. "Morning Mist does need to be cleaned, and I need to take care of myself."

Daniel understood her need to be private and use the outhouse beside the firewood shed. "It's right outside the door to your left."

He lifted Morning Mist from her mother's arms. She covered herself with one of the blankets and slowly stood up to leave, aching in every joint. The baby showed no fear and smiled at him again. Flooded with memories of the times he and Mary had held and changed little Lee, Daniel's hands began to shake, and tears again ran down his tanned cheeks. He was confused and angry and bitter and prayed for some relief from the pain that was tearing him apart. He changed the baby's soiled moss with a supply Mary had kept in the cabin.

The baby was cleaned and changed by the time the mother returned. Daniel had dressed her in a clean shirt Lee once used. The Indian woman stared at the shirt. Daniel justified his use of it: "The gown the baby had on was soiled. I hope you don't mind her wearing this."

She nodded her head in approval and sat on the bed feeling weak and unsteady. Daniel busied himself fixing something to eat. He made hot tea and placed a hot cup on the bench beside the bed. He cut up small pieces of dried venison and dried apples, mixing them in the iron kettle with the boiling rice. A few minutes later, he served her a large bowl of the concoction.

She finished nursing the baby and wrapped her in the deerskin garment. "Would you please tie the laces so that Morning Mist will be securely dressed?"

"Of course," Daniel replied, gently tying the loose ends snugly. "So your name is Morning Mist. That's a pretty name for a pretty little girl." Daniel placed her back on the bed and offered to help her mother sit up to eat the food and drink some hot tea. "Take your time, but the quicker we get to the fort, the quicker the doctor can help you. My name is Daniel Cullen. May I ask yours?"

She accepted his offer to help and winced in pain. "My name is Ruth. I'm an Ojibwa."

They ate all the food he had prepared in the iron kettle in silence. Daniel banked the fire and carried blankets, dried venison, and apples to the canoe. It was going to be a sunny day for the trip to the fort. Ruth allowed herself and Morning Mist to be carried out to the canoe. Daniel carefully laid her on soft blankets on the bottom of the canoe and placed a pillow under her head. Then he returned to the cabin for his rifle, powder horn and bullet pouch, placing them within easy reach in the stern out of Ruth's line of sight.

Hours later, Daniel's strong powerful strokes landed them at Fort Number Four. The canoe climbed onto the low bank of the large meadow next to the fort. Daniel waved to the sentinel on guard at the watchtower lookout. He placed little Morning Mist on her mother's stomach and lifted both of them from the canoe. He ran through the main gate to Doctor Hastings' quarters. The doctor motioned him to place Ruth on an Army cot and turned inquiring eyes to Daniel. Avoiding eye contact, he hurriedly told the doctor the whole sordid story. Doctor Hastings frowned at hearing about the cold calculating method of executing Indians. He asked Daniel to leave while he examined Ruth.

Relieved that he had finally brought her to the best possible place for care, Daniel wandered into the stockade of the fort. The wagon supply train he had agreed to join was getting ready for the long journey to the Hudson River. Wagons were being carefully packed and the wheels checked for proper bearing lubricants. He located the wagonmaster, Jason Downs, to find out what his duties as a scout would be.

Downs was a tall, bearded man with small bulging eyes that looked Daniel up and down several times. "Mostly your job will be to scout ahead on the trail which is quite clearly marked, and to circulate enough so that our flanks are covered from a surprise attack of Indians. You'll be responsible for selecting sites for night encampments with an eye for us to be able to defend ourselves if attacked. Are you married?"

Daniel turned away from Jason Downs' intense scrutiny. "I was up until a week ago. My family was wiped out by Saint Francis Indians."

"I'm sorry, Daniel," the older man replied softly. "I'll be glad to take you on. Once we get to Fort Anne, we'll leave some of our teams and wagons and proceed as a smaller group to the Hudson. It's up to you."

"Consider the job taken, Mr. Downs," Daniel said, shaking hands with the hardy frontiersman.

"We'll be pulling out early in the morning, Daniel."

Daniel left the stockade and walked to the trading post in Charleston to renew his supply of gunpowder and lead. The small collection of cabins was filled with teamsters and merchants preparing for the morning departure. He saw a team that looked familiar to him and recognized Thom Cameron driving a heavily loaded wagon pulled by Andy and Gabe.

"Mr. Cameron," Daniel called out. Thom Cameron pulled on the reins and looked around. At first he didn't recognize Daniel with his heavy beard. "Is that you, Daniel Cullen? Well, I'll be... I could have driven right by you and never have known that it was you." Thom jumped off the wagon and shook his hand. "It's good to see you. How's the wife?"

Daniel told Thom about what had happened. "I'm so sorry for you," Thom replied, shaking his head. "Every time something like this takes place, it makes it harder and harder for my wife and daughter."

Daniel was uncomfortable talking about his family's death and asked about his Uncle Lee and Aunt Maureen.

"Your uncle is becoming a respected voice in the Portsmouth community with his newspaper. He describes complex issues such as the limitations imposed by the Crown on manufacturing items in the colonies with great clarity. I must tell you though, lately, I've noticed that he has slowed down a little. When he led Andy to my place several days ago, he was limping slightly. It was probably his old leg wound."

"I never knew he was wounded."

"He doesn't talk very much about himself. You know that."

Daniel nodded, remembering his uncle's modesty with affection. "You're right, Mr. Cameron. How's Lavina?"

"That's why I came to the fort with this supply train. I had planned to meet Lavina, who is coming from Vermont. This meeting was planned a year ago when she left for the frontier. A close friend of hers at school is supposed to meet us here, also. She and Lavina were to meet at Hanover and then come down to Number Four. We were specific about our dates so as to not be confused. The beginning of the third week in April, 1753. They'll return to Portsmouth with me. I hope that everything is all right with them. Anything can happen on the frontier, as you well know. Lavina had sent a message to us a few months ago that everything was on schedule. Her friend was with child that should be about six months old now."

Daniel listened with mounting anxiety. "What's the name of Lavina's friend?"

"Her name is Ruth..."

Chapter Twelve

Daniel's heart sank. He had shot Lavina's friend. "Have you ever met this Ruth?" he asked Thom with mounting despair.

"Yes, what's wrong, Daniel? What do you know about her? Has something happened to Lavina?"

Daniel reached out to reassure Thom Cameron. "I haven't seen Lavina since the wedding in Portsmouth. I'm afraid I do know Ruth. I shot her yesterday, Mister Cameron."

"You shot her!" Thom Cameron cried incredulously. Daniel explained what he had been doing since Mary's death. "Where is Ruth now?"

"She's with the doctor at the fort. I hit her in the arm," Daniel admitted shamefully.

They both rushed to Doctor Hastings' quarters. He was too busy working on the woman and brusquely requested that they come back later. Thom Cameron looked over the doctor's shoulder at the patient.

"It is Ruth," he said, leaving the quarters.

"I'm sorry, Mr. Cameron. I've been sick about the incident ever since it happened," Daniel admitted.

"Your vengeful acts are out of character for you, Daniel," Thom Cameron accused, studying him closely with his penetrating eyes. "Lee and Maureen will be saddened to hear of Mary's tragic death. They'll also be concerned to learn of your murderous acts, no matter how justified you may have felt in committing them. How can you rationalize your behavior? You know that not all red men are evil." Thom stopped, seeing the pain on Daniel's face.

Daniel stood before Thom, unable to answer, and simply shrugged his shoulders in despair.

"You worry me, Daniel. Hate and revenge are two emotions that can only leave you more unfulfilled or dead, probably both."

"They were more than murdered," interrupted Daniel with trembling lips. "I've come to grips with what I must do and I don't need to be preached to by someone who has never experienced what I discovered that day when I returned to the cabin."

A fire burned in Thom Cameron's deep eyes. "You're wrong, Dan... You're wrong. Someday, when things settle down, maybe I'll tell you how wrong you are." Thom turned to leave, "Right now, I've got to transfer the load from my wagon to another one. I need to talk to Ruth about Lavina. I'm worried about her. Good luck on your trip to Fort Anne. I'll tell Maureen and Lee that you're thinking about them." He climbed into his wagon and left Daniel standing alone.

Later that afternoon, Daniel paid a visit to Doctor Hastings' house. He found the doctor sitting at his desk in the corner of the room and inquired about Ruth's condition. "I set her arm the best I could. There may be some bone fragments that will eventually work their way through the skin. She'll have some disfigurement, but should be able to regain partial use of it when completely healed." The stern set to his jaw clearly showed he was upset by the incident. "How could you shoot an unarmed woman?"

"I have no rational explanation, sir. May I speak to her?" Daniel requested. "I'm leaving in the morning and want to apologize again for my actions."

"She's in the room down the hall," the doctor pointed to his right. "It's up to her if she wants to see you. Her daughter is being cared for by my wife in the kitchen."

"Thank you, sir." Daniel entered the room and saw Ruth lying on the bed, staring at the ceiling. Her arm was heavily bandaged and supported by a sling around her neck. "May I come in for a moment?"

"You're already in, Mr. Cullen," Ruth answered with a blank stare.

"I've come to apologize for what I've done to you. A while ago I met Mr. Cameron. He told me that he was supposed to meet you and Lavina here at Number Four."

"He was in and has asked about Lavina," she looked into Daniel's eyes and saw the torment that gripped him. "Perhaps you will better understand if I tell you my story. My husband was killed while working as a scout for the rangers. I had pleaded with him to not leave with our baby so young, but he did anyway, claiming that we needed the money for supplies. He had promised to escort me to Hanover, where a small school is being considered for Native Americans. I had promised Lavina, my friend, to meet at Hanover. News of my husband's death has changed our plans. I sent a message to Lavina to meet at Number Four instead of Hanover. She should be along in a short time. We've known each other for many years. She even told me about you, Daniel Cullen."

"About me?" Daniel asked. "I know that what I did was wrong, and I apologize. I'm leaving for New York in the morning. Will you give Lavina a message for me?"

She nodded her head.

"Please tell her what happened to my family and ask her to look after my dear Aunt Maureen and Uncle Lee?" Daniel paused for a moment and then added, "Lavina was my best friend in Portsmouth. She'll be sad and angry to learn what I've done to you."

"Could you expect it to be otherwise?"

"No, not really," Daniel had run out of things to say to the lady. "I just wanted to apologize to you. I'm glad that Mr. Cameron is here to look after you. He's a good man. I wish you and little Morning Mist the very best. Good-bye."

"Good-bye, Mr. Cullen," Ruth said, turning her head towards the wall away from him.

Very early the next morning, Daniel wrote a letter to his aunt and uncle and went looking for Thom Cameron to deliver it for him. A line of men were forming to eat breakfast in the center of the stockade. Daniel saw Mr. Cameron among them and took a place at his side. A thick hasty pudding was cooking in a large cast-iron pot hanging over the fire. The aroma made them hungry.

"I'm glad to run into you, Mr. Cameron. Would you please give this letter to my aunt and uncle?"

"Yes, they'll be happy to hear from you," said Thom Cameron in a sober mood. "If I was too judgmental towards you yesterday, I apologize, Dan. I could not help thinking that it could have been my Lavina that you shot. I'm worried. She still hasn't come into the fort yet."

"Where was she coming from, Mr. Cameron?"

"Like I said yesterday, this meeting has been set for a year and confirmed a couple of months ago. She was leaving the northern region for Fort Number Four. Lavina has been diligently working at a

Moravian mission school in the northern New Hampshire Grants. She frequently travels in relative safety to the large Abenaki Indian encampments near Odanak, Canada. She has already negotiated the release of several captives from the encampment. At the same time, she seeks out those who want to learn to speak and write English, like Ruth, who has helped her."

"I can picture Lavina doing that kind of work," Daniel exclaimed.

Thom Cameron was nervously fingering his tin cup and plate. "I don't know how long I can wait for her. I'm worried that something has gone wrong since she spoke to Ruth."

"Is there anything I can do, sir?" Daniel asked, sharing her father's concern.

"You've already made your commitment to the train leaving this morning. I appreciate your offer of help. If she does not show within a couple of days, I'm going to take Ruth home to Portsmouth. Then I'll come back, prepared to enter the wilderness in search of her. In the meantime, I'll send out word by the friendly Abenakis around the fort for information on her whereabouts."

"I can't leave here knowing that Lavina may be in need of help," Daniel said resolutely. "I'm sorry, sir, but the wagon train can get by without my services. I'll let them know after we eat. Do you have any idea where we could start looking for Lavina? Please, let me be a part of the effort. She's my best friend, and I owe her that."

Thom and Daniel were served heaping bowls of hasty pudding and steaming hot mugs of tea. They took a seat on the ground against the stockade fence to eat.

Mulling over Daniel's request, Thom said, "My first act would be to go to Hanover where there are quite a few friendly Indians and half-breeds. Most of them speak some English. We could start looking there. If we don't learn anything there, we could leave word and let it be spread by the wilderness travelers between New Hampshire and Canada. Eventually something will show up."

"I'm prepared to leave right now, Mr. Cameron. Somehow the trip to New York hasn't seemed right to me. There'll be other opportunities. Captain Stevens told me that supply trains are leaving weekly for the Hudson and beyond."

Daniel and Thom both felt better now that a plan of action had been decided on. They collected their supplies and headed north on the

Connecticut in Daniel's canoe. With the two of them paddling, they made better time upstream against the flow than Daniel had made downstream with Ruth in his canoe.

The Hanover settlement was a small collection of cabins and a sawmill on the river bank. They inquired at the trading post where Daniel occasionally purchased supplies. The clerk had heard of the Indian woman known as Whispering Wind. He told them that a trapper had just come in from the Memphremagog Lake region. "Just a minute, I'll get him, he's in the back storeroom."

Thom looked at Daniel. "I hope we came to the right place," he said, nervously watching the storeroom door.

A middle-aged Delaware Indian looked through the door at Thom and Daniel before entering the room. He was tall and lean with graying hair and feverish-looking eyes. He spoke in an Algonguin dialect that Thom could speak. They conversed vigorously for several minutes. Daniel did not understand a word that was spoken, and anxiously awaited to learn what was taking place. Finally the Delaware spoke in precise measured words and in a tone that had an ominous ring to it.

Thom hailed the Delaware and turned to Daniel with a troubled expression on his face. "He just told me that he knew of Lavina and was quite certain that she had been taken to the Moravian mission by students after having a canoe accident."

"Then she's all right?" Daniel asked bluntly.

"As far as we know. The Delaware warned me that the wilderness is filled with French and Abenaki Indians on the prowl for scalps, and that we should exercise extreme caution." Thom and Daniel left the trading post.

"Do you have a plan, Mister Cameron?" Daniel asked, placing his rifle in the canoe. "I'd be willing to travel to the mission for Lavina."

Thom thought about the situation. Lavina's safety weighed heavy on his mind. "Ruth, as well as Lavina must be considered in our plan. It would not be wise to keep Ruth at the fort for a long period of time. The question is, how do we serve them both without neglecting one?"

"The river is high, and I could make it to the headwaters of the Connecticut by nightfall," Daniel stated decisively. "If I made camp there, I could make it to the mission in two, maybe three days. I was there two years ago. You can take the canoe back to the fort and escort Ruth and the baby home with you. I'll follow as quickly as Lavina's condition allows. I'll borrow or buy a canoe here at the trading post. If you don't mind, I'll take most of the supplies with me."

"What you say makes sense, Daniel. It'll be a long and arduous trip at this time of year before the leaves are out," said Thom, looking doubtful. "The ground is wet and cold. I hate to see you go it alone."

Daniel sensed his dilemma. "I'm your friend and neighbor, Mr. Cameron and I'm Lavina's friend, also. It will be a privilege to help her knowing that she is in need. I owe much to your daughter. I would not be able to rest until she's safe with her family. Now go, sir. Leave the supplies on the shore for me. One way or another, I'll get a canoe." Daniel placed his large hand on his friend's shoulder.

All of a sudden, Thom Cameron felt his fifty years. "If I were younger, I would go to Lavina myself, but your logic is sound, Daniel, and I thank you. Bring our daughter home to us. May God be with you."

Daniel shoved Mr. Cameron's canoe from the shore and waved as he headed downstream back to the fort. An hour later, Daniel returned to the riverbank with a canoe held high over his head. Placing it in the water, he loaded the supplies into the center of the craft and positioned his rifle close by.

It was mid-afternoon by the time Daniel left Hanover. Dark clouds were beginning to thicken overhead. The threat of rain would make his journey northward that much more difficult. One lesson he had learned with the rangers was that, more than anything else, the forest traveler had to pay close attention to his personal health. Isolated for long periods of time with no one for miles around, a bad cold that turned to pneumonia could be the kiss of death. Keeping as dry as possible was a high priority. A bad fall or a careless step could demobilize him at any moment if he did not remain alert. A healthy fear of the unknown was a necessity. It bolstered a person's awareness for survival and an instinctive readiness for the unexpected. The mark of the forest was on Daniel. His step was light, and his sharp eyes constantly scanned the surrounding wilderness. He had found a serenity in the forest that alluded him in the settlements. Returning to the endless wilderness was always a welcome retreat.

Heavy banks of fog rolled down the river valley, making visibility nearly impossible. Daniel guided the canoe within sight of the Vermont shore and stayed there until darkness terminated his progress. He pulled the canoe ashore across the sandy riverbank into a thick stand of white pine and hemlock that would provide shelter from inclement weather. He removed the supplies from the canoe and turned it upside down on top of them, leaving enough room for him to sleep without being in the open.

Lying snug and dry in his protective cocoon with his rifle beside him, Daniel ate pemmican that Thom Cameron had made. He listened carefully to the sounds of the night. Each camping place had its own peculiar sound and feel. The rushing water of the river drowned out most of the nocturnal animal sounds that were unique to the northern wilderness. Weary from the exertions and worries of the day, Daniel fell asleep as soon as he closed his eyes.

He awoke at daybreak, righted the canoe and prepared to continue on his way without delay, eating as he went. The fog was lifting from the river. Between powerful strokes of the paddle, he shoved a fistful of pemmican into his mouth. He felt an urgency to locate Lavina and relentlessly drove himself to his physical limits. The river was high and fast and it required strong arms to thrust the fragile canoe against the current. He plunged the paddle deep into the water and pulled the canoe northward at a rapid pace.

The farther north he traveled, the smaller the Connecticut became and the current slowed. Daniel decided it was time to end his river travel and pulled to shore to complete the remaining distance on foot. Rocks and rapids were becoming too numerous for him to take a chance of ripping the bottom of the canoe. He dragged it to a small depression ten feet from the river bank and unloaded the supplies. He made up a pack with enough food to make the trip northwesterly to the mission, and stored the rest under the canoe. Before leaving the area, he surveyed it carefully from all perspectives, locking it into his mind so that he could easily find it on their way back.

For two days, Daniel followed his compass on a bearing that would take him to Lake Memphremagog. At the end of the second day, he climbed a tree located on a small hill and saw the large lake ahead of him. The mission was located at the southern extremity of the lake. It was a wooden structure with a log stockade around it. He plowed through the forest without regard to his own safety in order to reach the mission by nightfall.

Several eruptions of musket fire echoed through the wilderness at the mission. Daniel instantly stopped and surveyed the area around him. Something was up, and he proceeded with caution, taking careful measures to be silent. The sun was setting, and he was getting nervous that he might not be able to reach the mission before darkness.

Without warning, several painted Indian warriors passed close to Daniel's hiding place behind a large beech tree. They were heading south and seemed excited about something. Slowly and silently, he made his way closer to the stockade. At the edge of the clearing around the fort, Daniel saw several men in uniform – French officers, huddled around a campfire making tea. They were discussing something with a few Indians and were animated in their expressions. Moving away from the conversing group, Daniel went westerly to intercept the lake, planning to approach the mission from the north.

He felt confident that he could make it to the stockade and request an entrance at the gate. If he was refused, he planned to go deeper into the surrounding forest and try again in daylight. There was a gate opposite where he had first seen the French uniforms. He crawled on his hands and knees every few feet, stopping to listen to the sounds of the night. So far, he had good luck in approaching the mission while it was under siege. He boldly crept to the gate where he stood and pressed himself flat against the large stockade poles. He heard a sentry's footsteps on a platform above his head, thirty steps to the right and ten steps to the left.

Just as the steps passed over him, he called in a loud whisper, "Ahoy in the stockade. May I come into the mission?"

There was a rustle of steps along the platform and several men looked down at him. "Who goes there?" asked one of the guards.

"My name is Daniel Cullen. I've just come from Fort Number Four. I'm alone," Daniel answered, feeling very vulnerable while talking on the outside of the stockade with hostile forces so close by.

An authoritative voice gave an order to open the small door in the gate for Daniel. Daniel breathed easier the second he stepped inside the stockade. He was confronted by a young husky ranger who wore the dark forest green uniform of Roger's Rangers. "You were lucky to get through the lines without being discovered, Mr. Cullen."

"I took my time," Daniel smiled.

"Come with me, sir," demanded the ranger, pointing to a doorway leading to a room with a lantern burning brightly. "The head of the mission will see you shortly. You may remove your pack and rest here. I've got to get back to my post on the wall. By the way, are you related to that Cullen guy who writes editorials in Portsmouth?"

Daniel smiled to himself. This was not the first time he had been asked that question. "He's my Uncle Lee," Daniel proclaimed proudly.

"We get copies of the newspaper every once in a while. Well, I'm glad you made it in safely, Mr. Cullen," the ranger said, leaving the room in a hurry.

A few minutes later, he was greeted by a small balding man with black wire-rimmed glasses. He had an energetic demeanor and a curious way of wrinkling his nose when he spoke. Daniel liked him instantly. "We don't have many visitors after darkness. Welcome to our humble mission, Mr. Cullen. I'm Reverend Blynn. What can I do for you?"

"I came in search of information of the whereabouts of an Ojibwa woman called Whispering Wind. I know her as Lavina Cameron. Her father sent me from Fort Number Four to locate her and bring her home," Daniel explained.

"She's in the mission now," Reverend Blynn told him. "I'll bring you to her, but first, may I offer you some refreshments? Maybe some hot tea?"

"Reverend, I'm starved, and your offer of food is humbly accepted," Daniel replied. "I'm relieved to know that Lavina is safe."

By the time Daniel removed his pack and outer jacket, a young Abenaki Indian maiden of twelve or thirteen entered the room with a tray of food and a hot pot of tea. He ate all the food. After three hot mugs of tea he was ready to see Lavina. The same Indian maiden motioned for Daniel to follow her to the library where he was requested to sit down. He was impressed with the size and variety of the volumes lining the walls of the wilderness library. A minute later, Lavina slowly walked into the room. Her right arm was in a sling, and she had cuts and bruises about her face, yet Daniel would have recognized her under any condition.

"I can't believe it's you," she cried, embracing him with her left arm.

"I've come to take you home, Lavina."

Chapter Thirteen

It was a poignant moment for both of them. Daniel told her what had happened to Mary, Lee and John Akins.

"I'm so sorry, Daniel. What a horrible tragedy. My dear friend, Mary, was a very special person. I shall pray for you, Daniel. It seems as if the world is tearing itself apart. The forest wilderness is alive with atrocity after atrocity. Who knows when it will all end?" Lavina cried in that soft melodious voice he remembered so well. She looked tired.

"Your father has returned to Portsmouth from Fort Number Four. He took Ruth with him, but, enough about me," Daniel said, looking at her bandaged arm and battered face reminding him of what he had done to Ruth. "What happened to you, Lavina?"

"I had an accident on the river and went over a waterfall. My arm was broken and I was injured on the rocks. Thankfully, one of the students at the mission pulled me to safety. I've been recovering slowly. I'm not strong enough to walk out of the wilderness, Daniel," she told him truthfully. It was more a question than a statement.

"If I have to, I'll carry you to the Connecticut River where I hid the canoe. Once we arrive there, the trip down the river should be quite smooth. If necessary, we could go all the way to the ocean, and then take a ship to Portsmouth."

"I could not impose upon you like that, Daniel."

"What else would a friend do?" Daniel answered quickly. "If I made arrangements for a horse, and guided it to the canoe, would you be able to do that?"

"Yes, I could stay in a saddle," she answered hopefully. "How is my friend, Ruth?"

Daniel avoided her searching eyes. "I might as well tell you right up front that I shot her." Daniel recanted the tale of what he had done and explained his hatred against the Abenaki.

Lavina listened and was mortified about Ruth, but she became more upset about the hate in Daniel's heart, and how it would change him. The silence in the room was compelling as she studied her friend under the dim candles. There was a hardness and tenseness in him that was new and out of character. Her gaze made him uncomfortable, and she began in a calm voice free of judgment. "I can never know the depth of your painful loss, Daniel. To seek justice for Mary's death is a natural human desire. The danger of being the instrument of justice is where the line between revenge and retribution is drawn. Are you capable of knowing when enough is enough, or is this episode in your life going to define you as an Indian-hater from this point on?"

"I don't have the answer for that, Lavina," Daniel replied in a wavering voice. "Right now, the hatred and bitterness is so wrapped up in my head that I'm unable to pass judgment on myself."

"Do you hate me?" Lavina asked curtly.

"You know better than to ask that," he replied angrily.

"Do you hate what I am, an Indian?"

Daniel was uncomfortable with the intensity of the discussion. "I'm too tired to debate you tonight, and we've been over that situation before, Lavina."

"I apologize, Daniel," Lavina said, seeing the fatigue in his eyes. "You can rest here in this room. There's a bunk in the corner behind you. Soldiers and rangers sometimes use it. I'll see you first thing in the morning. I'm so glad to see you again."

"I'm relieved to find that you're not more seriously wounded. I've been worried about you ever since your father told me that you failed to show up at the fort. I am tired. Goodnight, Lavina. It has been a difficult week."

He sat down on the bunk and rested his rifle against the log wall. The second Daniel laid his head against the straw mattress, his eyes closed. The night passed without incident from the besiegers beyond the stockade. He slept soundly until the first rays of a new day entered the room through a small knot hole in the wall. For a moment the strange setting confused him, then he recalled his conversation with Lavina. He reviewed the options available to getting her back to Portsmouth and came to the conclusion that a horse would be the best way to transport her to the canoe. None of the trails were good enough for a wagon, but if she was strong enough to stay in the saddle until they made it to the river, then it was a smooth canoe ride to the fort.

Daniel lit a candle on a small shelf containing a basin and pitcher of water. He quickly cleaned himself and left the room in search of someone who could loan him a horse. Climbing the ladder to the stockade platform, the first person Daniel met was a ranger he had known two years ago in the mountainous region of central New Hampshire.

"The night is gone," claimed Ted Sloane with a wry grin. "We can expect more attempts on the walls. How have you been, Dan?"

"It's good to see you again, Ted. I've come to bring the lady called Lavina back to Portsmouth. Her father would have come for her, but I insisted on taking the trip in his place. Do you know where I could get a horse for a one-way trip to the Connecticut?"

"Sure. Most of the horses in the stable belong to us," Ted claimed. "The brown mare with the white star on its face would be a good choice for your use. She's as gentle as a lamb and can handle loud noises, even gunfire, without being skittish. You're welcome to her if you want."

"I only need her to get to the river. What do I do with her then?"

"Leave her on the western side of the Connecticut at the junction of the Ammonoosic. Hobble her with a short rope so that she can reach water and has some grass to eat. I'll see to it that she's picked up within a couple of days on one of our regular patrols."

"Thank you, Ted," Daniel answered. "I'll remember the favor and do the same for you some day."

"Glad to be of help, Dan. Be careful out there. The Ohio Valley is going to be the spark that rips the frontiers apart from the Ohio to Canada. Mark my words, old friend, be careful!"

"Thanks again, Ted. I've got lots to do and will see you later," Daniel promised. "By the way, how tight is the siege out there?"

"When you and Lavina get ready to leave, let me know. We can clear a passageway for you so that the Indians will never know that you've left the mission. I'll be on watch until noontime."

Reverend Blynn had prepared blankets and food for the dash through enemy-infested forests for Lavina and Daniel. The two large saddlebags could be attached to the saddle on the star-faced mare affectionately called "Lightning." The breakout from the mission had already been planned by the rangers and Reverend Blynn, who would initiate an exchange of fire at the south wall of the stockade.

Lavina entered the compound hanging on the Reverend's arm. It would be easier for Daniel to lead the horse while Lavina lay low over the saddle. He carried his rifle in one hand and Lightning's short halter rope in the other.

"Good morning," Daniel acknowledged Lavina and the Reverend. "As soon as the shooting starts, we're going out at a hard run with me leading the horse. If we get into trouble, you take the reins and push Lightning to the limit. I really mean it, Lavina, you leave me without a thought. Is that understood?" He was dead serious and Lavina noted the determination behind the request and the hard look he gave her.

"Yes," she replied solemnly.

Ted Sloane shook Daniel's hand, tipped his hat to Lavina and climbed the south wall of the stockade. Shots fired from behind the large logs invited fire from the forest. Soon withering musket shots filled the air and a decoy horse was sent through the lines from the south gate. The frightened animal entered the safety of the forest in a hail of bullets from the Indians.

That very moment, the north gate was opened enough for Lightning, with Lavina in the saddle, to squeeze through. Daniel held the reins with his right hand and grasped his primed rifle in his left. They walked at an easy run so as to keep noise to a minimum. A small ridge a half mile from the mission was their immediate goal. When they arrived behind its protective cover, Daniel motioned to Lavina that he wanted to stop and make sure that they had not been spotted.

Five minutes later, Daniel signaled to her that they had left the mission unobserved. He headed easterly toward the Ammonoosic River using a local landmark known as West Mountain as a guide. They skirted several small ponds and streams following the trail that had been heavily used in the past.

Mid-day Daniel picked a small knoll north of the trail as an ideal place to stop for a rest and to eat lunch. They could watch the trail without being noticed. Daniel led Lightning into a small spring that flowed down the hill and across the trail, obliterating any evidence of tracks. He hobbled Lightning at a small clearing of grass and helped Lavina out of the saddle.

"We should be safe here for awhile, Lavina," Daniel announced. "How are you feeling? Tell me the truth. Don't hold back to make me think that everything is all right when it is not."

"I am tired, and I'm not very strong, Daniel. You can see that for yourself. This will be a long trip for me, but I intend to make it. If I felt that it would be better to stop and hold over for a day or two, I'll tell you. That's the truth."

He pulled one of the packs from Lightning and laid out a blanket for Lavina so that she could sit against a yellow birch tree and be kept warm. She shyly excused herself for a call of nature and returned to the blanket with a smile. "You're going to spoil me if you keep this up, Daniel."

The remark pleased him. It was a part of the positive spirit she always had, and he was glad to see that it was still with her. They rested for an hour, eating pemmican and dried venison. Lavina had rested her head against the yellow birch tree and closed her eyes. Within a few seconds she was sleeping. Daniel studied the rough map he had of the area and calculated that at the rate they had traveled that morning, it would take three days to reach the Connecticut.

Daniel gently woke her. "Lavina, it's time we continued on our way."

She opened her eyes and nodded her head. Daniel collected the blanket and left-over food and packed it away. This time, Lavina climbed onto Lightning without his help and pulled on a pair of deerskin gloves. She coiled the reins around her wrists and held onto the saddle horn. The day was sunny but still raw and damp. Whenever they broke out from the over-topping-canopy, the warm rays of the sun felt good. Daniel controlled the horse, and they methodically, step-by-step, made their way towards safety.

Two days after they left the mission, they had already passed West Mountain and expected to reach the Connecticut by nightfall. Their progress had been about as Daniel had expected. They intersected the river late in the afternoon of the third day. Daniel studied both sides of the river and concluded that he had left the canoe south of where they were and turned Lightning slightly inland from the bank so that they would not be noticeable to anyone on the opposite shore. Shortly, they came to the spot where he had hidden the canoe. It was intact.

If he left Lavina here, she would be alone for a few hours while he went upriver to hobble Lightning at the designated spot across from the Ammonoosic River. He looked at Lavina. She was exhausted and was barely able to keep herself in the saddle, but not once did she complain. He helped her out of the saddle.

Daniel dipped a tin cup into the river and passed it to her. "I have a problem, Lavina. My canoe is here in the brush. Ted Sloane requested that I leave Lightning upstream several miles. Will you mind being left alone?"

She turned to him. "I'll stay at the canoe site while you leave the horse at the rendezvous. I'll be all right, Daniel."

"I hate to leave you alone, but it's a better choice than having you try to walk the distance. I know that you're tired, and I promise that you'll be able to rest once we're on the river. Are you hungry?" Daniel asked, unfastening the packs from the saddle.

"No. Thank you for the water. I was thirsty."

"Maybe I can rig a fish line and catch a trout or two from the river. Fresh fish would taste great to me."

"I'd like that too, Daniel," she answered, smiling at his thoughtfulness.

Daniel retrieved the fish line he always kept in his pack and cut a piece of dried venison which he fastened to the fishhook. He tied the fish line to the canoe and threw it in the water. "Maybe we'll get lucky," he grinned. "Why don't you rest in the canoe? I'll place a few branches over you so that it won't be noticeable from the river."

"I'll be all right resting while you're gone," she answered bravely.

Daniel lined the bottom of the canoe with the blankets and helped her into it. "I'll leave my rifle and knife with you here in the canoe. I have my pistol. I'll ride Lightning back to the rendezvous. He's in for a surprise; he'll have to work up a sweat for a change," Daniel chuckled to himself much like his Uncle Lee did and broke several hemlock branches to cover Lavina lying in the canoe. "I'll be back as quickly as I can."

Lavina returned his smile as he mounted Lightning and turned him northward along the river from where they had just come. After a short jog, the horse broke into a full gallop and easily covered the distance to the drop-off point. Daniel picked out a grassy spot next to the river and hobbled Lightning, being sure that he had enough travel on the hobble to drink from the river. With a friendly slap on the rump, Daniel left the horse to fend for himself and was off at a run back to the canoe.

Daniel made the return trip as fast as the horse had taken him north. Completely exhausted and sweaty, he checked the river banks for evidence of intruders and pulled in the fish line. It had a beautiful brook trout thrashing at the end. He removed it and threw it on the shore as he reeled in his line. He carefully removed the branches from the canoe. Lavina awakened with a sudden cry.

"It's okay, Lavina. Rest easy. It's just me," Daniel said, sorry that he had alarmed her. "I'm going to start a small fire with very dry wood a hundred feet or so from the shore. We've got a trout to eat."

An hour later, they had consumed the trout with relish and made preparations for the night. Lavina remained in the canoe while Daniel slept on the ground beside it. Darkness was closing in on them. They were in that portion of the American border, that land between the settlements and Indian territory, where tragedy and death could suddenly erupt with ferocity. It was a lonely and frightening wilderness that cultivated fear of the unknown and the unseen. Daniel kept a lone vigil throughout the night, half asleep and half awake with his rifle clutched in his hands.

The morning dew was moist and chilly in the thick glen where they had spent the night. Daniel gently awoke Lavina and asked her to get ready to leave as soon as possible. They could eat once they got on the river. He positioned his rifle close to the stern and dragged the canoe into the water. Lavina was lying on her back watching him as he climbed in the stern paddling position and placed the pistol at his feet. A cool breeze accompanied them down the Connecticut River.

Daniel felt better now that they were on their way. "Here we go, Lavina. Our next stop will be Fort Number Four!"

Chapter Fourteen

The vast wilderness scene of spruce, white pine, and deciduous trees that Daniel and Lavina were traveling through was a sparsely settled area stretching from the Saint Lawrence River in Canada to the Gulf of Mexico. It was claimed by both the French and the British, and a clash of nations was inevitable in a land far away from the western civilized centers of Europe. During the early 1700's, France instituted a determined policy of defending their claim with military presence by building forts and settlements along the Mississippi River and the Ohio River Valley region. The British were rapidly expanding westward into the very area specifically claimed by France. Conflict was never in question, only its hour of eruption.

The French came to North America primarily as trappers and traders. They freely circulated and lived with the Native Americans; consequently, the French were able to enlist a large number of Indian tribes as their allies against the British and Spanish. The British proceeded to supplant the Indians and occupy the land. Therefore, the French were viewed as less threatening to the Indians' way of life. Cultural survival was at stake.

Daniel saw much more traffic on the Connecticut River. Many settlers were temporarily abandoning their isolated tracts and traveling in heavily laden canoes and rowboats for the safer, more populated areas to the south. Attacks such as Daniel's family experienced were becoming more frequent and more savage. Ranger forces from New Hampshire were constantly on the move within the contested region between the line of settlements a few miles north of Portsmouth and south of Canada. Their presence maintained a certain level of protection, but they could not be everywhere at the same time. Daniel's service with them for a year before he married Mary, had taught him valuable lessons of how to fight and survive in the hostile environment. Their most valuable contribution to safety on the frontier was the intelligence information they gathered of Indian movements and their intentions.

Lavina was lying in the canoe with her eyes closed when Daniel pointed the nose of the canoe into the landing of the large meadow beside Fort Number Four. She awoke and looked around, recognizing the familiar surroundings. Daniel helped her out of the canoe and up the pathway leading to the main gate of the fort. Doctor Hastings' quarters were just inside the gate. Daniel was anxious for Lavina to be checked by the competent physician. They knew each other well and Dr. Hastings greeted her with open arms. Daniel left them alone.

Daniel inquired of the fort commander, Captain Stevens, about the possibility of trains or individuals returning to Portsmouth. There were none, but an Army sailboat was returning to New York the next day. It had a crew of four men, enough to drag the ship across the few portages necessary to navigate the Connecticut all the way to the ocean. Once there, it would have been easy to hitch a ride to Portsmouth on one of the merchant ships plying the eastern seaboard. It was an option he would present to Lavina.

In the meantime, Daniel took a bar of soap and clean clothes and went to the river where he thoroughly scrubbed layers of dirt and grime from his powerful body. The water was frigid, but it felt good to be clean again. When he returned to the fort, Daniel noticed Lavina sitting in the sun with her back against the stockade near the gate.

She looked tired and asked, "Is there anyone going to Portsmouth?"

"Not for a while, Lavina. What did the doctor say?"

"Nothing new. The bruises and abrasions will just have to take their time healing. He thinks I could have a couple of broken ribs, which explains why my chest hurts so much and my shortness of breath. It hurts every time I breathe," Lavina admitted with a sigh of resignation.

"Maybe the ride from the mission was not such a good idea after all." Daniel was concerned for her, and felt helpless. "There's an Army ship going to the coast tomorrow. You could take it and eventually get to Portsmouth by boat."

She was not enthused about the long protracted journey such an option entailed. "That would take a long time."

"What do you suggest then, Lavina?"

112

"Was my father coming back for me?"

"He returned to Portsmouth with Ruth and her baby. I doubt that he would return so soon, but you know how anxious he would be for word about your safety. It may be that he's on his way, but it would be a dangerous trip for him alone."

"I don't know," she cried, closing her eyes against the sun. "I just want to go home. I'm so tired and I hurt all over... I've never felt so miserable in my life. I just don't know, Daniel," she said, discouraged and exhausted.

He placed a comforting hand on her shoulder. "Come now, Lavina. We've come this far, be strong a little longer. It is not safe for two people traveling alone."

Daniel had never seen her so dejected. He was at a loss about what to do. "Do you want to stay at the fort until a ride is available, or do you want to try it in a single horse and wagon? Whatever you decide, I'll agree with."

"Poor Daniel, I'm only thinking of myself. I have no right to place demands on you. Forgive my selfishness."

"I understand your condition. I told your father that I'd bring you safely home, and I intend to do just that, one way or another. If I can find an easy riding wagon in the village, would you be able to handle a ride home?"

"I think so. I prefer that to waiting here. I don't want to put you in danger though, Daniel."

"You be patient for a while, Lavina. I'm going to inquire around the area. I'll be back as soon as I can. Captain Stevens told me that meals are being served up in the great hall. While I'm gone, why don't you get something to eat."

Daniel pulled up an hour later in front of the gates driving a spirited trotting horse with a slender body and long legs. It was pulling a four wheel wagon with a large seat close to the front for a driver and a passenger and a small cargo area behind the seat with two mattresses piled on top of each other. The wagon chassis was originally used on a fancy touring carriage. It had two large springs capable of absorbing many of the bumps on the rough road ahead of them. It was a strange looking rig, but Daniel thought it was the best he could find in the area.

Lavina was sitting at the gate again and saw the strange looking carriage Daniel was driving and smiled. When she saw the mattresses in back, she started to laugh. It hurt inside her chest, but it was nice to share a light moment with Daniel.

"I think I've found an answer to our problem," he said, still grinning. "I bought the whole setup for the promise of herding two Jersey cows to Charlestown from Londonderry next month." He laughed at the good deal he had just made.

Lavina recognized the young man she had known so well in the printing shop years ago. "Thank you, Daniel. I promise to never complain, no matter how long it takes."

"On good stretches of road, this horse can really make good time," he bragged. "Come, let's get our packs and travel as far as possible before nightfall."

His enthusiasm was contagious. He had already purchased enough food to make the trip, and placed extra blankets on the mattress. He gathered their packs from the canoe, offering it to Captain Stevens. Daniel insisted that Lavina ride lying flat on the mattresses with her head close to the front seat to minimize her pain and for protection from branches.

For their first night's stop, Daniel selected a small open area on a hill overlooking the Connecticut River. They had already passed through the small settlement of Walpole. The black flies and mosquitoes were severe, and the breeze at the hilltop would help to keep them at a minimum. Lavina climbed out of the wagon at every stop to exercise her sore muscles. Not to do so would only result in greater pain later on. She was adamant about doing her share of the work. She collected firewood and cooked their meals. She hated being idle and helpless. Daniel was heartened that she was getting stronger.

That evening, he talked a lot about the life he and Mary had. Lavina listened, feeling it was important for him to relive those times. She was a sympathetic listener. It was the first time he had been able to talk freely about the tragedy. The hate and hardness that had pushed him to the edge of sanity was slowly ebbing, and she saw glimpses of the gentle young friend she had spent so much time with copying newspapers in the print shop. They had both changed; yet, that portion of their adolescence was like an ocean of stability in a sea of chaos. They both returned to that period at different times in their lives for strength and direction.

That night, Daniel slept beneath the wagon more soundly than he had since Mary's death. Sharing grief with a friend that truly cared was a consoling experience. That evening their friendship matured beyond what it had been years ago.

Three days later, Daniel turned down the path leading to Lavina's home. Lavina had insisted on riding on the seat beside Daniel while they passed through Market Square in Portsmouth. She would have been embarrassed lying on the mattress like an invalid. Daniel let the mare trot all the way to the Cameron house.

Thom Cameron heard the trotting horse approaching the house and looked out the window to see who it was. He instantly recognized his daughter. "Melinda... Come Melinda, our daughter has come home to us."

Melinda Cameron quietly took her place beside her husband and watched Daniel come to a stop in front of the house. Tears of thanksgiving formed in her dark eyes.

Thom Cameron reached up to lift Lavina from the wagon. He closed his eyes and wrapped his long arms around her. Letting her go to her mother, Thom looked up at Daniel. "Words can't express what's in our hearts, Daniel. Thank you. How can I ever repay you?"

Daniel jumped down from the wagon and shook his hand. "It was a privilege, Mister Cameron. Just to see the joy on your faces is payment enough."

Daniel also embraced Mrs. Cameron. She had a little more gray in her hair. In many ways, she was more beautiful than ever. "Thank God both of you have returned safely. Our prayers have been with you, Daniel. Your aunt and uncle will be pleased to see you."

"It's nice to be home, Mrs. Cameron," Daniel said, looking over her head at Ruth standing in the doorway of the house. A heavy sense of guilt came over him. "How is Ruth doing?"

"Why don't you ask her yourself, Daniel," suggested Mrs. Cameron, releasing him.

Ruth greeted Lavina with relief and happiness that she had been brought safely through miles of wilderness. "I was afraid for the worst, Lavina. The border is becoming so dangerous." She looked at Daniel as if she was still searching for the reason that he shot her. "My wound is healing, Daniel. My daughter, Morning Mist, is doing well."

Lavina spoke to Daniel. "Home looks so good to me. Thank you, Daniel. Tell your aunt and uncle that I'll be over to see them soon. What are your plans now?"

"Well, I've got a commitment to return to Number Four with two Jersey cows from Londonderry within a couple of weeks," he casually replied.

"Are you going to return the wagon, or are you going to keep it?" she asked with a big grin.

"Maybe your father or Uncle Lee can find a use for it," he chuckled. "I'll ride the mare back to Charlestown," he said, turning to go.

"Thank you for making my homecoming possible." Lavina kissed him on the cheek and let her parents guide her into the house.

Daniel turned the mare into his uncle's barn and unhitched the wagon. Old Andy curiously watched the mare walk into his stall and begin to eat some of Andy's hay in the manger. Daniel closed the stall door and picked up his pack and rifle. He had arrived undetected.

Aunt Maureen answered his knock on the door. At first, she did not recognize him with his beard. Then she looked into his eyes and swept him into her arms. She had been afraid that she would never see him again.

"It's nice to be home again, Aunt Maureen. You haven't changed a bit since Mary and I left for the cabin," he told her. Just being here without his Mary made him feel alone. The poignancy of the moment was also felt by his aunt.

She faced him, looking into his sad eyes, and a moist film clouded her vision. "We've been so worried about you, Daniel. My, you've grown much this past year. Come into the kitchen. Your uncle is in the print shop."

"How is he, Aunt Maureen?"

"He's doing well for a man his age. The hard life he lived as a soldier has been taking its toll over the years. He's a little slower than he used to be, but his mind is as sharp as ever. Go to him, Daniel. He'll be relieved to have you home."

The scent of drying ink could be smelled before he opened the door. The familiar print shop had been Daniel's favorite place in the house. Opening the door slowly, Daniel saw his Uncle Lee with small glasses on the tip of his nose, bending over a copy he had just removed from the platen, "Hello, Uncle Lee," Daniel announced, closing the door behind him.

Lee Cullen turned towards the familiar voice and uttered a cry, "Thank God! Now I can breathe easier, lad. Come, let me take a better look at yea."

Daniel embraced the man he loved and respected more than any man alive. His hair was whiter, and the shadows beneath his eyes were longer and darker, but his eyes were clear and bright as ever.

"How good it is to see you, Daniel. Your aunt and I have been sick with worry since Thom told us about Mary and the baby," Lee was filled with emotion. "What is there to say that you haven't already heard? My heart grieves for you."

Daniel released him and looked over his shoulder to see what he was printing. "You've developed quite a reputation as a crusader and spokesman on current events. Even way out in the sparsely settled areas, people have heard of you or have actually read a copy of the Coastal Beacon. It always makes me proud to call you my uncle."

They sat in the print shop and talked about his trip back with Lavina. Daniel truthfully admitted to shooting Ruth. Uncle Lee shook his head and met Daniel's look of remorse. "Don't let the revenge consume you, lad. In the end, it will destroy you, too, and what would your Aunt Maureen and I do if that should take place?"

It was a simple and honest admission of the love they held for him. Daniel was moved to tears by the sincere statement. "The moment that Ruth was hit, I lost much of my fervor for revenge, Uncle. Right now, I'm not sure that justice has been done or not. It's hard to rationalize the bestial way Mary and John died. Individuals that carried out the brutal acts can hardly be classified as human beings."

"I don't have any answers for that, Daniel, except that the Lord tells us that we should leave vengeance to Him. Eventually those in need of punishment will receive what they reaped. It's too heavy a burden for a mere mortal to carry," Uncle Lee advised him.

Daniel nodded his head in agreement. He was exhausted and hungry from the long arduous trip. "Do you think that Aunt Maureen might have any apple pie left over?"

Uncle Lee laughed and grabbed Daniel around the shoulders. "My boy, I'm sure she does, because I had a hearty serving this morning.

Come, let's have something to eat to celebrate the safe return of you and the lovely Lavina."

For several days, Daniel slept and ate to the point where he was afraid of getting fat and lazy. His Aunt Maureen was pleased to push food in front of him to satisfy his large appetite. He drank glass after glass of cool milk fresh from the spring cooler beside the woodshed. He shaved his beard off on the second day, hardly recognizing himself in the mirror.

Uncle Earl, Aunt Ursula, and his cousin Ellen all came one day to celebrate his safe return home. His two aunts put on a feast in his favor that was fit for royalty. Fresh baked bread from Aunt Maureen's oven and succulent lobsters from Uncle Earl's traps on the York River were enjoyed by all. Daniel would always remember the family's show of affection with fondness. Ellen wept in his arms when she saw him. He was always proud to carry the Cullen name, and the celebration seemed to elevate him as a select member of the clan. He knew that he had truly come home!

Right after Uncle Earl and his family left for York, Lavina and Ruth stopped by for a visit and met him in the barn. He had told them earlier that he was ready to return to Fort Number Four with the cows from Londonderry. Both of the young women carried an arm in a sling. Daniel was still self-conscious around Ruth. "It's good to see you again, Ruth. Is the arm improving?" he asked awkwardly.

"I believe it is," Ruth answered. "Mrs. Cameron took me to see a doctor in Portsmouth. He seemed to think that it was healing satisfactorily. It'll leave me disfigured for the rest of my life."

Daniel winced when he heard the words. "I'm sorry. I don't know how to say it so that you'll believe me, but it's true."

"I do believe you," Ruth answered. "But it doesn't change the fact that you shot me deliberately without reason. It makes me feel cheap and disposable."

"Now, now," Lavina interceded. "Ruth has been grieving the loss of her husband. You, more than anyone else, Daniel, should understand what she's going through. You both have had great losses and should have compassion for each other's pain."

"I know how she feels, and I don't take her anger personally, but the fact remains that I did try to kill her simply because she was an

Indian. In my rage, I confused justice with vengeance, and I was wrong. I hope that someday she'll be able to forgive me."

"I'm sure she will, Daniel," Lavina added. Ruth quietly left them and went in the house to see his Aunt Maureen. "I'm glad to see you looking so well, Daniel."

"And how are you, Lavina? You look less drawn and tired than the day I dropped you off."

"I'm much better. The broken ribs will take time mending. As for my arm, it doesn't hurt anymore. Mother is babying both of us, and we're loving it," Lavina giggled impishly.

"I'm leaving tomorrow for Londonderry. I'll ride the mare instead of walking. I don't know why, but I believe that I'm going to travel west towards the Ohio Valley. I can't sit around doing nothing, and I'm not yet ready to help Uncle Lee in the print shop on a steady basis. It's hard to explain. Right now, I'm too restless to settle down."

Lavina looked into his eyes. "I'll worry about you, Daniel Cullen. However, I understand your need to follow your heart and dreams, wherever they take you. Nothing else can guide us to fulfillment. Just remember that you have friends here that are praying for your safety and welfare. I hate the French, but they have a nice way of saying good-bye. Bon voyage, my old friend. May the north star guide you and lead you safely back home." She kissed him on the cheek and slowly walked away.

Chapter Fifteen

Five Months Later (October 30, 1753)

Daniel had a strong desire to be at the center of events which were shaping and molding the new land he had come to love. He took a job guiding several supply wagons to an isolated outpost on the northern border of Maryland called Wills Creek, a border settlement located on the Potomac River containing a large warehouse. It was the base of operations for the Ohio Company, a speculative land organization.

When the supply wagons arrived at Wills Creek, Daniel was met by Christopher Gist, a legendary frontiersman, actively involved in establishing settlements in the Ohio Valley. He was a sturdy well-built man, a little on the lean side, with dark blue eyes. He didn't talk much, but when he did speak, people listened.

"Where are you going from here, Cullen?" Gist asked him, casually evaluating the sturdy youth.

"I haven't planned that far ahead, Mr. Gist," Daniel answered truthfully.

"Would you be interested in signing on as a scout for a journey into French territory on a diplomatic mission?"

"A diplomatic mission, by whom?" Daniel asked with interest.

"Well," Gist slowly began, spitting out the tobacco he had been chewing. "It seems that a settlement I had organized on the Ohio River a few years ago triggered a response from the French who are pushing an ambitious policy building a line of forts that will eventually run from the Saint Lawrence River to New Orleans. Their intention is to eliminate any English settlements from taking place west of the Allegheny Mountains."

Daniel was interested about the prospects of being at the center of contentions between the French and the English, and listened carefully.

After all, he had left New Hampshire to see new places and to overcome the emptiness he felt.

Gist continued in his slow moderate way. "An old friend of mine, Major George Washington of the Virginia Militia, has been commissioned to carry an official document from Governor Dinwiddie of Virginia. The message is an official request for the French to vacate the Ohio Valley, because the French are restricting the rights of English subjects to settle the area."

"You mean a small group of diplomats are traveling over a hundred miles into French territory teaming with large numbers of French soldiers and unfriendly Indian allies, and they're asking them to leave?" Daniel asked in disbelief.

"That's right, Cullen," Gist answered. "If the French win control of the Ohio Valley, the English will be limited to the land between the mountains and the Atlantic Ocean. Fortunes paid out in land speculation would be lost, and dreams of an English Empire would be dashed to pieces."

"It sounds like a fool's errand to me," said Daniel, shrugging his shoulders.

"I'll leave that for the politicians to decide. Right now, I've been informed by a dispatch rider that Major Washington is on his way here with a small group of men. Would you like to join me on this venture? Travel over the mountains will be difficult in the wintertime. The mission will take us into next year, possibly until spring."

"If we live to tell it," Daniel smiled wryly. "Sure, I'll go along with you, Mr. Gist. I have my own mount if you're going by horseback."

"We have a few pack horses and a couple of riding horses. Personally, I'm a believer in traveling by foot through Injun territory. A man can walk just as fast as a horse, and he doesn't leave a traceable trail behind." Christopher Gist carefully watched Daniel for his response.

"I agree, sir. When is this diplomatic mission going to start?" Daniel asked.

"I expect Major Washington within a few days. He plans to take on more supplies and add a few extra hands. I'm going along as his guide. You'll help me get them safely there and back," Gist replied, appraising this serious young Scotch lad.

Daniel settled his account with the warehouse for the wagon train he had just escorted and placed his trotter horse in their livery stable for the duration of his mission with Gist. Then he purchased some bars of lead to melt down in his bullet mold. It was difficult to find bullets to fit his caliber rifle. Most of the frontiersmen used the British Brown Bess long musket, which used a larger caliber.

Two days later, Washington rode into the Ohio Company compound. He was a large man with a commanding presence, but he was most conspicuous by the way he rode his horse. Horse and rider were in complete harmony with each other. It was a picture of grace in motion. The man was over six feet tall with wide powerful shoulders and a narrow waist. He exuded strength and agility.

Daniel was certain that it was the much awaited Major Washington, and was surprised that the man was about his own age. Washington dismounted and was sincerely pleased to see Christopher Gist. The two men were friends. Daniel's instincts told him that something important was about to take place, and he was thrilled to be a part of it.

The mission left Wills Creek the last day in October under sunny skies, heading northwest into the Shenandoah Valley. They left Maryland and entered southern Pennsylvania. Warm, cheerful days in November were a rarity, and from the first day the party was chilled by freezing rains, making it difficult to keep their weapons dry and operable.

Daniel took his orders from Gist, who was an experienced traveler in that part of the country. He told Daniel that Indians were certainly watching their progress from hidden locations. The small nine-man party was being run like a military operation. Pickets were posted every evening around their encampment, and once underway, flank walkers secured the main column from surprise attacks. Daniel was assigned to the right flank where he kept abreast of the column a few hundred feet parallel to the trail. Gist was usually in front of the column about the same distance to provide advance warning of an ambush.

On their first night encampment beside a clear bubbling stream, Gist introduced Daniel to Major Washington. He wore his dark brown hair in a cue at the back of his head and was dressed in well-worn buckskin pants and shirt, like most of the party. Washington's angular face was pock-scarred. Daniel later learned it was from smallpox while he was in Barbados with his half-brother Lawrence a few years before.

Gist told Daniel that Washington had recently leased a large plantation on the Potomac River from his sister-in-law. His brother Lawrence had died two years ago. Daniel was impressed with the man, not just for his strength and robust physique, but for his regal countenance and mild manners. He was always a gentleman and interacted with each member of the party with sincere humor, making them feel that they were important to him and that he enjoyed their companionship.

The difficulty of traversing the steep hills and dark, sunless valleys worried Daniel and Gist. It was going to be a physically demanding journey, especially with the onset of winter in the mountainous regions of northern Pennsylvania. The prospect of becoming snowbound was not unrealistic and they could never carry enough food to last the party through a long winter. Game was scarce during the winter months, especially in the higher elevations.

The party pressed onward with an urgency commensurate with their situation. Each day became colder and colder, and the snow became deeper and deeper as they climbed through the mountains. About thirty miles from the Ohio River, they came to the Monongahela River where they spotted the cabin of an English trader. Washington spoke to the trader about Indian activity in the area. The trader told him that Indian allies of the French were always on the prowl, and travelers should take prudent measures for their safety. Washington was also informed that the highest ranking French officer had died and was being replaced by an officer who was located farther north at Fort Le Boeuf near Fort Presque Isle on Lake Erie.

Thanking the trader, Washington left with a renewed sense of urgency to reach the Ohio River as quickly as possible. Three days later, they reached the confluence of the Ohio, Monongahela and Allegheny Rivers. They heard the loud roar of the swirling waters before they could see the rivers. Daniel was the first to see the three-river juncture and was mesmerized by the turbulence and power of the treacherous stretch of water. Washington rushed forward.

"It's a sight to behold, Major," Daniel exclaimed, sweeping his arm before the boiling water.

"It is that, Cullen. We've made good progress. I'd like to pause in our journey to study this area. It's a logical location for a fortress to help us control the Ohio Valley."

"You're correct, Major," Daniel replied. "Evidently, the French are not strong enough this far south in the valley, or they would have already established some type of bastion at this important water cross-road."

Washington shook his head in agreement. "My sentiments too, Cullen. I was able to study and observe several forts constructed in Barbados a few years ago when I visited the island with my brother, Lawrence. I'm not that experienced in military affairs, but it seems to me that the best location for a fort should be the defensive command of a large portion of the surrounding landscape, with reasonable proximity to firewood and water. Well, Cullen, why don't we set up camp right here and get on with our survey of the area?"

"Okay, Major," Daniel complied.

Washington explored the area thoroughly and noted in his book that he had found a site that was perfect. The proposed fort could be called Fort Prince George after the King's son. The next day, they continued northwesterly along the Ohio River banks and ran into a blinding snowstorm, the worst encountered so far. The swirling wind and snow penetrated their clothing and fragile tents. That night, Daniel wrapped himself in a bearskin to keep warm.

Two days from the forks, they came upon a place known as Logstown where Washington met an old acquaintance, Half King, a Seneca Chief and an envoy for the Six Nation Confederacy made up primarily of Mohawk and Iroquois tribes. The Chief had been sent to negotiate with the French, but was rudely treated by the French commander who told him that France would repulse with force any Indian or English attempt to invade or settle in the region or who questioned their authority.

After patiently listening to his complaints, Washington assured Half King that he would convey the message to the Governor of Virginia when he returned.

Half King and several of his companions accompanied Washington northward. About a hundred miles north of the forks, the party arrived at Venango, which had been a trading post and was now occupied by several French junior officers. They cordially greeted

Washington and his party. The horses were weak and in need of rest and nutrition. The French provided forage and grain for the horses. The officers explained to Washington that they were not able to receive his message. Their new commanding officer was staying at Fort Boeuf, several miles north on French Creek. Washington requested permission to leave a part of his team at Venango while Gist, Daniel, and the interpreter Jacob van Braam, accompanied Washington to Fort Le Boeuf.

Washington's reduced party left Venango the next day in another blistering snowstorm. They were generously fortified by the food and fine French wines from the French officers. Washington had removed his buckskin clothing for a more appropriate attire for a representative of the King of England to meet with a high ranking French officer. Fort Le Boeuf was a rectangular fortress bristling with cannon and manned by one hundred French soldiers. It was built on French Creek about twenty miles from Lake Erie. It had been a difficult day's journey, and they arrived at the height of the storm.

The French graciously received them. Washington and van Braam were led to the commandant's quarters, while Gist, Daniel, and Half King were directed to the enlisted men's quarters. Hot food, tea and wines were lavishly provided. Half King immediately began to consume large quantities of wine. Given the circumstances, the rest of the party were circumspect. Washington had warned them beforehand to work hard at maintaining warm and friendly relations with their guests. That evening, Daniel and Gist, to their great relief, carried Half King to a bunk where he slept off his drunkenness.

Daniel and Gist had no way of knowing what was taking place in the Commandant's office. For three days, they rested and gorged themselves with massive amounts of roast venison and all the hot tea they could drink. They were also treated to a drink Daniel had never tasted before – hot chocolate. He instantly liked its sweet flavor. The commissary soldiers told him, in broken English, that it was made from cocoa beans grown in South America.

On the third day, Major Washington informed Daniel and Gist that they were ready to retire to Venango. He quickly changed his clothes back to buckskin and left with generous supplies of food and wine. Recognizing that French Creek was beginning to freeze over, they furiously paddled southward. Gist was most anxious to learn what had taken place. Washington was sober and quiet for several miles.

They made a brief stop to eat some delicious blueberry pemmican and wine. Washington finally spoke. "You've been wondering about our mission, Christopher."

"I hope it's good news, Major."

"The Commandant informed me that my request for the French to abandon their fort-building-policy in the Ohio Valley was, in his opinion, outrageous. He would convey the message to Marquis Duquesne for an official answer. My gut feeling is that they're going to expand their ability to control the area, which means building more forts." Major Washington paused and watched the water passing by. "I'm most anxious to return to Virginia. The Governor has been given authority by the King to forcibly evict any French forces from the valley that interferes with British settlements or land speculation in the disputed area."

"You mean there could be war?" Daniel asked.

"I'm afraid it might, Cullen. I have a hunch that the Governor will immediately commission the construction of a fortress strategically located to partially control the territory. I would not be surprised if the French have the same idea. Therefore, it's imperative that we get the job done first."

They placed the two canoes back in the water, anxious to link up with the rest of their party at Venango. Once they arrived, Gist determined that the horses were still too weak to make a forced march back to Wills Creek. Washington decided to push on alone with Gist and two of the strongest horses. The balance of the party could travel at a more leisurely pace the animals could maintain. The two leaders each filled a pack and turned to Daniel and Jacob van Braam.

"I'm going to depend on the two of you, Jacob and Daniel, to bring the rest of the party to the Ohio Company warehouse at Wills Creek," Washington said in a sober tone.

"We'll follow in your tracks as quickly as the animals allow," Jacob replied.

"You can depend on us, Major," Daniel added. "May I request that as soon as you determine what is going to take place, leave word for us at the warehouse? I'm not ready to return to New Hampshire yet. If you are to embark on another mission, I would be proud to accompany you, Major."

"I appreciate your offer, Cullen. You are a credit to the other hearty New Hampshire men that I respect. I promise to send a dispatch rider with orders and news as it becomes available."

"Thanks, Major. Good luck on your journey. That goes for you too, Gist, you've been a good trail companion, and I'll miss your wise and experienced ways."

The return trip south to Wills Creek was slower and more difficult than the northern trek for Jacob and Daniel. Deep snow, half frozen streams and swamps and rugged terrain through the mountains exhausted man and beast. Jacob van Braam slipped on an icy rock, injuring his leg at the forks. Daniel then took primary responsibility for guiding the party out of the treacherous mountains to safety. It was a contented and relieved group of men who finally walked into the compound at Wills Creek.

They arrived in mid January, ten days after Washington and Gist. Christopher Gist had left instructions for the party to be given the best in accommodations available at the Warehouse. Daniel and the rest of the team ate a hearty meal of venison stew and hot tea, then collapsed on the bunk assigned to them in a warm room with a fireplace. They slept without waking for twenty-four hours.

Chapter Sixteen

Daniel awoke, wiped his tired eyes, remembered where he was, and climbed out of the bunk. At the end of the room was a large washstand with a glass basin and several pitchers of water. He washed and dressed in a clean set of buckskin pants and a soft doeskin shirt Lavina had given to him before he left Portsmouth.

The small mirror above the washstand reflected a bearded face he hardly knew. Daniel searched his pack for a straight razor and shaved himself. He found it convenient and warmer to let his beard grow on the trail, but it always itched. The clean shave felt good. He now felt more respectable as his Aunt Maureen used to tell his Uncle Lee when he needed a shave.

While he was organizing his pack, a young employee of the Ohio Company entered the bunkhouse. "I have a letter that came to you this morning, Mister Cullen."

"Thank you," Daniel accepted the letter anxiously. "By the way, if I wrote a letter, how soon would it be picked up by a dispatch rider?"

"Every other day, sir. The dispatch packet goes directly to Alexandria, Virginia," the boy replied. "Whenever you're ready, there's always hot food in the kitchen beside the bunkhouse."

"Thank you again, young man," Daniel said, examining the envelope. It was a letter from Major Washington.

Dear Daniel Cullen,

Our return to Virginia involved a couple of exciting events which Christopher Gist may relate to you at his convenience. I want to thank you for your loyal and steadfast performance assisting me in carrying out a very delicate diplomatic mission. I do not have any specific news that I am at liberty to divulge at this time, but I'm certain that within a few days decisions will be made and implementation directed. I'll inform you via dispatch courier.

Again, thank you for your loyal service.

Sincerely,

George Washington

Major, Virginia Militia

Daniel spent several days at Wills Creek evaluating his situation and checking out the prospects for future work. Everybody he talked to believed that a conflict with the French was inevitable. War had not been declared, and the wealthiest province in the British colonies, Virginia, was reluctant to accept war as a possible resolution for the border disputes. Faced with the same situation, Daniel had a feeling that the people of New Hampshire would not hesitate to declare war on France. Virginia was still vacillating even though the Governor had been authorized by the King of England to exercise force to solve the encroachment problem west of the Allegheny Mountains.

One day while Daniel was grooming his horse, Blackie, Christopher Gist entered the livery stables looking for him. "I've looked all over for you, Dan."

"Hi, Mr. Gist," Daniel greeted the frontiersman.

"I've just been informed that the Governor of Virginia, Robert Dinwiddie, has authorized the construction of a fort at the forks of the Allegheny and Ohio Rivers."

"You mean the structure Washington roughed out?"

"Aye, the same," Gist nodded his head and continued. "The proposal to build the fort has been given to a fur trader by the name of William Trent. He'll be commissioned a major in the Virginia Militia. He is authorized to raise a work force of forty men and the necessary equipment and supplies to complete the job."

"That sounds interesting. I've been thinking that if something for work doesn't show up soon, I would head back to New England. Are you offering me a job?"

"I don't have the authority, Dan. Trent is an old friend, and I'm sure he would like to take you on as a scout and guide. After all, you just came back from that country."

"I would prefer going as a private citizen rather than a member of the militia. If I ever join any military outfit, it'll be the New Hampshire Militia. My loyalties are strong in that area," Daniel proudly proclaimed. "I served a year or so with the New Hampshire Rangers. If the frontier is going to explode, I'm returning to New Hampshire."

"I like a man who's loyal." Gist slapped him on the back. "Trent will be in touch with you when he arrives. He's going to need a lot of building material and a number of heavy draft animals, which are difficult to come by on the border. May I convey your approval to Trent?"

"Sure, Mr. Gist. It sounds like an interesting operation." As soon as Gist left, Daniel sat down and wrote a letter to his Aunt Maureen and Uncle Lee. They had been in his thoughts more than ever.

January 21, 1754

Dear Aunt Maureen and Uncle Lee,

It has now been almost a year since Mary's death. Much has happened to me in the ensuing months. The hurt is always with me, and I'm afraid that time has not diminished the horrific specter of the way she died.

I can honestly tell you that I am no longer seeking revenge and am still horrified that I fired upon Ruth and her child with the sole intention of killing her simply because she was an Indian. That cowardly act has curbed my desire for retribution. If you see her, please convey my apologies, again, and tell her that I continue to pray for her complete recovery.

I miss all of you very much. You seem so very far away from this desolate wilderness. For some reason I cannot understand, I had a desire to leave New England after Mary's death. Perhaps I'm searching for the peace of mind and serenity that filled the short time we spent together. I also miss

130

the harmony and support that was so much a part of growing into manhood within your home. Someday you'll look out the window and I'll be there. Until then, please keep me in your prayers.

I don't have enough paper to adequately describe what I have been doing. It is just possible that I have participated in a very historical journey to the Ohio River Valley. I'll fill you in on the project when I come home.

Please take care of yourselves and never forget that I love you both more than life itself. I shall always strive to be worthy of your love and respect. Love to both of you.

Daniel

Wills Creek,

Maryland

A week later, Daniel was mounted on Blackie, leading a column of workers, militiamen, and heavily-laden supply wagons towards the Monongahela River. The column consisted of forty men commanded by Ensign Ward, a young energetic carpenter who knew most of the men in his company. Daniel liked Ward and the two soon became good friends. He was comfortable with the responsibility and treated the contingent like a large family. Ward was firm, fair, and confident that he was going to succeed in his assigned mission of constructing a fort.

The absence of Captain Trent from the column, Daniel believed, was significant. Trent had excused himself from the company the first day out from Wills Creek. When he left, he spoke briefly to Ward who had remained silent about his departure. Daniel felt uncomfortable with a commander voluntarily leaving his command for no apparent reason.

They had just left the plantation belonging to Mr. Gist, where they picked up two teams of Clydesdales and three matched teams of Shire horses, each hauling sturdily constructed wagons filled to capacity with grain and forage. The powerful work horses were some of the most beautiful animals Daniel had ever seen, especially the Clydesdales with their large white fur-covered hooves. The teams showed no exertion in pulling the largest and heaviest wagons in the column.

The trail George Washington had used was not wide enough for some of the wagons, so several woodsmen and a team of horses led the column to widen the road as needed. Daniel's job was to ride the point and scout in advance of the column. Militia riders patrolled their flanks. When trees or rocks blocked the wagons, the road widening crew went to work extracting the trees, roots and all. Even though it was winter with a foot of snow cover, the depth of frost in the ground was only a few inches, not enough to prevent the crew from uprooting the trees.

When a tree had to be removed, a woodsman climbed the tree as high as possible where he attached a heavy chain around the trunk affecting a powerful leverage advantage. Most trees up to fourteen inches in diameter could be readily tipped out of the ground with roots attached. When the teams were pulling down trees, the teamsters controlled their animals with firm voice commands. They told Daniel that a nervous horse was capable of killing or badly injuring a teamster. The animals responded by digging into the snow-covered ground, their powerful muscles straining with their stomachs almost touching the snow. The exhibition of the superbly trained animals and professional teamsters impressed Daniel.

They crossed the swift-running Monongahela River at a convenient fording area. So far, the trek to the forks had been uneventful, and they reached the proposed fort site without incident. The site Washington had selected for the fort was located at the forks of the Ohio and Allegheny Rivers, and had requested that it be called Fort Prince George in honor of the heir apparent King of England.

Ensign Ward ordered the column to set up an encampment as close to the proposed center of the stockade as possible. Pickets were established at several crucial locations around the designated fort area. Daniel and Ensign Ward discussed their plans to secure the construction site.

"Starting tomorrow at first break of day, I plan to begin a perimeter patrol of up to six miles to the north of the fort. We saw little or no sign of activity south or west of the Monongahela River. The river itself will act as a reasonable defensive feature. I'll check with you every day, Ensign. Do you have anything to add to my duties?" Daniel asked.

Ensign Ward looked at his young guide. "You've laid out a sound plan, Daniel. I like the idea of you constantly patrolling our perimeter. That will make our work easier and give the men a little more peace of mind knowing that they'll be forewarned about any approaching parties, hostile or friendly. I never expected to use you as a worker, so follow your instincts and do not attempt to make contact with strangers. You're more valuable to us sounding the alarm than initiating conflict. Good luck and be careful out there."

"I plan to, Ensign," Daniel smiled and left to attend to Blackie.

Tents were set up to temporarily house the company and to store their supplies and equipment. Daniel was assigned to a tent with several teamsters who owned the beautiful Clydesdale draft horses. Most of them were as sturdy and fit as the teams they drove. Daniel enjoyed their camaraderie. They collected pine and hemlock branches to serve as mattresses to cover the frozen ground. Daniel slept on his heavy bearskin and covered himself with two British Army woolen blankets. There was no heat in the tents, so most of the men slept fully clothed.

Work clearing the site of trees and brush began immediately. Day after day, the site was a beehive of activity with the constant "chomp" of sharp axes fitting trees and logs into useable shapes to build the stockade fence and other structures. The tempo never ceased, for the men were anxious to get the fortification to the point where they could turn it over to Virginia Militia or regular British Army forces. Occasionally, the weather was cold and blustery, but as time passed, each day became warmer and the snow and frost were beginning to disappear, turning the site into a muddy hole.

Daniel paid special attention to the area to the north, the most likely direction for French or Indian intrusion. He knew that Fort Le Boeuf was on French Creek, which flowed into Allegheny River at Venango. His main worry was that they would come by boat or canoe, and the construction crew at the forks was ill prepared to hold off a major force. The only ammunition available was carried in each man's horn and bullet pouch. As spring approached, Daniel's vigilance increased.

One day in mid-April, Daniel spotted a large number of boats and canoes coming down the Allegheny River. Patiently waiting until he could determine the identity of the occupants, he was alarmed. It was an armada consisting of several hundred French troops. Some of the lead boats even had swivel cannons attached to the gunwales.

Daniel immediately left his hiding place and rushed to spread the alarm. He was three miles from the fort construction site and ran as fast as he could, shouting to isolated tree-felling crews on his way that the French were coming.

Ensign Ward heard Daniel yelling and ran to intercept him. "What is it, Daniel?"

Daniel reported what he had seen. "They outnumber our construction company ten to one, Ensign."

A frown crossed the soldier's face. "Well, we can't say that it is unexpected," Ensign Ward exclaimed. He turned to the men at the fort site. "We can at least take defensive positions and see what develops." Ward shouted orders for the men to take their pre-arranged defense positions and to double check their powder and flints.

Daniel quickly left the construction site, following along the river bank. A half mile from the forks, he met a group of three French soldiers carrying a white flag. A young Captain approached Daniel and spoke in broken English, "I am Captain Pierre Contrecoeur, commandant of the French forts on the Ohio. Would you take me to your commanding officer?"

Daniel was aghast. The officer had a friendly demeanor and was very polite. "Yes, you may follow me," he answered, leading the way toward the fort site.

Ensign Ward saw Daniel and the French soldiers enter the cleared area, and waited for them to approach. There was a proud confident look on the Ensign's face as he announced himself to the advancing troupe. "I am Ensign Ward of the Virginia Militia. We are in the process of building a fort at this location under the direction of the Governor of Virginia and the King of England."

Daniel thought the Ensign handled himself with great dignity.

"I am Captain Pierre Contrecoeur. I have over five hundred French marines staged a short distance down the river. I come to request that you leave this area and return to wherever you came from. England and France are not at war, therefore, I will allow you to take whatever equipment and supplies you can carry, including your horses."

"And if I refuse, Captain?" Ensign Ward asked.

"It is not my desire to attack your company, Ensign, but if you refuse my offer, I shall do so. I must warn you that we also have several swivel guns with us. The bloodshed would be heavy and meaningless, Ensign. You have already shown great courage and fortitude by coming here to build your fort. You have nothing to gain by refusing, except dead Virginia soldiers."

Captain Contrecoeur checked his watch and continued. "It is now 11:20 A.M. I shall give you forty minutes to reply."

Ensign Ward turned around and surveyed the men under his command. He knew it would be irresponsible to fight. His company was mostly workmen, not soldiers. The thought that he would lose many of them was frightening. He drew himself to full attention and turned back to the French party with a grim set to his jaw. "I accept the terms you have given us, Captain Contrecoeur. It will take us a couple of hours to strike our tents and harness the teams. Will you give us time to do that?"

"Of course, Ensign Ward." Captain Contrecoeur shook his head. "Do not take this personally, Ensign Ward. You have made a sound decision, and I understand how difficult it is. Soldiers the world over are pretty much the same. I will grant you the courtesy of leaving with your command intact. Simply inform your superiors that we intend to complete the structure and call it Fort Duquesne."

"I will do that," Ensign Ward replied, saluting the French officer. Daniel noticed a nervous twitch under Ensign Ward's left eye as he again faced his men, instructing them in a clear strained voice. "Strike the tents and pack the wagons men. We're moving out."

It was a stirring moment when the proud Virginians were forced by the sheer preponderance of French troops to abandon the site. Ensign Ward warned the men not to be foolish and try something that might bring destruction down on themselves and their comrades, and admonished them to obey his orders to leave as soon as possible.

Daniel packed his personal belongings and helped his tent mates take down the tent. He fastened his pack on Blackie's saddle and mounted, holding his rifle across the saddle. Captain Contrecoeur carefully watched him. Their eyes met, and for a split second, he saw understanding and compassion in the young French officer. Daniel acknowledged him and turned Blackie eastward towards the rising sun. It was a bitter moment. Captain Contrecoeur saluted him and Ensign Ward as they evacuated the compound across the river.

After Daniel led the company across the Allegheny River, he reined Blackie off to one side and waited for Ensign Ward and his adjutant to come abreast of him.

Tears of defeat and humiliation ran down Ensign Ward's face. "You did the only thing you could, Ensign. I thought you handled the situation with grace and dignity. It has been a privilege to have served under your command."

Ensign Ward nodded his head acknowledging Daniel's words. "I didn't think it would hurt so much, Daniel."

"You saved your command from annihilation, Ensign. Our day will come. We'll just have to be patient," Daniel counseled.

"You have a quiet wisdom, Daniel," Ward replied. "We should use even more diligence on our return to Wills Creek. I did not see any Indians with the French. I'm not sure what that signifies, but we should be alert to potential ambushes. Would you continue your scouting ahead of us? I'll see that adequate flank riders are posted."

"I'll ride ahead and locate a suitable place to stop for the evening, Ensign," Daniel replied.

"Thank you."

The trail leading past Gist's settlement and over the mountains was easier on their return trip. Unbeknown to Ensign Ward or Daniel, a Virginia Regiment had been authorized and funded by the Virginia Congress to limit the encroachment of French forces in the Ohio Valley. Lieutenant Colonel George Washington was made second in command of the regiment, and left Alexandria, Virginia, on April 1, 1754, arriving at Wills Creek at about the same time that Ensign Ward was forced to leave Fort Prince George. Washington heard of the surrender from a dispatch runner before Ward's company arrived at Wills Creek.

The Commander of the Virginia Regiment, Colonel Frye, had left Winchester, Virginia with the second half of the regiment's troops. He accidentally fell off his horse and was killed, leaving Washington in full command. Washington was waiting for the additional troops at the Ohio Company's warehouse at Wills Creek.

Upon his return to the warehouse, Daniel decided to return home to New Hampshire once the company was safely encamped at Wills Creek. He was purchasing supplies for the journey when Colonel

Washington sent him a note requesting a visit. Daniel dropped what he was doing and accompanied the orderly back to Washington's command tent located on the Potomac River.

Washington was studying some maps when Daniel announced himself. "I'm glad to see you again, Daniel," Washington exclaimed. "Ward has told me about your humiliation. Do you have anything to add?"

"Nothing, Colonel. Ensign Ward handled the situation with great courage and wisdom. His competent performance saved his command. I never understood what happened to Captain Trent. He sent us on our way and simply disappeared."

"Ward mentioned that, too," Washington shook his head, making no further comment on the subject. "As you may have heard, I'm waiting for reinforcements. It is our intention to advance to the site of Fort Prince George, and take it back from the French and complete its construction."

Daniel thought it was a little optimistic. "Captain Contrecoeur claimed that he had five hundred French marines with him. I was not able to count them, but it was a large force armed with several swivel guns. The Virginia Regiment of three or four hundred men will be outnumbered."

Washington thought about what Daniel had said. "We'll cross that bridge when the time comes. In the meantime, I sent for you hoping that I could enlist your services as a guide for the regiment. Right now, you probably know as much about the territory as anyone alive, except Gist."

Daniel was anxious to go home, but found it awkward to refuse the imposing Colonel Washington. "I'll do it for you, Colonel, but I must warn you that I'm not interested in a prolonged campaign through the summer. I'll agree to guide you to the forks, then I'll take my leave."

"That's satisfactory to me. Welcome to the regiment, Daniel. I knew I could count on you."

Chapter Seventeen

Daniel left Colonel Washington's tent feeling that the commander was too impatient to take his regiment to war. He also had reservations about signing on for another scouting job with the young commander, this time on an offensive military formation.

Washington had requested that he be prepared to move within a few days, for it was his intention to encamp the regiment west of Wills Creek. He wanted to be closer to the French forces. Daniel questioned the wisdom of the precipitant move of the regiment fifty miles west of Wills Creek to a place called Great Meadows before the rest of the regiment under Frye joined them. Great Meadows was a swampy, open stretch of land with a running brook for water. Washington had taken the position that the French had committed an act of war when they evicted Ward's command, and he was preparing to redeem their soiled honor, regardless of the cost.

Daniel accompanied the regiment to Great Meadows, acting as a flank guide north of the line of travel. The selection of Great Meadows as an encampment defied elementary military tactics. Daniel could not understand why Washington did not choose a location with a higher elevation that would have been easier to defend, but he never said anything to the regal Washington.

The mission of the Virginia Regiment was to travel to the forks of the Ohio and Allegheny Rivers to assist the workers building Fort Prince George and to garrison the structure once it was completed. The French had arrived there first.

While Washington was waiting for Frye's troops to arrive at Great Meadows, Half King, his old friend from the diplomatic mission, arrived with news that French soldiers were hiding in an obscure glen nearby. Ever since Daniel and Gist had witnessed the drunken antics of Half King, Daniel remained skeptical of the Indian chief's trustworthiness.

About forty soldiers from the regiment were assembled by Washington for the march to the location Half King proclaimed was only about two miles from Great Meadows. Daniel was a part of the task force that left Great Meadows in the middle of the night, in a driving rain storm, for a forced march in the dark. Amid much confusion of their whereabouts, the main force had veered off the correct path. Washington ignored Daniel's report that the task force was off course. Finally, he ordered them to wait until early dawn when they could realign their forces. They arrived at Half King's camp shortly after daybreak.

That morning, Washington called a conference with Half King and Daniel. Prudent tactics would have dictated a cursory estimate of the French force's strength, positions, and possible intentions, before initiating an attack. Washington refused to do so, basing his attack solely on Half King's word. Daniel voiced his misgivings, but was overruled by Washington and Half King. Their adrenaline was high in anticipation of the hunt and the kill.

The French troops were eating breakfast sheltered in a tree-studded glen protected by a high ledge to the west. The potential for a disaster was not lost on Daniel who had made up his mind to not participate in the attack on the French troops. By contrast, Half King and his fanatical Indian companions were out for blood. It brought too many ugly images of Mary, Lee II, and John Akins for Daniel. He was not a soldier, and the enemy was not threatening him or the Virginia Regiment. He was hired as a scout and wanted no part in an ambush of unsuspecting French soldiers.

The French camp was attacked by the Virginia soldiers firing down the slope into the glen at the main camp. Half King's Indians had gone around the encampment to cut off any possible escape route. The firing was furious and of short duration, not more than fifteen minutes. The firefight killed ten French soldiers, wounded one and netted the Virginians twenty one prisoners. Ensign Coulon de Jumonville, the French commander, was one of those killed. Half King had intentionally selected him as a victim, burying his hatchet into the young French officer's skull. One French soldier was able to escape injury or capture, and fled the scene. One Virginia soldier was killed and buried near the battle scene.

All of the dead French soldiers were viciously scalped by the hysterical Indians under Half King. Daniel watched them in disgust jumping from body to body with their knives poised for the removal of scalps, dumbfounded that Washington did nothing to stop the Indians from defiling the corpses.

Daniel saw no difference between the tactics of the British or French Indian allies. Butchery of human corpses was a part of their culture. Washington learned from the prisoners that the French troops had been on a peaceful mission to warn the British and colonial forces to leave the Ohio Valley. A mission not unlike the one Washington had recently carried out without incident. He also learned that Jumonville had sent runners back to Fort Duquesne that he had located Washington's encampment.

Later that same day, they returned to Great Meadows. Washington frantically ordered the men to build a stockade, proposing one about fifty-three feet in diameter. He also sent an urgent request to Wills Creek for reinforcements. Within three days the stockade was completed. Colonel Washington called the structure Fort Necessity.

During the construction of Fort Necessity, Daniel maintained vigilant patrols of the northern and western flanks of the encampment looking for enemy sign. He also watched the Indians with Half King. They were all sneaky, devious, and unpredictable, and he did not trust any of them. While Fort Necessity was being built, he noticed that the Indians were leaving, deserting Washington when he needed them the most.

News of the death of Colonel Frye came to Washington at Great Meadows after the attack. Christopher Gist was the bearer of the sad news and led the remaining three companies of infantry from Frye's command into the compound. Washington now assumed complete control of the regiment. That fact worried Daniel, for he now viewed Washington with great skepticism. His inability to stop the desecration of dead soldier's bodies still bothered Daniel.

The day after Gist's arrival, a contingent of South Carolinian militia marched into the camp under the command of Captain James McKay, who was, also, a regular British Army officer. Daniel was present at the conference when McKay refused to place his troops under Washington's command. He was there to reinforce their efforts but he alone was responsible for his troops. The expectation of a French retaliatory attack was very real, but most thought it was not an immediate threat. The troops now needed to have something to do. Discipline was becoming difficult, so Washington ordered the regiment to widen and improve the road leading past Gist's settlement toward the Monongahela River.

The day after his arrival, Gist visited Daniel out on one of his patrols to the north. They sat on a hilltop looking across a ravine while they ate jerky and pemmican. Gist was concerned about Daniel. "You're not happy about the situation are you, Dan?"

Daniel thought for a moment and replied cautiously. "I have some reservations about Washington's military judgment. I know that he's young, my age, but I think he has trouble aligning his priorities."

"What do you mean?"

"Well, first of all, his selection of a swampy vale for a stockade leaves much to be desired and defies basic military defensive tactics. He should have placed it on a hill or knoll or at least on a piece of land that dominated an area. The stockade is too small to hold his regiment and is very weak for a determined siege or attack. The fort needs protective measures more than the road improvements to your place." Daniel was quick to outline the basis for his discontent.

"I agree with your assessment, Dan."

"The thing that sticks with me the most is how he attacked the French without any indication that they were a threat to anyone. I know that they could, potentially, have been a threat, but he could have easily surrounded them and asked for a surrender. Instead he ambushed them and allowed Half King's thugs to do their dirty work without one restraining order from him. I like the man but his ability as a troop leader is very thin at best. I'm not sure if he seeks glory or is simply indecisive. Either way, it spells trouble for the men in his command."

"Wow, I wish now I hadn't asked you," Gist exclaimed.

"What are your thoughts on the subject, Chris? Now that Washington is the commander of the regiment and has all of his companies in the encampment, he should be able to disperse them in such a way to put up a good fight when the French arrive. Captain McKay looks like a professional to me. I'd feel better if he was in command instead of Washington."

Chris leaned his head against the tree and thought about Daniel's question before answering. "It's a certainty that the French will hit us with a major force. I'm not sure if Washington has thought about the significance of his attack, but it was the opening salvo of a war that could rip this frontier apart and set it on fire. The repercussions are eventually going to be felt by the British and the French all over the world."

"I hadn't thought of it in that context, but you're right about the big picture. It's not a pleasant one to think about," Daniel answered, impressed with the frontiersman's quick mind.

"The French have more troops in the Ohio Valley than the British, so for now, they'll dominate the scene. As soon as England gets its act together, more troops will be forthcoming. Given enough time, the British will prevail by sheer numbers. The French along the Ohio, the Champlain Valley, and in Canada proper, are spread pretty thin and will not be able to sustain an active campaign."

"Your prophecies for the immediate future are a little discouraging, Chris."

"Cheer up, lad. Within a short time, we'll either be dead or pushed back to civilization. Nothing is forever. Change is always taking place."

"I didn't know you were such a philosopher, Chris," Daniel smiled at his friend and stood up. "This cold ground is stiffening me up. I'd better be on my rounds. Thanks for stopping by. I apologize for being so critical."

"Take care of yourself," urged Gist, lumbering off in that peculiar gait he had.

The date of July 3, 1754, was one that Daniel would always remember. The Virginia Regiment knew that a large formation of French troops were on their way to seek battle with the Virginians. Daniel was with Washington near Gist's settlement when they first heard the news. Washington made a snap decision to fall back to Great Meadows with orders for the men to dig defensive pits and reinforce the stockade so that they could repulse a determined attack against the fort. Daniel thought that such elementary measures should have been taken long before the attack.

The Virginians' retreat to the stockade was hastily made and wore the men down. Much of the equipment was left behind. The realignment move was a debacle. Discipline was almost nonexistent.

The pitifully small Fort Necessity soon became a refuge instead of a fortress.

The French surrounded Fort Necessity to block any retreat. They had learned what tactics worked in the forested country. Instead of marching to battle in smart formation, they took positions behind rocks, brush and trees, and began sniping at the fort from a distance. The random shots rang out for hours during a heavy rain storm. Both sides had trouble keeping their powder dry. The French outnumbered the British and had more firepower in the form of swivel guns and small caliber horse-drawn cannons.

Darkness began to set in, and both sides were concerned about their supply of ammunition. The tempo of small arms fire continued unabated. The French were the first to propose a parley. Colonel Washington immediately sent Jacob van Braam to negotiate for a capitulation. Van Braam returned that evening with a draft from the French commander. Washington read it and made a few changes. Ultimately, that evening the terms of capitulation were agreed upon and signed. The provisions of the declaration were that the Virginia Regiment would be allowed to leave the field of battle with anything they could carry. They would be allowed to leave in safety the next morning, July 4th. Two hostages were given to the French, van Braam and a soldier named Stobo. They would be released when the British returned the twenty-one French prisoners in their custody.

While negotiations were taking place, Daniel had been huddled in one of the trenches hastily dug outside of the stockade walls. He had used up most of the ammunition for his rifle during the sniping period. When the cease fire was ordered, he knew that Washington was going to surrender, so he made sure that he had his pack on Blackie who was nearby and ready for a rapid exit if it became necessary. He walked out with the regiment and headed back towards Wills Creek. Daniel gave one final glance back at Fort Necessity as the French tricolor was being raised on a post outside the fort. The Indians were turned loose and shortly, the fort was in flames. The French had already burned Gist's settlement and the large warehouse of the Ohio Company at Wills Creek.

Washington took the regiment to Wills Creek where he ordered them to help build the nearby Fort Cumberland then in progress. When it was completed, the regiment garrisoned it. They were in a somber mood as they settled in for a long siege.

The French now controlled all of the territory west of the Allegheny Mountains. The frontiers in Pennsylvania and New York were about to experience a blood bath. The Indians preferred to ally themselves with a winner, so they sided in large numbers with the French. Forays against the English settlements would soon set the frontier ablaze. No man, woman or child on the frontier was safe from the tomahawk, the scalping knife or the torch.

Daniel's last act with the Virginia Regiment was to resign. Washington paid him in full and cordially thanked him for his services. The large warehouse was still burning when he left Fort Cumberland and pointed Blackie at a gallop into the rising sun. It was time to go home!

Chapter Eighteen

Leaving the Appalachian Mountain region was a welcome relief for Daniel. He had seen enough of hardships and debilitating toil on the trail, especially when those sacrifices accomplished nothing. If his experience under Colonel Washington was typical of the efforts of the colonies to thwart French intentions in the area, he was afraid for the eventual outcome.

Daniel rode the faithful horse Blackie across three hundred miles of virgin forests and unsettled wilderness sprinkled with rugged peaks and dark lonely valleys that blocked out the sun. During these early days of summer, heavy mists rose from the damp earth and hung still in the air. Daniel remembered that Lavina had told him that the native Indians believed that the mists were filled with spirits of the dead. The thought always sobered him.

Christopher Gist had given Daniel a map covering the area from Pennsylvania east to New England. It took him two and a half weeks to travel to the Hudson River. There, near Newburgh, he was able to hitch a ride on a supply barge with a large single sail. The barge was bound for Hudson Falls about a hundred miles north. Daniel agreed to help the crew stand watch for his passage. He rode all of the way sitting in the bow with his rifle ready. Indians were a threat, but recently, thieves and pirates were even more numerous and deadly. They had successfully hijacked several cargoes from the company that owned the barge, and they were glad to have an experienced hand like Daniel on board. Blackie was fed all the hay and oats he could eat.

The trip was plagued with very little wind, which meant that the crew had to resort to poling the barge upstream against its normal flow. It was laborious work. Daniel was exempted from the task and maintained his vigilance in the bow looking for anything that appeared suspicious or out of the ordinary. The passage up the Hudson River on the slow, lumbering barge was a spectacular experience. He witnessed some of the most beautiful countryside he had ever seen. It rivaled his beloved mountains of central New Hampshire. The rough, undulating landscape ended abruptly at the edge of the river, creating precipitant cliffs that rose sharply out of the water. Many new homes were being built close to the river. Some were modest log cabins similar to the one he had built for his family, but many were ostentatious, even grand. The southern portion of the Hudson Valley, by then, was relatively stable from French or Indian attacks. In the absence of constant danger, the area was becoming prosperous, and, according to Daniel's standards, excessive in their statement of wealth.

The barge docked at Albany for one night. Daniel went ashore to explore the bustling town located at the juncture of the Mohawk and Hudson Rivers. Here, in the middle of the wilderness, the town was becoming a metropolis of trade and shipping companies. He slept that night at an inn next to the dock where he was able to take a bath and shave off his heavy growth of beard. The tavern below his room was filled with boisterous voices that kept him awake for most of the night.

The next morning, the barge continued its journey north. A few miles north of Albany, Daniel said good-bye to his genial mates and led Blackie off the barge on the east side of the river. Daniel checked his compass and headed due east, where he picked up remnants of a well-used trail wide enough for small wagons.

Several days later, he arrived on the west bank of the Connecticut River opposite Fort Number Four at Charlestown. He turned Blackie downstream to a fording area he was capable of negotiating without swimming. Daniel held his pack and rifle high over his head to keep them dry and gently nudged his faithful mount into the water. The instant he arrived on the New Hampshire side of the river, Daniel felt that he had come home. The familiar fort had not changed. The outpost sentry in the lookout tower waved to him. Daniel returned the salute wondering if Captain Stevens was still in command of the military contingent. The sentry at the main gate confirmed Daniel's query that Stevens was still very much in command, and that the fort was on an elevated alert. Raids by Indians from Canada had increased in numbers and in ferocity.

Captain Stevens was genuinely pleased to see him again and invited Daniel to share his simple quarters. He insisted that Daniel clean up and enjoy a decent meal before he plied him with questions about his travels.

Daniel didn't need any coaxing from the gracious and courageous soldier. After a bath and a fresh shave, Daniel enjoyed a meal of hasty pudding and venison stew with fresh-dug potatoes, one of the first crop of seed potatoes from Scotland in the area.

Captain Stevens smiled at Daniel's appetite. "You know, Daniel, I saw your Uncle Lee earlier this summer when he was part of a supply train from the coast. He's a remarkable man. Tell me about this debacle you experienced first-hand with a Colonel Washington from Virginia."

Daniel took a sip from his tea cup and shook his head. "That meal was delicious, sir. Thank you for your kind hospitality. What have you heard about Virginia's failure to build a fort on the Ohio River?"

"All we know is what we've read in the dispatches that have come to us from Baltimore and any newspapers that the couriers bring to us. They claim that Washington is under a lot of pressure to resign his commission in the Virginia Militia. He apparently displayed a certain amount of ineptness and inexperience commanding a military mission that surrendered to the French forces. Was it as bad as it sounds?"

"My inexperienced opinion is that the colony and the men in his ranks were poorly served by Colonel Washington," Daniel claimed, watching the authoritative figure before him. "He seemed a little too anxious to close with the French, and his knowledge of tactics was minimal at best. All that drove him, in my opinion, was a desire to make a name for himself. Evidently he lived under the shadow of his brother, Lawrence's achievements, and I believe that his inferiority complex motivated him. Having said that, I always found him cordial and very respectful. I don't wish him any bad luck; he simply needs to be patient while he's gaining experience in leading soldiers in combat."

"Your perspective is unique, Daniel," Captain Stevens remarked, emptying his pipe in an ash receptacle. "Things have gotten a lot worse this past year. New York and Pennsylvania are not the only places that settlers are being driven off the fields they've cleared and out of the cabins they've built. In the midst of all this unrest, I was concerned to see the daughter of Thom Cameron, the one they call Whispering Wind, embark on a trip to the Moravian Mission in northern Vermont. She was accompanied by another Indian woman called Ruth."

"I know both of them," Daniel said with interest. "When did they leave, Captain?"

"About a week ago. They were alone except for Ruth's small child. They assured me that they would be safe in the wilderness. They are quite well known for their interest in helping native people learn to read and write English," Captain Stevens smiled, thinking about the young ladies. "Their enthusiasm and dedication is remarkable. What are you going to do with yourself, Daniel?"

"I'm going home to Portsmouth, but first, I want to visit my cabin on the river to see if it's still standing," Daniel replied.

"Well, you should exercise caution, but you already know that. My superior has just informed me that we are getting additional men assigned to the fort. They'll be here soon. Now, let me make arrangements for you to stay the night in the great room, Daniel."

"Thanks Captain. It's nice to be back among familiar faces. I've been away too long." He followed Captain Stevens to the stairs leading to the great room over the main gate.

The large hall was filled with travelers seeking refuge within its walls. Daniel spread his blanket on the floor. The room was surprisingly quiet and free of idle chatter. He carefully placed his rifle on the blanket and stretched out beside it. He was tired and fell asleep soon after he closed his eyes. The next morning he rose before sunrise and descended the stairs to the stockade. He ate a hearty bowl of oatmeal and jerky offered by the sentries warming themselves around a large fire in the center of the stockade. He also accepted a mug of hot tea and sipped it slowly. It tasted good, for the morning was damp and cool. There was a nip of fall in the air that morning. Thanking the sentries for the food, Daniel silently slipped out of the main gate and walked to the corral. He whistled for Blackie.

A few minutes later, he climbed into the saddle and walked Blackie around the fort heading north along a well-defined pathway on the east shore of the Connecticut River. Daniel kept his rifle primed and ready across the saddle. His instincts became alert the minute he left the relative safety of the fort. Every sound and sight within range of his eyes and ears were evaluated and catalogued in his mind. The canopy of deciduous trees was filled with chirping birds welcoming the sun rising in the east. Daniel was pleased that a slight breeze blew down wind of him out of the north. Blackie could sense the presence of people or animals close by and would warn him if any strangers approached on the same trail. The horse's senses were more developed than Daniel's. Therefore, he rode with confidence that the path ahead of him was relatively free of surprises.

As the sun began to climb higher in the east, the day warmed, and a soft breeze blew out of the north. It felt good against Daniel's face. His mind wandered to the tragedy that had taken place at the cabin. All the way up the trail, past the trading post at Hanover and beyond, Daniel could feel Mary's presence. He wondered if the dead are still near their loved ones. He believed in God and the teachings of Christianity, but he was skeptical about where the spirits of the dead went. Was he actually feeling her spiritual being, or was he remembering the way it had been between them? Images of Mary sitting in the rocking chair beside the fireplace nursing their son, Lee, filled his eyes with tears. He had forgotten how happy they had been. For the past year he had kept himself occupied and denied the images that cried out for recognition within his soul. How could he ever forget?

Daniel passed his neighbor's cabin where he had executed the Indians that had forever altered his life. Now, directly in front of him was the cabin he had built for his bride and newborn son. John Akins had helped him turn a patch of wilderness into a home, a small piece of mother earth that nobody else could claim, except the native population who extracted a high price for his ownership.

The clearing next to the river made it possible for Daniel to check for intruders. He dismounted and tied Blackie to the oak tree in front of the cabin door. The graves at the edge of the clearing were undisturbed. As he walked towards them he noticed that fresh flowers had been planted on the three graves. He knelt beside Mary's grave and touched the gentle blossoms on the lily-of-the-valley. Each of the graves also had a small planting of rosemary, the traditional flower of remembrance. The rosemary touched a tender part of him that unleashed a torrent of tears. For a long time he laid across the three graves grieving anew. It was a catharsis that he needed to cleanse his soul and to accept the loss that he had been denying for a year. The hurt had never left him, he had simply pushed it deeper in his soul and tried to forget. Now, face-to-face with the physical graves, the pain could no longer be held back, and he wept until there were no more tears to shed.

Daniel never knew how long he laid prostrate across the graves. He opened his eyes and saw the bell-shaped white flowers of the lily-of-the-valley. Their scent was pure and sweet. A light breeze gently brushed his face, and he knew in that moment that his Mary was with him. It was a closeness that drained away all of the pain and sorrow that he had stored for so many months. Daniel sat up and looked at the cabin. He could imagine Mary standing in the door, motioning for him to enter the way she had done so often. There was a sad look on her face, and when Daniel wiped the tears from his eyes, the apparition had disappeared. He walked to the cabin, opened the door and stepped inside.

The interior was as he had left it. On the table near the fireplace, Daniel noticed a piece of paper. He rushed to it and read a note from Lavina:

Dear Daniel,

Ruth and I have just stopped by your cabin seeking shelter from a hard driving rain storm. We are on our way to the mission bringing supplies of medicine and as many books as we can carry in our canoes.

My first thought upon walking through the door was of Mary and little Lee II. How sad it is to recall. I feel their presence here in this cabin where you were a happy family. My prayers are for Mary to find peace in that land beyond the horizon that awaits all of us.

And you, my dear friend, are always in my prayers, too. Your family and friends have no idea where you are or what you're doing. We don't even know for certain that you are alive or dead. I try to be positive and am leaving this note in the hope that you may return from your illusive wanderings to this place.

I pray that someday I may find, once again, that dear friend I've known for a long time. Come back to us, Daniel. Let your family and friends help you carry your burden of grief. You search for solitude, but you're never truly alone. We are with you in spirit.

Your Uncle Lee and Aunt Maureen are doing as well as can be expected, but the truth is they're sick with worry over you.

Ruth and I are excited about the potential of a permanent school at the mission and are working hard to make it possible.

Thinking and praying for your welfare.

Lavina, Ruth,

and Morning Mist

Daniel placed the letter on the table. It brought a smile to his lips and filled him with a desire to go home. The note was so typical of Lavina. Without hesitation, he left the cabin and mounted Blackie, carefully oriented himself with his pocket compass, and turned towards Portsmouth with a determined sense of purpose.

He crossed the Merrimack River at the Concord ferry and arrived at Portsmouth the following day. Once he saw the church steeple in the square, his pulse beat faster. He was thrilled and excited to be back, but he also had a strange feeling of detachment as he walked Blackie along the familiar streets. It was almost as if he was returning as a stranger. The Market Street Wharf at the river was the same as he remembered it. A large four-mast freighter was tied up to the dock, and several men were busy unloading its cargo.

A light mist rose from the river as he turned to take the road to the Cullen home. It was late in the afternoon and a light was burning in the print shop. He passed the house to the barn undetected and quickly turned Blackie into a stall. Daniel fed him a large helping of oats and fresh hay. He patted the faithful horse that had carried him so many miles. Then Daniel emptied the gunpowder from his rifle's primer pan, the first time he had done that for a year. Placing the rifle on a shelf in the barn, Daniel took his pack and rushed to the front door of the house where he knocked lightly.

"Hello, is anyone at home?" he asked in a wavering voice, opening the door. He dropped his pack inside the hallway and looked up. His Aunt Maureen was standing in the doorway leading to the kitchen looking at him. Her eyes instantly lit up and filled with tears when she recognized him. Daniel ran to embrace her. The shock of his sudden appearance left her speechless. He grasped her and gently held her to his chest. It was a powerful moment for both of them. He noted that her hair had turned whiter than he remembered, and he caressed the white strands. "How nice it is to be back home with you, Aunt Maureen."

She caught her breath and looked into his deep eyes. "Oh my, our Daniel has come back to us," she cried with trembling lips. "Our prayers have been answered, you've been spared. Let me look at you."

"The last few days have been tiring and long, and I'm desperately in need of a bath and a change into fresh clothes," he replied.

Aunt Maureen ran her long fingers over his face and said, "Your eyes have that same blank stare that I used to see in my Lee's eyes whenever he came home from the wars. How wonderful it is to have you home. Your Uncle is in the print shop. He'll be so excited to see you."

"How is he, Aunt Maureen?"

"He's much better now. He was very sick for a long time, and we feared that he might have caught smallpox, but he pulled through. He has a strong constitution. I can honestly tell you that ever since the day you left for destinations unknown, he's been a changed man. We were so afraid of losing you, Daniel. When you left it was as if he had lost another son. Go to him, Daniel, he needs you."

"I saw the light in the shop," Daniel answered, embracing his aunt one more time. "How lucky I am to have you two in my life."

"I'll put on some water for tea and fix you something to eat," Aunt Maureen promised. She gently pushed him towards the door leading to the print shop.

The door was slightly ajar. Daniel carefully opened it to see his Uncle Lee leaning over a freshly printed sheet, intently inspecting it. The room smelled of printers ink and linseed oil, bringing back fond memories of the happy days he had spent there. His Uncle had not seen him, so Daniel knocked lightly on the door.

Lee Cullen lifted his eyes to Daniel and dropped the sheet he was holding. "My God, ye have come back to us, lad," he uttered, reaching out for his beloved nephew. "How good it feels to see yea again. We were afraid you were swallowed up in the atrocities on the frontier, and lost to all of us. We prayed for yea every day, Daniel."

"I know, Uncle Lee, your prayers have been answered," Daniel smiled, feeling the strong arms embrace him. He looked closely at his Uncle in the dim light of the room. Slowly the harsh lines around his face softened.

"Seeing you again like this is a shocker to this old heart of mine. Come," Lee requested, putting an arm around Daniel's waist, escorting him toward the kitchen. "Your Aunt Maureen has some vittles ready. I can smell them now."

Daniel let himself be led into the kitchen where his Aunt had a crackling fire going in the fireplace, boiling a tea kettle full of water. She grabbed him and sat him down to the table. She served him baked codfish and fresh rye bread and beamed, watching him eat as if he hadn't eaten in days, which he had not. He noticed an interesting transformation take place with his Aunt and Uncle. When he first arrived, there was a drawn sallow look about both of them. Now, within a short time, their eyes were bright with happiness, and their cheeks ruddy with color. Their smiles were the best homecoming gift he could ask for. How dearly he loved these two gentle people.

Chapter Nineteen

The three of them sat around the kitchen table late into the evening listening to Daniel's experiences with George Washington. Lee questioned him in detail about life on the Pennsylvania frontier.

"As far as I could tell, Uncle Lee, the western border is much more explosive than our New Hampshire border, possibly because there are a lot more settlers pushing into the area. The soil is easier to work than our New England rocky hillside farms. The French have used the Ohio River Valley as a gateway to the western lands as far west as the Mississippi River, and the southern lands to Louisiana. They've successfully gained the loyalty of just about every Indian tribe in the Northeast. It's primarily the native warriors that make the French such a formidable adversary. The Indians act and fight the same way regardless of which side they're on. I seriously question their commitment to any ideology or cause, except their own duplicitous treachery," Daniel explained with forceful conviction.

"But, Daniel, what does that mean about our long-term relationship with the native tribes?" Lee asked with a frown. "After all, this land was theirs before we took it away from them. They have a legitimate claim that has not been recognized by England or France, except for the right of overpowering force. I know that you have been subjected to an unforgivable tragedy that will probably always influence your feelings towards the Indians. I pray that you don't let that consume your better judgment or cloud your reason."

"I don't disagree with you, Uncle. I admit that the way Mary died has influenced my outlook. I also think of Ruth and Lavina who left me a note at the cabin," Daniel paused to fill his clay pipe with tobacco he had purchased at the Wills Creek warehouse. "Try some of this tobacco, Uncle Lee. It's a burley variety that smokes smooth and light."

Lee accepted the pouch and filled his favorite Meerschaum pipe. Maureen silently listened to the exchange, thinking how nice it was for

Daniel and Lee to be back together. She thought that Daniel had matured beyond his young age, but she occasionally caught a glimpse of the enthusiastic young Scottish boy who had assimilated very well to the demanding environment of the colonies. He had grown into a tall muscular heavy-framed man with soft, gentle ways much like his father and his Uncle Lee. "Could you eat some apple pie, Daniel? Your Uncle ate half of it for his dinner," she smiled at her husband.

"Your apple pie would go good with this tea, Aunt Maureen. Frequently on the trips to Ohio when food was not plentiful, I used to dream about your apple pies and always woke up hungry," he chuckled softly like his Uncle Lee.

"I remember how it was on the campaign trails," Lee exclaimed. "Soldiers the world over are hungry most of the time. They tolerate poor rations because there's no alternative, and most never cease to yearn for their favorite foods."

Daniel and his uncle ate the remaining piece of apple pie while Aunt Maureen looked on contentedly. They talked of many things taking place in the region. Daniel was surprised to learn that Lavina's mother, Melinda, had died suddenly of smallpox. The news touched Daniel, remembering the proud, attractive Ojibwa lady. "I never knew. Lavina did not mention a thing about her mother in the note she left me at the cabin. How's Mister Cameron doing?"

"He's had a difficult time," Uncle Lee added. "Thom has withdrawn more than ever since her death. Now, with Lavina gone, we look in on him occasionally. He did play the violin for the last solstice fair, but it was evident that he was hurting a great deal."

"I must stop by to see him," Daniel promised. "Lavina told me how her parents met and of their perilous return in the dead of winter. I'm saddened to hear of Melinda's death. She was a wonderful person and a most beautiful lady."

"I know that you've just come home, lad, but do you have any plans for the immediate future?" Lee asked, fidgeting nervously with his empty tea cup.

"I don't really know what I want to do, Uncle Lee," Daniel replied. "My first goal was to come home here with the two of you. I haven't thought of anything beyond that. I plan to clear some of my land, but to be really honest, I'm not too anxious to do that right now."

Lee looked across the table at Maureen. She smiled and nodded her head acknowledging the question she knew her husband was going to ask. "Your Aunt and I have been thinking about the print shop. The paper has done well enough that we anticipate purchasing another press so that we can double our capacity to print."

"That sounds like a great idea," Daniel enthusiastically endorsed.

"If you're willing to help in the print shop, we're offering you a full partnership. It would mean a lot to both of us. Your aunt and I are aware that this is a difficult period of readjustment for you, Daniel. You know that our home will always be your home. We are not getting any younger and your youthful energy will be a tonic to our aging bodies and minds. You don't need to answer right now lad. Take some time to think about it, and no matter what you decide, we'll support your decision."

Daniel had not thought much about the future. The prospect of a partnership with his aunt and uncle was almost too good to believe. An expansion with a new press would have unlimited potential. The privilege of working with his uncle as an equal excited his senses.

"I don't need to take any more time to think about the proposition. To work with you in a partnership will be an honor. I'm a lucky man to be offered such a generous proposal. I believe it's an answer to my wanderlust. It's time I accepted Mary's loss and faced the future. How can I ever repay you two for all that you have done for me?"

That evening a pact was made between Daniel and his Uncle Lee and Aunt Maureen. He would be a full partner in the enterprise. Lee insisted that the pact be made official with an appropriate document that also served as a will for his aunt and uncle. Daniel was to be sole heir of all their possessions and properties upon the time of their death. It brought peace of mind to Lee and Maureen knowing that the future was taken care of. As for Daniel, he was overwhelmed with their generosity and made a promise to live up to the standards of integrity and fair play already established by the COASTAL BEACON.

They began building an addition to the print shop between the house and the barn to hold the second press, the drying lines, and additional space for the expanded operation. By the time the press arrived from Boston, two weeks later, the new room was ready. Uncle Earl had arrived from York to help them maneuver the heavy press into position and to firmly anchor it to the floor.

Daniel began a weekly column in the two-page paper in which he described his travels to Pennsylvania and Virginia. Uncle Lee told Daniel that in order to write well, a writer has to have something he wants to say. That simple premise was the heart of good writing. Under his experienced eye, Daniel's writing improved. He had a flair for detail and description of personal traits. Daniel limited himself to describing events with a minimum of commentary, but when the occasion cried out for criticism, such as George Washington's leadership, he did not hesitate to write his opinion. Daniel even went so far as to predict that Washington would soon fade into obscurity after his first confrontation with French troops. The attack on French forces had the potential of becoming a worldwide problem. The columns became very popular.

Daniel wrote several columns pertaining to his concern about the "correctness" of Washington's promise to the French that he would return the twenty-one French prisoners, which to that date, he had failed to do. Daniel wrote several letters to the governor's office in Williamsburg, Virginia, inquiring about the disposition of the exchange. He never received a reply.

Therefore, he concluded that the Virginia Militia had broken the agreement between the two combatants. Daniel protested in eloquent terms that the future and physical well-being of the two British subjects, Captain Stobo and Jacob van Braam, taken by the French to insure a timely exchange of prisoners, had been compromised. The failure of the militia to honor its agreements had far-reaching implications for the conflict that was about to erupt on the colonial frontiers. The prisoner issue, as described in the COASTAL BEACON, drew wide attention and increased circulation of the paper. The Cullen partnership quickly became a leading source of information for the greater seacoast region of the northern Massachusetts Bay Colony, primarily New Hampshire and Maine.

Daniel labored long hours writing, setting type, and printing copies. He and his uncle were establishing a network of people in Boston, New York, and Philadelphia who, on a regular basis, sent dispatches of important events from their area by mounted couriers and occasionally by boats destined for Portsmouth. They added several more advertisements from local merchants, increasing the profitability of the partnership. Lee also worked hard in the shop and spent a lot of time soliciting ads. He was pleased with the way Daniel seized responsibility, and soon proved himself capable of running the shop. They both agreed that they needed more help in the composing and printing phase of the operation, and decided to advertise for responsible applicants.

The colorful foliage of the deciduous maples, beech, and birch trees had dropped from the trees and blanketed the earth in rich tones of red, yellow, and orange, leaving the trees naked to the harsh winter that was about to descend on the area. One day late in October, Daniel was occupied printing a page on the new press when a visitor silently appeared at the door and watched him work. Daniel felt that someone was near and turned to see who was at the door.

His jaw dropped when he saw Lavina smiling at him. He released his heavy grip on the press handle and turned to her. He embraced her and exclaimed, "Lavina, I've been worried about you."

She kissed him on the cheek. "Your Aunt Maureen told me that you were here. It's so good to see you again."

The sound of her voice brought back fond memories. "Come, sit down." He nervously directed her to the long narrow table and chairs beside the fireplace where he often wrote his articles for the paper. She was as beautiful as ever but had dark circles beneath her eyes. "You look tired and drawn, Lavina. How have you been?"

Lavina answered the question with a long sigh and sat facing him. "Ruth and I have been working hard for the mission school. There's so much that needs to be done and so little time to do it. The Reverend ordered me to come home for the winter months. I reluctantly conceded and brought Ruth and the baby along."

"I read your note at the cabin," Daniel told her. "It was a nice surprise to hear from a friend after being absent for so long."

"I was hoping that you'd find it. We had no way of knowing if you were alive or dead. I spoke to your Aunt Maureen before coming to the print shop. She told me about your agreement with your Uncle Lee. I think it's wonderful for both of you."

"Uncle told me about your mother, Lavina. I'm saddened for you and your father. You have my sympathies. She was a wonderful woman, loved by all who knew her. You inherited her spirit of independence and her remarkable beauty."

She smiled at him and blushed. "Thank you, Daniel. I wasn't sure what kind of person I'd find in the print shop. It's nice to know that the youthful Scottish boy that was my best friend has returned to us. Welcome home, Daniel."

He squeezed her hands in his. "Did you say that you're here for the winter?"

"Yes. Father needs me. He's not well."

"Would it be appropriate for an old friend to ask another old friend if she would be interested in helping him work in the print shop? After all," he chuckled softly. "You made better copies than I did, and you never spilled as much ink on you as I did. Aunt Maureen still asks me if I swim in the stuff."

They laughed at each other. How nice it was. She replied in a serious tone. "I'd like that, Daniel. Maybe Ruth will be able to help too. On our way back we stopped in Londonderry where we saw a copy of your paper at the Inn where we stayed. Ruth was impressed with the power of your writing, and of course, so was I. I always knew that someday you'd find yourself."

"Did you stop at the cabin on your return to Fort Number Four?" Daniel asked.

"No, we were escorted down the river to the fort by some of the rangers from the mission area. Do you remember Ted Sloane?" she asked in a nervous tremor.

"Sure, we served together on the northern border a few years ago. We became quite good friends," Daniel answered.

"Well, you're the first person, besides Ruth, to know that Ted Sloane has asked me to marry him!"

Chapter Twenty

"Ted Sloane?" Daniel involuntarily blurted out.

"Yes, you're the first to know. He remembers you," she added quickly.

"Sure I know Ted. He's a good person. Isn't this kind of sudden?" The question was more a demand for clarification. The announcement left him with a sinking feeling that shattered his composure. He nervously fidgeted with the press handle searching for the right words.

Once again, Lavina avoided his penetrating stare and continued to defend her situation. "Ruth thinks the same thing. Ted has been most attentive to me and has been helpful to Ruth and me in our work with the northern Indian tribes throughout the region. I had hoped that you would be happy for me," she added quietly.

"You know that I am, Lavina. It's just that it came as a shock. Ted was raised somewhere around Exeter, if I remember correctly. He's a lucky man to win your heart."

"I haven't given him an answer yet," she said. "You and Ruth are probably right, more time is needed for us to get better acquainted. I don't have much practice with affairs of the heart. I'm really not interested in being married just to have a husband. I want what my mother and father had. Their commitment to each other was sincere. I would like for my children to experience the same level of love and respect I shared with them."

"You've set your goals high, Lavina. I understand what you mean. Your desire for a meaningful lifelong commitment is the way things should be," Daniel replied. "I do wish you much happiness and that comes from my heart. You're worth any sacrifice Ted has to make, and I pray that he honors you the same way your father honored your mother. I, too, found their relationship inspiring and heartwarming."

Lavina smiled at his words and knew that they were spoken with conviction. "Thank you, Daniel. It's important that I have your support." She clasped his hands in hers on top of the table. "I'm so glad to have a chance to work in the shop with you and your Uncle Lee. The winter months will pass quickly. In the spring, Ruth and I are planning to return to the mission."

There was a soft glow about her that made him feel good just being with her. "I agree, it will be fun working together again. How's Ruth and the baby?"

"She's in the kitchen now with your aunt and uncle. I told them I wanted to speak to you alone. You and Ruth are the only ones to know about Ted and me. I plan to tell my father when we return to the house. I wanted you to be the first to know," she said.

"Old friends always wish each other the very best."

"I knew I could count on you, Daniel," she replied. "Come, Ruth and Morning Mist are waiting to say hi."

He followed Lavina into the kitchen where Ruth was talking with Uncle Lee and Aunt Maureen around the large kitchen table. Ruth was dressed the same as Lavina in trail clothes of soft doeskin shirt and pants with intricate bead designs across the front of the shirt.

She saw Daniel enter the room and lowered her eyes. She was self-conscious about her disfigured left arm and held it beneath the table. He noticed her efforts to hide it. The arm had healed so that she could move her wrist and fingers, but she was unable to bend her arm at the elbow without assistance. She grasped the injured arm with her right hand to place it where she wanted.

Daniel spoke first. "I'm glad to see you again, Ruth... I hope you feel the same way."

She lifted her eyes to confront him and replied in her unique soft voice. "I do not bear you any ill will, Daniel Cullen, and I'm pleased to see you safely at home. This is my daughter, Morning Mist. She came into the world very early in the morning when the land was still embraced by the spirits of our deceased loved ones. Misty, this is Mr. Cullen. You probably don't remember him, but I'm sure that he remembers you. He is a friend of Whispering Wind."

Daniel watched the child listen to her mother. Then, she looked up at Daniel with large brown eyes and smiled at him much the way she did on that fateful day so long ago when he found her lying alone in the canoe. She was dressed the same as her mother with her hair in two

161

braids hanging down her back and a pink ribbon tied to the end of each braid. The wide-eyed child stared at the strangers in the room.

Daniel held his large hand out to Misty and returned her smile. "I'm glad to meet you, young lady. I remember when you were just an infant. My friends call me Dan. Can you and I be friends?"

Morning Mist looked at Daniel and then at her mother. She shrank from him, yet she held on to his strong fingers and continued to smile. "We friends…"

Daniel released her hand and motioned Lavina to take a seat at the table. He sat beside Misty. She continued to watch him as she walked to Ruth and clung to her legs. Aunt Maureen left the room for a few seconds and returned with a small rag doll about twelve inches tall. Misty spotted the doll in her hands, and her eyes opened wide.

"Misty is a lively two-year-old," Aunt Maureen declared, holding out the doll to her. "You may have it, Misty, but first, you've got to give me a hug and say thank you."

Misty's reaction to her request was instantaneous. Misty left her mother's side and opened her arms wide to Maureen who swept her into her lap. Misty accepted the rag doll and said, "Thank you," in her small voice. She hugged the doll and placed it against her cheek.

"I'm glad the three of you are safe from the wilderness for the next few months," Daniel said. "Lavina has accepted my offer to help us in the print shop. She's much better at typesetting and spelling than I am."

"That's wonderful, Lavina," Lee Cullen was quick to show his pleasure at the arrangement. He greatly admired her intellect and quick mind. "It'll almost be like old times. Daniel has been doing very well describing his experiences on our western frontier. It'll be nice having ye on our team, lass. We have plans for a larger newspaper and there will be lots of work for all of us."

"That sounds wonderful," added Aunt Maureen, placing an affectionate arm around Lavina's shoulders.

Morning Mist had been quietly listening to the adults around her and yawned with her mouth wide open. Daniel saw her and chuckled to himself.

"Perhaps we should be getting back to your father, Lavina," Ruth suggested.

"I know, we just wanted to drop by to say 'hello' and to make sure that you were all right," Lavina explained, rising to leave.

"You look tired, little Miss Morning Mist," Daniel smiled and held his hands out to her. "How about it, may I carry you to Mister Cameron's house? I could give you a ride on my shoulders."

Without hesitation Misty raised her arms. He lifted her in the air and sat her on his shoulders. She grasped him tightly around the forehead, smiling down on her mother and Lavina.

"I do believe you've made a new conquest, Daniel," Ruth observed, pleased with his natural response to her daughter.

The evening air was warm with a light breeze from the ocean. The night was filled with fresh scents from the sea. Daniel, Lavina, and Ruth leisurely walked abreast of each other. Daniel held onto Morning Mist's small legs so that she would not fall off his shoulders. He was impressed with the delicately decorated moccasins on her tiny feet. She was so precious and so innocent. Holding her touched the raw emotions he had suppressed for his own child. She was about the same age as Lee would have been if he had lived. It was all he could do to contain his tears.

Ruth walked on Daniel's left so that he could not see her left arm. He again witnessed her self-conscious effort to conceal it and hated what he had done to her. "I have to ask you so that I'll know, Ruth. Can you use your left arm at all?" he asked, hoping that the answer would be positive.

"I can use my fingers and thumb. It hurts when I try to extend my arm in front of me. It's much weaker than my right arm, but I'm adapting to the limitations," she replied without a trace of malice or anger.

"My God, I'm sorry for my irresponsible act. I'd take that bullet myself if it was possible." Daniel still agonized over the incident.

Even in the dim light, Ruth was able to see the torment on his face. "I believe the things you say, Daniel. You've told me before. I don't hate you for what happened. I forgive you, and now you must forgive yourself. We cannot change the past."

"Your Christian charity exceeds mine, Ruth," he replied, shaking his head. "I can't say that I'm ready to forgive myself just yet."

Lavina listened to the exchange and placed an arm around Daniel's waist. "I was afraid that your personal tragedy and loss would turn you into a monster and make you cold and hard. I'm gratified to know that my fears were for naught."

They arrived at the Cameron home, and Daniel effortlessly lifted Morning Mist from his shoulders. He gave her a warm embrace before passing her on to Ruth. "She's a precious child."

Ruth held her daughter with her right arm. "She's a tired little girl. It has been a long trip. Thank you, Daniel."

"It was my pleasure," Daniel answered.

Lavina kissed him on the cheek. "Good night, Daniel."

"It's nice to see you again, Lavina." He embraced her briefly and turned to walk away.

The winter of 1754-1755 was long and cold. Snow accumulations amounted to twenty feet. It had been difficult for families in the villages and towns to send their children to school or for any other activity that involved moving beyond the shelter of the homes and barns. For those people who were unprepared or had insufficient firewood or hay for the animals before the heavy snows of December and January, the winter was a struggle for survival. Borrowing hay or firewood from neighbors was an arduous task. The commodities had to be dragged over the snow in sleds or toboggans.

The Cullen print shop continued to be resourceful and productive. Lavina had an artistic flair for laying out articles and stories on the pages. Once she had set the type, Lee faithfully proofread the first sheet, holding up the printing process until he had checked every word. Once the printing process began, Lavina removed each sheet from the platen and hung it on the lines to dry. Daniel then inked the type before placing another clean sheet on the platen. By then, Lavina was in position to swing the platen, holding the paper down on the inked type. Daniel compressed the paper against the type by turning the screw handle. As soon as he released the heavy press, the cycle started all over again. They worked quietly most of the time, each carrying out their task in concert with their partner. They developed a routine that was productive and produced a quality product. Monks on the COASTAL BEACON were a rarity.

One blustery morning in late February 1755, Lavina struggled through the deep snow to the print shop and instantly began to build a fire in the fireplace. Within minutes, flames ignited the dry pine kindling and began warming the room. Lavina placed an iron teakettle over the dancing flames to heat the water for tea.

Daniel quietly entered the room and saw her kneeling beside the fireplace. She had removed her bearskin coat and was dressed warmly in doeskin shirt and pants. Her braided hair fell over the front of her shoulders. Daniel looked for the red ribbons tied on the ends of the braids and smiled at her adherence to tradition. She had not noticed him, and he stood observing her from a distance. The room was dark except for the light from the fire. Dark shadows and flickering light illuminated her face. She was watching the flames, still unaware of Daniel's presence.

He continued to study her sad and reflective countenance. The normally proud and confident tilt of her chin was gone. For a moment, she closed her eyes and bowed her head as if she was praying. Daniel felt like an intruder, yet did not declare his presence. She wiped tears from her eyes, as he greeted her, "Good morning, Lavina. Are you all right?"

She was startled and rose to face him. "I was just waiting for the water to boil for tea," she answered in a wavering voice. He came to her side and detected the unique aroma of bayberry in her black hair. She was troubled, and it saddened him. "What's wrong, Lavina?" he asked, taking her in his arms.

She shook her head denying that anything was wrong, and laid her head against his chest. He could feel the tenseness in her body, and it worried him. She lifted her head to look into his eyes. He saw the angst and turmoil she was going through and held her even closer. Her sensuous lips were trembling, and he kissed her. She returned his caress and immediately began to cry.

Daniel took a clean handkerchief from his pocket and pressed it in her hand. It was the first time he had ever kissed her. It felt like the most natural thing to do. "I'm sorry, Lavina," he said, not sure what to say.

She dried her eyes and left his embrace to throw a handful of tea leaves in the boiling pot. "I don't know what happened to me," she explained in her soft resonant voice. "These past few days have been difficult for me. I've been impatient with my father, and I've snapped at Ruth and the baby several times when there was no real justification for doing so."

"But why, Lavina?" Daniel persisted to question her. "Have I done anything to upset you?"

She sat on the long bench near the fireplace and confronted him with a nervous tremor in her voice. "Please sit with me a moment, Daniel. It's time we talked about a subject that I've avoided for a long time. Please sit," she pleaded, directing him to the bench. "Would you like some tea?" She reached for the hot kettle to pour the tea.

"Yes," he said, taking a seat beside her, a puzzled look on his face.

She began after a long sip of tea, grasping the cup with both hands. "Two days ago, I received a letter from Ted Sloane telling me that he was going to join forces with a Major Robert Rogers who was forming a battalion of rangers under his command. They will be part of the New Hampshire contribution to a Colonial task force assigned to attack and occupy Fort Frederick on Lake Champlain this coming summer."

"Yes, I've heard about the plans," he said.

"Well, Ted is planning to come to Portsmouth as soon as the snow cover has melted to the point where travel on horseback is possible. He wants to marry me on that visit," she paused.

"So soon?" Daniel questioned.

Lavina placed a finger over his lips. "Please let me finish, Daniel. This is not easy for me, and if I don't complete what I've started, it will probably always remain unsaid."

"I promise," Daniel saw the troubled look in her eyes and yielded to her plea.

"Ruth and my father told me that I should be pleased that Ted has followed through on his commitment to marriage, for it proves how much he thinks of me. I'm flattered by his proposal, of course, but working here with you and your Uncle Lee this winter has given me time to rethink the future. The thought of marrying Ted is frightening because I don't love him. Oh, he's a good person, but he will never have my heart." she paused and stammered. "I...I...fell in love with you, Daniel, years ago on that first day when my mother and I were accosted," she finished, gasping for breath. She turned to look at him. "What I'm trying to tell you is that I will not marry Ted, and I'm asking if you have feelings for me. I'm desperately aware that it has been less than two years since Mary's death, and I realize how painful her loss has been for you..."

"Are you asking me if I love you, Lavina?" Daniel asked in a shaky voice.

"Yes, I'm asking if there is any hope for you and me. I'm not of your race and I know that I'm being very bold in confronting you this way. Can you look into your heart and tell me what you honestly feel?" she pleaded with large tears forming in her dark eyes.

Daniel was not surprised that she brought up the subject, but he was shocked by the depth of her expression of love towards him. He had always known that it was there, and he had been indifferent to her feelings ever since they were teenagers. He recalled the softness of her lips and how he felt when she told him about Ted's proposal. It had bothered him and he had spent restless nights thinking about it. When he was with Lavina he felt a completeness that gave his life meaning. It really hurt when he thought he was going to lose all of that to another man. He was searching for a suitable answer when she suddenly ran from the room, crying hysterically.

Daniel sat on the bench and stared at the flames, feeling helpless and a little confused. She had interpreted his silence as an answer. When she mentioned that Ted Sloane wanted to marry her, it made him feel uncomfortable, and the thought of her belonging to another man threw him off balance.

He was not sure if his feelings could be interpreted as love for Lavina or if it was simple jealousy that someone else was claiming his best friend. Was he confusing love with friendship? He admired her character, her intelligence, and her warm, generous disposition. If she was to marry Ted and never again be a part of his life, he knew that would be difficult.

Daniel analyzed his own feelings towards the beautiful and winsome Indian maiden, and left the print shop. His Uncle Lee and Aunt Maureen were in the kitchen trying to console a despondent Lavina. He went to her and lifted her from the chair she was sitting in. Lavina looked into his eyes and saw the answer she had been praying for.

Chapter Twenty-One

The spring of 1755 was a welcome relief after the long, harsh winter. Anxious to shed the confinement of their snug homes, the colonists looked forward to outdoor activities such as spring planting time when they could work with the soil and grow food for the winter ahead. Spring brought a fresh, new start to life in the seaport town of Portsmouth. More ships from Europe began to stop at the docks. Crossing the north Atlantic in winter was not contemplated unless absolutely necessary. Spring brought a renewed flurry of activity to the docks. It was the time when the print shop normally purchased their year's supply of paper.

Daniel had promised Lavina and Ruth that he would accompany them to the mission on Lake Mempgremagog in the New Hampshire Grants, so that they could continue their tutoring work among the native tribes. Daniel was not happy with Lavina's decision to place herself in jeopardy on the explosive frontier. They frequently discussed the issue, but he was unable to change her mind. Ultimately, he supported her desire to make a contribution.

He had explained the situation to his Uncle Lee, so that his absence from the print shop would not unduly overload him, regardless of why he would be absent. After depositing the two women at the mission, Daniel intended to take a few days to girdle trees on his land in preparation of planting crops that spring. The girdling would kill the trees and permit sun to reach the ground. Later, when the trees had seasoned, he could harvest them for firewood. The land near his cabin was part of the river's flood plain with rich, fertile soil capable of growing native crops such as corn, squash, and flax.

That winter, Daniel and Lavina discovered the love they shared for each other. Both agreed that they had nothing to lose in waiting a year or two before marrying. Daniel was torn between his work on the paper and his desire to develop his own piece of land. Lavina had to make a hard decision about her excursions to the wilderness armed only with spelling and arithmetic books. She wanted to work one more year. No matter what the future held for them, knowing that they would face it together was a source of strength and comfort. Everyone who knew them experienced the respect and affection they held for each other. Their love had expanded their capacity to function as a pair instead of separate beings. They were in tune with each other's thoughts and feelings to the point where they could accurately complete each other's sentences.

Daniel and Lavina had found peace and harmony. That was in direct contrast to the storms brewing all across the frontier wilderness. Lands from the Kennebec River in Maine to the Allegheny River in the Ohio Valley were unprotected by any effective British or Colonial forces with the exception of localized ranger groups. The frontier was more dangerous than ever. Reports received in Portsmouth and Exeter of isolated cabins being ravaged were daily occurrences in the New Hampshire land grants. Daniel had good reason to be concerned about Lavina's safety while conducting her classes in small tribal villages, viewing the French as more of a threat than the Abenaki.

Early in 1755, the English Parliament had finally been aroused by the desperate cries for help from her colonial brethren. If help did not arrive soon, the French conquest of North America would succeed. Their colonial subjects were desperate. Unless immediate measures were taken, the French and their fanatical Indian allies would control New England, if not all of North America.

Reports of activity along the Hudson River were especially alarming. The French were building forts from Montreal south to Lake Champlain and down the Hudson River. It was a logical invasion route enabling the French to cut the colonies into two pieces. England had finally risen to the threat, and in February had sent a General Edward Braddock to Virginia with orders to plan a campaign against the intruding French. Braddock commanded a large regiment of British regulars. If it was well handled, it was assumed by all concerned that it would be adequate for the task at hand, provided local militia groups were formed to augment the British regiment. Braddock studied the situation and came to the conclusion that if the colonies were to survive, the French threat would have to be met on three fronts.

Lee Cullen was able to obtain summaries of Braddock's recommendations within a week after they were printed by several Virginia presses. Braddock's first suggestion was to build a series of forts in northern New York on the Hudson River to counter the French thrust southward. The second proposal was to seize Acadia and remove the heavy French influence on their northern flank. Over six thousand people loyal to France occupied the area. The third front involved attacks along the Great Lakes region of western New York and an attack on Fort Duquesne on the Ohio River. These thrusts should contain a large enough force to permanently oust the French from the region.

After a winter of forced inactivity, a great deal of planning had taken place within the colonies to confront the border problems. When Daniel read about plans to enlist able-bodied men from New Hampshire, Massachusetts, Connecticut, and Rhode Island for a summer campaign in the Champlain Valley, he was torn between his loyalty to Uncle Lee and the paper and his desire to be a part of the effort. He and Lavina had talked often about his urge to join up with the New Hampshire volunteers. She shuddered at the prospect of his going into combat again, but declined to demand his refusal.

One evening in May, after Lavina had left the print shop and gone home, Daniel was cleaning out the stalls in the barn and feeding the horses. On his way back to the house, he noticed that a light was still burning in the print shop and entered to turn it off. He found his Uncle Lee lying on the floor beside the new press. Frightened and thinking the worst, Daniel knelt down beside him and listened for a heartbeat. His uncle was breathing normally. "Thank God for that," he cried aloud. Daniel kept speaking to him, praying for some answer or recognition, but there was no response!

Several seconds passed, and Daniel began to perspire. His uncle was still not responding to his voice. Not wanting to alarm his Aunt Maureen, Daniel prayed in quiet desperation. "Oh, Lord, do not desert me now. Help this wonderfully kind and gentle man. Give me the strength and ability to help him. Do not take him from us now, for we need him as only You must know. Please, Lord, help us!"

It was the first time in his life that Daniel experienced real unadulterated fear. The prospect of life without the steady hand of his uncle was beyond comprehension. Tears of impotence and frustration swelled in Daniel's eyes. Then, all of a sudden, he felt his uncle move. Wiping the moist film from his eyes with his shirt sleeve, Daniel looked into Uncle Lee's face and saw him smile. Daniel silently thanked his God.

"Uncle Lee," he exclaimed as calmly as possible. "Are you all right?"

Lee braced himself and sat against the press. "I had a dizzy spell and lost my balance, Daniel, I'm okay. I must have banged my head on the floor or the press. We Cullen's have hard heads ye know..." he smiled at Daniel, seeing the concern on his face.

"You had me worried, Uncle. How long have you been here? I left an hour ago to do some chores in the barn, and you were reading at your desk then."

"I remember," Lee recalled closing his eyes. "I got up from my chair to go over the latest article drying on the line when the room seemed to turn around and upside down on me. The last couple of days I've had some trouble walking without the aid of walls and railings. It's bothersome."

Daniel listened carefully. "What's causing it, Uncle Lee?"

"I've had an earache for sometime. Lately, it has kept me awake."

"Why didn't you say something to me or Aunt Maureen? We could have had the doctor look at you," Daniel scolded him softly.

"I know, your Aunt made me promise to do that, and I was going to," Lee sighed.

"Come, Uncle. Let's get you into the house. Whatever it is you were doing can wait until morning," Daniel said, lifting his uncle from the floor.

That evening, Lavina stopped at the Cullen house to bring them some fresh bread that she and Ruth had just made. It was still warm, and Daniel insisted on sampling it immediately. While he and Lavina were sitting at the kitchen table, he mentioned his uncle's earache and dizzy spells. She asked to look at his ear, and Daniel led her into the large sitting room where a fireplace was crackling. Uncle Lee was quietly reading beside the fireplace holding a warm cloth over his ear.

"Uncle Lee, do you mind if Lavina checks your ear?"

"Tonight, my ear is hurting more than ever," Lee told them.

"I don't mean to pry, Mr. Cullen," Lavina said in a calm voice. "Both Ruth and I have been studying herbs and their use in treating many human ailments." She placed a candle near his face and used a small pewter dish to reflect and concentrate the light in his ear. Daniel watched the serious look in her eyes. After examining his ear canal, she set the candle on the table.

"What is it, Lavina?" Daniel asked.

"You have an infection in the ear canal, Mr. Cullen. It looks like a boil to me. Would you object if I go to get Ruth? She's more experienced in these kinds of things than I am. I truly believe she can help you."

"I'll take any help I can get right now," Lee replied in a strained voice.

Ten minutes later, Ruth entered the house carrying a small deerskin pouch containing her medical instruments and herbal medicines. She calmly studied Lee's ear with interest. She spoke to him in soft tones and described his condition, confirming Lavina's diagnosis. "You have a boil growing in your ear, Mr. Cullen. It is probably putting pressure against your inner ear, which is making you dizzy. The boil needs to be drained. That will relieve the pressure. Do you object if I lance the boil? It will hurt some."

"If you think it's for the best," Lee replied with a shrug.

Ruth wiped the sweat beads from his forehead. "I would not attempt it if I didn't think it would help you, Mr. Cullen. It would be easier if you could lie down on the cot beside the fireplace. I'll get things ready."

Daniel helped his uncle to the small cot, while Ruth checked to see that there was plenty of warm water and soft cloths available. Maureen assured her that they had an adequate supply. Ruth lit a candle and placed a small razor sharp scalpel in the flame to sterilize it. Her slender fingers were steady and precise as she held the scalpel to the flames. Daniel was acutely conscious that she did not use her left hand except to place it on Lee's head. "Daniel, would you help me hold your uncle's head steady while I lance the boil?"

Daniel met her eyes and felt strong guilt pangs. "I'd be glad to help," he replied, lowering his eyes.

Lee gritted his teeth and held himself still as Ruth deftly pierced the swollen boil. As soon as the incision was made pus oozed from it-. "Quickly, Daniel," Ruth demanded firmly. "Help me turn his head so that the pus can drain from the canal." Daniel complied by lifting his uncle over on his side while Ruth placed his head on a warm cloth.

"The warm cloths will soothe the inflamed tissue and thin the pus remaining in the boil so that it will completely drain itself."

Ruth explained that once the infected boil has drained, she would turn Mister Cullen over and fill the ear canal full of a warm salt solution. She warned Lee that it would be painful for several minutes, but it was the only way she knew of fighting the infection. She promised he would have relief from the pain after she drained the salt solution. Then, she planned to bathe the ear canal with warm flaxseed oil to soothe the infected area and lessen the pain.

"The flaxseed oil will make you smell like a freshly printed paper from your press," teased Ruth.

"I really appreciate your help, lass," Lee said, grasping her good hand in his. "Ye have a soft touch that reflects the goodness in your heart. I admit that I was frightened by my condition, but thanks to your skills and knowledge I feel much better. God bless ye, lass."

Later that evening, Ruth administered the same warm salt water solution every hour on the hour and substituted a distilled witch hazel liquid for the flaxseed oil. The latter treatment brought noticeable relief to Lee, and he praised her efforts one more time and fell asleep on the cot.

Daniel had been a silent observer watching Ruth and Lavina work on their patient. He shook his head in admiration, not solely for their skills, which were evident, but for their willingness, even eagerness, to help a person in need. The fact that Ruth labored under a difficult handicap sickened him, and he silently cursed at himself: "Imagine, Daniel Cullen. You almost killed a lady, a stranger to you, who does nothing but give of herself to others..."

Aunt Maureen also observed what was taking place, and being of a pragmatic nature, she began preparing something to eat. She added more tea and boiling water to the teapot and warmed some apple pies she had made earlier that day. Daniel had recently purchased a twenty pound tub of cheddar cheese recently arrived from Scotland. The Cullens had a fondness for cheese and kept a supply of it in the house.

They ate what Maureen Cullen had prepared while Lee rested quietly on the cot. Ruth had never eaten cheese and tried a piece. Her smiling eyes lit up, and she took another piece. "It has a smooth texture and a hearty flavor," she explained. "It's also a little tangy... is that a proper word to describe it?"

"My husband says the cheese is sharp with a snap," Maureen laughed softly.

Lavina had enjoyed the cheese for many years. "This combination of apple pie and cheese is a tasty combination and very filling. My father likes to take cheddar cheese on long trips because it keeps well."

Ruth told Maureen that she wanted to stay for the evening so that she could administer to Lee. It was important that the moist bandages be maintained and the infected area be treated on a regular basis for maximum healing. Maureen protested that it was too much for her and offered to do it herself, but Ruth was adamant, telling her that she was more rested than anyone else in the room. Ruth was concerned for Lavina, also, who had worked hard all day in the print shop. They agreed that Ruth would stay with Lee.

"I'll walk you home, Lavina," Daniel offered, turning to Ruth. "Do you want me to bring back Misty? I could put a feather mattress on the floor near the fire for you and her to rest between treatments."

Lavina knew how close mother and child were. "Misty will rest better with her mother."

A warm smile formed on Ruth's lips. "If it's no bother to you, Daniel, you may bring her back."

"It's nice to have children in the house," Maureen Cullen exclaimed. "I've been feeling helpless in all of this. Is there any way I could take over from you later in the evening, Ruth? You need your rest, too."

"I'll come to get you when I need to sleep, Mrs. Cullen. Perhaps you can take over mid-morning. That will give me a chance to rest while Misty is still sleeping soundly."

Lavina made Ruth promise to send for her if necessary, and left with Daniel. A half moon shone through scattered clouds in the dark void filled with stars. It was chilly, and Lavina clung to Daniel as he placed his strong arm around her. She felt happy when she was with him. "It was amazing how your uncle responded to treatment. I was very concerned when I first looked at his ear."

"I have to confess, Lavina," Daniel said. "Seeing him lying on the floor gave me a mighty fright. Ever since I came to his home as a young boy, he has been so invincible. Finding him unconscious made me wonder what I would do if my uncle became unable to direct the day-to-day affairs of the paper. He still does most of the outside advertising work and maintains a phenomenal amount of correspondence with friends and acquaintances throughout the colonies. You and I do the printing, but without his input, we'd have a hard time."

"You're right, Daniel," she agreed with a sigh. "What else are you thinking?"

"We never did complete our conversation about my joining the New Hampshire militia for the coming campaign in the Champlain Valley." Daniel stopped in front of the Cameron home and looked down at Lavina. "If I was to do that, which I admit appeals to me, I'd leave Uncle Lee alone, and he might have to close down the COASTAL BEACON or at least reduce the size of the paper."

"Would that bother you, Daniel?" Lavina asked.

"It would make me feel as if I had let him down. I've captured some of the same pride and responsibility he feels towards the community. He's worked hard to be a source of enlightenment, news, and above all else, a standard for truth. He loves New England and the greater English community in this new land. He's a proud Scot, but he's also a very proud American."

Lavina traced the lines in his face with her fingers. She loved him for the strong ideals he represented and championed. She was particularly proud of the way he interpreted his responsibility to his uncle. "I'm afraid I don't have a definitive answer for you, Daniel. Do you suppose that you may serve a greater good by remaining at work on the paper with your Uncle Lee, than whatever you might accomplish in a military campaign?"

He nodded his head contemplating her statement. "You're a remarkable woman, Lavina. You posed a question that's at the heart of the dilemma."

Before Lavina could answer Daniel, little Misty opened the door and called to them, "Is that you, Aunt Lavina?"

"Yes, Honey," Lavina answered moving from Daniel's embrace. "Daniel and I have come to see if you want to stay for the night with your mother at the Cullen's house?"

"Is Mr. Cullen sick?" she asked.

"Yes, but your mother is making him feel well again," Daniel told her. "I'll give you a piggy-back-ride back to the house if you want."

Misty liked riding on Daniel's shoulders where she could see the world around her from a high vantage point. She answered by running into his open arms. Over the winter he had come to love the child, and she had responded to her Uncle Dan's sincere devotion. A warm glow filled his heart as he lifted the small Indian child to his shoulders.

Chapter Twenty-Two

Several days after Ruth treated Lee's infected boil, she told him that it was healing satisfactorily. He no longer had throbbing pains in his inner ear canal. She had refused to leave his side except for brief occasions, assuming complete responsibility for his condition. When the infection appeared to be under control, she agreed to check on him mornings and evenings.

Two days later, Lavina had a visit from Ted Sloane, who wanted to personally hear that she had rejected his proposal of marriage. Thom Cameron met him at the door. Their paths had crossed often on the frontier. Thom was glad to see the young border man, and knew that he was in for a disappointment. Thom liked Ted, but he saw Daniel and Lavina as more suited for each other. "Lavina isn't here, Ted. She's down the road a ways at Cullen's print shop. Things don't look good out there do they?"

Ted looked at the house Thom pointed to and answered in his unassuming way. "The frontier is going to burst wide open this summer, Thom. You probably know why I came by..."

"I'm sorry how things worked out, Ted. Lavina can explain it to you," Thom answered awkwardly.

"Much obliged, Thom," Ted replied, shaking his hand.

Ted knocked on the door of the print shop. "Come in," a voice he recognized as Lavina's spoke from the corner of the room. Ted entered the shop and saw her leaning over the bins of lead type. She was startled by his unexpected appearance. "Ted, what a surprise to see you!"

"I just wanted to talk to you," he said, approaching her.

"Didn't you get my letter?" she asked hesitantly.

"Yes, that's why I had to come. You didn't give any real reason why you called it off. You simply said that it was over. Why?" Ted asked, feeling out of place.

At that emotionally filled moment, Daniel entered the room carrying an arm full of firewood, which he placed in the woodbin. "Hi, Ted," said Daniel. "I didn't expect to see you. Lavina and I have been working in the print room helping my Uncle Lee," Daniel explained. "I know that you two have things to talk about. Good to see you again, Ted." With that, Daniel left the room and closed the door behind him.

"Is Dan the reason you cancelled our plans?"

"You deserve the truth, Ted. Yes, Daniel is the reason. I did not mean to hurt you, and I've valued your friendship very much. You're an honorable man. Daniel had my love long before I met you. I'm sorry that I've hurt you. Can you forgive me?"

"Well," Ted pondered her answer, nervously fingering his long black rifle. "I had some business in Exeter and figured I'd stop by to hear you tell it to my face. Dan's a lucky man." his voice trailed off. The room was filled with unexpressed feelings. Ted quietly walked out the door without saying another word.

Lavina followed him to the doorway. "You take care of yourself, Ted. I'm so sorry to do this to you."

He turned to look at her, cradling his rifle in his arms. "I'm on my way to the Champlain Valley area with Roger's Rangers. He's assembling recruits in Londonderry. I understand that he's a hard driver and a renowned Indian hater. If we had married in the spring as planned, I probably wouldn't be going with him. Now, I kinda look forward to the challenge. I'll always be your friend, Lavina." Ted waved and continued down the road. Lavina stood in the doorway watching him walk away.

A short distance from the house, Daniel hailed Ted and ran to him. "I wanted to speak to you before you left, Ted. I'm sorry the way things turned out. Lavina is a wonderful person; anyone would love her. I hope you and I can still remain friends."

"If it was anyone else, Dan, I'd feel worse," the quiet border man answered, offering his hand. "The two of you have my blessings."

"Thanks, Ted. I wanted to check with you about conditions along the Connecticut. I'll be escorting Lavina and Ruth back to the mission school in a few days. How bad is it out there?"

Ted told Daniel about the meeting of prominent leaders from the thirteen colonies at Albany. The main reason for the session was to discuss and make provisions for the colonies to work together against the French and Indian threat on the western and northern borders. The proud colonies were suspicious of giving too much power to the Crown. The Crown, in turn, rejected any proposal for a union because it gave too much power to the colonies. The congress was at a stalemate, but they did send William Johnson, a popular Indian agent from New York, to the Iroquois to persuade the Five Nation confederation to maintain their loyalty to the Crown.

The colonies were generally on their own and went their separate ways. Ted described the situation as very explosive throughout the wilderness region. He mentioned that New York and New Hampshire were in the process of raising militia forces to help control events on the frontier. "If you ask me, it will take ten times more armed men to make the frontier safe again. The French are much stronger than they were a year ago. I don't have to tell you that caution is necessary when you take Lavina and Ruth to the northern portion of the land grants. Number Four is bustling with activity right now."

"I'm obliged, Ted. I had a feeling the situation had deteriorated from when I was in Virginia. I wish you the best of luck, old friend. Watch your back trail."

Ted shook his hand again and left with a heavy heart. It was the last time Daniel or Lavina ever saw Ted Sloane.

After speaking to Ted, Daniel had no doubts about Lavina's desire to return to the wilderness for the summer months. From Acadia to the Ohio, the frontier was ready to burst into full scale warfare. Just thinking about it sent cold shivers through his spine. He brought up the subject to Lavina the next day.

"I've seen with my own eyes how savage the French and Indian allies can be, Lavina. They ask for no quarter and give none either," he claimed as they were drinking their first cup of tea in the morning.

"The savagery you describe does not apply to every Native American in the forest." she replied in measured tones. "I fully understand how the French have manipulated some of the tribes for their own purpose. The French gave their Native American allies complete autonomy and freedom of action, without consequences. The shrewd French needed them to augment their war machine in the new world, and as long as the Indians killed the British, the French ignored their bestial tactics. You, more than anyone else, understand the

179

enduring hatred that has grown within the white population, for anything French or Indian."

"Knowing all of these things, how can you want to continue with your work?" Daniel asked impatiently. He was seeing a determined and stubborn side of her that frustrated him.

Lavina placed her tea cup on the bench and faced his searching eyes. "Listen, Daniel, the educational movement Ruth and I have helped to organize, along with many dedicated Christian ministers and lay people, will help the native population better understand our western culture and give them a chance to participate in a future beyond these ugly years of conquest, killing, and maiming. It would not be fair for Ruth and me to desert the dedicated men and women who have sacrificed all for this noble movement. To abandon it now would be unthinkable, and I'm surprised that you cannot see that."

Daniel looked into her fiery eyes. "I'm not asking you to abandon your mission, Lavina. I only question the prudence of doing it now."

"Someone has to counter the terror that is circulating all over the wilderness. What would all of the students we've touched over the past few years think about us if we were to abandon them? We're trying to help them define us, and we cannot do that by running away. We believe we're making a difference." She placed her arms around Daniel. "I was hoping you could understand that. Your support for our efforts is important to me."

He caressed her shiny black hair. "I do support you, Lavina, I really do... It's just that I'll worry about your safety, because I can't protect you."

Lavina ran her fingers through his hair and kissed him. "I love you very much, Daniel Cullen, and it is my dream to be with you always. Right now, your work on the paper is very important, not just for you and your uncle, but for the community, too. Without your coverage of events taking place in our new world, the people will not be well-informed. Information is power, just as knowledge empowers everybody."

"Uncle Lee told me he doesn't see how France and England can avoid a war. Both countries are sending more troops to our shores to resolve the conflicting claims of who will control the land." Daniel felt Lavina tense in his arms. "What's wrong?"

She took a deep breath and stepped back from his embrace to better look into his eyes. "You and everybody else talk about claims to the land. What about the native tribes that met the white man as he first came ashore from their ships? This was all their land before you came. The English, Spanish, and French now look upon the Indians as individuals to be assimilated into their society or as obstacles to expansion policies that must be overcome.

"The claims of the native people for the land they've always lived on and their desire to govern themselves are discredited and ignored. Maintaining cultural integrity is difficult when faced with annihilation, or the threat of displacement in small groups to areas far inferior to the land now controlled by the white man, strangers to the land."

Daniel listened to her passionate monologue. She was able to understand that complex dilemma better than most, and he listened to what she had to say with great interest and compassion.

"I am a proud Native American," she continued. "My mother was a proud Ojibwa whom I loved and admired with all my heart. The Scottish blood of my father, whom I also love, runs through my veins. I feel the injustices against the Indians more than any white man could possibly understand. Your western culture has much that is good and even noble to offer to the native population, but appropriation of the land, simply because you are stronger and have more soldiers and deadlier weapons, does not make it right. The concept of victor reaping the harvest is inherently wrong if it destroys a culture or a way of life that has existed for centuries." She rarely spoke with such conviction and emotion.

"I didn't mean to offend you, Lavina. You know me well enough to realize that I hold similar views of the situation. I also respected and admired your mother. Melinda's daughter is much like her, and I love her very much."

She again came into his arms. "I'm sorry, Daniel. I didn't mean to imply that you or your Uncle Lee hold those prejudices. I was merely speaking of national policies and the way they are administered. Does my racial heritage ever give you cause to regret when you think of what happened to Mary?"

"Lavina, how could you ask such a question of me?" Daniel gasped incredulously. "I'm not going to give it the dignity of an answer. You already know how I feel about you."

She had made him angry and regretted her impetuous question. "Forgive me, Daniel," she cried, holding him. "I've been upset lately thinking about the contentious period ahead, and it frightens me. Ruth and I were discussing this subject last night, and we've had doubts about our role in the conflict that's descending upon the frontier. We've come to the conclusion that education and the ability to read and write are more important than ever if the native population is to become a vibrant part of western society. Assimilation appears to be the best hope of preserving some of the more noble elements of their society. Before that can be achieved, appropriate communication skills are desperately needed."

Daniel kissed her on the forehead. He was proud of her commitment to the Indians. Lavina and Ruth were the vanguard of educators for the native peoples. He saw it as an awesome task, but one worthy of their efforts, and he pledged to support them any way possible.

Lee had recovered from the boil infection and was soon as active as ever in the print shop and in town affairs. One afternoon he returned from a Portsmouth council meeting in an exuberant mood. He confronted Daniel in the print room. "Daniel, when are you going to take Lavina and Ruth to the mission school?"

Daniel glanced at the calendar on the wall near the new press. "We were thinking of sometime in the middle of next month, Uncle Lee. We haven't set an exact date. As you know, the spring has been a cold and wet one, so the trip has been delayed more for weather than anything else. I was planning on talking with you before deciding. I don't want to create a problem with the paper."

"Well, I've just had an offer I can't refuse," Uncle Lee exclaimed. "I've just heard of an expedition being mounted to seize Acadia."

"Acadia!"

"Yes, and I've been asked to go along as an observer by an old acquaintance, Captain Jameson, who will command one of the supply ships. A Lieutenant Colonel Robert Moncton from Massachusetts is in command of the ground troops. Captain Jameson has assured me that I can return to Portsmouth with his ship when he has delivered his cargo of militia and supplies, or I may stay on to cover the land campaign as I please. Colonel Moncton approves of the arrangement."

His Uncle Lee nervously paced the room. "I haven't told your Aunt Maureen yet. I believe she'll approve as long as I don't carry a musket."

"How long would you be gone?" Daniel asked.

"Probably a month. I plan to limit my stay so that we can continue with the paper. I should be able to provide some first-hand accounts of the operation. It sounds exciting to me."

Daniel smiled at his uncle. "It sounds like a wonderful idea, Uncle. That will give us time to get out two editions before I leave with Lavina for the frontier. We'll be able to prepare the readers for a lapse of publishing. Will the advertisers be disappointed?"

"No more than the readers. The anticipation of being the first to learn about our assault on Acadia should generate renewed interest in the paper once we resume printing," Lee replied, heading for the door, where he turned with a devious twinkle in his eyes. "I've got to inform ye Aunt about the plans. I may have to use me Scottish charm to convince her, but it will be worth the effort." Daniel shook his head and chuckled.

That evening, Lee reviewed for Maureen's and Daniel's benefit the situation in which he was about to embark. France was preparing to defend the territory with three thousand more troops. They had set sail from France for Canada earlier that spring. The fleet carrying the troops was intercepted by a British Admiral Edward Boscowen, who had stationed his squadron off the mouth of the Saint Lawrence River.

The blockade became enveloped in a heavy fog bank just as the two fleets met. In the ensuing blind melee, most of the French ships escaped from the blockading British squadron and sailed up the river toward Quebec and to Louisbourg. Two of the French ships were quickly overpowered by the British. They captured two battalions of French marines and a large amount of military supplies. Fast ships had brought the news to Portsmouth, which introduced an element of urgency to their planned response. Acadia had to be neutralized because it presented a constant danger to British shipping in the north Atlantic.

Lee left Portsmouth early the next morning with Captain Jameson. Daniel accompanied his Uncle to the Market Wharf and carried his duffel bag aboard the ship to the Captain's quarters. The tide had passed ebb and was starting to recede as the Captain shouted orders to release the lines from the wharf. The swift current soon swept the heavily loaded craft down the river faster than it could ever travel under full sail on its own. Uncle Lee stood on the starboard side and waved to Daniel.

The ship stopped briefly at the largest island a few miles from the mouth of the Piscataqua River known as the Isle of Shoals. There, they filled their holds with dried codfish. The fishermen on the rugged wind-battered islands had a flourishing codfish business. Their reputations were not very admirable, and the mainland considered them a few notches above cutthroats and thieves. Several pirate ships operated from the islands with impunity. The ship then headed northeasterly toward the Bay of Fundy.

According to the plan, Lieutenant Colonel Moncton had already left Boston Harbor with several regular British officers plus two thousand militia troops from Massachusetts, New Hampshire, and Rhode Island. The main force from Boston included three frigates and a sloop-of-war. Captain Jameson joined the main fleet off the coast of Mount Desert Island and positioned his unarmed ship in the middle of the heavily armed British Royal Navy ships, driving toward the Bay of Fundy under full sails.

Several days later, they arrived in Chignecto Bay early in the morning and unloaded the militia on the isthmus connecting Acadia with the mainland of New Brunswick. Lee was not allowed to go ashore until Fort Beausejour on the isthmus was captured. Several French troops manning a blockhouse on the shore were captured shortly after the militia landed. The French soldiers escaped, burning every dwelling between the blockhouse and the fort. A small force of three hundred men proceeded to the fort with several field pieces for support. They surrounded the fortification and periodically fired at targets of opportunity. The siege phase of the operation had begun.

While the siege troops maintained their pressure on the fort, Lee was allowed to roam at will within the ranks of the soldiers. He observed the area and the massive walls of the fort. The militia periodically fired their field pieces at the fortress. By mid-June the French capitulated. The fort was soon occupied by the militia and renamed Fort Cumberland. Lee was in the fort when the British flag was hoisted up the flag pole. It was a solemn moment, and he proudly saluted it.

Within a short period of time after Fort Cumberland flew the Union Jack, the balance of the French troops were evacuated from Acadia. The British Navy and the New England militia had won a stunning victory with very few casualties. Anxious to return to Portsmouth so that he could describe the well-planned and executed expedition, Lee boarded Captain Jameson's ship in the Bay just as they were lifting anchor to sail home to Portsmouth.

Chapter Twenty-Three

Lavina and Daniel rushed to complete the printing and drying of the last issue of the COASTAL BEACON before they left Portsmouth for the trip to Lake Memphremagog. They packed all of their supplies and belongings on three horses. He had selected his faithful Blackie for Ruth, because he was dependable, gentle, and had a lot of heart. Blackie was still his favorite horse. He then selected two sturdy mares from Thom Cameron's stables for Lavina and himself. They carried about a hundred pounds each plus the riders.

Daniel insisted that Misty ride with him. He had constructed a small seat for her that could be attached to the horn of his saddle so that she rode in front of him. That way she was secure within his arms. He had also been busy making a scabbard for his rifle and two pistols. The rifle was attached to his saddle under his right leg with the butt pointing to the rear so that he could remove the rifle without getting off the horse. The two pistols from his father were always with him, and he tied them on both sides of the saddle beneath the seat for Misty.

The day before they left Portsmouth, he rode to the Cameron home with the new seat and holsters attached. Ruth answered the door, and he asked her if he could take Misty with him to see how she liked the arrangement. Misty heard her name mentioned and poked her head out the door. She saw Daniel on one of Mister Cameron's horses.

"Would you like to take a short ride with me, Misty?" he asked. "I'm going across town to Strawberry Bank to run an errand. You can come with me to check the seat you'll be using on our trip. What do you think of that?"

She ran down the steps and held her arms up to him. He reached down and lifted her into the small seat, and strapped her in so that she could not fall. She giggled and looked down at her mother. "I go for a ride with Uncle Dan on my seat."

"You can hold on to my arms if you want, Misty, or you can steady yourself by grasping the sides of the seat. It's important that you tell me exactly how you like riding like this. Do you understand?"

She shook her head and said, "Yes."

He gently nudged the mare to a slow walk while he wrapped his arms around her. She was relaxed and leaned against him. For an hour he pushed the mare at a full gallop, then down to a trot and a walk, all the time twisting and turning to see if he was going to frighten Misty. Her black braids blew in his face as she laughed and seemed to find it exciting. Not once did she exhibit anxiety or discomfort. Dan waved to an occasional passing rider or wagon whom he knew. He was satisfied that Misty was ready for the trip and took her back to the Cameron house. He dismounted and lifted her out of the seat.

Lavina came out to greet them. "My, my, Misty," she exclaimed happily. "You look like you've had fun with Uncle Dan."

"We rode fast down the street," she answered.

"She's a strong little girl. She's going to be fine on the mare with me," he said.

"I can see that, Daniel. It's nice to see how the two of you get along. Does this mean that tomorrow is still on?"

"We'll go tomorrow as planned, Lavina. Get a good night sleep and eat a hearty breakfast in the morning. I'll have the two horses ready and packed by daybreak at your front door."

"We'll be ready won't we, Misty?"

"Is Mommy coming, too?"

Dan knelt down to her level. "Yes, your mommy is coming with us. It will be a long trip and sometimes you'll be tired and maybe a little impatient. Are you going to be a strong little girl for Mommy and Aunt Lavina?"

"If you want me to be, Uncle Dan," she answered seriously.

That next morning, the weather was warm and sunny without a cloud in the sky. It was a good omen. He had predicted that the trip to Fort Number Four would take three to four days. He intended to keep a steady pace that the horses were capable of maintaining without frequent stops to rest the animals. He wanted to avoid rapid travel at a gallop over the roadway. A lame or injured horse would seriously jeopardize their safety. Consequently, Daniel was as concerned for the animals as he was for the comfort of the travelers.

Twenty minutes from Portsmouth, Misty leaned her head against Daniel and fell asleep. He steadied her with his left arm and remained alert to a potential ambush on the trail. He knew that traveling groups with young women were subject to a higher incidence of ambush by roving Indians or thieves and bandits who saw the females as worth any risk. If they were held up by either type of enemy, Daniel had described a plan that they were to follow without question or hesitation.

Lavina always rode at the rear of the column of three, with Ruth in the middle. If they were stopped or threatened, Lavina was to come abreast of Daniel on his left side so that she could take the reins of his horse in her right hand. Misty was to remain lashed to her seat, for Daniel intended to surprise any potential threat by rolling off the horse with both of his pistols and the rifle. For a fraction of a second the intruders would be confused. At that moment, Lavina and Ruth were to whip their mounts into a rapid gallop and follow the trail as fast as the horses could go. Their safety and that of Misty depended on the speed upon which they left the scene. Daniel made them promise not to look back or stop until the horses were exhausted.

Daniel's survival also depended on the shock of the horses leaving the scene. He calculated that he had several seconds to use the two pistols, then one shot with the rifle which he could use as a club to defend himself. He was as fleet of foot as anyone they might meet in the forest. He intended to do as much damage as possible to the intruders and outrun them. It all depended on the element of surprise, and he was confident of his ability to at least accomplish enough of a skirmish for the women to escape untouched.

The afternoon of the third day, they rode up to the main gate at Fort Number Four on Charlestown in a driving rain. They were exhausted and shivering. Daniel had sheltered Misty from the rain with a woolen hooded parka. She was warm and dry and full of smiles, but she was anxious to exercise. It had been a long trip for her. The first person Daniel saw at the gate was Captain Stevens.

"It's not a fit day for man or beast," he exclaimed, signaling for them to enter the fort. He was as personable and friendly as ever.

"We're happy to be here, Captain Stevens," Daniel leaned down to shake his hand.

The commander directed Lavina, Ruth, and Misty to the great room above the main gate, where they could get something to eat and change into dry clothes. In one section of the hall, blankets were hung to provide privacy for the women. A few British soldiers and several travelers were also using the room that evening to sleep. Daniel helped carry bags containing dry clothing for Ruth and Lavina to their designated sleeping area at the east side of the hall.

"The Captain asked me to come to his quarters as soon as I got you settled," Daniel straightened out three blankets that enclosed their sleeping space. "I'll take care of the horses and check in with him afterwards. You are safe here, so rest and eat all you can. There is always food and tea available at the fireplace across from your sleeping area."

"Where are you going to spend the night?" Lavina asked.

"I'll settle down with the soldiers at the western end of the great room. Try to relax and eat well. I know the three of you are exhausted."

"Thank you for being so patient with us, Daniel." She circled his neck with her arms and kissed him.

"I like that kind of reward," he smiled at her. "I'll check in with all of you when I finish with the Captain. I'll be able to dry out at his quarters."

Daniel knocked on Captain Stevens' door announcing himself: "Captain Stevens, it's Daniel Cullen."

"Come in, Daniel."

Daniel entered the familiar room and felt the warmth of a fire crackling in the fireplace. "I don't know what we'd do if we didn't have Number Four to use as a refuge. The fort is almost like home to me," he smiled.

The Captain directed him to take a seat next to the fireplace. "I wanted to talk about conditions in the colonies. I've read a few copies of your paper over the years. We're at the extreme end of the information circuit and value any information we can discern from the travelers who visit us. How are things in Acadia? Have you heard anything new?"

"I've spoken to a merchant captain who had been shipping men and supplies there. The last time he was in Acadia, the main fort in the Bay of Fundy was occupied by our forces. My Uncle Lee is there now. When he returns, he'll have much to say about events that took place.

I'm bringing Lavina Cameron and her friend, Ruth, north to the mission school on Memphremagog. What is your assessment of the frontier between here and the mission, sir?"

Captain Stevens filled his pipe and offered tobacco to Daniel, who obligingly filled his clay pipe and lit it with a firebrand from the fireplace. "You're embarking into dangerous territory, Daniel. There's no protection available for settlers or travelers in the area. Vigilance and luck are all you have. All of our New Hampshire Rangers have pulled out from the New Hampshire land grants for duty in the Champlain Valley. The border is wide open for the French and their Indian allies to do as they please. The Crown has let all of us down."

The two men talked and smoked their pipes until early evening. Captain Stevens told Daniel of the sudden urgency to begin construction of forts along the length of the Hudson River. Fort Edward had just been completed at the Hudson Falls, an important portage point between the Hudson River and the Champlain Valley. Daniel also knew that Maine had built three forts on the Kennebec River during the past two years.

A General Braddock had arrived in Virginia with a regiment of regulars for a campaign against Fort Duquesne. The move towards the Ohio stronghold was underway as they spoke. It was the only positive piece of news they shared.

Daniel questioned Captain Stevens about Ted Sloane, for he was concerned and sympathized with his friend of many years. Evidently Sloane had passed by Number Four on his way to Lake Champlain with the rangers. Stevens had little respect for the very popular Indian fighter, Captain Robert Rogers. He was one of the fiercest fighters on the frontier. Having praised him for his audacity and effectiveness, Stevens complained that Rogers and his band of irregulars were little different from the marauding Abenaki. Stevens had witnessed an Indian encampment that had been wiped out by Rogers and his men. The butchery was unspeakable. It included infant children and pregnant women with their unborn fetus removed from the womb of the dead mothers. Daniel learned that Ted Sloane was killed in the forests west of Lake Champlain while serving with Roger's Rangers. Indians had captured him and slowly tortured him by roasting him over a roaring fire. His captives delighted in eating portions of his body!

"Perhaps the struggle on the frontier has reached that point where unwanted slaughter begets more butchery, but I can't believe that man has to slide to the lowest level of animals," Captain Stevens spoke with a firm distaste of the horror that always seemed to accompany the famous fighter. "I'm not able to call Roger's Rangers soldiers, for they have betrayed every standard of civilized behavior. The things they do to opponents is common place. I would never tolerate such conduct from any man in my command."

"I've heard rumors here and there about the man, but was never able to substantiate anything," Daniel added.

"Don't get me wrong," Stevens continued. "Perhaps we need such men at this crucial time in our development. If that is the case, then it has tarnished the nobility of our efforts. I'm saddened to know that he has taken to the field with a large body of men."

Daniel listened to the able soldier with interest and respect. He was a man much like his Uncle Lee. Both had served the Crown with distinction and valor. The inhabitants of the area surrounding the fort depended on him and the fort for protection. They had taken his measure and made it possible for him to remain at his post.

Darkness came early that first night at the fort. It was still raining and did not bode well for traveling the next day. Daniel had supplemented their food supply when he purchased ten pounds of pemmican at the trading post near the fort. He liked the staple food for its taste as well as its ability to maintain freshness for weeks at a time. He made a point of checking with Lavina and Ruth to see that they were settling in for the night. Then, he retired to the west corner of the great room near the stairs leading to the lookout tower and laid out his blanket on the floor.

He had just closed his eyes when he heard Misty call for him in a hushed voice. There was a candle burning in a lantern near the stairway beside him. He told her to walk toward the light, and he intercepted her.

"What's wrong, Misty?" he inquired, picking her up. "Are Mommy and Aunt Lavina sleeping?"

"They snore, and I was afraid of the dark," Misty answered, holding on to his neck.

"They are very tired and need their sleep. Do you want to stay with me for the night?" he asked in a low voice. The room was filled with

191

soldiers and travelers of all types, and he could understand how she might feel uneasy.

"Yes," she answered quietly.

He smiled at her in the limited light. "I have room for you on my blankets. We'll have to get up very early to tell your mother where you are, or she'll be worried about your absence."

"If I'm with you, she will not be worried," she replied.

The words touched him and he embraced the child. Minutes after they retired to his bedroll, her breathing was steady and relaxed. Misty slept with her head resting on his arm for the remainder of the night. His Uncle Lee had once told him that to be loved by a small child is the ultimate compliment for a human being. He was inclined to agree with that sentiment.

Lavina was the first to wake at first light and noted that Misty was not on the blanket between her and Ruth! She began to panic and looked throughout the great room. Privacy blankets prohibited her from seeing very much. She threw a shawl around her shoulders and began to systematically search the room. Lavina located Daniel and saw Misty curled up on his arm with a blanket around her. A broad smile crossed her face, and a sigh passed her lips. Not wanting to disturb them, she retraced her steps to her sleeping area.

Ruth was sitting up on the blankets when Lavina returned. "Don't worry. Misty is with Daniel. They're sleeping soundly."

Ruth nodded her head, understanding what Lavina had said. "Isn't it nice to see how those two have taken to each other?"

"It truly is," Lavina answered in a whisper, lying down on her blanket. "She's such a good child."

Within an hour the great hall was emptied as soldiers were ordered to their posts and the travelers and visitors began to prepare for the new day. Misty opened her eyes and saw her Uncle Dan looking down at her out of the corner of his eyes. "Now that you're awake, little girl, we had better get you back to your Mommy."

"I have to go potty," she whispered in his ear.

"Hold on a little longer, Misty, mommy can take you to the place where you can do that," he said. "Come, let's find your mother and Aunt Lavina." He held out his hand to her. She grasped it tightly.

Daniel delivered Misty to her mother and went outside to check on the weather. It had stopped raining, but the sky was heavily overcast. He decided that they could attempt a run to his cabin on the banks of the river. He returned to let Lavina and Ruth know that the weather was suitable for travel, and they should prepare for the day with a good breakfast. He then left to attend to the horses in the corral east of the fence. Always alert for danger, Daniel carefully searched the surrounding area when a soldier leaned over the top of the stockade: "I've checked the area, sir, and it looks clear to me. Occasionally, the Indians sneak into the corral and make off with the horses at the crack of dawn. I see no evidence of them this morning."

"Thanks," Daniel hailed the soldier. "I'm going to saddle three horses for a trip north along the river."

"You'll want to be wary," the soldier warned.

Once the horses were fed and saddled, Daniel returned to the interior of the fort for something to eat. He found Lavina and Ruth eating beside a large fire burning in the center of the stockade with a heavy cast iron pot hanging over the flames. He helped himself to a bowl of Scottish stew made with venison instead of beef or lamb such as his mother used to make in Scotland.

Twenty minutes later, Daniel urged his party to gather their blankets and follow him to the waiting horses. He felt a sense of urgency to make the trip to his cabin as early in the day as possible. He was unsure of what he would find or if the cabin was even standing. He was in a sober mood as they mounted the horses, and he warned them to be vigilant of anything that looks suspicious. The horses could outrun any person on foot, unless the well-worn pathway was blocked with fallen trees. In that event, he urged them to immediately turn towards the river and plunge the horses into the water, keeping a low profile by hugging the horse's neck.

Lavina was seeing a more demanding and protective Daniel on this trip than she had ever seen. She attributed it, accurately, to their destination, the cabin where he and Mary and Lee II had lived. She remained silent and followed his suggestions, for she knew that he was an experienced forest traveler.

Misty sensed the tensions driving Daniel. "Are you angry at me, Uncle Dan?" she asked innocently.

He held her closer with his left arm. "No, I could never be angry with you, Misty. I'm just concerned about what we might find at my old cabin, that's all. I didn't mean to make you worry."

How could he tell her what was really in his heart? Not only was he approaching the area where his family had been butchered almost beyond recognition, it was also the same place where he had shot Misty's mother, endangering the baby he now held in his arm. The magnitude of his recklessness still bothered him, more than ever, since he had become better acquainted with Ruth and her baby. Was his affection for Misty generated by guilt of what he had done? It was a question that made him feel unsure of himself, for Misty deserved to be loved for herself, and he hoped it was the case with him, but he could not be sure.

A few hours after leaving Fort Number Four, they passed the trading post at Hanover, which looked like an armed camp. Guards were posted all around the simple cabin. Daniel avoided the post with the intention of increasing their pace to his cabin. Midday they stopped at a prominent hilltop beside the river to eat and rest the horses. He had carried a ration of oats for the horses and fed it to them during their first stop. Daniel and the women ate pemmican and drank water, watching the river flowing south to the sea.

Lavina sensed Daniel's uneasiness and sat beside him while they ate. "I didn't realize it was going to hurt so much," he revealed, grasping her hand in his.

"How could it not be painful, Daniel? If I could wipe away all the grief, I would do it. I can't say I know how you feel, but I share your sorrow and agony," she replied in that soft serene voice that always comforted him.

"If everyone's finished eating, we should push on," Daniel declared, loading the rest of their food on his mount. "We should be at the cabin within an hour."

When the cabin south of Daniel's came into view, it brought back memories of the way he had avenged the murder of his family. As they passed spot where Ruth came ashore after he had shot her, he reluctantly looked at Ruth. Their eyes met, they were remembering the same scene. Daniel turned away first.

Ruth reined Blackie to a stop. "This spot will always be painful to me, Daniel," she revealed what was in her heart. "I see the regret in your eyes, and I can understand the depth of your sorrow. You must know that I, as a Christian woman, forgive you for what took place here. I admit that I carried hatred for you in my heart for a long time, but now that I have come to know how kind and generous you are, forgiveness comes easy. If I can forgive you, then you must forgive yourself, Daniel. Will you do that for me?"

Her remark unleashed all the pent up emotion he had carried with him for so long. Tears filled his eyes and ran down his face. Little Misty heard her mother talk to Uncle Dan in a serious voice, and she knew that something important was taking place. She looked up at him and saw the large tears dripping off his chin. She reached up and wiped them with her small fingers. "Don't cry, Uncle Dan. Everything is going to be all right."

He hugged her and glanced at Ruth. "I will try to be as strong as you are, Ruth. My faith is not as deep as yours and Lavina's. Your words are comforting, and I thank you for your generosity. Now, let's see if the cabin is still standing."

As the cabin came into view, Daniel crouched to look through the brush on the trail. Something did not feel right. He held up his arm to stop Ruth and Lavina and whispered to Misty, "Listen Misty, we've got to be quiet. The yonder cabin is mine, but I see smoke coming from the chimney, and we're not certain who's inside. For now, we're going to back-track on the trail to hide the horses while I see what's going on." Misty looked up at him as if to say that she understood.

He selected a sheltered location with grass and water for the horses and immediately dismounted to tether them to nearby saplings. Daniel gave Ruth and Lavina each one of his primed pistols while he pulled his rifle from the saddle scabbard. "I plan to walk up and look inside the window on the east side of the cabin. You three be quiet and stay here until I come for you. The horses should remain quiet grazing the green grass by the river. If something happens to me, promise that you'll ride out of here towards the trading post."

"I can't promise, Daniel," Lavina answered, calmly fingering the pistol in her hand. "Be careful and don't worry about us."

Ruth was studying the cabin as she kneeled on the ground with Misty clinging to her waist. Daniel was satisfied that they were well-concealed and said, "I'll be careful, and you two should be alert for any intruders that may be in the vicinity." With that, he was gone.

Chapter Twenty-Four

Daniel skirted the open area between the cabin and the sheltered hiding place where Lavina and Ruth were waiting. He moved swiftly, keeping low to the ground to avoid detection. The small, three-sided shelter he had erected for the Jersey cow that was butchered by the Indians, hid his presence in case someone was looking out the window on the east side of the cabin. He crawled along the ground close to the shelter until he reached the cabin where he placed his ear to the pine log walls and listened.

He heard two or three people inside talking in French. He did not understand what was being said, but two of the voices were Abenaki. Their sharp guttural speech was distinctive, and he was familiar with it. There were three men inside, and that worried him. He had not seen any sign of horses around the cabin, so they either came by foot or by canoe on the river.

Reluctant to take a chance to look into the window, Daniel continued to listen to the voices and made a mental picture of where the men were located inside the cabin. Convinced that he knew their location, Daniel retraced his steps back to Ruth and Lavina.

"There are at least three men in the cabin. They're talking French, but two of the men are Abenaki. I don't understand French, so I don't know what they were discussing," Daniel informed them in a calm voice. "My guess is that they came down the river and stopped for the evening."

"Why don't we simply bypass the cabin and continue a mile or so north until nightfall?" Ruth suggested, concerned about a deadly confrontation.

Lavina echoed her sentiments for the same reasons. "What is accomplished by facing the visitors?"

Daniel was inclined to establish his ownership rights, and was reluctant to leave enemy elements on his back trail. "If I crash through the door with the two pistols in my hands, I would be able to get inside while they're still startled at my sudden presence. I'm surprised that they do not have a guard outside." Daniel paused and watched the reaction from the two women. They were troubled and frightened at his proposal. He continued, "If I leave you with my rifle, you would be able to stop any one who tries to flee from the cabin."

Lavina was still reluctant to contribute to a confrontation, but Daniel's determination to enter the cabin held firm. She gave in with a hesitant sigh. "If you think this will work. What are you going to do with the men inside?"

"That depends on them. If they're reasonable, we can send them down the river unarmed and without food. The three men are our enemies, and we have an obligation to at least thwart their efforts to continue killing innocent people," Daniel explained, fully aware of the imminent danger to the two women and Misty. He shook his head as if there was simply no other way.

The three planned a precise sequence of events. Daniel was certain that he could break through the door and get inside without any trouble. Once he was inside, he could hold the men prisoners until Lavina backed him up. He knew that Lavina was an excellent shot with either rifle or pistol. Misty was instructed to stay with her mother who would remain secluded until the situation in the cabin was under control. All three understood what was to be done.

Daniel kissed Lavina on the cheek and silently crawled to the cabin. He reached the small clump of birch saplings that had sprung up since he had cleared the area several years ago. There, he carefully inspected the pistols. They were loaded with double lead bullets and fully primed. He cocked the hammers and ran to the door. His two hundred and twenty pounds easily smashed the door off its hinges. He rolled onto the floor with both arms aiming a pistol at the three men sitting at the table in front of the fireplace. It was as he thought, two of the men were Abenaki warriors. The third person was a surprise to him; it was a Jesuit priest in a black robe.

The warrior closest to Daniel had instinctively drawn his tomahawk, and was poised above him prepared to strike. Daniel fired the pistol in his right hand, hitting the Indian square in the chest, driving him backward against the table. He was dead before he hit the floor. The room filled with smoke from the discharged weapon. He raised himself from the floor and directed the priest and other warrior to place their hands behind their heads. They saw the seriousness in his eyes and did as he demanded.

Seconds after the pistol shot, Lavina appeared at the doorway with the rifle primed and ready. She winced at the body on the floor and studied the two prisoners with their hands clasped behind their heads. The priest was fluent in the English language. He was a short, energetic man with bulging eyes that searched out everything around him, and a protruding Adam's apple. He was not frightened; indeed, he had an insolent smile on his lips and was disgusted at the way he was being treated.

Daniel instantly disliked the priest. "What are you doing on my land and in my cabin?" he asked in a slow voice not wanting to be misunderstood.

The priest laughed at him. "How dare you question a Jesuit priest? I'm allowed to travel wherever I please."

"Not on my land," Daniel growled at his overbearing air of superiority. Images of Mary and little Lee flashed through his head. Death and desolation on the frontier followed in the wake of the rabid black-robed Catholic priests. Daniel held a deep hatred for them. They knew that their measures were contrary to the true teachings of Christianity, yet they arrogantly persisted in their debaucheries. "Your record of butchery on this frontier dispels any notion that you are a man of God. Your God is one of fear, death, and hatred. I do not recognize your credentials; therefore, I'll treat you like the lowly beasts you and your brothers have become."

The sturdy Abenaki standing closest to the door did not understand what was being said, but he discerned the tone of the conversation. He surveyed the situation and estimated that he could knock Lavina out of the door before she could fire the rifle, or Daniel could take aim with the pistol he held on the priest. It was a desperate attempt to take flight. The warrior leaped towards the door. He had underestimated Lavina's reflexes. She pointed the barrel of the rifle at

198

his midsection and pulled the trigger, releasing the hammer. In that fraction of a second before the powder in the barrel ignited the charge, the warrior tried to push the rifle to one side. He was too late. Daniel had charged the weapon with two bullets, and they tore a large hole through the Indian's stomach. A look of horror crossed his face when he realized that he had lost the gamble and crumpled to the floor.

Lavina's blood drained from her face, and she felt faint. Daniel saw that she was troubled by the incident and rushed to her, taking the rifle from her hands and leaning it against the wall. He took Lavina in his right arm and turned to the priest. "You stay where you are, Jesuit, or I'll send you to eternity with pleasure."

The priest was worried and took on a more conciliatory attitude. He looked mournfully at the dead Indians on the cabin floor and sat down at the table in silent resignation.

Daniel carried Lavina to the cot beside the fireplace, all the time watching the wily priest.

Ruth heard the sound of gunfire coming from the cabin, remaining out of sight in the brush, frightened at what might have happened to Daniel and Lavina. She held Misty close to her and softly kissed her on the forehead. "Be quiet, my baby girl, and don't be frightened."

Lifting a branch to one side so that she could see the cabin more distinctly, Ruth gasped in horror. An Abenaki warrior was approaching the cabin from the riverbank with a string of fish in his left hand and a tomahawk in the right. He passed within twenty feet of their hiding place without noticing them. He kneeled to study the partially opened door. Ruth's heart beat so rapidly she was afraid the warrior would hear it.

Fearful that Misty would make a noise and give their position away, Ruth made a desperate decision to attack the warrior. She released Misty and placed her on the ground where she could look into her child's eyes. Misty seemed to sense her distress and remained silent as her mother placed a trembling finger over her lips to signify that she must not make a sound. Then, Ruth propelled herself at the warrior. Leaping into the air from her hiding spot, she drove the hunting knife she always carried, into the Indian's back. Twice her right arm arced through the air driving the razor-sharp knife to the hilt. Twice the warrior gasped in pain.

The Abenaki died silently, not realizing that an Ojibwa maiden had eliminated a dangerous threat to the safety of her daughter and her friends. It was an extraordinary act of courage that made her feel nauseous and weak the moment she pulled the bloody knife from the inert body. Misty was terrified and began to cry hysterically, running quickly to grasp her mother by the legs, shaking and screaming out of control.

Daniel was comforting Lavina when he heard the cries outside. The desperation of the screams alarmed him, and he leaped for the door. He saw Ruth holding Misty. At first, he wondered what was wrong, then he saw the still figure at her feet. "My God, Ruth," he cried. "Are you and Misty all right?"

Lavina heard his sudden outburst and rose from the cot. "Ruth, Ruth," she screamed and ran to them. Quickly surveying the scene, Lavina enclosed Misty and Ruth in her arms. Tears of desperation filled their eyes.

Daniel looked on helplessly, not daring to take his eye off the wily Jesuit. The priest was praying over the dead bodies inside the cabin when Daniel brusquely grabbed him by the collar. "Drag these two bodies out the door and place them at the edge of the clearing." Daniel pointed through the door near where he had buried Mary and Lee II. "Afterwards, you can gather the third member of your party and start digging a grave for each of them. Move, or you'll get the same treatment."

The priest snarled at him and began dragging a body out the door just as Lavina directed Ruth and Misty to the cabin. Ruth, still in a state of shock, saw the priest and mocked him. "You so-called man of God. You are responsible for the fiendish brutality unleashed by my people upon the white settlers. It is you and your evil kind that have incited and encouraged the vile acts. God will punish you for your deception." Ruth spit in his face as she entered the cabin. "It's you who should be dead, not your companions."

Lavina ushered the distraught Ruth to the cot while Daniel took the priest outside to bury the bodies. An hour later, Daniel returned to the cabin and observed Ruth and Lavina calmly drinking hot tea. "It's getting dark out there. I've tied the priest to a post in the woodshed where he can spend the night."

"The animal doesn't deserve to be treated so well," Ruth insisted with a viciousness that surprised Lavina and Daniel.

Daniel sat beside Ruth on the cot and accepted a warm cup of tea from Lavina. "Why are you so harsh against this Jesuit? Do you know him?"

Ruth pondered his question a second and responded with carefully measured words. "My husband was a gentle and proud Delaware warrior who had found contentment and peace when he studied about Jesus Christ. His conversion to Christianity was sincere and heartfelt, and he did not hesitate to share his convictions with others. He was a member of a small hunting party made up of Abenaki and braves from other tribes including Delawares and Ojibwas from the Saint Francis village at Odanak. Leading the small party was a Jesuit priest who had planned an attack against a white settler's cabin on the Ammonoosuc River. My husband vocally refused to be a party to the torture and rape of a woman and her daughter. The priest went into a tirade calling him a traitor and buried a hatchet in his skull. I am not enough of a Christian to forgive the Jesuits for killing my husband."

It was a declaration of pain and suffering that revealed a great deal about Ruth as a victim and as a person. Daniel now understood, for the first time, how this devoted Ojibwa could forgive him for disfiguring her. He got up from the cot and looked at Misty lying close to her mother. He smiled at her, but she was still so traumatized that she could not reciprocate with her traditional wide smile. He gently patted her on the arm and placed another log on the fire.

It was a sober party that prepared for the night at Daniel's cabin. He told Lavina and Ruth that he could defend them and the cabin better by taking a position just outside the door. He left the lighted room and paused until his eyes adjusted to the darkness. Checking the rope fastenings on the Jesuit, he fed the horses and selected a location in a small clump of white ash sprouts where he could see the horses and the door to the cabin.

The night was dark and still with a heavy overcast that threatened rain. It was chilly for a July evening, and Daniel was glad that he had brought along a doe pelt to wrap around himself and his rifle. He had left one pistol with Lavina, the other one was in his right hand beneath the deerskin. His thoughts were with Lavina and Ruth. Both were troubled by the death of another human being. He had tried to explain that they had acted in self-defense. They listened to what he had to say, but they were little comforted by his words.

A half hour after Daniel had settled into his secluded vantage point, he saw the shadow of a person approaching him. His thumb tightened on the hammer of the pistol when a soft voice called, "Daniel, it's me, Lavina."

"Come forward a few more steps," he answered in a whisper. He reached for her hands and pulled her close to him.

She kissed him and whispered, "I simply wanted to tell you how much I love you, Daniel. I know that you worry about Ruth and me. We worry about you, too."

"I'm so sorry that our journey has turned out this way," he confided in a low voice. "I should have taken your advice and by-passed the cabin. I'm sorry, Lavina. My Scottish pride still gets the best of me at times."

"Hush, Daniel," she answered. "I came out tonight to reassure myself that you were all right, and to see if you were comfortable in this damp air. I didn't come to criticize events of the day. Keep as dry as you can, and take comfort in the fact that we're more than halfway to our destination. Goodnight, my love." She kissed him warmly on the lips and disappeared into the night.

The night proved uneventful. An hour before dawn, Daniel quietly patrolled in a circle several hundred feet from the cabin. He found no evidence of anything unusual and waited another hour for the sun to come out. Retracing his steps around the cabin, he checked the bindings on the priest. Smoke rose from the chimney, and he knew the women were awake. He remained silent and extra alert, aware that the first hour of dawn was the preferred time of attack for the Indians.

An hour later, Daniel and his charges were leaving the clearing of the cabin with the priest walking behind Daniel's horse. His hands were tied, and a rope around his waist was attached to Daniel's saddle. Ruth and Misty followed the priest, while Lavina brought up the rear armed with one of the pistols. They made good time following a well-worn path within sight of the Connecticut River. In the middle of the day, Daniel pulled the party to a stop at an elevated plateau where they could see a long section of the river.

He suggested that they hold up for a brief rest and eat. The pemmican mixture tasted good to the hungry travelers as they sat watching the river. Ruth directed Daniel's attention to two canoes traveling south on the river in mid-stream. The lead canoe held two men, and the second contained one. Daniel studied the three men with his telescope, estimating that they were either trappers or traders, so he hailed the canoes and ran to the shore to get their attention. The men in the lead canoe pointed to the shore, directing the trailing canoe to steer closer to Daniel. Before the canoe landed, Daniel ordered the priest to come down the bank to the river, and cautioned Lavina and Ruth to remain out of sight.

The canoe with two men remained off shore while their companion landed his canoe on a sandy stretch of the bank. Daniel noticed that the two men were holding their muskets at the ready. He did not blame them for the precaution. He presented himself and the priest to the occupant of the beached canoe. "I'm Daniel Cullen," he announced. "I was hoping that I could impose upon your generosity to take this priest off my hands. I found him and three Abenaki at my cabin. The Indians are dead now."

"We'll be obliged to take him to Number Four," the tall, thin man spoke with an Irish accent. "I'm Lane Stewart. We've just come from Lake Champlain where we served with Robert Rogers and his rangers. The despicable behavior of these French clerics is well known. We'll be happy to see that he gets his just dues."

Daniel breathed a sigh of relief. "I'll be obliged to you, Lane."

"You may be interested to know that just before we left the Champlain Valley, a courier told us that the large British force under General Braddock has been wiped out by the French near Fort Duquesnes on the Monongahela River. There were very few survivors. The post rider was especially concerned about the Champlain area because the French captured Braddock's documents, disclosing British plans for the Hudson Valley."

"My God, Braddock had over twelve hundred men," Daniel exclaimed.

"Well, British troops are almost extinct on the frontier now. God help the settlers. The French and Indians now have free reign," Lane Stewart said, shaking his head sadly.

"So, in your opinion, the border will be more dangerous?" Daniel asked thinking about Lavina and Ruth.

"How can it not be worse than ever?" Stewart answered, clearing a place in his canoe for the priest.

Daniel picked up the Jesuit and dropped him in the canoe with a parting threat. "If I ever see you again in the company of Indians, I'll kill you."

With a wave to the departing canoes, Daniel returned to the camp mulling over what he just learned. The ominous news troubled him.

Chapter Twenty-Five

Daniel safely escorted Lavina and Ruth to the mission on Lake Memphremagog without incident. Before he left to return to Portsmouth, he solicited a promise from Lavina that she would stay close to the school and give up the missionary trips she and Ruth traditionally made throughout the northern wilderness area to small tribes and clans. Daniel left Lavina with a heavy heart, for he had taken her to the most dangerous region in North America.

Braddock's massive defeat on the Monongahela sent shock waves throughout the countryside. The destruction of the British force and the death of General Braddock emboldened the French to even greater efforts to remove the English presence on the continent and leave France in control. The climate of fear on the frontier was high for good reason – the Abenaki and French were free to plunder at will.

On the return trip to Portsmouth, Daniel rode one of the mounts from Thom Cameron's stables known as a Narragansett. It was the first time he had ridden the horse. Lavina had selected it for her mount on the trip and suggested that Daniel return it to her father's string of horses. Blackie and Ruth had gotten along just fine, as Daniel had anticipated, so he gave Ruth the horse as a gift. The Narragansetts were known for their endurance, gentle dispositions, and comfortable gallop. The small mare proved to be a champion, and the longer Daniel rode her, the more respect he had for her willingness to perform. She never faltered when he saw a smooth stretch of path ahead and urged her to a fast gallop. He admired the proud heart that allowed her to give when more was asked of her. Daniel was determined to have Thom Cameron locate a Narragansett for himself upon his return.

He was concerned about his Uncle Lee and the Coastal Beacon. Now, in this most recent period of crisis, he knew that the paper played an important role in guiding the colonists through the unsettled days ahead by providing the most up-to-date information possible. He and his uncle agreed that an informed citizenry was a more responsible citizenry.

For months, Daniel had been debating whether he would be more valuable to the English cause by joining a militia or a ranger formation, or helping his Uncle Lee continue publishing the newspaper. The trip to the mission had given him the opportunity to think about the options, and he had made up his mind to help his uncle increase circulation of the COASTAL BEACON. The paper could become a clear voice informing the people, and at the same time, representing their positions and feelings on current issues. The more he thought of the potential, the more excited he became, and the harder he rode the gallant Narragansett toward home.

One day, shortly after Daniel had returned to Portsmouth, he and Uncle Lee were in the print shop where they had been training two young men in the art of typesetting and printing. The added help would free Lee and Daniel from long, painful hours of repetitious work and allow them the freedom to travel and collect the news and compose copy. Daniel was most pleased with the direction the paper was taking.

Both Daniel and Lee proofread the first printing of a new edition of the paper and retired to the kitchen where Aunt Maureen had poured a hot cup of tea for them. "You two have a contented look about you," she observed with a cheerful smile. "Sit. The tea is just right."

They willingly took their seats at the table. Daniel acknowledged his Aunt with a kiss on the cheek. "Thanks, Aunt Maureen." He turned to his uncle. "I was down at the waterfront on Market Street earlier this morning talking with your old friend, Captain Jameson. He told me that on his most recent trip from Acadia, two days ago, he had a boat full of relocated French Acadians. Evidently, the British command up there is forcefully shipping them out a boatful at a time. Jameson said he left some of the passengers at Portland and some have headed inland from Portsmouth. They had limited belongings and not much in the way of funds to care for themselves. He felt sorry for their plight. What's happening in Acadia, Uncle?"

Lee Cullen anticipated the question. "I share your concern and that of Captain Jameson. The relocation policy of the Crown in Acadia is not a proud one. It came about as a last-ditch attempt to reduce French influence in the province. The uprooting of families has been successful in curbing resistance to the English claims on the province. The French inhabitants refused to pledge allegiance to England. Fort Louisbourg on Cape Breton Island remains strongly in French hands, and is a thorn in the side of the Royal Navy. It rules the entrance to the Saint Lawrence River. Since relocation has been introduced, many families have fled to other parts of Canada and the colonies in New England. Most, however, have made their way to French-controlled Louisiana. Jameson said that over six thousand Acadians have been forced to give up their homes and land. It's the price they pay for allegiance to France. An attempt was made by the Crown to help the people make that transition, but they adamantly refused. Now, they're poor victims of the undeclared war between England and France."

"It's a rotten policy if you ask me," Aunt Maureen added forcefully.

Daniel shook his head. "I don't agree with the policy either, Aunt Maureen, but I can't think of any viable alternatives right now."

"Mark my words," Lee predicted, his eyes focused on the burning embers of the fireplace. "The Hudson and Champlain Valleys are going to be the flash point for this confrontation between France and England. Several hundred men from New Hampshire are already in the area serving with militia units, or they're with Robert Roger's Rangers. My opinion of him as a man is less than complimentary, but he has proven to be a dynamic and successful leader of irregular forces. Fort Number Four will become an important distribution center and supply conduit to the Champlain area if the campaign unfolds as I expect it to."

Daniel smiled at his uncle and marveled at his ability to visualize events on a large scale. He had a passion for maps and historical documents and was always studying them with his reading glasses held on the tip of his nose. Dan knew that the Champlain and Hudson Valleys were not only the most direct route to the colonies along the coast, they also divided the colonies. The French were already telegraphing their intentions by the number of troops entering the Lake Champlain area. They were building a new fortification, called Fort Frederick at the crucial choke point at the southwestern end of the lake.

Dan and his uncle talked about how the British countered the move by sending a large force under Major General William Johnson, a noted Indian agent from northern New York, to attack and eliminate

Fort Frederick. Fortifications had been built all along the Hudson by the colonies up to the Hudson Falls, a strategic portage between the Hudson River and Lake George. Johnson named the fort built at that location, Fort Edward. At that time, it was the most northern fortification under English control. Lee had based his ominous prediction on the fact that both nations were establishing strong points that could be easily defended and were capable of challenging any further claims by their opponents.

"An explosive clash is inevitable," he declared, shaking his head. "Diplomacy won't work, there's too much at stake. This will be a fight in which the victor takes all. Right now, I fear that the French hold the stronger hand."

"I should never have left Lavina and Ruth at the mission," Daniel admitted his mistake and agonized over the decision. "Even if I went up there to get her, the trek back would be more dangerous than ever."

Maureen listened to the two men in her life with pride. They were so alike in temperament and demeanor. She smiled at the way Daniel listened to every word his uncle spoke. From the moment Maureen and Lee first met, Lee was constantly reading and sought to learn about those things in the world that interested him. As a self-taught man, he had gained respect and admiration from a large number of scholarly friends and acquaintances. His modest and gentle ways even earned him a begrudging acceptance by the Tories who opposed his strong conservative principles.

The COASTAL BEACON had grown in circulation since Daniel had returned from Vermont. During the summer, Daniel and Lee were quick to visit every vessel that anchored in the Portsmouth harbor. They talked with crews and ships' officers for news, gossip, etc., regardless of their port of origin. The brisk trade between Portsmouth and other ports on the Atlantic seaboard, gave them a very up-to-date picture of events throughout the Atlantic colonies. Every week, they received papers from Boston, Baltimore, Virginia, and New York. The volume of news increased to the point where the BEACON, on occasion, became an eight-page weekly paper. When Daniel first came from Scotland, the paper was a single page of local news, weddings, births and other important events along the coast.

One clear day late in September when the autumn leaves were just beginning to become colorful, news arrived from New York that

General William Johnson had defeated a large contingent of French forces at the southern end of Lake George. The French lost over four hundred men killed, to the English loss of two hundred and sixty men, and the French force retreated to Fort Frederick on Lake Champlain. Immediately after the battle, General Johnson ordered the construction of a fort at the southern end of Lake George. He named it Fort William Henry after one of the King's grandsons.

In the aftermath of the battle, the French began construction of Fort Carillon at the extreme end of Lake Champlain where the narrows drains into Lake George.

The fall of 1755 was cold and blustery, and Daniel was worried sick about Lavina. Neither he nor her father had heard from her since he left them at the mission. Consequently, Daniel made preparations to go to the mission to bring her back home, or at least determine if she was safe and well. Before he left, Daniel wrote several news stories for the paper so that, in his absence, Uncle Lee would not be overburdened to get the paper out on schedule.

The day he left Portsmouth was a sober and fearful day in the Cullen household. Aunt Maureen wished him well and gave him a long embrace. His departure brought up the memory of when their son, Robert, had left for the last time. Partings were especially painful for them. Uncle Lee did not say much except to tell Daniel not to worry, that he could handle the paper while he was away.

Thom Cameron was an expert on horses, and he insisted that Daniel ride the Narragansett he had liked so much. The small mare was a good choice. Her surefootedness in the wilderness was without equal. He drove the mare hard all the way, and not once did she waver.

Daniel did not take the trail to Fort Number Four, instead he traveled in a northwesterly direction across the southern tip of the rugged mountain chain in central New Hampshire, intersecting the Connecticut and Ammanoosuc River junction. He was driven by worry and fear for Lavina and thought of little else during the long trip. He had a feeling that something had gone wrong, and he could not help blaming himself for placing her at risk.

The stockade at the mission was heavily guarded with sentinels on the narrow catwalk surrounding the compound. Daniel rode up to the main gate and announced his presence in a clear, urgent voice. A heavily whiskered frontiersman looked down at him for several seconds before asking, "Are you alone?"

"Yes, I'm alone," Daniel quickly replied.

The gate opened enough for him to ride through and immediately closed behind him. Daniel was confronted by the burly guard holding his musket at the ready. Daniel had grown a beard and much of his clothing was tattered from the rapid passageway through the wilderness. He was tired and exhausted and presented a rather shabby appearance.

"I'm Daniel Cullen, and I've come to the mission to see Reverend Blynn," he declared.

"I'll take you to him, Mr. Cullen," the guard lowered his musket and motioned Daniel to follow him. "Leave your horse here, I'll take care of it for you."

"Thank you," Daniel said, following the guard into the interior of the large structure to a room with a small cot where he had stayed the last time he visited the mission.

"You may rest here if you want, Mr. Cullen. The Reverend will see you shortly," the guard told him.

"I'm much obliged," Daniel said. "Is the mission school still functioning?"

"Oh yes, there are more students than ever, especially young girls," the guard replied stepping out the door.

An hour later, the courtly Rev. Blynn entered the room. "I apologize for keeping you waiting, Mr. Cullen. It's good to see you again."

"Rev. Blynn, I've come to see about Lavina Cameron and her friend Ruth. We have not heard a word from them all summer, and are concerned for her safety and well-being. May I see them?"

The kindly minister studied Daniel with sad eyes and a frown. "My dear Mr. Cullen," he began.

"What's wrong?" Daniel demanded, frightened by the grave demeanor of the man.

"Lavina is all right," the minister was quick to reply, "but, she is not here right now."

"Where is she?"

"There's no way but to tell you straight out," the minister replied. "Our dear young Ojibwa, Ruth, has been taken captive along with her daughter, Morning Mist. We have reason to believe that they are hostages and are at the large Indian encampment on the Saint Lawrence River known as Odanak. The information came from reliable sources. Lavina left two days ago with a small escort to determine the situation. We've heard nothing from her yet!"

Chapter Twenty-Six

Daniel could not believe what he was being told. "You mean Lavina is out there in the wilderness with only a few guards?" he cried incredulously.

"There are two armed guards with Lavina," Reverend Blynn explained to Daniel. "One is a Penacook and the other is an Abenaki, and I trust both of them or I would not have allowed her to leave. Ruth and her daughter were seen by some of our students at the mission school who had passed through Odanak. Lavina insisted on a small party to avoid detection. She has on her person a number of gold coins to purchase Ruth's release. It has become common practice on the frontier to pay for the release of a hostage. It's a sordid practice that only encourages more hostage taking, but I also believe that it has decreased the number of deaths of women and children. It's a gamble, I know, but Lavina insisted on taking the chance."

"If they know that she's carrying gold that places her at an even greater risk of being taken captive, too," Daniel replied, agitated at the turn of events. "I should have come sooner for them."

"I understand your concern, Mr. Cullen, but you must remember that up to this time, Ruth and Lavina have been able to move freely between small groups of Abenaki because of their goodwill as teachers and healers of the sick. Word came to the mission that sickness, probably smallpox, had almost wiped out a small band of Indians on the Saint Francis River south of Odanak. Immediately after learning of the outbreak of smallpox, Ruth left with her daughter and three companions for the encampment of sick people. She told me that she may visit her family on the Saint Lawrence, if weather and conditions are favorable."

Daniel listened carefully to the minister and realized how the situation came about. "I thought she was a Chippewa?"

"Ruth is an Ojibwa, like Lavina, but her father was an Abenaki. The Abenaki at Odanak, Canada have a long history of personal ties to the New England tribes and the Iroquois Confederation in New York. There has been much intermarriage between tribes. All natives have a strong desire to learn to read and write, and that is what gives Ruth and Lavina such an immunity from harm. They have been powerful instruments for good by spreading the value and power of an education."

"Reverend Blynn," Daniel cried impatiently. "I don't blame you for what has happened, but please don't preach to me about the Indians. I've seen their handiwork up close and I'll be frightened for their safety until I can be assured that they are all right. I'm going to Odanak first thing in the morning."

"There are a few rangers in the mission," Reverend Blynn said. "I could arrange for one who knows the area to accompany you."

"I prefer to travel alone," Daniel said, thanking him. "I've been over some of the area years ago. It's about a hundred miles from here," Daniel paced the room, laying out his plan. "The horse will cut my travel time in half."

"The horse will also make you more visible to forest travelers. Deep snows could come anytime in the Saint Lawrence region. You're running out of time, Mr. Cullen."

"How about Ruth and Lavina? What are they running out of?" Daniel snapped back, leaving the room to check on his horse.

Early the next morning, Daniel left the mission with a small pack of extra blankets, gunpowder and a large bag of pemmican. His baggage was scrupulously selected to meet his survival needs and yet as light as possible for rapid travel to Odanak.

He followed a heavily worn path on the east side of Lake Memphramagog leading north until he intersected with the Saint Francis River. Then, he followed along its bank toward the Saint Lawrence River.

Daniel drove the faithful Narragansett recklessly over the rough forest paths, uncertain of what he was going to do and what he might find once he arrived at the large Indian compound. He planned to conceal the horse a few miles from the village and resume his journey on foot so that he could watch the compound for some sign of Lavina and Ruth and remain undetected. He arrived at the bank of the Saint

Francis River shortly after noontime. The path was still easy to travel and he maintained an easy trot most of the time. The horse seemed tireless.

Several miles up the river Daniel located a small hilltop just off the main pathway where he decided to stop for the night. He watered the horse in the river and climbed the hill where a few scattered openings contained some grass for the mare to feed. He ate a handful of pemmican and removed a bearskin hide from his pack and laid it on a bed of balsam fir boughs. The location was perfect. Daniel could sit on the bearskin robe beside a yellow birch tree and see the horse and the river. The mare was hobbled, but Daniel was taking no chances on being stranded if the mare was spooked, so he tied the mare's lead rope to his leg.

Darkness settled over the wilderness quickly. Daniel observed the half moon rise above the trees and listened to the silence of the night. He shivered from the dampness that penetrated his clothing and wrapped the bearskin tighter around him. All he could think of was Lavina and Ruth. He prayed that he was not too late. It seemed a long time since he had left them at the mission. His love for Lavina had grown steadily. He could still see her playing the violin at the summer solstices gatherings at Portsmouth. Fatigue finally displaced the pleasant memories.

For two more days, Daniel followed the winding river northward until he estimated that the Indian village was a few miles away. On the third day, he veered from the pathway and picked a route through the thick spruce-fir forests that would better conceal him. He climbed a large sugar maple tree on a hilltop so he could survey the area. He could smell smoke and dried fish, which indicated that he was close to the village. He noted a small island in the middle of the river heavily covered with birch and maple trees. It looked like a good spot to leave the mare. After darkness he carefully made his way across the pathway and entered the river. The current was swift and cold, and Daniel held his powder supply high over his head. Luckily, the river bed was only three feet deep.

The moon was hidden behind scattered clouds so that Daniel could not survey the island as thoroughly as he would have liked, but it seemed to give adequate cover for the mare. He repackaged his pack with bare essentials and slung it over his shoulders. There were aquatic plants, marsh grass and standing water all over the island, so the mare would be able to eat and drink. Daniel tied her to a sturdy maple in the center of the heaviest growth and affectionately rubbed her neck before he left the island and waded ashore.

Traveling through the thick forest at night was difficult, so Daniel decided to follow the pathway. The local Indians stayed close to their fires after dark. Twice he noiselessly passed longhouses with fires burning in their fire pits. Every fiber in his body was alert to possible danger as he crept deeper into the Indian encampment. An opening in the tree canopy in front of him was illuminated by several fires located in a semi-circle in front of a single longhouse. It was difficult to distinguish its significance, so he lingered to observe the situation from a small alder grove at the rear of the longhouse until daylight. He was aware that he may have already walked into a situation he could not get out of without being discovered.

Focused and worried about what the day might bring, Daniel checked the charges in his rifle and both of his pistols. They were primed and ready for use. Ben's knife was secured in the legging on his right foot. A heavy dew settled over the land, and Daniel began to shiver from the cold. At times his teeth chattered, and he was afraid of being heard by someone or a stray dog from the village.

An orange hue on the eastern horizon signaled that the sun was about to announce itself. Daniel heard a twig snap behind him and turned toward the noise, lifting his rifle in alarm. A club struck him across the side of his head, glancing to his neck and shoulder. He lost consciousness and fell to the ground on top of his rifle.

As Daniel lay slumped over his rifle, Lavina was lying on a reed mat covered with a doeskin in one of the tepees beside the longhouse. She was afraid for her life and for little Misty's. She was too frightened to cry and was tormented by images of what was planned for her. Her lips trembled, and every muscle in her body vibrated out of control. Ruth had been brutally murdered. A Jesuit priest had taken over the small band of Abenaki and ruled them with a level of depravity that was rare on the frontier, even for renegade Abenaki bands.

Lavina and her escorts had walked into the compound the way they had several times in the past. Most of the families she knew by name had abandoned the village when the priest assumed complete power over his trusted bodyguards. As soon as they came near the council fire in front of the longhouse, they were intercepted by the priest who lifted his arm ordering the death of her two Indian escorts. Sharp tomahawks smashed through their skulls before anyone could speak. It was a preferred method of execution, swift and deadly. Lavina felt faint and cried out in protest. The priest called her an instrument of the devil and viciously taunted her. Lavina sneered at the priest, repulsed by his bad breath. Her insolence infuriated him, and he ordered her thrown into a teepee for safe-keeping. Lavina cowered in silence, frightened and angry. She knew that food was scarce in the native villages that winter, and extra mouths to feed were a burden. She hoped that they would ransom her.

The day after her capture, Lavina was gathering firewood with an elderly lady from the village who told her that the families had relocated further north on the Saint Lawrence River. She also confided that little Misty was in her teepee and had been crying most of the time. The child was scared and missed her mother; otherwise she was all right. The woman had promised Lavina that she would try to bring Misty to her, but they had to be careful. Punishment for disobeying or displeasing was severe.

Loud cries from the women in the village outside Lavina's teepee the next morning, alarmed her. There were cries that a white enemy had been found spying on the village. She peaked through an opening of the flap and noticed the guard sitting in front of her tepee. She watched as several Indians carried an unconscious white man into the longhouse. Even in the limited light, she recognized Daniel as the prisoner.

Daniel had come to get her. Immediately her spirits rose, yet the thought alarmed her, because she knew it was only a question of time before he would be put to death by the priest. Lavina learned that the mad priest liked to have the death blow delivered while the victim was conscious, and in his twisted mind found pleasure in watching the victim's eyes while he was dying. He was a sick and dangerous psychopath. Just the thought of such a death sent chills throughout her body, and fear filled her heart. She had to find a way to escape. The very thought of escaping filled her with hope.

Lavina summoned the guard in front of her teepee and asked for permission to visit the elderly woman who was caring for Misty. The guard seemed more interested in eating his bowl of smoked fish than refusing her request. He pointed out the wigwam of the woman and child, and continued his eating. She crossed the cleared common ground, acting noncommittal to the activity taking place at the longhouse. She looked, but couldn't see anything in the longhouse.

As soon as Lavina lifted the flap of the teepee, Misty stopped crying and ran to her. The traumatic child was a nervous wreck. Her long flowing tresses were soiled and disheveled. Tears streaked down her unwashed face. Lavina held her in a tight embrace softly whispering in her ear that everything was going to be all right. Slowly her tears stopped, and Misty's fragile body relaxed. Lavina stayed for an hour comforting her. The venerable Indian woman watched how Lavina had calmed the frightened child and smiled approvingly.

Lavina remembered that she had once seen the elder woman at the mission and gambled that she might be willing to help them. Lavina asked if she had a sharp knife in the teepee. Their eyes met in mutual understanding. Without a word, the lady pulled a small sharp skinning knife from a bundle of hides beside the fire pit in the teepee and handed it to Lavina. Lavina held Misty with one arm and accepted the knife, placing it under her doeskin frock. Then she asked the woman if she could take Misty to her tepee for the rest of the day if the guard did not object.

The woman nodded her head in approval and embraced them both. "Be very careful. The Jesuit is crazy in the head, and he will not hesitate to kill both of you. Now go and may Jesus Christ guide you."

Touched by her words, Lavina kissed her on the temple and turned to leave. "May God be with you, dear lady."

The guard saw Lavina crossing the common and approached her as if to object to Misty being with her. Lavina quickly told him that the elderly lady was tired and needed to rest. The child's crying had made her weary. The guard patted Misty on the head and motioned them into her teepee.

A plan was beginning to form in Lavina's mind. The first thing she had to know was Daniel's physical condition. Later in the day, the guard entered the teepee with two gourd bowls of fish and corn meal for Lavina and Misty. For a long time he stood quietly, staring and admiring Lavina. She remained outwardly calm and rational even though she was completely unnerved at the guard's boldness.

"Maybe you can be my squaw," he said in Abenaki.

Lavina knew that she had to play for time and kneeled to place the bowls on their robes. She casually loosened the rawhide lacings at the top of her frock so that the warrior could look down and see the top of her breasts. "Perhaps I can warm your blankets some night, but right now, I'm frightened for this child who needs me to care for her. If I agree to come to your blanket, will you assure me that the child will be released without harm?"

The guard triumphantly smiled at her and answered, "If the mission will pay ransom for you and the baby girl, then you will be exchanged. It is often done. Until then, you can be my squaw. . ."

"Does the Jesuit agree with what you say?" Lavina boldly asked.

The guard hesitated and checked the flap of the teepee, then turned to answer in a low voice. "The priest only wants gold and powder, not hostages. He can be very dangerous."

"What is happening in the council house now?" she asked, casually making conversation.

"The white man was found spying on the village and will be running the gauntlet very soon. I have heard him speak angry words to the priest. His head is bleeding, but he seems to be strong enough to survive the gauntlet. If he does not, then he will die from the blows of many clubs."

Lavina turned to help Misty eat as if she was unconcerned about what he was telling her. "Thank you for the food. I know how to reward men who are good to me," she answered with a coy look of submission.

The guard took a step towards her. She saw what he had in mind and firmly placed her hands against his chest. "No, not now in front of the child. When the moon is full, I will come to your blanket. Until then, you must take good care of us."

The guard again surveyed her lithe body with hungry eyes and smiled his approval. The conversation and her lewd promise sickened her, and she asked God for forgiveness. Hopefully her hint of sexual favors had purchased precious time to put a plan into action.

Midday, Daniel was paraded through the village while women were taking positions with their sticks and clubs along a line stretching past the longhouse. The gauntlet was a familiar test of manhood and physical courage. The women that wielded the clubs were intent on inflicting pain and injury to the hostage. A stumble or a fall was commonly fatal, for the women continued to pound on the hapless individual until every bone in his body was broken.

The contest was about to begin when Lavina casually held Misty in her arms and stood in front of her teepee to watch the festive occasion. She studied Daniel without being too conspicuous, and drew a mental map of the layout of the village. She noticed out of the corner of her eye that an Abenaki had left the longhouse with a rifle, powder horn and an armful of clothing. She noticed a pistol in his hand and recognized it as Daniel's. The guard entered a teepee beside the longhouse and momentarily came out empty handed. She noted the location of the teepee.

The village people were in a celebrating mood and began chanting and dancing around Daniel mocking and trying to intimidate him. It was a ritual in which the entire village participated. The tempo of the ritual increased, and the taunts to Daniel became more and more threatening, degrading and insulting. Daniel ignored the dancers around him as he carefully surveyed the layout of the village. His eyes met Lavina and passed as if she were a stranger. She knew he was protecting her.

The dancing and chanting stopped when the village chief and the Jesuit exited the longhouse to watch Daniel's performance. Several well-armed warriors surrounded the common ground to stop Daniel if he tried to run away. The chief instructed the men to take him to the starting position and then let the Indian maidens prepare for the sporting event. He was pushed to the middle of the village at the start of the long line of club-wielding women.

Daniel knew what was ahead for him. He had witnessed it before. He was most worried about his head which was still bleeding. The blow that had knocked him out had left him with a massive headache and a severely bruised neck and shoulder. He was having trouble focusing his eyes and worried that he might be knocked off balance before he completed the gauntlet. The two warriors released him and stepped back. Daniel straightened his back and looked down the line of women. He could not see them clearly. It was as if the line was waving back and forth. He uttered a silent prayer for God to be with him and leaped into the fray.

Chapter Twenty-Seven

Daniel sprinted down the line orienting himself with a large spruce tree beyond the village proper. The passage route was about three hundred feet long lined with women and adolescent children armed with clubs and sticks. The blows from the women and children were deadly accurate. Daniel tried to cover his head with his arms and hands, only to have them severely pounded. It saved his already bleeding head, but he was afraid both arms would be broken by the vicious blows. He blanked everything from his mind and plowed toward the spruce tree in the distance.

Part way down the line, Daniel staggered and faltered. Lavina saw him and wanted to cry out to stop the cruel madness, but she remained a silent observer. The moment he slowed down, the cries increased in intensity and the blows were aimed to cripple him. The pain in his arms and shoulders was almost too much to bear. He prayed to be knocked unconscious so that he could die without pain. He tried to locate the tree again and was unable to distinguish the canopy from the sky. Then, a sharp pointed stick was rammed into his stomach, sending a burning pain through his body. The attempt to disembowel him made him angry, and he found a new reservoir of strength to complete the running of the gauntlet. His rally to the end impressed everyone watching him. A few feet beyond the finish line, Daniel tripped and fell to the ground. His inert body was covered with blood.

Lavina held Misty so that she could not see the barbarous exhibition. Her strong discipline kept her from going to Daniel's side, knowing that her beloved was badly hurt. To remain a casual observer tortured her soul. Several warriors carried Daniel to the lodge next to the longhouse where his weapons were located. Lavina wrapped her arms around Misty and walked back into her teepee.

She had come to the village on an errand of mercy. The gold coins were still fastened to her waist beneath her jacket. Now, Ruth was dead, and her two escorts had been murdered, and winter was descending upon the northland, a time of destitution when deep snow blankets the earth. Misty was in need of better care, and Daniel was in a nearby teepee, possibly dying. Fear gripped her. Something had to be done and soon. What was she to do? She also knew that the guard would not wait many days before he forced himself upon her. The thought nauseated her and inspired a bold attempt to escape from the village.

That night, the guard outside her teepee was changed shortly after sunset. He was a very young warrior who wrapped himself in a bearskin and soon fell asleep. Lavina heard him snoring. Misty was heavily wrapped in soft doeskin hides sleeping soundly. Lavina saw this as her chance to implement the first part of her plan. She quietly used the skinning knife to cut the moose hide wall of the lodge opposite the main flap entrance.

She poked her head out through the opening and looked all around. It was raining a steady drizzle. The village was quiet as she crawled toward the teepee where Daniel had been dragged. The ground was wet and cold. Lavina took a long time checking where Daniel's guard was and saw him beneath a clump of alders near the longhouse. Slowly, she made a long incision in the moose hide tent covering opposite the guard and carefully entered the teepee.

Holding her arms at full length, she nimbly felt her way to a deerskin in front of her. With trembling fingers, she explored to see if anyone was lying on it. She touched an arm and pulled back frightened that it might not be Daniel's. There was no response. She could hear heavy breathing and threw caution to the wind. Her nimble fingers ran over the person's shoulders and neck into the head. She felt a sticky substance on his head. It felt like blood — the person before her had to be Daniel.

She placed her ear over his mouth and listened to his breathing. It was heavy and steady. That encouraged her, and she kissed him on his dry lips, then held a finger over his lips and whispered in his ear, "I'm going to get us out of here. Can you move?"

He nodded yes, lifting his bound hands to her. She swiftly severed the rawhide bounds with the skinning knife. He also directed her to his feet where she carefully placed the knife between his ankles and cut the bindings. Now he was physically free.

"Listen carefully, darling," she again softly whispered in his ear, "I'm going to collect your weapons in the teepee and take them down to the river. I'll be back as soon as I can to get you and Misty so that we can leave the village. Do you understand me?"

Daniel again nodded to her. He took her hand and pointed behind him. She crawled a short ways and felt his rifle. She continued to extend her arm exploring the area and was pleased to locate his two pistols, rifle, powder horn, and bullet pouch. She wrapped the weapons cache in a single moose skin. A few minutes later, she was outside the teepee crawling toward the river skirting the village proper. Lavina placed the weapons in a sturdy canoe, then quickly made her way back to Daniel's teepee on her hands and knees. She was thoroughly chilled and shaking. The dreary weather was perfect for their breakout from the village. It helped to screen their movements.

Daniel laid on his robe calculating what Lavina had in mind. His head was still bleeding. Blood had collected around his neck and shoulders. He slowly moved his arms and feet. Though every movement was painful, he did not believe he had any broken limbs. He was fortunate. Lavina returned and crawled through the opening. She took a rabbit skin from her jacket to wrap around his head and fastened it lightly with deer hide lacings. The covering would absorb the blood and provide some warmth and protection for his injured head.

"Come, my love," she whispered. "Follow me as quietly as you can. We'll crawl through your teepee to the one where Misty is sleeping. Do you understand me?"

He nodded again and whispered, "I love you, Lavina."

His words quickened her pulse and increased her resolve to succeed. "Follow me."

They exited the teepee and crawled to the rear of the one where Misty was sleeping. Lavina again whispered in his ear, "Wait here, I'm going in for Misty."

Lavina very carefully climbed through the opening, collecting as many robes as she could find. Suddenly, the front flap was pulled open. She deftly buried herself under the robes and feigned sleep next to Misty. The guard carried a firebrand to check on her. He saw the two charges supposedly sound asleep and quietly left the teepee. Lavina's heart was pounding. If the guard had happened to touch her and see that she was soaking wet, she cringed to think what might have happened to them. She was prepared to use the skinning knife to silence the guard if necessary.

Feeling Misty move beside her, Lavina was afraid she would cry out, and the guard would come back. She softly warned the frightened two-year old that it was very important for her to remain silent, no matter what happened. She clasped her small arms around Lavina's neck and held on tightly. Lavina wrapped her in a heavy deerskin and crawled out of the teepee to where Daniel was waiting for them. Lavina was terrorized by the stark reality that she might be caught. The wet ground numbed every muscle in her body. They slowly crawled around the village to the canoe.

The three of them reached the river bank undetected. So far, so good! Lavina held Misty in her arms and tried to slide down the embankment. She slipped and pitched forward into the deep water, still holding Misty. Daniel was close behind them and saw her fall. He quickly threw the bundle of robes he was carrying into one of the canoes and grabbed her by the shoulders, lifting her head out of the water.

At that point Misty began to cry. The tiny cry in the night was probably drowned out by the babbling stream of water, but if she continued, her screams would give them away. Lavina clasped her hand tightly over Misty's mouth. Daniel decided it was time for decisive action. He lifted Lavina and Misty out of the water and deposited them in the canoe filled with robes and another wrap he assumed to be his weapon cache. He ripped the mooring cords free and climbed into the stern of the canoe with help from the paddle.

Lavina replaced her hand over Misty's mouth with her lips, kissing the child and beseeching for her to be quiet, for they were in grave danger of being discovered.

Daniel guided the canoe into mid-stream, straining to see ahead of them. The night was pitch dark with a low-hanging mist covering the river. He was unfamiliar with the channel and afraid they would tear the fragile bark canoe on some rocks. He prayed that the canoe would hold together until they reached the island where he had hobbled the horse. Every bone and muscle in Daniel's bruised and battered body throbbed with each stroke on the paddle.

Misty had stopped crying, and Lavina used the lull to cover each of them with the dry robes. They were both shivering uncontrollably.

The cold November night had penetrated her wet clothing. Lavina's teeth chattered; she had never been so cold and paralyzed. Daniel reached out to reassure her. "Remove your wet clothes beneath the robes, Lavina. The night is getting colder, and we don't want you getting sick," he whispered to her. "We've done well so far. About an hour from the village, I left a horse on a small island in the middle of the stream. We'll pull into it and wait until dawn."

Lavina stripped Misty first and wrapped a dry bearskin robe around her. Then, she did as Daniel requested, and wrapped herself in a bearskin robe. Soon their bodies began to warm, lifting their spirits as they snuggled beneath the large robes.

The fragile canoe traveled the distance from the village to a small island vaguely visible to Daniel. He was uncertain if it was the same one and was considering staying in mid-stream when the canoe slammed into a rock ripping a large hole in the bottom of the canoe. He directed the damaged canoe to shore at full speed, cautioning Lavina to keep Misty quiet until he could reconnoiter the area.

As soon as the canoe grounded, he leaped out to pull it ashore to keep the contents as dry as possible. He quietly felt through his gear, grasped his knife and left to check if they were alone on the island. A hundred yards away, he crawled through an alder thicket which he believed to be where he had left the Narragansett. A second later, he heard a whinny - it was music to his ears. He knew that they had been lucky again. The horse was cold, and Daniel was glad that he had left the saddle and blanket on the mare. He wrapped his deerskin robe over the head of the horse and continued around the small island to insure that they were alone.

Satisfied that the island was deserted, Daniel returned a half hour later to find Lavina and Misty still buried under the robes in the canoe. Daniel suggested that they try to get some rest until early dawn. He took a place under the robes beside Lavina. He arranged the skins so that they were covered to the maximum and carefully placed Misty between the two of them. Their collective body heat would even help to dry some of their wet clothes. While they were snuggled beneath the robes, Daniel opened a small bag of dried pemmican and venison he had left in his saddle bags on the horse. They ate all of the contents of the bag in a short time. The warm enclosure and nourishing food contributed to a comforting sense of well-being, and they all slept soundly for the rest of the night.

Daniel woke everybody while it was still dark and rushed them out of the canoe, carrying the contents near the horse. Then he dragged the damaged canoe out into the current where it was swept downstream out of sight. They fastened everything onto the saddle. Lavina and Misty were dressed in their regular clothes, which were partially dried, and wrapped themselves in robes for added warmth and protection from the wet brush.

As soon as the trail was visible in the dawn light, Daniel nudged Lavina into the saddle and passed Misty to her. "We've got to get out of here quickly," he announced. He checked the two pistols, making sure they were primed, and placed one in his belt under his shirt and gave the other to Lavina. The rifle was also primed and placed in its scabbard beneath her right leg.

They stepped off the island into shallow water and walked for a half mile in the riverbed before climbing the bank to travel on the same pathway he had used on his way north. Daniel led the Narragansett at a slow trot for miles, disregarding the pain that screamed from his body. The only thing in his mind was the safety of Lavina and little Misty, and their chances improved with each passing mile.

Midday they stopped at a small overview of the river where they could see in both directions. The sun was slowly drying their wet clothing. November in the north woods was usually wet and cold. There was a distinct possibility of everybody becoming ill from chills and the severe cold nights. The sun temporarily lifted their spirits as they ate more of the pemmican and venison from Daniel's provisions.

Daniel was leaning against a tree facing the sun, eating a strip of venison when everything around him began to slowly turn in circles. He looked at Lavina resting on a bearskin and could not focus his eyes. His legs no longer supported him, and he crumpled to the ground, unconscious.

Lavina was watching him, concerned about the punishment his battered body was taking. He had been going on iron will ever since the grueling run past the club-swinging squaws of the village. She sprang to her feet and went to him. He was unconscious and wet from perspiration. Her first instinct was to protect him from the cold and she immediately wrapped him in robes. Thank God they had the presence of mind to salvage the number of robes they did when they left the village.

Fear and desperation gripped Lavina. She was deep in the forest alone with very little food, an unconscious two hundred pound man and a child to care for, and was being pursued by angry Abenaki tribesmen! She embraced Daniel's unconscious body and wept. Despair and frustration triggered a flood of tears. Then, a small hand touched her on the shoulder. Misty said, "I'm cold and want my Mommy."

Lavina picked herself off the ground and swept Misty in her arms. "Oh, my dear little girl. Your Aunt Lavina got you into this mess and with God's help, will find a way to take you back home. You've got to be a big girl, for I need your help. Uncle Daniel is very ill, and we've got to help him."

"Is he sleeping on the ground?" she observed.

"Yes, darling, he's simply exhausted," Lavina told Misty, wrapping her in a doeskin robe, kissing her on the cheek.

A plan of action that seemed feasible had formed in Lavina's head. She released Misty and took Daniel's heavy knife from his legging. It was impossible for her to lift Daniel into the saddle, so she began to make a simple travois to drag him behind the Narragansett.

She checked the area around them, selecting two maple saplings about two inches in diameter and cut them into two lengths about twelve feet long. The two long poles would serve as the main rails running from each of the two stirrups to the ground. Another sapling of smaller diameter was cut six to seven feet long. These she fashioned to the main poles in the form of a cross, which would help support Daniel's body. Lavina attached a moose hide on top of the crossed bows and to the main rails with rawhide lacings she had cut from the robes. She spent a long time cutting strips from the hides that were needed to fasten the main poles to the stirrups, the cross pieces to the main drag poles, the moose hide to the travois, and finally, she used the strong bindings to hold Daniel on the drag. Two of the five hides were used to make the travois.

Once the travois was completed, Lavina asked Misty to help her place Daniel on the crude platform. It was all they could do to drag his inert body onto the travois, and after a struggle, they were satisfied that he was far enough on the drag so that his feet were completely suspended from the ground on the platform. Lavina used several feet of heavy rawhide bindings to secure him to the platform. Then, she placed their extra robes and their packs on the travois with Daniel. That left the saddle for Lavina, Misty, and the firearms.

Without delay, Lavina climbed into the saddle and leaned down to lift Misty off the ground. Everything now depended on the stamina and courage of the small Narragansett mare. Slowly, they began their journey toward the sea and home. It was past midday, and they had exhausted their supply of pemmican that morning. Only a few strips of venison were left, and Lavina was keeping them for Misty. They had two hundred miles to travel. Starvation was a very real threat to their survival. Lavina had a pistol under her shirt primed and ready to fire, and asked Misty to play a game watching for any animals along their pathway.

Lavina had occasionally traveled the area and was familiar with some of the major landmarks. Their chances of meeting unfriendly war parties decreased if she selected a more easterly route to the coast. Therefore, she left the well-traveled path along the Saint Francis River for a southeasterly direction toward the Androscoggin River. She planned to follow that south to the great mountain chain that separated them from the coast.

Lavina had passed this way once with her father who had led them through a valley between towering mountains with sheer cliffs. It was desolate country with few settlers. Her main worry was food. She estimated that it would take three days to reach the pass through the mountains. All that remained of Daniel's supplies were a few dried tea leaves which Lavina placed in her jacket pocket. It provided little nourishment, but it made the clear spring water more inviting and could still invigorate the body when steeped in hot boiling water.

The Narragansett required a minimum of direction from Lavina as they wound in and around trees and rocks, picking as smooth a path for Daniel as possible. Lavina desperately urged the sure-footed horse onward. The sun was dropping behind the hills to the west, and it was getting colder. Lavina looked for a good location to make camp for the night, fully aware that food and water requirements for the horse were the highest priority in selecting a suitable campsite. Without the mare, they were doomed to disaster. She saw a small sheltered glade ahead with a small pocket of clear water surrounded by meadow grass. She urged the horse to the grass and water and climbed out of the saddle.

Lavina and Misty gathered small sticks for a fire in the sheltered area beside the horse. There was enough forage for the Narragansett to feed on all night, but Lavina took no chances and hobbled her with the rope Daniel had used on the island. Daniel was still lying unconscious on the travois. She was frightened, cold, and hungry. Tears of helplessness again fell on her bronze cheeks. Wiping them away with the sleeve of her jacket, Lavina assembled small twigs into a large pile and sprinkled a small amount of gunpowder in a concentrated area of the smallest twigs. Covering the ignition hole of the pistol, she cocked it and pulled the trigger holding it sideways beside the pile of twigs. The powder ignited a small fire. Seconds later, they had a warm fire snapping and cracking. It was like a friend, and Lavina's spirits picked up.

They heated water in the small metal can Daniel always carried with him. Lavina chose two leaves from her tea supply and crumbled them into the tin suspended above the flames on a stick of green hardwood supported by two large rocks. The aroma of hot tea brewing was welcome.

Suddenly, the Narragansett whinnied and lifted her head in the direction they had just traveled. Lavina's heart beat wildly as she reached for her pistol. Lifting her eyes towards the trail, she saw three men with muskets pointed straight at her!

Chapter Twenty-Eight

"Please don't shoot," she screamed at the three men. It was dark enough that she could not determine if they were white or Indian. Her greatest fear was that they might be French or Canadian stragglers or deserters.

"Do not be afraid," one of the men answered in an authoritative voice, coming closer to the fire. He was not as tall as Daniel, but he was muscular and lithe of build. He cautiously made his way to the fire, studying Lavina and Misty, then looked at Daniel lying motionless. "This is a white man," the stranger said, kneeling beside Daniel. He turned to the other two men behind him and said in a gentle voice, "Come, we must help these people."

Lavina sighed and thanked God that the strangers were friendly. "Daniel was injured when he ran the gauntlet at Odanak. We just escaped from there," she told them.

With those few words, the men came forward and started to remove their packs. First, they collected more firewood and added it to the stack Lavina and Misty had already gathered. One placed a small cast iron skillet on the live coals of the fire.

The leader of the group introduced himself as Captain John Stark. "We are members of a Ranger company from New Hampshire."

Her prayers for help had been answered, Lavina sighed. "Oh, Daniel Cullen and I are from Portsmouth," she breathed easier.

Stark seemed puzzled with her reply. "The name Cullen is familiar to me, but I can't place it now."

"Perhaps," Lavina explained. "You've seen copies of the COASTAL BEACON, which is published by Daniel's Uncle Lee Cullen." She told the ranger what had happened to Ruth and about their escape from the Saint Francis Indian village.

Stark continued to study Lavina, watching the flickering flames of the fire. "You must be the one they call Whispering Wind," Stark said, helping to lift Daniel from the travois to a deerskin placed beside the fire. "I have heard of your good deeds. Do not worry, we have food and will escort you south as far as the Mountain in the Clouds. Then we must return to the Lake Champlain area. We are scouting for the British Army," Stark assured Lavina with his moderate tone and calm voice.

One of the rangers poured a small amount of gunpowder from his horn into his palm and placed it under Daniel's nose. A few seconds later, Daniel moved his head away from the hand and opened his eyes, sneezing twice.

Lavina saw his reaction and cried, "Oh, Daniel, I've been so afraid for him. He was so badly beaten in the gauntlet, yet he ran for hours this morning, leading us out of the village." Her love for him was evident.

The young ranger smiled. "We picked up your trail near the village and saw where you built the horse drag. Our curiosity was aroused, so we followed you here. You've been very courageous to attempt an escape in late November."

The rangers shared their supply of pemmican and dried moose meat with the weary travelers. The food and hot tea warmed and filled their stomachs. Daniel had rallied some after Lavina fed him warm broth made from boiling small chunks of moose meat. He was able to sit up without assistance.

Throughout the evening, Lavina was impressed with Captain Stark. He was a roughhewn frontiersman, obviously in command. He was slightly older than Daniel and Lavina. Stark remained untalkative, even reticent. There was a silent efficiency about the man that earned respect. His dark, deep-set eyes with shaggy eyebrows were constantly searching the surrounding campsite. Experienced bordermen, like Stark, were the personification of the new Colonists, self-reliant people of the forest. Stark and Daniel both held the same virtues admired in the old world, mixed with the strength and innocence of the wilderness. They were a new breed of men cultivated by the raw frontier.

That night, the rangers took turns posting an all-night vigil. Lavina shared her robe with Misty, next to Daniel and slept soundly. She had been assured that the northern half of the New Hampshire Grants were relatively free of French or Indian combatants. They were too busy building fortifications and fighting the British and colonial forces west of the Connecticut River.

The following day was warmer than usual. They ate quickly and broke camp. Daniel was still too weak to climb into the saddle, so they again tied him to the travois. Captain Stark set the pace walking ahead of the party, while the two younger rangers took positions on both flanks and watched for game to supplement their food supply. A few hours later, one of the rangers shot a small doe. They quickly dressed it and cut the meat into small portions, placing it in Daniel's empty saddle bags on the travois.

For three days and nights the stalwart rangers guided them to the Androscoggin River, following it until the river turned sharply to the east. The land was lonely, wild and remote, and it proved to be free of hostile bands of men. Captain Stark continued to guide them to the pass through the great mountains. They could see the Mountain in the Clouds off to their right. Lavina told Stark that she had traveled the area and felt confident that she could lead the way back to Portsmouth.

Daniel was feeling stronger at that point and was able to ride in the saddle holding Misty, and the travois was discarded. Lavina insisted on walking ahead of the Narragansett. That last night they made camp in the shadows of the tall mountain covered with clouds. Generally, Captain Stark remained aloof and quiet, but that evening he was a little more talkative. He spoke affectionately of his family living on the banks of the Merrimack River in Derryfield, and told them of his own experience as a captive of the Abenaki Indians at Saint Francis, Canada, four years ago. He also had run the gauntlet and was lucky to have come out of it relatively unharmed. He was ransomed by Captain Stevens, the Commander of Fort Number Four, for one hundred and three dollars.

That night Lavina lay wrapped in her doeskin robes, thanking God for sending the intrepid scouts to their rescue. Her stomach was filled with venison and she had a warm feeling that her prayers had been answered. She had successfully executed an escape from the Indian village in wintertime. She was convinced that the appearance of Stark and his companions was an act of God. The fact that she and Daniel could dream of the future filled her with thanksgiving.

The next morning, Stark and his men left Lavina and Daniel. They exchanged pleasantries and bid each other good luck. Daniel shook hands with them. Lavina embraced Stark and kissed him on the cheek. He smiled at her and turned to leave. A bond had grown between the two parties. Daniel, Lavina, and Misty owed their lives to the hardy frontiersmen.

The sheer granite cliffs that towered above the three forest travelers looked down upon their passage with indifference. Many voyagers had taken the same well-worn path through the notch between the massive mountains. Their strength and timelessness made the travelers seem insignificant and small. In time, the people would turn to dust, while the granite cliffs still maintained their precipitant hold on the side of the mountains, standing in silent testimony to the fragile mortality of man. The valley thundered with rushing water plunging over granite formations.

Daniel rode in the saddle humbled by his weakened condition. Every step made by the gentle horse sent a stab of pain through his chest. The first day after Stark left, Lavina selected a location beside a small pool of water to stop for a midday rest. There was water and grass for the horse and ample firewood nearby. She quickly started a fire for tea. It became a ritual at every stop. Stark and his men had given them a supply of tea leaves to last until they arrived home. The day had begun cloudy and damp, but within a short time, the sun burned through the heavy mists shrouding the pass. While they were eating a ration of deer meat they had cooked over the open fire, a shimmering rainbow arced overhead. It lasted only a few minutes.

Daniel pointed it out to Misty who clapped her little hands in joy. "It's a good sign for us, Misty. The rainbow will bring us good luck."

"Will the rainbow bring back my Mommy?" she asked.

Daniel and Lavina looked at each other, seeking some way to tell the child the truth. Lavina spoke first. "The rainbow could be a sign from your mother who will always love you, Misty. If it pleased you, it pleased her, too. Your Mommy is never going to come back and be like you or me, or your Uncle Daniel. She's part of a world we cannot see, but we can feel in our hearts when the ones we love are with us. Don't you feel that sometimes?"

Misty looked at Lavina and thought about the words. "Mommy comes back to me in my heart. When I think of her, I can remember how she looked and the way she smiled at me and kissed me goodnight when she put me to bed," Misty replied with a serious demeanor.

Daniel was a silent witness to the scene. He placed an arm around Misty and said, "You keep those memories of your mother and always remember how she looked and how the sound of her voice always made you feel special. Your mother lives in all of our hearts and is a part of everything that is beautiful. When a soft breeze blows across your face, believe that it's a kiss from your mother in another world, and once again she's telling you how much she loves you."

It took four days for them to traverse from the mountains to Portsmouth. Each day became noticeably warmer as they moved south to a lower elevation. Lavina led the Narragansett all the way. The passage from Dover Point on the Piscatagua River to Portsmouth generated excitement and a great sense of accomplishment. They had cheated death and had lived to tell of it.

It was late in the afternoon when Lavina led them along the river bank to the rear of Lee Cullen's farm. She led the mare into the barn unnoticed, and tied her up in an empty stall. They were home! Tingling with the anticipation of being reunited with their families, Lavina helped Misty and Daniel from the saddle. His condition had improved, but his chest still hurt, and his breathing was labored. She told him that he had several broken ribs, and only time and rest would heal them.

Misty recognized the familiar Cullen home. While Lavina helped Daniel from the horse, Misty walked out of the barn and knocked on the front door. Maureen Cullen opened the door and saw Misty smiling up at her. Looking up, she saw Daniel and Lavina walking toward the house. A cry of joy pierced her lips. "Our prayers have been answered," she cried with tears forming in her eyes. She saw that Daniel was having trouble and ran to him. "What's wrong, Daniel? Oh... we have been so afraid something terrible had happened to you three. Come in... Lee is in the print shop."

Lavina helped Maureen and Lee put Daniel in a bed. They were both exhausted and hungry, and she was anxious to assure her father that they were safely home. She embraced Maureen and Daniel and excused herself and Misty and hurried to her home.

Daniel slept for twenty-four hours. When he woke up, he ate large servings of fish and apple pie and several pieces of cheese. Fresh cold milk was a real delicacy, and he drank several full glasses.

Lee and Maureen insisted that a doctor come to see Daniel. The local doctor reinforced Lavina's diagnosis of cracked ribs. He was amazed at the number of deep black and blue marks on Daniel's body. The doctor recommended that Daniel refrain from physical exertion until his body had healed. There was a possible danger that one of the broken ribs might puncture his lungs, or more seriously, his heart. Thus, Daniel reconciled himself to an inactive recuperation.

One week after they arrived home, Lavina and Misty walked into the print shop where Daniel was helping with typesetting. It was impossible to keep him idle for a long period of time. When he saw Lavina and Misty enter the shop, he warmly embraced them. His breathing was slowly getting better, and his normal color had returned. That had bothered her more than the cracked ribs. All the way home, she saw his sallow complexion and had been worried that he might die before the journey was over. Now, that haunting memory was dismissed, and she rejoiced at her good fortune.

Daniel casually asked her to print the first clean sheet under the press. She agreed, and checked the alignment of the paper, inked the type and turned the handle to lower the press. After a slight pause, she released the handle lifting the press and removed the sheet. She glanced at what she had printed, and almost dropped it on the floor!

WILL YOU MARRY ME, LAVINA?

Daniel placed his arms around her and waited for her reply.

"You've made me the happiest woman in the world, Daniel Cullen," she cried softly in his arms.

"Well, is your answer yes or no?" he asked.

"Of course, it's yes," she replied with tears forming in her eyes. "I've loved you for a long time," she said, hugging him.

"I want you to know that I'll always treasure your quiet courage and your generous heart, Lavina," said Daniel, looking tenderly into her eyes. "Misty and I would have perished if it were not for your bold spirit and determination. I'll always be grateful for your love. I love Misty as if she were my own."

"I know, Daniel."

That night, Daniel and Lavina agreed to marry in the spring. Daniel needed the remainder of the winter to recuperate, and it gave them time to plan their future. Lavina's father was pleased with their decision to marry. He suggested that it would be nice if one of the Moravian ministers marry them, and recommended a Rev. Frederick Post whom he had occasionally guided in years past. Rev. Post was widely known for his missionary zeal and his ability to act as an emissary for the rights of the native population. He was a true Apostle for Peace. Rev. Post had married a converted Delaware woman when he lived among them.

The Moravians were disciples of peace and were very successful in weaning the Indians from many of their more savage-like habits. The Canadian missions, in contrast, encouraged the natives to fight as they were traditionally inclined, especially against enemies of the Catholic Church. Rev. Post preached Christianity and emphasized peaceful means of resolving differences of all kinds. Post had heard of Lavina's desire to be married. He often visited the mission at Lake Memphremagog where Ruth and Lavina had met him. He was very popular with the tribes and spoke most of their dialects. The French were suspicious of his intentions and never gave him the same respect they gave to Catholic priests.

The winter of 1755-56 was severe and long with heavy snows that kept many New Englanders snowbound for days at a time. Lavina spent her time caring for her father and Misty. She also helped in the print shop on a regular basis. The first month of the new year, they learned that the British and the French had officially declared war with each other. It was a joke to the colonists who had been fighting the French continuously for years without a declaration.

The campaign for dominance of the New World between the French and the British was not going well for the colonists. They had fortified most of the Hudson River Valley as far as Lake George to counter any attack from the French. The Champlain Valley north of Lake George was increasingly being fortified and manned by French soldiers. The same was true along the Ohio Valley and the Great Lakes. The British had miserably failed to protect her colonies. Apprehension and disappointment was rampant on the western frontier. The future of the colonists' hold on the continent was in grave risk of being terminated.

Daniel's and Lavina's wedding was set for late May, 1756. They were married in the Cullens' living room by Rev. Frederick Post. He was a tall, soft-spoken man of God who ministered to a far-flung flock of believers. The British idolized him while the French were envious of the high esteem the natives held for him.

The wedding was a very simple and solemn occasion attended by Lavina's father, Daniel's Uncle Earl, Aunt Ursula and Daniel's cousin Ellen. The highlight of the ceremony was, of course, the vows, but they were supplemented by a most pleasant secret that had been kept from Lavina and Daniel. Late in March, Lee and Earl had contracted for a small home to be constructed at the northern edge of Lee's farm property beside the Piscataqua River. It was completed a week before the wedding and presented to them during the reception where toasts to their happiness were raised.

The new home was only five minutes walking distance from the print shop. The COASTAL BEACON was a wedding gift to Daniel from his Uncle Lee. Lee agreed to stay on as writer and consultant and was ready to leave the daily operation of the enterprise to younger blood. Daniel had lost some of his urge to "be where the action is," and he was content to follow in his uncle's footsteps as a publisher and printer of the respected newspaper.

As soon as Lavina got their new home organized, she began scheduling violin lessons to a select number of students in the area. She divided her time between her home, music lessons, and the print shop. She was Daniel's most efficient typesetter, and she took her job seriously. The workers who printed the copy and dried the printed sheets soon found that she demanded perfection. She did it by working with them and praising them when a good job was done.

The news they received from other papers and sources were disappointing. Advances of the French and defeat of the British dominated the news for the summer. There was one story that warmed everybody's hearts – the heroic feats of New Hampshire's own Roger's Rangers. They roamed the area around Lake Champlain, Lake George, and the Great Lakes, scouting, gathering intelligence, and striking at vulnerable enemy targets with lightning fast blows. Regardless of what one thought of the leader's personal attributes, his feats were the only bright spot on the British colonists' horizon against the French that summer of 1756.

Lavina entered the print shop one day, late in August, and motioned Daniel to close his office door. He complied to her request with a questioning glance.

"I have some news for you my dear husband." She embraced him warmly and looked into his eyes. "I just came from Dr. Jenkin's office. I've been feeling a little off lately, and he confirmed that I'm pregnant!"

Chapter Twenty-Nine

Three and a Half Years Later
(November, 1759)

Daniel and Lavina were sitting in the composing room of the print shop reviewing copies of the COASTAL BEACON. For the past three and a half years, they had been the primary publishers of the popular regional newspaper. Much had taken place since the day they were married.

Their home was filled with peace and harmony. Happiness was shared by their two-year-old son, Daniel Cullen, III and their adopted daughter, Misty. The children were the center of attention with their grandparents. Grandfather Cameron was raising a very special Narragansett colt for the children. The colt's mother was the Narragansett mare that Lavina and Daniel had used to escape from the Odanak Indian village. The colt reflected the same gentle spirit as her mother.

Daniel recovered from his ordeal with no lasting limitations, dedicating himself to his work with the same intensity he brought to most tasks in his life. Lavina was a perfect complement to him. He had a tendency to be a workaholic, but she gently helped him set limits to his daily toil and balanced his life with family, friends, and adequate leisure time to rest and dream. The dream part was important to him, and Lavina recognized that early in their marriage. She loved the studious part of her husband and scrupulously made it possible for him to exercise that side of his consciousness. The ability to find solitude in his home was greatly appreciated by Daniel. As he grew older, he discovered that those quiet moments enriched the rest of his life, and he loved his wife for the insight to quietly make it possible for him.

Most of the headlines in the papers were about the conflict of which they had been an intimate part. There was much jubilation within the colonies that fall. The British regulars had successfully captured Quebec, and all of Canada would soon fall. The French had lost their bid for an empire in the New World. For several years, the colonists had doubts about the outcome of the conflict.

Each campaign after the summer of 1757 had contributed to the supremacy of the British and the colonists over the French forces. The turnaround came, ironically, with the capture and destruction of Fort William Henry by French forces under the Marquis de Montcalm. The ensuing massacre of innocent prisoners released from the captured fort by the French Indian allies was an outrage that motivated the British to greater efforts. The French, to their credit, also deplored the senseless murder of so many innocent people.

That same summer of 1757, a force left New York harbor to assault the Fortress of Louisbourg in Acadia. The fort controlled the gateway to the Saint Lawrence River and central Canada. Uncle Lee followed the campaign in Acadia with more interest than Daniel. Lee could still remember the courageous assault and capture of the fortress by a rag-tag assembly of New Englanders back in 1745. Their sacrifice had been in vain, when England returned the fortress to the Acadians. When it was recaptured in 1758, Uncle Lee celebrated loudly. He had written most of the stories pertaining to the campaign and all of the editorials about the significance of the victory.

The British forces under a brilliant tactician, Brigadier General James Wolfe, destroyed the massive walls of the fortress with tons of explosives, rendering it unusable for years to come. The French fleet was destroyed in Canadian waters at the same time. The loss of Fort Louisbourg in Acadia was the beginning of the end for France.

1758 had been a great year for the British and the colonies. The fall of Fort Louisbourg and the destruction of the French fleet was followed by the capture of Fort Duquesne on the Ohio River by a large force under Brigadier General John Forbes. The French were demoralized and abandoned the fort. General Forbes immediately occupied the structure and renamed it Fort Pitt. Daniel had followed the campaign with interest and recalled an earlier campaign commanded by the young Colonel Washington. Daniel still was not convinced that Washington had been fit for command of troops.

The PENNSYLVANIA GAZETTE wrote extensively about the campaign. Daniel quoted a paragraph in the BEACON:

Colonel George Washington commanded a Virginia regiment attached to General Forbes' command. Washington was most critical of the general's selection of a route to fort Duquesne. Washington wanted to use the Braddock route to the fort from Virginia. Forbes chose a route from Pennsylvania, and Washington became most critical of his ability to command.

Immediately following the British success in the west, Fort Carillon on Lake Champlain and Fort Niagara on Lake Erie were captured. The British Crown was now in full control of the western frontier. The celebrations and euphoria that accompanied the success of the British regular forces augmented with Colonial militia units were encouraging, but the doom of French influence in the New World was not decided until General Wolfe captured Quebec. The fall of Quebec sealed the fate of Canada. It would be several years before the politicians met and signed the necessary terms of surrender in Paris. The control of Canada and all of the French claims east of the Mississippi River became British territory. Sporadic fighting would continue in Canada for a few months, but the end result was preordained. They had won.

Lavina was proud of the achievements and accolades Daniel received from other publications for his vivid and real descriptions of the battles raging along the frontier. They were responsible for a much larger distribution of the paper. It had doubled in numbers since Daniel took over the BEACON.

He had kept in touch with other prominent journals and newspapers in the colonies, maintaining the contacts his Uncle Lee had established. The VIRGINIA GAZETTE, MARYLAND GAZETTE, and the PENNSYLVANIA GAZETTE shared news reports with the COASTAL BEACON on a regular basis. Practically every ship that tied up at the Portsmouth Market Street wharf carried a packet of bulletins and copies of regional newspapers for Daniel. It paid handsome dividends in keeping northern New England informed of current events.

Daniel and Lavina's pride of achievement gave them hope for the future. The past summer, they had traveled to Daniel's cabin on the Connecticut River to assess its condition. A veteran soldier from Fort Number Four was interested in purchasing or renting the tract. Lavina knew that Daniel held deep feelings for the property and urged him to rent it for now, and see what the future brought.

While Lavina and Daniel were reminiscing, the door to the print shop was slowly opened. Misty and Daniel, III, looked around the door jamb at their parents. Daniel held out his arms, and the two children gleefully ran into them. Lavina had suggested that they call their son something besides Daniel, III. She said it sounded snobbish and elitist. Daniel had smiled at her and impishly suggested that they call him "DC." The nickname rolled off the tongue well and soon became permanent.

"All right, gang," Daniel picked them up on his lap. "Your mother and I were just reminiscing about where we've been with the BEACON. Have you two been pests for your Grandmother and Grandfather Cullen?" he asked playfully.

"No, Father," replied Misty with her winning smile. "Grandmother sent us in to get you and Mother. She just took a hot apple pie from the fireplace oven and is making tea."

"Oh, then your Mother and I are everybody," Daniel winked at her.

Misty shook her head and rolled her eyes at him. "No, that means DC and me, too! You're teasing me again."

"Hot apple pie and tea sounds good," Lavina said, placing several newsprints on the large composing table. She turned to look at her family. Seeing them so happy touched her heart.

Daniel saw his wife's loving gaze and gently placed the children on the floor and embraced her. "I love you, Mrs. Cullen," he whispered in her ear.

She kissed him as DC and Misty watched with approving eyes. "I love you, too, Mr. Cullen. Every day I count my blessings, and am thankful for the happiness that fills my heart. I pray that our children will be able to find the fulfillment that has been ours to share. There are signs on the horizon that give me some misgivings, and I pray that the future will be more placid than these past years."

"I'm sure God will listen to your prayers, my love." Daniel kissed her again and gathered the children to go and enjoy a sweet dessert with his beloved Aunt Maureen and Uncle Lee.

The colonies had suffered greatly from the ambitious designs of the French and their Indian allies. The Colonial militia that was formed to protect local interests performed well but lacked the professionalism of the British regulars. England had not served her colonies very well. Once William Pitt became Prime Minister, England began taking steps to defeat the French in North America.

While that war raged on the western frontier and the maritime provinces of the north Atlantic, seeds of discontent were sown that eventually would grow to unmanageable proportions. Shots fired in the Pennsylvania wilderness had ignited a world-wide war between England and France. The flickering flame that had been lit in that far-away Pennsylvania wilderness would eventually become a blazing torch.

The fight for empire was not over when the troops raised the British flag over Quebec. A crucible of far greater intensity and cost would have to be waged before the true temper of the colonies could be judged.

The future that Lavina prayed for was destined to be cataclysmic. They could not know, but it would define a nation and a way of life, unique in the history of man.

THE END

Other Historical Romance Novels
BY
Clifton LaBree

A Song for Lisa   A Historical Romance

This is the story of a young American woman captured by the Japanese in the Philippines, 1941. Like most prisoners, she was brutalized and sadistically treated with a cruel disregard for human life. Three years later, Lisa and her companions had reached the low point of starvation and abuse .....

Lake of Three Sorrows - A Historical Romance

A warm spiritually uplifting story of courage, commitment, and sacrifice. This is the story of Dale Cooper, a battle-weary American soldier who served in two world wars.

Raising the Torch *(Colonial Series Book Two)*

A continuation of the saga from Flickering Flame, Colonial Series book one, of the Cullen family in Colonial Portsmouth. This is a moving story of love and sacrifice when a small colony had the audacity to fight for independence from their motherland...

NON-Fiction Books

By

Clifton LaBree

NEW HAMPSHIRE'S GENERAL JOHN STARK,

LIVE FREE OR DIE: DEATH IS NOT THE GREATEST OF EVILS
Publisher - Fading Shadows Imprint

A fresh look at one of America's staunchest defenders of liberty
and freedom. John Stark was a courageous New Hampshire citizen-
soldier who fought in both, the French and Indian War, and the
Revolutionary War. His pursuit of leadership excellence on the
battlefield distinguished him as one of the most successful combat
commanders of the war, and one of the least appreciated.

His selflessness, modest life style, and devotion to the cause of
freedom are an inspiration that time has not diminished. He remains
today the embodiment of the frugal, independent, and cantankerous
New Hampshire Yankee.

GENTLE WARRIOR, GENERAL OLIVER PRINCE SMITH,
USMC.

Published by - Kent State University Press. Kent, Ohio, 2001

The Story of one of the United States, Marine Corps best General
Officer. His flawless performance in Korea is a story that needed to be
told.